Praise for Kimberly Duffy

"Duffy is an author to watch. She presents a unique look at society's expectations for women in two different cultures in the late 19th century. . . . This historical romance is recommended for readers of Tracie Peterson and Jody Hedlund."

—*Library Journal* on *A Mosaic of Wings*

"In this exceptional novel, Duffy tells a powerful story about personal transformation and legacy. From the picturesque falls of Upstate New York to stunning sites in India, Duffy shines in elegant, flowing prose and delicate precision that underscores the nineteenth-century setting. *A Mosaic of Wings* examines the rhythm of change, the sense of loss that accompanies a passing season, and fear and excitement of journeying into the unknown. Science, culture, and romance intersect enjoyably in Duffy's tale of academia, while the tensions of gender and social norms circa 1885 add complexity to her memorable characters."

—*Booklist* starred review for *A Mosaic of Wings*

"A nineteenth-century entomologist is caught between social expectations and desire in Kimberly Duffy's *A Mosaic of Wings*, a novel about wanderlust and women's empowerment. . . . India's allure is captured with appreciative details of its spices and embroidered saris. . . . *A Mosaic of Wings* is a religious romance that pays tribute to trailblazers and field research as a captivating, down-to-earth bluestocking dares to let her own dreams take flight."

—*Foreword Reviews* ˹ ˺ings

"The excursions through the Indian ˹ ˺ Ithaca, New York, are well detai˹ ˺The stakes are high, and so are the ˹ ˺ choices Nora makes. The book had ˹ ˺ on with its trailblazing female lead and he˹ ˺ill climb. Recommended."

—*Historical Novels Review* on *A Mosaic of Wings*

Books by Kimberly Duffy

A Mosaic of Wings
A Tapestry of Light

A TAPESTRY OF LIGHT

KIMBERLY DUFFY

BETHANYHOUSE

a division of Baker Publishing Group
Minneapolis, Minnesota

© 2021 by Kimberly Duffy

Published by Bethany House Publishers
11400 Hampshire Avenue South
Bloomington, Minnesota 55438
www.bethanyhouse.com

Bethany House Publishers is a division of
Baker Publishing Group, Grand Rapids, Michigan

Printed in the United States of America

Library of Congress Cataloging-in-Publication Data
Names: Duffy, Kimberly, author.
Title: A tapestry of light / Kimberly Duffy.
Description: Minneapolis, Minnesota : Bethany House Publishers, a division of
    Baker Publishing Group, [2021]
Identifiers: LCCN 2020046124 | ISBN 9780764235641 (trade paper) | ISBN
    9780764238178 (casebound) | ISBN 9781493429943 (ebook)
Classification: LCC PS3604.U3783 T37 2021 | DDC 813/.6—dc23
LC record available at https://lccn.loc.gov/2020046124

Unless otherwise indicated, Scripture quotations are from the King James Version of the Bible.

Scripture quotations labled NIV are from THE HOLY BIBLE, NEW INTERNATIONAL VERSION®, NIV® Copyright © 1973, 1978, 1984, 2011 by Biblica, Inc.® Used by permission. All rights reserved worldwide.

Cover design by Jennifer Parker
Cover image of woman by Lee Avison / Arcangel

Author is represented by the Books & Such Literary Agency.

21 22 23 24 25 26 27   7 6 5 4 3 2 1

To Hazel,
my sweet homebody whose light just might
change the world. We may never live in one of
those mansions you love looking at on Zillow,
but I'm giving you one in this book. And that gift
can never compare to the one God gave us
when you were born.

"Truly I tell you, if you have faith as small as a mustard seed, you can say to this mountain, 'Move from here to there,' and it will move. Nothing will be impossible for you."

—Matthew 17:20 NIV

Pitying I dropp'd a tear:
But I saw a glow-worm near,
Who replied, "What wailing wight
Calls the watchman of the night?

"I am set to light the ground,
While the beetle goes his round:
Follow now the beetles hum;
Little wanderer hie thee home!"

—William Blake, "A Dream"

1

CALCUTTA, INDIA
NOVEMBER 1885

Hardly anyone was buried at South Park Street Cemetery anymore, and yet Ottilie Russell had spent more time there during her twenty years than any other soul living in Calcutta. The plaque on the front gate said it had been closed in 1790, but the board occasionally allowed the burial of august persons. Persons like her father, superintendent of the Imperial Museum, who had died five years earlier when cholera swept the city.

It hadn't taken only him. Two tombs nestled against his—Jemima's and Nathan's. So much grief enclosed in stone. And now her mother.

Reverend Hook stood before the mausoleum's open door and performed a eulogy Ottilie didn't hear. He'd traveled all the way from Lal Bazar Chapel for the burial. She should pay attention to his words and find comfort.

But comfort seemed a long way off. Certainly not something that could be had with the stringing together of a few pretty words, even if those words came from the Bible.

Ottilie slipped her hand from her little brother's and wiped it on the black silk of her skirt. She'd pulled this dress from the top shelf of the wardrobe last night, wishing she'd never had to see the hideous thing again, hoping the differences in her body between fifteen and twenty were enough that she'd be forced to wear a white sari like her grandmother.

But there was no grace for her these days. Here she stood, surrounded by the dead, with the same slim frame. The same narrow hips and shoulders. The same pain snapping at her heart.

A sniffle beside her drew the morbidity from her thoughts, and she took Thaddeus's hand again. "*Maji.* Mama." The Hindi and English words slipped from his lips like a prayer.

Ottilie could hardly make sense of their mother's death— there in the morning, enjoying tea and making *cholar dal* with their servant, Dilip, her voice bouncing around their little house as she called for them to wake up, then gone by midafternoon, struck down as she crossed the street, her arms full of the paper-wrapped dresses she was delivering to a client. Struck by a drunk Englishman riding a horse through the city, heedless of pedestrians, said the witnesses.

If Ottilie could barely comprehend it, how could a six-year-old work through the horror of his suddenly upside-down world?

She knelt beside Thaddeus, indifferent toward the dust coating her skirt, and wrapped her arm around his thin, quaking shoulders. "Do you know, little glowworm, I think Maji is looking down on us from heaven. I'm sure she can see you and is pointing you out to the angels. Can you hear her voice? Close your eyes and listen for it."

Thaddeus screwed his eyes shut, and Ottilie leaned in closer. "Listen for her. She's not too far. Heaven is only on the other side of the veil."

Reverend Hook's somber words hung heavily, like the vines draping the hundred-year-old gravestones and obelisks. "'The righteous perisheth, and no man layeth it to heart: and merciful men are taken away, none considering that the righteous is taken away from the evil to come. He shall enter into peace: they shall rest in their beds, each one walking in his uprightness.'"

Ottilie pressed her head against Thaddeus's side and squeezed her own eyes shut. *Please, Maji, please let me hear you. Please be near. I don't know what to do. How to live. What will happen?*

Nothing. She heard nothing.

"I hear her, *Didi*!" Thaddeus said, his exultant cry drawing indulgent glances from the people huddled around them. "She says, 'There is Thaddeus, our little glowworm, bringing light and joy to everyone.'"

Ottilie smiled, tears dripping from her nose and splashing her bodice. Thaddeus heard what Maji said to him every morning. It was how she greeted him each day, holding out her arms as he rubbed sleep from his eyes. It felt right that she should leave him with those words.

"You see, you only need to listen, and you'll hear her." Ottilie tapped his heart. "Right here."

Thaddeus stood on his tiptoes, trying to peer past the pastor and into the gaping mouth of their family's final resting place. "Even though she's in that house?"

Nānī, standing straight-backed beside Ottilie, tsked. "She's not in that house, *navasa*. She's in heaven." Her words were strong in their certainty. That was how Nānī spoke. It made Ottilie feel safe. Not everything had changed. Not everyone was lost.

Ottilie stood and leaned against her grandmother's side. Not too heavily because, as small as she was herself, Nānī only met her chest. But height and breadth didn't account for support.

Sometimes little things held more strength than the grand.

"I don't like to think of Sonia moldering away in that stone monument." Nānī swiveled her head, taking in the fallen gravestones of long-dead colonizers, and shuddered. "Bodies everywhere. Surrounded by them."

"She's not there, you said."

Her grandmother's eyes snapped. "You know what I mean. Her spirit is free, but the temple that housed her? No. When I die, take me home to Benares and scatter me on the river."

"You sound like a Hindu, Nānī. You'll scandalize the reverend."

After her husband had left her, Nānī had thrown off British clothing and customs, saying they made no sense in India and that Jesus hadn't addressed such things in the Bible, so why should she embrace foreign ways? She was an anomaly in the Eurasian community, whose members wanted nothing more than to be thought of as English. But Nānī had been raised in a Hindu home in the holy city of Benares. Reverend Hook didn't seem to mind, but sometimes Nānī said things that made people question what she really believed.

Nānī flicked her finger against Ottilie's neck. "I'm as Hindu as the queen sitting on her throne. But when I die, I will go home. My spirit to God, and my body to the Ganges."

"Shush. Don't talk about this anymore. I've had enough of death." Ottilie pulled away and focused on the *krishnachura* that shaded her family's grave and the mausoleum of the British merchant resting beside them. In April, the ornamental tree would burst with thousands of red flowers, showering her parents and siblings in a *dupatta* of petals.

Thaddeus tugged at her sleeve. "He's done."

Reverend Hook had stopped his monologue and was standing with his hand against one of the mausoleum's columns. It was an elegant structure, purchased before Maji realized Father hadn't been nearly as good with his money as he had his artifacts and family. There was only room for five in it, though. Ottilie would be buried there with them. She wouldn't marry and would more than likely die before her brother. And Nānī was to be dust on the river.

Ottilie passed a trembling hand across the back of her neck where sweat had pooled in the dips of her high collar. The

Bengali custom of wearing simple white clothing in mourning seemed much more practical than the British one of black. Maybe, if she lived in the land of cold winters and cloudy skies, her attire would make sense. But precious little of this entire situation made sense to her.

The reverend was making his way toward her, his eyes drooping and steps heavy. Ottilie shuffled back, her gaze darting, looking for escape. But already the mourners were disappearing like specters, slipping down the pebbled path and over weed-strangled graves. She didn't want to speak with him, to hear his well-intentioned condolences that would likely consist of trite proverbs. They'd gust past her hastily erected barricade—the only thing keeping her from losing herself to grief—and she couldn't be accountable for the anger and hopelessness that would assault her. That would blast like a cannon against his tired words.

"Look, there is your English friend. Go to her. I will see to the reverend." Nānī shoved Ottilie forward.

Before she could make her escape, another man appeared. A soldier. He walked toward them, and Nānī hissed through her teeth.

The soldier stopped before Ottilie, his gaze skipping over Nānī and landing on her face. "Ottilie."

She drew herself up, not even reaching his shoulder, but tall enough to shield her grandmother. She clutched Thaddeus's sleeve and tugged him toward her, ignoring his wiggles and complaint. They could face this man together. A cord of three. Four, if you counted God . . . which she didn't.

"Hello, Colonel."

She'd never call him Grandfather.

For a moment the three of them stared at the colonel. He stared back—not at Nānī, but at Ottilie and Thaddeus, his mouth working as though he wanted to say something but found words too difficult to form. Ottilie didn't rescue him. She took a moment to absorb the sounds of the cemetery—the gentle murmurs of condolences as people continued to glide past them and out the gate, the rat-tat-tat-tat of a woodpecker, the tinkling of anklets.

Finally, he scrubbed his hand down one wiry muttonchop and said, "I heard about Sonia's death. I'm sorry."

"Who are you?" Thaddeus, finally succeeding in wrenching his arm free of Ottilie's grasp, looked up at the colonel with wide eyes. They hadn't been able to dispel him of his fascination with all things military. He loved nothing more than watching the sepoys practicing their drills on the Maidan parade grounds.

The colonel's lips twitched. "I'm your—"

"He's no one, Thaddeus." Ottilie glared at the colonel, urging him to contradict her, to give her an excuse to tell him exactly what she thought of his imposing uniform and unwanted presence at his daughter's funeral—a daughter he'd refused to acknowledge after he traded in her and Nānī for a proper British wife.

Instead, he said, "I knew your mother well."

Nānī snorted.

"I shouldn't have come. I can see that now." His voice gave no indication of the dejection stooping his shoulders beneath the heavy epaulets of his uniform, but Ottilie had made a habit of studying people, of deducing their moods by almost imperceptible changes in expression, posture, and tone.

She steeled herself against the slight softening of her heart. He didn't deserve it. His next words proved it.

"Do you need anything? Money?"

Ottilie laughed. "Money?" She didn't elaborate but could see her point hit home. He closed his eyes. "You need to leave. Let us grieve in peace."

The colonel looked past Ottilie's shoulder. "I'm sorry, Gitisha. Truly."

Nānī said nothing, and he left.

Ottilie turned and caught her grandmother just as she began to sway. "It's fine. He's gone."

"He left. Again. But now my daughter is gone too." Nānī's body shuddered against Ottilie, and the earthy scents of the henna and mustard oil she religiously rubbed into her hair each week sent Ottilie back a month, a year, a decade, to evenings spent rubbing the mixture into her mother's hair, detangling it with a wooden comb, massaging her scalp in tight circles and listening to her sighs.

"Maji, Maji," Ottilie whispered. Tears clogged her throat, coming thick with Nānī's cries.

They hadn't cried since the police chief had come to the door twenty-four hours earlier. There had been no time. But now, with Maji's body interned, their three-room house empty of her constant prattling and the sound of her bare feet slapping against the stone floors, and the reverend's shadowy words filling the crevices of the cemetery, there was room for tears.

Ottilie dissolved against Nānī, and they crumpled to the grass. Thaddeus wiggled between them, his wiry arms creeping around their backs, the glue holding together the remaining women of the family.

Ottilie rested her chin on Nānī's shoulder and through swollen eyes took in the mausoleum. During the service the sun had crept high, and now its rays glinted against the pale stone. It warmed Ottilie's face. And her spirit. Maji and Papa, together again. And with the two children they'd lost along the way.

No, they hadn't been lost. The lost remained on earth, captive to dust and starlight.

Papa's voice, bubbling with laughter, filled her mind. *The heart of a poet—an artist—beats in that ever pragmatic chest of yours, Ottilie. You are just as nimble with words as you are your fingers and beetle wings.*

And they had laughed because Ottilie always was the perfect mixture of Papa and Maji. Hard and soft. Poetry and practicality.

Which was good, because now she'd have to be both for Thaddeus.

A firm hand gripped her shoulder. "Dear friend."

At the sound of Damaris Winship's solid voice, Ottilie extricated herself from her brother and grandmother. Damaris's embrace was just as weighty, just as reassuring, as her tone. Ottilie's head barely reached her friend's chin, but their friendship allowed for no self-consciousness.

They could not have looked more different—Damaris with her thick red curls and pale skin dotted by freckles against Ottilie's long dark curtain of hair and skin the color of dried soapberries—but they had forged a deep connection. One that still, two years later, surprised Ottilie.

"I'm so very sorry. Your mother was lovely." Damaris stepped back, and her hands cupped Ottilie's face. "She was one of the best women I've ever had the pleasure of knowing." Her thumbs wiped away the tears streaking Ottilie's cheeks. "You *will* get through this. You have her strength."

Nānī and Thaddeus stood and brushed the dirt from their knees, and Damaris eyed them. "I like the way you grieve. There's no pretending or adopting a stiff upper lip. It's a more natural expression. You don't seem embarrassed by your outward showing of emotion."

"Death is inevitable and common," Nānī said, coming to stand beside them. She pulled Thaddeus to her side. "There is no pretense in it. Not in birth either. There's no reason to hide grief or joy."

Damaris pressed a kiss against Nānī's cheek. "You're right. I'm going to allow myself that opportunity." She walked to the mausoleum, gave a short nod to Reverend Hook, then stepped inside.

When she was lost to the shadows, Ottilie met the reverend's eyes and sighed. She couldn't avoid him forever. They still attended his church every Sunday, despite the thirty-minute walk.

When she approached him, though, he gave no tired excuses for their loss.

He took Ottilie's hands. "I'm sorry. Your mother was loved, and you've experienced too much suffering already."

Ottilie dropped her head and inhaled deeply. "I admit I don't understand this. I can't make sense of it."

"I don't think we can ever make sense of the evil things that happen in this world. And it was evil. The man who killed your mother may not be brought to justice on this earth, but he will be held accountable before God."

She didn't think those words would comfort her, but they did. Because, in the end, they had so little control over how life played out. And God, despite his distance, was righteous. She knew that. It didn't ease the roiling anger that seemed so close to the surface, but it did send a shaft of light through it. A promise of one day finding peace.

Damaris appeared in the mausoleum's open door, wiping at her eyes. Reverend Hook patted Ottilie's hand. "I'll take care of everything here. You go home and rest with your family."

Her family? So reduced. So small. She looked at Thaddeus, sitting on the ground and piling stones into a tower, and Nānī, who watched the clouds with a blank expression. A strand of three. Her family seemed like a fragile thing. But it was enough. She'd make sure it held together.

And Nānī was strong—not even sixty. She carried the wiry strength of her Indian forebears. Her black braid showed only a few strands of gray, her face even fewer wrinkles. She would be with them for years yet.

Their cord would remain unbroken.

Damaris joined her. "I've hired a *tanga*."

Ottilie squeezed her friend's hand, grateful for her foresight and compassion. The horse-drawn carriage would have them home more quickly than walking, and they could avoid the crush of people going about their day in Calcutta's crowded streets. "Thank you."

Damaris helped lift Nānī into the back of the cart just outside the cemetery gates, and the rest of them squeezed around her, Thaddeus on Damaris's lap. The driver slapped his reins against the tired-looking horse, and they jerked into traffic.

Nānī dozed, her head hanging at an awkward angle, a wheezy snore escaping her open lips, and Thaddeus leaned over the side of the cart and made a game of trying to touch cows with red-painted horns and women carrying heavy loads atop their heads.

"What will you do, Ottilie?" Damaris asked. "Will you continue your mother's work?"

Their eyes met and they smiled, both knowing she'd done the brunt of her mother's work for a year, since Maji's sight had begun failing—brought on by the almost constant fancywork she'd needed to take on to keep them in food, clothing, and shelter.

"I'll try. It's the only way I can continue to support us." Ottilie could become an *ayah* for a wealthy English family—her education at La Martiniere for Girls would make her in high demand. She knew French and English, math and history, and years at her father's knee and exploring the museum had given her what amounted to a fairly advanced understanding of natural sciences.

But she couldn't sacrifice her pride to the snobbishness. The constant innuendos about her birth, references to being dark for a Eurasian. *"Is there any British blood in you?"*

As though her father's inheritance could only reveal itself in her skin tone and eye color. His love of poetry pumped through her blood. His beautiful watercolors were expressed through her embroidery. She was her father's daughter, no matter that she looked just like her grandmother. Thaddeus, with his fair skin and sun-tinted brown hair, might *look* like their father, but Ottilie claimed Edwin Russell's heartbeat.

"The lieutenant governor is throwing a Christmas ball at the

Government House next month. I'll persuade Mother I need an embellished gown." Damaris's father, a man whose family had grown rich on Indian spices, could well afford the cost of an embroidered dress.

Ottilie pressed a kiss to Damaris's cheek and grabbed for the back of her brother's shirt just before he tumbled beneath the carriage wheels. "Sit down, Thaddeus, or you'll make us a weak strand of two." Thaddeus furrowed his brows, and she pulled him off Damaris's lap and into her own, wrapping her arms around him and squeezing him tightly.

The tanga jerked to a stop outside the narrow lane leading to their house, pressed in on all sides by others.

"I will leave you here," Damaris said. "Come to the house Monday morning, and I'll see that Mother is swayed by my sudden interest in fashion." She smirked and gestured at her simple skirt and bodice. Damaris, much to her mother's disgust, never wore a stitch of impractical clothing.

That she would willingly wear a ball gown—and Ottilie was sure Damaris's mother would leverage her daughter's desire to help a friend and make it the most ridiculous ball gown ever sewn—spoke leagues about her character. Damaris Winship was a friend like no other. And Ottilie felt safer in the world for her presence.

2

Ottilie had been staring at the ceiling for hours by the time the fruit *wallah*, calling for people to buy his perfect winter oranges, made his way past their alley. When the sound of people shuffling by the window and the quick, aggressive barks and growls of two fighting dogs drowned out his cries, she carefully slipped from her mat and rolled it up.

Behind the carved teak screen, she pulled on a *choli* and draped a sari around herself. She'd don her British-style mourning dress before she left, but for now she wanted the freedom Indian dress provided. She wanted to breathe this morning. Not to fuss with clasps and buttons and heatstroke before breakfast.

Walking with light steps, Ottilie stood over Nānī as she slept, taking in her pale, drawn face and the deep circles shading her eyes. She'd wept in the middle of the night. Ottilie smoothed her hand over Nānī's hair, then crept from the main room and into the antechamber that served as the kitchen.

Dilip sat in the middle of the room before the small hearth, his legs bent around a grinding stone. Dilip, the only servant Ottilie's mother had been able to retain after Father's death, did most of the cooking and housework. He'd been somewhat adopted by Ottilie's father, who'd offered him a position after Reverend Hook had found him abandoned at the train station, an underfed child of eight who walked with a limp due to a clubfoot.

Initially, Dilip did minor jobs around the house, fetching or running errands for one of the other eight servants. But when Father discovered how quick his new servant's mind was, he relieved Dilip of his duties and spent the next seven years tutoring him. When Father died, Dilip grieved for him like a son. And when they lost their house and other servants, Dilip promised to follow them the way he had followed Father—with complete loyalty and a love born of finding a family when he had none.

"Good morning," Ottilie whispered, not wanting to wake Nānī in the next room.

Dilip stood and bowed his head. "Ma'am, good morning."

Ottilie sighed. They'd grown up as siblings, but she'd given up trying to erase Dilip of his deep-rooted sense of inferiority. They sat beside each other, and Ottilie picked up the poker and stuck it into the flames dancing in the hearth.

A spark flew from the tinder and fell on her hem. Dilip's finger squashed it. "Have a care, ma'am," he said. "I don't want you injured."

She gave him a wry smile. "Always looking out for me." Despite having just woken, she felt exhaustion sweep over her, bowing her shoulders and head. "Do you sometimes wish we were children again? Father gathering us all together and telling stories about English kings and extinct animals and discoveries made by archaeologists halfway around the world."

Dilip didn't answer her question—she didn't expect he would. They weren't children anymore. Father could tell no more stories. And the press of her siblings, who filled her life with laughter and belonging, had long since disappeared.

Ottilie extended her hands toward the flames, eager to release her gloomy thoughts to the heat. Dilip lifted a spoon and stirred the *khichdi* that bubbled in a copper pot.

With an impatient grunt, she stood and slipped through the

door that led to the verandah, her feet scraping against the sun-soaked stone and the sharp scent of the peppers Nānī had hung to dry tickling her nose. Bunched together like wind bells hanging from a temple, they were a noiseless promise of normalcy.

Except everything had changed. And Ottilie couldn't find her bearings. Nothing felt normal anymore. Maybe it never would. She pulled the edge of her sari more tightly around her waist to ward off the sudden chill that traveled the length of her spine.

A soft padding drew her attention back to the house. Nānī stood in the doorway, and though she still looked tired, a soft smile rested on her lips. "I had a dream last night."

Ottilie reentered the room, leaving the door open to allow air to circulate, and leaned against the wall. Other people had dreams, but Nānī was *given* dreams.

Dilip limped to the cabinet in the corner of the room and took the stack of rolled *dhurries* from the shelf. He unfurled one and placed the mat on the floor not far from the fire. "Here, *Dida*. Have a rest."

Nānī sat with the sound of creaking bones and a groan while Dilip spooned breakfast onto plates. Ottilie sat cross-legged beside her and took Nānī's hand. She rubbed her fingers over her grandmother's knobby knuckles and the bulging veins crisscrossing beneath her brown skin. Weathered and calloused, Nānī hadn't been born to hard work, yet she remained faithful in her burden.

"Tell us your dream," Dilip said as he tossed cumin seeds into the ghee that popped in the iron pan. He pinched some seeds from the bag and dropped them into Ottilie's open palm, then set their plates before them.

Ottile crunched the seeds as Nānī's voice, thin from age and exhaustion, pierced the sadness blanketing the room. "I dreamed of Edwin. Of Sonia and the little ones who've been called away. And great peace filled my heart. Joy too, because God doesn't give us half measures."

"Is that all?" Dilip pulled cooked lentils from another pot and added them to the simmering vegetables and spices.

"No. There was more." Nānī's eyes turned sad, and she patted Ottilie's hand. "But it isn't the time to tell."

Ottilie helped her grandmother to her feet so she could check on her pickles. She wouldn't ask Nānī to reveal the rest of her dream. There was no point. Nānī would do what Nānī chose to do.

Ottilie would have rather taken a cart the three kilometers to Damaris's large home near the Imperial Museum, but she didn't want to spend the coin, so she walked. She set out after breakfast, carrying brown paper-wrapped parcels, her black gown sweeping the dusty road beneath her feet.

Nānī had helped her choose examples of her best work—a lightweight cotton shawl, a pair of shoes Ottilie had planned to give Maji at Christmas, and a reticule. All embroidered with vibrant green beetle wings, all by Ottilie's hand.

The shoes, in particular, Ottilie took great pride in. She'd spent countless hours by lamplight, long after Maji, Thaddeus, and Nānī had gone to sleep, working the silver thread around tiny glass beads and wings clipped into geometric shapes. The shoes were an old pair of Maji's, worn to the parties Papa had been invited to. Once Ottilie had them reshod and created magic with her needle, they looked ready to be danced in again.

Ottilie sniffed and tightened her arms around her packages. Maji would never wear the shoes, but maybe they would bring her family blessing. If her work impressed Mrs. Winship, they wouldn't starve. All she needed was one customer to start. Then, when other wealthy wives and daughters saw her work, she'd surely have more. Maji had been able to meet their needs after Papa died. Ottilie would take up that mantle.

The Winships lived just north of the museum Papa had loved

and worked at. Though it was still early, the city was already teeming with life. Cows with red-painted and bell-tipped horns shared the crowded streets with carts and wallahs and women wearing vibrant saris, their ankles, noses, ears, and wrists tinkling with silver.

Entally, the neighborhood Ottilie and her family lived in, wasn't fashionable like the one they resided in while Papa lived, but it was her favorite. No uppity British officials or rich *babus* looking down their noses. Just a crush of Arabs, Jews, Indians, and Eurasians of every shade. The chatter of a dozen languages was a tapestry woven by an expert hand.

Soon, though, the dusty lanes leading past crumbling buildings and clusters of men in *lungis* smoking and playing *pachisi* turned into wide boulevards. The scent of freshly baked pastries drew Ottilie's eyes to the Federico Peliti confectioner, where wide windows revealed cakes, sweets, and foreign delicacies. Ottilie had been there a handful of times with Maji, and she could still taste flaky tart crust and cinnamon cream.

She set her eyes forward, ignoring the longing to step into the building and inhale the scents of fond memories. She had work to do, and spending her remaining rupees on treats wasn't in her plan.

Fifteen minutes later, she arrived at the Winships' palatial bungalow, its pleasing façade rising two stories, fronted by marble columns and a wraparound verandah.

Damaris lounged on a chaise, flipping through a magazine, which she set aside when she caught sight of Ottilie. "You made it! I'm so glad. I told Mother to neglect her calls this morning, and only the promise of letting her decide on the design of my new gown persuaded her to stay put."

Ottilie climbed the steps and joined her friend at the top. She shifted her packages to one arm, wiped her sweating palms against her skirt, and leaned in to receive a kiss on the cheek. The fan manned by the *punkawallah* stirred Damaris's curls, and they brushed Ottilie's skin. "Does she know it's me coming?" Damaris shook her head, and Ottilie picked at the twine wrapped around a package. "You couldn't ease the way for me? Just a little bit?"

"It's not that I didn't want to, but I wasn't sure how she would respond. You know my mother's prejudices run deep. The only reason she patronized your mother was because the quality of her work was excellent. I'm hoping once Mother sees your samples, she'll recognize your talent. I didn't want to chance her saying no before you can impress her."

Ottilie blew out a hard breath. "Well, let's hope it works out that way."

Damaris's throaty laugh filled the verandah's airy corners. "You already sound so defeated, and we haven't even stepped foot in the house. Optimism, my dear friend."

She took Ottilie's hand and tugged her over the threshold. As they crossed polished floors and gold-bordered Agra carpets, Ottilie straightened her shoulders, tried to adopt Maji's effortless grace in her walk and posture, and forced her lips to relax into a slight smile.

But the pressure building beneath her breast grew with every step. And by the time they reached the back parlor—a large room filled with so much furniture and bric-a-brac that her eyes had trouble settling on any one spot—her smile and her shoulders had slipped.

Damaris pinched the inside of Ottilie's elbow and hissed, "Don't show fear. She'll bare her teeth."

At the sound of their entry, Mrs. Winship lifted herself from a reclining position on a cane-back settee. Her eyes widened when they rested on Ottilie. "Why, another Eurasian embroiderer. Calcutta is overrun with them." As she righted herself, she threw Damaris an accusing glance before looking back at Ottilie. "Damaris tells me you're talented enough to induce even her into showing an interest in fashion." As Ottilie drew closer, intending to unwrap the parcels and prove her competence, Mrs. Winship's eyes narrowed. "You look familiar."

Ottilie faltered.

"Of course she looks familiar, Mother. She's Mrs. Russell's daughter." Damaris shook her head, then pushed at the small of Ottilie's back, urging her forward. "You've met her half a dozen times. And you know she was trained by the very best."

Ottilie set her packages on the table beside the settee and drew the shawl from its wrapping. She carefully unfolded it and laid it over Mrs. Winship's lap. As Ottilie pulled the reticule free, she watched Mrs. Winship's fingers trace the intricate embroidery edging the ruffle, her nails catching the elytra splayed in a floral pattern.

"Your mother was quite good. How do I know she didn't do this work?"

Ottilie's brows rose. "You don't, I suppose, but why would I take on work I'm not qualified to do?" She held out the reticule.

Mrs. Winship didn't reach for it. She picked up the shawl and shoved it at Ottilie before leaning back against the settee. With an elegant yawn, she gave a wave. "I'm sure you're *qualified*, but I'm looking for something exceptional. Damaris is reaching an age where even our money won't be enough to turn a man's head. She needs to look stunning. Especially with all those Fishing Fleet girls coming and stealing the Raj's best men." She pressed her fingers to her temples, and her eyes drifted shut. "It's a shame your mother is no longer here. I had something spectacular in mind."

"Mother!" Damaris's rebuke covered Ottilie's small gasp.

Ottilie focused on the paper-wrapped shoes she held in her arms. She didn't want to show this foreign woman the gift she'd made for the most precious person in Calcutta. Didn't want her pale fingers prodding the embroidery and picking apart the memories Ottilie had tucked away of hours snipping wings and beading thread and giggling in the lamplight, impatiently anticipating Maji's joy and pride and the sight of her small, perfectly arched foot slipping into something beautiful again.

"Mrs. Russell didn't set out to be run over by a horse just to inconvenience you." Damaris plucked the package from Ottilie's hold and carefully peeled back the paper. She stared at the shoes, her large hand resting for a moment over the trailing flowers made of wings and glass. Her friend's quick glance assured Ottilie that she knew what she held. Understood the precious thing Ottilie was about to reveal. Knew her own mother wouldn't appreciate the skill or sacrifice or grief. She began folding the paper back around the shoes, tucking the edge beneath the heels.

"You needn't be so vulgar, Damaris," Mrs. Winship said. She removed her fingers from her head, and Ottilie wondered if the woman's jaw tightened with regret or irritation. "Let me see what you're holding." She motioned for it.

Damaris narrowed her eyes. "If you've decided against hiring Miss Russell, I'm not sure it matters what I'm holding." She held the package out to Ottilie and, when she took it, raised her shoulders in what might have been called a shrug on another woman but took the form of a sloping kind of hunch on her.

Ottilie's heart constricted at her friend's goodness. Damaris could work her mother—most people and situations, in fact—with a finesse that struck fear in those with ill intentions and admiration in those who campaigned for good.

Mrs. Winship was neither. "Oh, for heaven's sake." With a languid stretch, she got to her feet and lifted her brows. "I'd like to see this final product before making my decision."

Damaris released a dramatic sigh and muttered, "I don't see why. I'm no longer interested in a gown or the ball." All theatrics. Every word calculated.

Mrs. Winship snatched the package, and the paper fell away. She held the shoes between her hands, and Ottilie prayed. She despised the thought of working for this selfish woman, but she would do it to create something that accentuated Damaris's natural beauty. She would do it to feed her family. Would do it so she didn't have to ask the colonel for help.

"This is much different than your mother's work. Its simplicity is bold." Mrs. Winship drew her thin lower lip between her teeth, and Ottilie met Damaris's eyes, which glittered with satisfaction. "Yes, I think this will work. You've not done anything like this for anyone else?"

Ottilie ripped her gaze from her friend's and tugged her grin into the straight lines of a professional expression. "No. The shoes are the first displaying that style of embroidery. I think it's particularly suited to Miss Winship's impressive form. She can pull off a more daring look than other women, and because of that, she'll draw every eye in the room."

And maybe there would be a man there who would love not only Damaris's unfashionable figure and wild mane of red curls but also her kindness and intelligence.

Mrs. Winship handed over the shoes—this time gently—and slipped back to the settee with a sigh. "Damaris, ring for Colleen. I swear that girl is just as unreliable and lazy as an Indian."

For a brief moment, Ottilie had felt a kind of goodwill toward Mrs. Winship. A gratitude for her excellent taste and willingness to hire her. That fled in the face of her insensitivity, though Ottilie pretended otherwise. Just as her mother had. Just as her grandmother had. Just as every woman possessing a drop of Indian blood would have to. If it provided rice and lentils, Thaddeus's tuition, and a little to set aside, she'd swallow her pride and parade Maji's shoes in front of every British woman living on their soil. She would sew until she bled, if need be.

And then she'd take her bruised fingers, and even more battered heart, to Nānī's room, where she'd have her scalp rubbed. And where her grandmother's songs would ease the sting of rejection.

3

The day after Ottilie spoke with Damaris and her mother, she met with the dressmaker at her shop in Bowbazar. The small French lady eagerly watched as Ottilie pulled out her sketch. As the dressmaker's lame husband shouted demands from the back room, Ottilie and Madame Bisset compared designs and sketched one that worked for both of them.

A week later, the gown arrived at Ottilie's home, and she spent five frantic days embroidering it.

Each morning she rose from bed just as the sun peeked its face above the horizon, lit the kerosene lanterns, pushed open the shutters that kept the worst of the night mosquitoes out, and settled into her mother's favorite straight-back chair, yards of white satin draped over her lap.

She'd take a few moments to eat toast and drink tea when Dilip forced her to rest midmorning and again for lunch. Her dinner more often than not sat untouched on the table beside her until the light grew too dim to work without a lamp and her vision grew too blurry to work at all. Then she'd hang the dress in the wardrobe dominating the bedroom, eat her cold lentils and rice, and fall asleep the moment she fell onto her mat.

She poured every ounce of creativity into embellishing Damaris's gown. She stitched a pattern of spikes and zinnias around the hem and two feet up the skirt in gold thread. Then she began the tedious work of turning a pile of iridescent beetle wings into flowering vines and butterflies nestled within the branches, adding clouds of minuscule mirrors to represent the monsoon rains.

She left the chiffon insert and sleeves bare, but on the rest of the gown, from the bodice to the fabric at the back that would fall over a bustle, she spun nature. She poked holes through thousands of wings, fastening them to the fabric with stitches at the top and bottom. She fanned them and overlapped them and clipped them.

And when Damaris stood in the middle of her dressing room, the gown puddling the floor around her bare feet, Ottilie knew every minute of missed sleep, every pricked finger, and every skipped meal had been worth it. Not many women could pull off such a dress.

Damaris, though, did so with ease. The fashionable neckline, cut deep and overlaid with sheer muslin, revealed just enough décolletage, and Ottilie could imagine how the beetle wings would glimmer and sparkle in the gaslights.

"You will draw the eye of every man at the ball," Mrs. Winship had said, her expression calculating and detached.

"That's why I did this, Mother." Damaris looked at the mirror, meeting Ottilie's gaze, and rolled her eyes.

Ottilie had smiled, but she knew what Mrs. Winship's approval of the gown meant. More clients. More work. More money. Maybe enough money. Damaris looked stunning and would no doubt receive her fair share of attention, but she'd only done this for Ottilie's sake. And there was no woman more deserving of endless work and effort than her friend.

Even so, by the time Ottilie stumbled back home, her eyes were red from lack of sleep, and her dress hung limp around her waist.

The next morning she slept until sunlight spilled through the window and Thaddeus had tripped over her on his way toward the kitchen, drawn by the scent of frying spices and Nānī's singing.

Ottilie stretched and rubbed the tight muscles of her shoulders and neck, stiff from days of hunching. The street sounds a backdrop to her thoughts, she eyed the black mourning gown hanging from the hook on the wall, and grief clawed at the back of her throat. Turning her head away, Ottilie watched the sun and shadows play on the worn wooden floor planks, naked of carpets. No warmth or softness.

Maji's death had left a void much the same.

Why, Lord, do you make us suffer so much? Why have you forsaken us? Why do you hide your face from me?

The loss of her father and siblings had hurt. Had left her soul gaping with emptiness. The loss of Maji had thrown her world off its axis, and she couldn't yet believe it to be true. Her heart had frozen beneath her breast, and she feared it would never thaw.

Maybe when the monsoon came, with humidity that wrapped like a wool blanket and skies that wept, maybe then Ottilie could fully embrace the truth of her new life.

But now Christmas beckoned. Christmas was a time of birth, was it not? A babe rooting for milk and a mother's love. A father's plan.

Ottilie couldn't imagine Christmas without either. So she wouldn't.

She pushed up from her mat and, ignoring her mourning gown, wrapped herself round and round in the white sari. The gauzy fabric slid over her hips and swathed her shoulders. She pulled the neatly hemmed edge around her back and tucked it into her waistband.

There. Now that she was hidden and protected within a brilliant chrysalis, God could do something with her shattered spirit. With time, maybe a butterfly would emerge. When she wore European dress, expected of her because of her majority of English blood, she drew stares and abuse from British and Indian alike.

When she wore a sari, because she looked Indian, she could hide. No one noticed her. Her waist was uncrushed by stays, and her movements unhampered by bustle and heavy fabric meant for foggy days. Maybe the most Anglophile in their Eurasian community would raise their brows and the aunties would gossip about Ottilie behind raised hands, but no one would say anything. Especially in her grief. And today she wanted to be like Nānī. Wanted to distance herself from the feelings that came whenever she donned woolen gowns—as though she were a child playing dress-up. Clothing that didn't fit properly. A look that endeared her to no one and drew distrustful pale English eyes and resentful Bengali frowns.

A knock quickened her pace as she crossed the room. When she opened the door, Nānī stood on the other side. Her gaze traveled Ottilie's length before she gave a short nod. "Now that you are finished with your work, you will eat."

She led the way to the back room and motioned Ottilie toward Dilip, who sat on his heels, peeling papaya. Nānī handed Ottilie a steel plate piled with rice, *masoor dal*, and *begun posto*. Ottilie's stomach growled at the scent, and she mixed a small knob of eggplant into the rice and scooped it into her mouth. She made quick work of her first full meal in nearly a week.

When Nānī had married, she'd been the spoiled youngest daughter of a rich man. Never had her hands seen labor. And her new husband provided her with servants and a French chef who ignored local preparations for European dishes. But Nānī had been on her own for decades now and had returned to the food of her youth. These days Dilip did most of the cooking, except when Nānī wanted something. . . .

Ottilie, a fragrant slice of papaya halfway to her mouth, sent a sharp look at her grandmother. The lentils turned to rock in her belly. "Nānī . . ."

"*Navasi.*" She sang the word. *Granddaughter.* Not one of the numerous nicknames she'd bestowed on her grandchildren over the years. Only granddaughter.

Ottilie handed the plate to Dilip and stared at her grandmother. This couldn't be good. "Will you tell me what's on your mind?"

Nānī's face relaxed into innocent-looking lines. Her grandmother might have rejected a privileged past and spent many years struggling to survive, but she'd never released a stiff-fingered grasp on attaining her wishes.

Ottilie rubbed her forehead with her fingertips, easing the furrows that betrayed her worry. Nānī called her *Boodha* when Ottilie allowed little things to deepen the lines between her brows.

"You will have wrinkles before me if you hold your face like that." Nānī shoved a ceramic bowl, the last of Maji's set, onto a shelf before crossing the room, her bare feet slapping the floor. She settled between Ottilie and Dilip, her teeth flashing in a large smile. "I have news. Do you know Mingel D'Souza?"

Ottilie searched her memory until the image of a middle-aged man with a quick laugh put a face with the name. "The Luso-Indian from Kochi?"

Nānī nodded. "He has a good job with the railroad. He moved his widowed mother up here and takes care of her. His home is well kept—I was invited last month."

"That's nice." Ottilie hoped Nānī only wanted to tell her about a new friend but knew it was unlikely. Her grandmother wouldn't make breakfast for idle chitchat.

"Mingel is looking for a wife."

Ottilie's teeth bit into the soft inside of her lower lip. "Nānī, no."

"Oh, come now. You can at least meet him properly. He's a nice man, isn't he?"

"No." Although Ottilie had no idea. She'd hardly spent more

than five minutes in his presence since he'd arrived in the neighborhood a month ago.

"He's a hard worker. Catholic, but that can be forgiven, and perhaps he'll attend the Baptist church with us once you're engaged."

"I'm not getting engaged."

"He is older than you, but not by more than twenty years, and that's not so much, is it? His mother doesn't speak a lick of Hindi, English, or Bengali. Only Portuguese and a bit of Malayalam, but she seems like a nice woman. Not the type to hit a daughter-in-law. They have servants—Boodha, stop frowning before you damage your face—and five rooms. Five! We'll be living nearly as well as when your father was alive. It's not a palace, but you could do worse. He isn't the most handsome man I've ever seen, but you should marry a man whose beauty is on the inside. A man with a fine face usually hides ugliness inside."

"I don't care what he looks like. I'm not marrying Mr. D'Souza. I'm not marrying anyone." Ottilie ground the words between her teeth and crossed her arms. Her stomach clenched when she thought of Victor, the memory of his eyes and gaze and the soft brush of his fingers. She remembered how a man's touch could set off a fire that spread over her skin. But that was when she was fifteen and sixteen—little more than a child. She couldn't love someone now. Not like this, her heart a hard little knob that beat only a faint tempo, needing time to recover from the death. The betrayal.

Not Mingel D'Souza.

"You're young. There's no reason to say you'll *never* marry. Why? No. You will marry someday, and it might as well be someone who can feed us. Keep Thaddeus in school." Nānī crossed her arms, matching Ottilie's posture.

Nānī didn't know. Had never met Victor. Had never seen him resplendent in his gold-braided uniform. Had never been tugged into a dark corner of the Imperial Museum and held in his arms. Had never heard Ottilie whisper a frantic *yes* when he proposed. Hadn't noticed when Ottilie wept when it ended only four months after Papa's death. Because there had been so much weeping, and how would she know Ottilie shed tears over a cowardly soldier, not again for the loss of father and siblings?

She didn't know, and Ottilie wouldn't tell her. And even if Ottilie did, one day, set aside her vow not to marry, she wouldn't be coerced into a marriage of convenience. Not when she'd grown up watching the restrained passion and evident love between her parents. "I don't love him, Nānī. I never could."

"Psssh, love. What did it bring me but heartache? Even your mother suffered from it. Better to marry a man you merely *like* so that if he rejects you, you won't grow cold, and if he dies, you won't grow weak from grief."

Ottilie stood and looked down at her grandmother, able to see the fear in Nānī's drawn face. Her grandmother only wanted to spare them the indignity of poverty. Her stubborn meddling was birthed in love and concern.

Ottilie held out her hand and helped Nānī to her feet. Placing her hands on her grandmother's narrow shoulders, she pressed a kiss to her forehead. "I love you and would do almost anything to see you happy, but I won't do this. I'd rather marry no man than marry a man I feel as much for as I do a jackfruit."

The next day, a barefoot child came to the door. He lifted a letter. "For Miss Ottilie Russell, from Memsahib."

Ottilie pulled a note from the envelope and scanned the elegant script asking her to appear with her embroidery samples at a fashionable address near the Maidan the next day. It was simply signed *FL*.

"Who is the memsahib?" Ottilie turned to fetch a coin, but when she held it out for the boy, he had disappeared. She looked down the alley, empty save for the sow who'd taken residence in the constant puddle near the gutter, and shook her head.

The following day, Ottilie strode down Chowringhee Road, boxes secure in her arms, hoping the cryptic letter would lead to a generous client. The message sender didn't live as far away as the Winships, so Ottilie took a moment to pause outside the fence that gated the Manohar Das Tarag, an artificial lake built by a man from Benares to provide water for the city's cows. Beyond lay the Maidan parade grounds, Fort William with its beautiful gates and barracks full of red-coated military men, and, even farther, the Hooghly River, clogged with ships.

Calcutta was a beautiful place, a vibrant mixture of British and Indian architecture, traditional and modern, planned and chaotic. Where wealthy English roses lounged in palanquins and took the air on King's Bench Walk, and where bent women, their arms taut from decades of labor, washed clothing on the steps of the ghats.

Ottilie belonged to none of it. Neither had her mother, though that was softened while Father lived and held an esteemed position. Her grandmother, born into a tightly woven Indian family, had belonged. At least before she married. And again after her husband left.

Nānī knew who she was. Whose blood ran through her veins. Ottilie, with her Indian looks and British education and accent, traveled between worlds. Thaddeus, who looked so much like their father that Ottilie's breath caught every time she saw him, might have an easier time of it.

A breeze glided over the water, tickling her ears with a whisper. Maybe Thaddeus could pass. It had been done by Eurasians before. It would lead to a better life. But to deny one's heritage? To deny memories of Hindi lullabies and the soft curves of a mother wearing a sari and the click of anise seeds against teeth?

How could one betray that in favor of the pretention of an English life?

She sighed and set off again. Her steps ate up the distance, and she soon arrived at a marble-fronted palace. Whoever had summoned her would have connections. Maybe their financial burdens, at least, would be eased.

The door, opened by a white-swathed servant, swung into a wide hall leading to a teakwood staircase. He bowed his head and led her beneath a carved doorway into the parlor. A balanced mix of British sensibilities and Indian craftsmanship, the room exuded tropical warmth.

Ottilie set her boxes atop a carved trunk and took a turn around the room, admiring the rich textiles and heavy furniture. Soft steps padded behind her, and when she turned, she saw a plump woman carrying a terrier.

"Miss Russell?" The woman's voice held a timid note Ottilie didn't often hear in the English. Colonists and conquerors, they'd grown used to having their way.

"I am."

"Thank you for coming. I had tea with Mrs. Alma Winship and her daughter, Damaris, and was convinced I needed a gown embroidered by you. I wondered if you might have time to work on one before the governor's Christmas ball."

Ottilie counted the days. Three. She blew a puff of air from between her lips. She'd have to work day and night. Again. But if this customer liked her work, she'd tell others about it. The house, if not the timid woman herself, gave the impression of great wealth and influence.

"There isn't much time, but I can do a simple design. Who is your dressmaker?"

She named the little French lady Damaris had used. "But the gown is already made. I only want it embellished."

That would give her time to complete the project. "I can show you some examples of my work. Maybe I can embroider the bodice only and bring the wings down the torso like this"—Ottilie swept her hands down her middle and flared her fingers over her hips—"which would create a beautiful effect. I don't think an unadorned skirt would diminish it."

The woman nodded eagerly, her expression matching the little dog's in her arm. "That would be an elegant solution." She set the terrier down and motioned Ottilie to the settee before perching herself on the edge of a firm cushion.

Ottilie gave her a sidelong glance. She'd never been invited to sit in a client's presence. Neither had her mother in all the years Ottilie assisted her. But the woman patted the place beside her and smiled, the apples of her cheeks squishing her eyes. Kindness settled upon her round face.

Ottilie's fortification crumbled just a little. She found herself smiling back and reaching for the small packet that held Maji's shoes.

"These are lovely!" the woman said. When her little dog put his paws on her knees, she tsked and gently pushed him aside with her foot. "You mustn't get close to these special shoes, Cordelia."

"I made them for my mother before she passed."

The woman closed her eyes and held the shoes to her chest. "I'm so very sorry. I lost my mother, too, when I was very young."

Ottilie ignored the twinge of pain that asked her to withdraw and instead touched the woman's hand. "It's a hard thing to lose a mother before one is settled into life. It feels as though nothing will ever be right again."

"Tell me about her." The woman set the shoes on the table and pulled Cordelia into her lap.

"My mother?"

"Yes. She died recently, I know."

Ottilie drew her brows together. What an odd woman. Not anything like most of the upper class she'd worked with. Damaris must have mentioned Maji's death, but for this person to bring it up, to sound as though she cared? It unsettled Ottilie, and she began wrapping the shoes in their brown paper to distract from the oddness of it all.

"You don't have to speak of her, of course, but I remember how much it eased my heart to have someone to tell about mine."

Her voice, as syrupy as the *rasgulla* Ottilie's father used to bring home from the sweet maker, worked magic within Ottilie. She grew as soft as the *chhena* that formed the treats she loved so much but hadn't been able to eat in years. Grief had turned them bitter.

"My mother was . . . kind. In some people, life's hardness creates a brittle shell. A sharp defense. But Maji became *good* instead. She wasn't weak, though. She was so strong, I sometimes forgot she was human. I relied on her too much. We all did. So when she died, we became lost."

"You don't seem lost to me. I'm struck by your strength. Your mother raised you well." The woman patted Ottilie's knee.

Ottilie tilted her head and tried to read the intention behind her watery gaze. "Who are you? You've yet to give me your name."

The woman drew back, and her gaze darted from Ottilie to the dog in her lap. "I've not been completely honest with you," she said. "I've been so desperate to meet you, especially after I heard of your mother's death. I thought this might be a way to bridge the . . . separation."

Her words were spoken in a desperate whisper, and with each one, her accent grew thicker until Ottilie could hardly understand what she said, much less what she meant. Ottilie pushed off the settee and gathered her packages, unsure if the kindness had been a mad person's ruse.

"Please let me explain myself. I've bungled this so terribly." The woman pushed her face against Cordelia.

Ottilie inched toward the doorway just as a man entered the room.

"Darling, my meeting was canceled. Would you like to take a

ride before the heat makes the day unbearable?" The man caught sight of Ottilie, who stared at him, mouth agape. "Ottilie?" The colonel's gaze swung to the woman who still sat on the settee. "Flora, what is going on?"

The woman burst into tears. "I only wanted to meet her. To know her. There is no one else now."

Ottilie fled toward the door. The colonel held out a hand as she passed him, but she skittered away.

Before she could escape the grounds, however, her grandfather—no, the *colonel*—clattered down the verandah stairs and caught up with her.

"Ottilie, a moment."

She ignored him and kept her gaze focused on the tall iron gate fencing them in. And everyone else in Calcutta out. She didn't belong on this side. Didn't care what he had to say. She only wanted to go home and forget the image of that woman stroking her mother's shoes.

Ottilie scrubbed her free hand over her eyes, not wanting to see Flora's—Mrs. Lupton's—crumpled face. Her tears. She'd sounded so desperate. So broken. Ottilie jerked her elbow away from the colonel's grasp and pushed forward until she reached the street outside his residence. "Leave me be. I don't understand what your wife intended, but I want nothing to do with it. Or you."

"I had no idea of her plans, but let me tell you why she called for you. I think you might show her compassion."

He'd been a military man for decades, and the strength girding his words couldn't be ignored. She nearly obeyed him much the way she imagined those beneath him did, but she had despised him for so long. She wouldn't be undone by a commanding voice.

"Compassion? For her? For *you*? After what you did to Nānī and Maji? I remember. I *remember*. Do you? Your own daughter, and you sent her away."

Her father had only been dead a couple of months when they lost nearly everything. First their home near the museum, then the furnishings and artwork and, most painfully, the books. All but one. Evenings spent curled against Father's legs as he read poetry and history. The fairy tales illustrated with pastel princesses and hairy goblins. The scientific examinations of birds and plants and insects. Every volume tied to a memory. Every page swept by his fingers. Every word tangled with his voice.

And Maji had thought, before it came to that, her father might offer assistance. Maybe he held fond thoughts of her. He'd been a present parent during her childhood. Until he abandoned them. Found a more suitable wife among the Fishing Fleet girls. A plump woman who had skin like cream and lovely blue eyes.

"It wasn't like that," he said. "I hadn't told Flora about my past. That wasn't how I wanted her to find out. She stumbled into the meeting. I just wanted time to explain Gitisha and Sonia to her."

"Don't say their names! I hate to hear them on your tongue." Ottilie spun and stepped into the street, eager to escape.

A shout, the clatter of hooves, and she was dragged away from the wagon that had nearly run her over. "Have a care," the colonel said, his hands still grasping her upper arms.

Ottilie drew in a ragged breath, then clasped her fingers over her mouth when she saw her samples, torn from their paper, lying in the dust. The lightweight shawl fluttered after the wagon's wheels, dirt and cow excrement marring the fringe. And Maji's gift . . .

With a quick glance in either direction, Ottilie pulled away. The colonel, though, wouldn't release her and instead guided her toward the shoes. One lay ruined, the heel splintered and the toe box crushed.

"Oh no." Ottilie sank to her knees and gathered them to her chest. Colonel Lupton stood near, motioning traffic around her as she retrieved the shawl and reticule, thankfully undamaged.

But the shoes . . . only one remained. Her most beautiful work. Her last remaining bit of Maji.

She allowed him to help her to her feet and lead her back toward his house. "Let me get you something cool to drink. You don't have to come in, but you can rest on the porch."

Ottilie, drained and unable to refuse, nodded and followed him back to the verandah. She sank onto a wicker chair tucked into the corner, and he waved toward two servants. One stepped inside the house, and the other brought over a wide fan and began waving it before her.

Closing her eyes, she received the breeze against her face and neck until a clattering drew her eyes open, and she saw the second servant carrying a silver platter of glasses. The colonel handed her one, and she sipped at the minted sugarcane juice.

"Thank you," she murmured.

A wave of ice washed over her. She could have been killed just like her mother. Run over in the street. Her impetuous actions, goaded by anger, could have left Nānī and Thaddeus alone, with no protection. No way of feeding themselves. She peered at the colonel over the rim of her glass. Sitting in the chair opposite her, he didn't look away but watched with a guarded expression.

"All right. Tell me why your wife tricked me into coming here." His quick actions had kept her, at the very least, from serious injury. She could offer him five minutes of her time.

He settled back into his seat and took a sip of juice before sighing. "Flora has always wanted children. There have been . . ." He looked away, the skin beneath his muttonchops mottling. "There have been none."

Ottilie was able to fill in the blanks. Whether Mrs. Lupton had never conceived or lost her babies, the end result was the same. An empty house. Empty arms.

He set his glass on the tray that the servant, who had been standing in the shadows, held out. "I told her about your mother's death. I believe she feels a kind of commiseration with you. Her parents are both dead. Her sisters scattered across England. She only has me." His lips quirked. "And I don't think I'm family enough for her."

Bile filled Ottilie's throat, and she couldn't help the bitterness leaking into her response. "How dare she presume I'd want to be that for her! After usurping Nānī's place? After conniving her way into the heart of a married man?"

"It wasn't like that. My marriage to your grandmother had ended long before I met Flora. She's a good woman. She wouldn't have married me had she known about my previous life."

"You turned my grandmother into a polygamist."

"She pushed me away."

"I don't believe it."

"You don't have to. But I would ask that you allow me— my wife—to be part of your life now. With both your parents gone, I feel responsible for you and Thaddeus. And for Gitisha."

"After you sent us away years ago? We *needed* your help then. Maji was desperate for a relationship with you."

"I reached out later, after I told Flora about everything. My messages were sent back unopened."

Ottilie shook her head. She didn't wait for the servant but set her glass on the ground and stood, mangled packages in hand. "Why should I trust you now?"

She strode away, her heels clicking an angry staccato against the marble. His voice, heavy with authority and thick with emotions Ottilie hadn't expected from a man so bent toward his own desires, pierced the silence between her steps.

"I understand you don't trust me, but I hope to change that. I'm not sure you have much of a choice at this point."

Ottilie paused at the bottom of the stairs, the truth of his words weighing her shoulders and bowing her head. She didn't turn, but she could tell he drew nearer.

"If you find yourself in need of anything, come to me. Start with something simple—embroidering a dress for my wife. It will provide you with income and also future customers. Flora will see that everyone knows you embroidered her gown."

Ottilie straightened her spine and nodded. "I will do that. And if all goes well, it will be the only time I need to rely on you."

4

"Now that you're done with the dress, you can rejoin our family." Nānī shuffled into the front room and pushed the door open, allowing the late afternoon sunlight filtering between the buildings to dispel the gloomy corners.

Ottilie shifted on the flattened cushion of her father's chair—Maji had been unable to bring herself to sell it after his death—and lifted her head. She'd dozed after making the final stitch after lunch, unable to resist the effects of the quiet, the heavy air, and the rice filling her belly. Nor the exhaustion of sleepless nights.

"I'm doing this for the family." She grimaced at the twinge in her back and stood to stretch it out. "I need to do two gowns and half a dozen smaller items each month to keep us in food alone. Another gown for Thaddeus's school fees, lamp oil, needles, and wings. There is no scenario where I am not working day and night."

Nānī's face softened. "I know. Where would we be without you? Who is this one for? Another daughter of a rich merchant? Or perhaps the wife of a military official."

Ottilie swept her hair over her shoulder and busied herself with locating the pins that had dislodged while she slept. Nānī's accurate guess warmed her face, and she hid her guilty expression—her grandmother could ferret out the truth in a glance—by poking around the floor beneath the chair.

She stood, holding the hairpins between them. "Will you help me with my hair?"

Nānī noticed the tension in her voice and probably the way Ottilie evaded the question. She narrowed her eyes and studied Ottilie's face, but she inclined her head and went to retrieve Maji's hairbrush. Ottilie used the moment to settle her nerves. She knew her grandmother appreciated their precarious financial situation too much to forbid work, but Ottilie wanted to keep her contact with the colonel and his wife private for a little longer. She wanted to explore the situation before discussing it.

She wanted to know the truth.

And she wouldn't risk hurting her grandmother in the process of finding it.

When Nānī returned to the room, she pushed the shutters open, set a jar on the ground, and sat cross-legged on the floor. "Sit, Ottilie. How will I fix your hair if you tower over me?"

"You make me sound as tall as Damaris." Ottilie sank to the floor and rested her hands on her knees.

A small pop sounded when her grandmother pulled the cork from the bottle of hair oil, and the sharp scent of rosemary tried its best to overpower the musky, rotten smell of the marigold. Nānī credited the plants, steeped for months in mustard oil, for her still-thick and shiny hair. Each week, Nānī, Maji, and Ottilie had taken turns massaging the oil into one another's scalps. They all had the same curtain of heavy, dark waves that fell to midback.

As Nānī rubbed her thumbs in circles, starting at the base of Ottilie's neck and creeping outward toward her ears, Ottilie allowed herself to relax. The tradition of mother and daughter that had knotted hearts together and mended broken ties did its work.

Nānī's fingers, flexible and calloused, crashed through the

flimsy wall Ottilie had erected around her grief. She hadn't had time to miss her mother. Hadn't allowed herself the luxury of considering the injustice of losing her.

And now . . . now Ottilie smelled her in the oil dripping down her cheek. Felt her in the brisk strokes of the brush that smoothed and coerced. Heard her in Dilip's song, drifting from the kitchen as he ground spices and chopped vegetables for dinner.

As Nānī twisted her hair into place, Ottilie patted away the tears that trickled, not wanting to draw awareness to her suffering. But, of course, nothing could be hidden. Nānī saw much more than her tears.

"I know you weep, Navasi. You are allowed to weep." Nānī's words released the final barricade, and when the last pin secured her hair, Ottilie laid her head in her grandmother's lap. She closed her eyes, and Nānī drew firm fingers from behind her ears, down her neck, and over her shoulders, forcing the tension to release. Forcing the distractions to flee.

"Oh, Nānī, I thought when Papa died, I knew grief. But this . . . how can I go on without her?"

"You go on because you must. One step forward. One small act of faith." Nānī lifted Ottilie's shoulders, pulling her upright. "Do you remember why I went to Benares shortly before your father became ill? Before the children died?"

Ottilie nodded. "You wanted to visit your sister. To restore your relationship."

Nānī jiggled her head. "That. And I wanted to know I'd done my best to repair the damage my hus—the colonel had done. We'd grown in faith together, Niraja and I. We read the Bible, stolen from one of the dignitaries visiting *Pitaji* and smuggled into our room. But after the thing that was done—" She held up her hand when Ottilie interrupted to ask for more information. "I won't discuss that now. I will only say, I took your mother and Thaddeus so I could convince my sister that *his* actions weren't a reflection of God's. That the loss of life from the one didn't have to mean the loss of faith in the other."

Nānī took a deep breath, cradled Ottilie's face between her hands, and smiled. Such a sad smile. "My sister didn't listen, and when we got home, your father and the babies were gone. You were terrified, burdened with something too great. And do you know what Sonia said to me when I railed at the God who took everyone and everything away?"

"What did she say?" Ottilie needed to hear her mother's wisdom. Needed the comfort of hearing her deepest thoughts after losing her husband and children.

Nānī pressed a kiss to Ottilie's forehead, and when she drew back, the words made a sharp path through Ottilie's spirit. "She said, 'My Edwin is gone for only a moment. How much more tragic if he believed as Niraja does and became lost to God forever?'"

Ottilie let her lashes fall, remembered the shattered expression on Maji's face when she walked through the door, smile ready and arms extended, and found only Ottilie, rocking in the corner, still with breath in her body.

"They're gone. They're gone," Ottilie had cried, her words matching the rhythm of her movements.

Maji had shoved Thaddeus at Nānī, then clattered upstairs, calling, "Edwin, my darling. I'm home."

And then the cry when she found him.

Ottilie covered her ears now, just as she had then, a girl of only fifteen. Maji had spent hours upstairs, saying good-bye to her children and husband. So much grief. So much loss. Ottilie knew, even then, that the woman who returned to her wouldn't be the same person. And now Ottilie realized even more personally how true that had been.

When the undertakers arrived to prepare the bodies, Maji came out of the bedroom, her face washed and hair brushed. She gathered Ottilie to her and whispered, "They are only gone a moment, dearest. Only a moment. Death is not the end."

Ottilie parroted the words now. "They are only gone a moment. Death is not the end."

Nānī gathered her close and ran her hand over Ottilie's head. "And for you, life is about to begin. Happiness is around the corner."

Ottilie pulled away, a question on her lips, but a light rapping on the doorframe stole the words away.

A satisfied smile curved Nānī's lips, and she twirled the baby curls springing around Ottilie's temple.

"Who is it?" Ottilie hissed.

A square face framed by salt-and-pepper hair poked into the room. A pleasant enough face with a quick smile and wide-set eyes, but not a face Ottilie wanted to see.

Nānī shot to her feet and darted toward him. "Welcome, Mingel. Come in. Join us."

When Dilip entered the room carrying a tray of salted *lassi*, Ottilie knew Nānī was serious. They hadn't entertained since Papa had died. And mourning for her mother had hardly begun.

Mingel, sitting in Papa's chair, accepted a glass and brought it to his mouth. "Delicious," he said with a smack of his lips.

Dilip frowned at him before serving Ottilie and Nānī, sitting cross-legged on mats across from Mingel. When Ottilie reached for a glass, Dilip raised his brows, but she only shrugged. She could hardly believe Nānī's nerve. She'd expressly asked her grandmother to abstain from matchmaking. With Maji buried not even a month, it was socially unacceptable.

Ottilie sighed and took a sip of the refreshing yogurt drink, then looked at her lap. She'd play the modest Indian girl if it got her out of making conversation.

Nānī filled the quiet with her chatter, and Mingel's responses, girded in the musical rhythm of Kerala, danced in the pauses. Ottilie glanced at him from beneath her lowered lashes. He wasn't a bad-looking man, but he was entirely too old for her. When he flashed a smile her way, she felt nothing.

Nānī pinched the underside of Ottilie's arm, spurring her to join the conversation. "How do you like Calcutta? Kochi is very different."

"It is." The gleaming smile flashed across Mingel's face. "Kerala is more relaxed. The food is spicier. The heat invades every corner, and it's impossible to escape, even in December."

Ottilie nodded. "The weather in December is very nice here."

And off Mingel went, talking about monsoon season and rainfall and temperature. All things as exciting as tracing the path of a cockroach. Ottilie met Dilip's eyes, and a smile quirked one side of his mouth. They'd spent too many childhood hours together for him not to know her mind. He jerked his head toward the door.

"Will you excuse me?" Ottilie said. "I need to discuss tomorrow's Eurasian Club Christmas celebration with Dilip. We aren't going, of course, but he's offered to deliver treats on our behalf."

Nānī's hand shot out, but Ottilie evaded her grandmother's obstruction and scurried to the kitchen. When she reached it, Dilip stood with his back against the wall, his face a twisted mask of concern. Ottilie patted his arm. "It will be fine, Dilip. Nānī just needs to be convinced I know my own mind. She must know she cannot force me to marry."

"Your father wouldn't like you to marry against your will. He wouldn't like you to marry for comfort instead of love." His worry-filled brown eyes took in her face.

"Of course he wouldn't." Papa, despite his success in the scientific field, had been a romantic. He would have wanted a love match for her. She lifted the heavy jug of water from the cabinet and poured some into a brass cup. Lifting the jar of fennel seeds, she unscrewed the lid and shook some into the water. "Of all the ridiculous things she's done . . ." Ottilie rolled her eyes and pressed the drink to her lips, sucking the seeds between her teeth and crunching them to release their healing power. Nānī's manipulations had soured her stomach.

Turning, she set down the cup and gripped the edge of the cabinet. She hadn't recovered from Victor's betrayal four years earlier. Even had Mingel D'Souza been the handsomest, most charming man on the planet, she wouldn't have considered him.

Sharp, prying fingers grasped her arm, and Nānī's voice tore through her swirling throughts. "You've lost your mind. What do you think Mr. D'Souza thinks of your rudeness? We can still salvage it. He is interested. It is good you are beautiful. That makes up for your headstrong stupidity."

Ottilie jerked her arm away and turned to face her grand-mother. "I'm not marrying Mr. D'Souza. I'm sure he's a good man, but Maji just died. I'm not ready to think about this."

"What else can you think about? Our situation is precari-ous. And Mr. D'Souza is more than a good man. He is a well-respected man with a steady job."

"But shouldn't there be something more if you're to marry someone, Nānī? Shouldn't there be mutual affection and pas-sion?" Ottilie had that once, though it didn't last. But her parents proved love matches worked.

"Life doesn't work that way, no matter your father's modern nonsense. He was full of foolish ideas and couldn't even manage his own household."

From the corner of her eye, Ottilie saw Dilip stand up straight, his brows pulled in and mouth pinched. She shook her head, knowing his intense loyalty toward Papa. Knowing he would defend Edwin Russell even at the risk of alienating Nānī, who spoke more from fear than anger.

Ottilie could see it in the trembling of Nānī's shoulders and arms. In the jerky movements as she paced the small room.

"You don't mean that, Nānī. I know you loved Papa. I will marry whomever I choose or no one at all if that is what I decide. I am three-quarters British, Nānī, whether you like the notion or not. You don't have the right to arrange my marriage. Father wouldn't have liked it. Neither would Maji." Ottilie clasped and unclasped her hands behind her, unable to keep the quiver from her voice. Nānī had always been temperamental. Determined to see her own way. But they'd never fought like this. It filled Ottilie with impending dread. "You don't have to worry. I will take care of you."

On Nānī's next pass around the room, Ottilie held out her hand, her fingers grazing the fall of Nānī's sari. She tugged until her grandmother stopped. "Please."

Nānī yanked her sari from Ottilie's clasp. "You have it in your hands to ensure our safety, yet you choose to throw it away. I am tired of living without security. Tired of having nothing. Your mother tried, I know, but it was never enough. You have it within your grasp to give us enough. I am disappointed in you."

With a regal carriage, Nānī left the room.

Just as she disappeared, the door flung open, and Thaddeus rushed inside, swinging his books tied with a strap over his shoulder and then dropping them in the corner of the room. "Can I have something to eat, Dilip? I'm so hungry. Your lunch wasn't enough to fill me." He shot an accusing glare in Ottilie's direction.

She'd given what they could spare while still leaving enough for dinner. "You may have lassi, and Dilip has sliced a papaya."

"I don't want papaya. I want cake. Or biscuits. One of the boys had biscuits at school today. He had biscuits and a sandwich made with sliced meat and a banana *and* an orange, Ottilie. Both! Why don't we have biscuits? My stomach always feels funny."

Ottilie walked across the room and gathered her brother into a hug. Her fingers probed the dips and ridges of his spine, hoping he'd not lost more weight. "I'm sorry, glowworm. I'll try to do better."

Her eyes met Dilip's over Thaddeus's head. Maybe she should consider Mingel D'Souza. Her brother was worth the sacrifice, but she wanted to take care of her family on her own. She didn't like the idea of relying on a man. They'd proven less than dependable in the past.

5

Ottilie used to stop by the Imperial Museum once or twice a week on her way home from school. She'd walk up and down the halls of the bird gallery, reading the scientific names on their plaques in her admittedly weak Latin. *Perdicula asiatica, Gavia stellata, Ciconia nigra, Psittacula caniceps* . . .

She'd run to her father's office, swipe a black-and-white-striped humbug from the sweet dish on his desk, and launch into his arms. Then he'd show her new artifacts and send her on her way with a pat on her head.

Ottilie wandered the wide galleries now. She took her time at each of the glass cases lining the walls of the botany hall. Gaslights hanging from the ceiling illuminated specimens collected from all over the world. Showy tropical plants from her own backyard to desert cacti. She examined a *Dionaea muscipula*, a carnivorous plant from the United States displayed with a small ant about to become its lunch. She splayed her fingers over the glass, wishing she could touch it. Something tangible her father may have handled.

She walked on, allowing her hand to trail the cabinets. Feeling the same wood and glass her father had loved for so many years. Here, she could sense him most. His presence invaded every corner. She'd passed the three-story building after dropping off Mrs. Lupton's package and decided it had been enough time since her last visit. She hadn't been since before Maji's death. And there was no better place to find distraction.

She also wanted to forget the simpering gratitude in Mrs. Lupton's eyes when Ottilie pulled the burgundy gown from its wrapping. A simple design, it didn't warrant such effusive praise. Nor did it deserve the double fee the colonel's wife had pressed into her hand.

Ottilie wished she could have refused, but that morning when she'd reached into the little mustard jar, her fingers brushed only a few lonely coins. She'd pulled one out for the boy she'd hired to deliver a message to Damaris. The rest wouldn't have even covered food for the week.

Hunger was a greater motivator than pride. Especially when that hunger came in the form of a little boy's stomach growls. Thaddeus was already small for his age. He needed meat. Something that was all too often out of reach.

"Ottilie."

The call pulled her from her worries, and she turned to greet Damaris, handsome in a green plaid walking suit that played off the red curls piled beneath her hat. Since the room was empty of patrons, Damaris allowed Ottilie to pull her into a hug.

"How I love that you aren't too proper for physical affection. This would give my mother indigestion." Damaris pulled away and grinned. She took Ottilie's elbow and led her from the hall. "Let's go see the newest member of the Imperial Museum."

"Who is that?" Ottilie had spoken with Mr. Janssen, the slight, bespectacled Dutch botanist who'd taken over as museum superintendent after Father's death. He hadn't mentioned any new employees.

"Henutsen, daughter of Egypt." Damaris pulled Ottilie into the anthropology wing.

"The mummy. I forgot about her. She was to be delivered this month."

"Everyone at home is agog over everything Egypt."

They wound through the rooms, their silence companionable, until they reached the one that held this new wonder. Approaching the sarcophagus, Ottilie peered into the glass case. A shudder ran down her spine as she took in the open casket, the wrapped body swathed in strips of linen. Who had she been? A princess, it seemed, by the wealth buried with her. But had she been loved or despised? Content or burning with ambition? Every day, people filtered by, curious to see her. Enamored with the romance of the past. But Ottilie knew there was nothing romantic about death. Someone had mourned this life. Had taken care to clean her body and preserve her—not for future generations to ogle at but because they thought she was going on to life after. Life with all the jewels and food and household items she'd been discovered with.

Ottilie thought of her family interred in a stone building. Buried with nothing but the clothes chosen for them. She hoped Jesus had it right and not the ancient Egyptians. Otherwise her family was wandering around in the afterlife hungry and poor.

"I'm going outside." Ottilie pushed away from the exhibit and left the room, Damaris on her heels. Halfway down the hall, Ottilie paused before a stone relief of a dancing Ganesha carved out of basaltic stone. One of the less terrifying Hindu deities, his elephant head and round body spoke of goodwill.

With a deep sigh, she continued on, pressed through the door, and exited onto the verandah that ran the entire perimeter of the inner courtyard. Outside, she could breathe. Away from the gods and religious artifacts, she could relax.

The air, spicy with the scent of jasmine, cleared her lungs but not her mind. "How do we know what we believe is truth? That Christianity is the right path?"

Damaris didn't respond right away, and it was one of the things Ottilie loved about her. She wasn't given to idle chatter or trite answers. "I don't think we can. Not entirely. We can try to make sense of everything, and some people do, but there's a beauty in remaining faithful despite our doubts. If we had all the answers, that beauty would be diminished."

"I want answers." Ottilie's whisper held a hard edge. *Do you hear, God? I want answers. You saw fit to take nearly my entire family. Why?*

They walked beneath one of the archways onto the grass. A few families braved the midday sun and sat on blankets in the courtyard. Ottilie smiled at the hive of children playing a made-up game involving sticks and a lot of giggling. Parents and ayahs looked on, indulgent smiles on their lips.

"I wish I had an answer for you," Damaris said. "What you've been through . . . it's enough to damage anyone's faith. But sometimes I just don't think there are answers. All I know is that if it came down to following Christ, who sacrificed for love of me, or following a god who sows discord, expects more than I can give, or consigns me to a life of eternal works, I'm choosing Christ."

Ottilie nodded as though she agreed, but inside, desperate questions fermented. Bubbled up and begged for release. She couldn't say them. No proper woman would. And she wasn't sure even Damaris's liberal leanings could entertain her doubts. But inside, where no one could hear or judge her, Ottilie begged to understand. *How is it love to destroy my entire family? What separates you from the millions of gods dotting temples all over this country? Where have you been?*

A child screeched his glee at having scored a point in the game that made no sense. Ottilie hadn't expected to hear anything else.

"Why are we here?" Thaddeus whispered, tugging the collar of his too-small sailor suit. His large hazel eyes took in the room, from the plush carpets to the rich woodwork, and he shifted on the settee beside her.

Ottilie sighed. She had no idea. A week earlier, she'd received a letter from the colonel asking her to visit and bring Thaddeus with her. She ignored the message for a few days, but then she was contacted by two women wanting gowns embroidered . . . and both said Mrs. Lupton had referred her to them.

Ottilie hated to be obligated to anyone, especially to *that* man and his wife, but in truth, they'd be starving if it weren't for Mrs. Lupton. And Ottilie feared what would happen if she refused.

So when Nānī told them that morning that she was going to visit some of the sick in their church with a few other ladies, Ottilie forced Thaddeus into his best suit and hustled him out the door.

"We're visiting someone who . . . used to know Maji." She clicked her tongue and crossed her arms. "Don't ask me anything else. I can't explain. And don't tell Nānī about this. I will myself when the time is right."

Thaddeus looked at her askance. His mouth formed around the words he was thinking, but he thankfully let the matter alone and didn't voice them. Ottilie had no idea if Thaddeus could keep their visit quiet. He'd been reserved since Maji had died. He'd never been the type to prattle, so she thought he might listen to her, especially if she promised him a stop at the bakery on the way home.

A scratching sound at the door drew their attention, and when it pushed open, the terrier Cordelia pranced into the parlor. Thaddeus gasped, and a grin lit his face. Other than the occasional stray pariah dog, they hadn't interacted much with the animals. Most Indians didn't keep them as pets.

Thaddeus clasped Ottilie's arms. "Can I pet it, Didi?"

Before she could answer, Mrs. Lupton and the colonel entered. "Cordelia loves attention. Here." Mrs. Lupton lifted the dog and set her on Thaddeus's lap. "Hold your hand out and let her sniff you."

Thaddeus did as instructed, then laughed when Cordelia licked his fingers. Ottilie smiled. She hadn't heard him laugh in a month. If that was the only good thing to come out of this visit, it would be worth it.

"Thank you for coming," Mrs. Lupton said, her eyes shining. She settled into a rattan chair across from them. The colonel stood behind her, his hands on her shoulders in a protective gesture.

"Do you think we could get a small dog like this?" Thaddeus pressed Cordelia against his chest, not noticing when the animal squirmed.

"Nānī will never allow us to have a dog. She detests them." Ottilie extricated Cordelia from Thaddeus's hug and set her on the floor. "You know she says they are filthy and shouldn't be in a house."

Ottilie didn't know why she said it, except maybe to put the colonel's wife in her place. This foreign woman who stole her grandmother's husband and was now trying to steal her brother with pets and soft smiles. Even though Nānī hadn't spoken to Ottilie since their argument in the kitchen, a fierce protectiveness swelled beneath her breast.

Thaddeus screwed up his nose and bent down to pet Cordelia, who had put her front paws on his shins, her tiny claws piercing the fine cotton of his pants. "She doesn't look or smell filthy to me."

"A friend brought Cordelia all the way from England about ten years ago. She's been my dearest companion ever since." To Mrs. Lupton's credit, she ignored Ottilie's insult, and her voice still held warmth. "But if your grandmother doesn't care for dogs, it's best you abide by her wishes. You're welcome to visit here anytime you wish, though, to play with Cordelia."

Thaddeus sent a sly smile Ottilie's way, then said, "And where am I?"

Colonel Lupton's brows rose in question when he looked at Ottilie.

"It's just easier to leave the story untold." Ottilie lifted the dog and offered her back to Thaddeus. Distracted, he said nothing else.

Really, what did they expect? How could Ottilie explain them to her brother? He knew nothing of Nānī's previous life, nothing of the pain she suffered. Maji had never mentioned her father again after that disastrous visit when Thaddeus was a toddler, and Ottilie had no reason to pile another story of loss on top of all he had already suffered.

"Darling, I think Thaddeus would enjoy walking with Cordelia in the courtyard. Would you like to take him?" Colonel Lupton's question sounded more like a demand than a suggestion.

Mrs. Lupton clapped her hands and smiled. "Yes, what fun!" She stood and held her hand toward Thaddeus. Without even a glance at Ottilie, her brother, one arm still secured around Cordelia, took it and let her lead him from the room.

Ottilie scooted closer to the edge of her seat, poised to vacate it at a moment's notice. She picked at the frayed fabric of her cuff, rolling the black thread between her fingers, and shot the colonel a look she knew betrayed her wariness.

He took his wife's seat. Resting his elbows on his knees, he steepled his fingers. He said nothing.

Neither did she.

Whatever he hoped for, Ottilie felt little inclination to give it to him. She'd indulged his desire to meet Thaddeus. Surely that would be enough.

"I want to make things right." His voice held steady. Strong. "And my wife wants a family. We'd like for you and Thaddeus to move in with us."

Ottilie's mouth dropped open. Of all the presumptuous

things she'd thought he might say, that hadn't even entered her mind. "No."

"No?" He looked around his lavish parlor, then dropped an accusing glare at her threadbare sleeve. "You have nothing. We have everything, and no one to share it with."

"I am not left with nothing. I have my grandmother. I'll not abandon her the way you did."

He stared at her a moment. A tense silence filled with all manner of words. None of which Ottilie wished to hear. "I'll see that she's cared for. Not here, of course, but somewhere nearby so you can visit."

Not here, where it would be awkward. Two wives beneath one roof.

"I will not abandon Nānī." Ottilie hoped he'd hear the steel beneath her words. She wouldn't be bullied. Wouldn't be commanded.

The colonel slapped his hands against the armrests of his chair. "And how do you plan on paying for Thaddeus's school? His clothing and food? You make little with your embroidery."

"I make enough."

"Only because we've sent you work. How big do you think our social circle is? Flora has told everyone she knows about your skill, but there is an end to our contacts and influence."

Ottilie stood on shaking legs, for once grateful for voluminous British skirts. The colonel would see only what she wanted him to see, and that didn't include the tremors wracking her body. "I will take care of Thaddeus and Nānī. I will do it without your help."

"You've not inherited one iota of your mother's common sense."

"Maybe not, but I have inherited her virtue."

"You are so much like Gitisha." His face was red, whether from Ottilie's underlying insult or being defied, she didn't know. "You will regret this."

59

"Not as much as you will regret the way you treated Nānī and Maji."

Giggles and a clatter of footsteps interrupted the tension between them. Thaddeus, followed closely by Mrs. Lupton, tumbled into the room. "Ottilie, did you know we might live here? Won't Nānī be surprised when we tell her she will be sleeping in a real bed and eating with silver forks?"

Ottilie sent an accusing glare at Mrs. Lupton. Taking Thaddeus's arm, she said, "We will never live beneath the roof of such a man, no matter the luxuries he could give us. It would be a betrayal of Maji's love and Nānī's honor."

Thaddeus's lips squished toward his nose, but she ignored his confusion and stalked toward the door.

"For what it's worth," the colonel called, his words punctuated by Mrs. Lupton's soft weeping, "I only left because she told me to. And I tried to send money, but she never accepted it. She sent back all my letters unopened."

Ottilie paused at the threshold and swallowed the words that threatened to tumble from her lips—Hindi insults and Bengali accusations and English censure.

In the end, she decided on silence. Because nothing she could say would ever fully express her disdain.

Nor would it ease the pain that had lodged beneath her breast and grown ever deeper, ever wider, with each loss she faced.

The moment Ottilie and Thaddeus got home, she headed toward the back room where they slept and removed a sari from the cabinet. Not the white one of mourning but her favorite green silk. A paisley pattern shot through with gold threads embellished the rich color.

She set it on a chair behind the screen. With the removal of each layer, she shed her connection to England. First her skirt and bodice, which proclaimed to the world that she'd lost a loved one. Too common a color seen on the streets of Calcutta, but grief was an intensely private thing and went deeper than the shade of her frock. Then the corset, which stole her breath and forced her body rigid. She untied the ribbons that held the bustle to her backside and made her look like a preening peacock. And finally she pulled off her chemise and petticoats, wishing she could let go of the colonel's blood as easily.

She shook out the skirt and draped it over the back of the chair, resisting the urge to kick it into the corner. With quick movements, she undid the buttons lining her black boots and pulled out the pins holding up the twist of her hair.

And then she stood there, arms akimbo. A slight breeze swept through the open window—December was the only time this happened—and chilled the sweat dripping down the curve of her spine. Divesting oneself of unwanted associations was no easy task.

With deft fingers, she plaited her hair, tying it off with a piece of string, then pulled on her blouse. The snaps down the front made it easy to don. The short sleeves made it more suited to the climate than the layers she'd worn earlier.

A moment later, swathed in yards of airy fabric, she strode from the room and found Thaddeus playing with a couple of wood pin soldiers in the kitchen. Nearby, Dilip stooped and brushed the floor with a broom made of twigs. Something fragrant bubbled over the fire.

"I'm going to work on the verandah while the sun is still out. Nānī won't be here for dinner today. Something light will suffice." Without a backward glance, lest she reveal too much of the emotions simmering beneath the surface of her tranquil expression, she left.

Settling near the steps, legs crossed, Ottilie pulled her beetle-wing box onto her lap. Spanning the length and width of two hands, it had a flat carved top and sturdy brass clasp. It had been part of Nānī's dowry, and she'd gifted it to Maji on her marriage to Father. Maji had originally used it to store her jewelry, but there were no gems left, and now Ottilie filled it with jewels of a different kind.

Lifting the clasp, she flipped open the top and scooped her hand into the pile of green iridescent elytra. The box was filled halfway, so she had enough for another two or three projects. She needed to purchase more soon. She could find the *Buprestidae* jewel beetle wings in Calcutta, but they were cheapest in Benares, Nānī's hometown. Ottilie would send for a case and buy enough locally to get her through the interim.

Today she would work on fabric that would be fashioned into a reticule with black fringe and a tightly woven drawstring. Ottilie's client wanted something "native" to take home during her husband's year-long leave from military duty, so she'd asked for peacocks.

Never mind that Ottilie had never seen a peacock wandering Calcutta. They were all locked behind the walled courtyards and gardens of the rich babus on the other side of the city. She had nearly suggested embroidering the face of a cow on the front of the bag, but the woman seemed a sour sort, all deep lines and disapproving scowls. So . . . peacocks.

Ottilie drew golden thread through the needle's eye and outlined the face, neck, and chest of a bird. Then another. All around the bottom of the fabric that would be sewn by the French seamstress the British women adored into something that would hold nothing of importance. When a bevy of birds pranced in a cocky parade, she riffled through her box and pulled out elytra of similar size, pouring them into the dip of fabric between her knees.

"What are you making?" Thaddeus poked his head through the window to the main room. He hung his arms over the ledge and slapped the wall with his hands.

"A reticule for a fancy lady."

"Should I learn to embroider like you? Then I can help bring in money, and you wouldn't worry so much."

Ottilie dropped the wing case she'd been trimming with a pair of small scissors and met Thaddeus's gaze. "What makes you think I'm worried?"

Thaddeus drew a line between his brows. "It's always there and deep."

Ottilie smoothed her finger down the wrinkle marring her skin. "No, you don't need to learn my trade. You need to finish school and go on to university and become an important man."

A line—smaller and shallower than hers—appeared between his brows. "I want to be a scientist like my father."

Warmth flooded Ottilie. Thaddeus didn't remember Papa. Didn't remember the way he held him, cuddled to his shoulder, unlike so many men who feared babies as though they posed a larger threat than a hungry tiger. He didn't remember the way, even then, Papa called him his little glowworm. Didn't remember the tears in Papa's eyes when the midwife came out of the birthing room and announced another boy. But Ottilie counted it a success that Thaddeus loved him still. Loved him enough to want to follow in his footsteps.

She set her project aside and motioned for him. With a smile, he disappeared back into the window and popped outside a moment later. When he settled in her lap, she wrapped her arms around his thin shoulders and brushed back the swath of thick hair that always fell into his eyes.

"Will you sing to me, Didi?" he asked.

She knew which song he wanted. The Bengali lullaby Maji had sung to him most evenings before bed. She closed her eyes and lifted her voice, hearing her mother in the music. "*Ghum pharani mashi pishi . . .*"

It was a song about an auntie bringing a child sleep in exchange for sweet betel leaves that meant only as much as the memories tied to it. And Ottilie put every effort into making this moment one that would help Thaddeus feel closer to Maji.

After she finished, he sat there, quiet and eyes closed. She continued to hum the tune and, finally, pressed a kiss to his sweaty temple and pushed him off her lap. "Now I have to work, so go see if Dilip needs help."

She watched Thaddeus scamper off before turning back to her embroidery. With a pair of brass-handled scissors, she trimmed the little knobs that once connected the elytra to the beetle's body, then fanned them into feathers. Happy with the effect, she began the tedious task of attaching them to the fabric.

She fell into a rhythm. Piercing, pulling, knotting. Over and over until the birds took shape and seemed ready to make their horrid screams and hop onto the tiled verandah floor.

"Such a beautiful creature. Such an awful sound." She stabbed the needle through an elytron.

"Maybe," Dilip said, coming out of the house carrying a steel *thali*, "God expected the peacock would grow too prideful if it had both beauty and grace." He crouched before her and set the thali down, then tore a piece of *chapatti* and handed it over.

"I told you something simple would be fine for dinner. Why have you gone to all this trouble?"

"You need to eat. You work too hard."

"I work precisely so we can eat." She took the flatbread. Dinner was beautiful. Balanced. Around a mound of rice were small earthenware bowls filled with pickled vegetables, fish cooked in yogurt, fried eggplant, and lentils dotted with little puddles of ghee. "You spoil us."

He smiled. "Your father showed me so much love. He saved my life. I promised him I'd care for you the day he died."

"I didn't know that."

Dilip had been at the house, of course. Had spent that horrid night running between beds and bringing water to Ottilie so she could wash her father's and siblings' brows. He'd been the one to fetch the doctor. The one to force her from the room after first her brother, then her sister died.

"While you sat with Jemima and Nathan, I talked with him. He knew he wouldn't survive. And he knew you'd be alone, surrounded by death. He told me to care for you. To see that you didn't die of exhaustion and grief." Dilip pinched off a piece of chapatti and used it to scoop up some lentils. Holding it toward her, he said, "Eat. You must eat, ma'am. You get like this, and I'm afraid you'll disappear."

She took the food. Darling Papa, knowing death was present and thinking, in his final moments, of her. He had known her so well. And he'd tried to protect her from herself.

Dilip stood. "I've honored his request. I always will." Then he disappeared inside the house.

"Your papa loved you very much." Nānī's knees creaked as she stepped onto the verandah, her sandals making scuffing sounds against the tile.

Ottilie traced the dips and bumps of an elytra. "I know. My childhood was magical."

Nānī winced as she sank to the ground. "You have not suffered a deficit of love, which is why I think a marriage to a near stranger might work—you have a strong foundation for it. But I will not push you any more over it." She grasped Ottilie's knee as she pulled her *pallu* from beneath her and wrapped it around the back of her midriff. When she finished, she didn't withdraw her touch, her palm warm and knobby fingers stroking.

Ottilie knew she was forgiven. And she needed to release a burden from her chest, one that weighed heavily. "Do you remember when Papa took me to the Royal Botanic Garden?"

He did that once in a while—took one of the children somewhere, just the two of them. Ottilie had looked forward to their trip for weeks. She'd imagined the hours and hours she and Papa would spend exploring the acres of trees and plants. He loved botany. Loved sharing in the discovery of it.

They'd ridden the twelve miles in a *gharry*, eating sweets that left their lips and chin sticky. When they arrived, he helped her from the carriage as though she were a princess. He had an uncanny ability to make whomever he was with feel like the most important person in the world.

"We were exploring the banyan when a dreadful shriek sounded and a peacock charged at me. For a child of six, it was terrifying."

"Peacocks are horrible creatures." Nānī smiled at the story. By the time Ottilie and Papa had arrived home, they were clutching their sides from laughter over it.

"Papa swooped right over, holding his arms out and making himself big. He stood between me and that peacock." Ottilie smiled at the memory. Her studious, restrained papa, barreling toward that bird like a rhinoceros. "He always made me feel safe. Like everything was right when I was with him."

"Your papa was a good man."

"He was. But when he left, Nānī, he took that feeling with him. I haven't felt like everything is right in a very long time."

6

On the rooftop, above the night sounds and the ever-present noxious scent from the meat-packing factories a few streets over, they celebrated Christmas Eve.

Their Christian neighbors jumbled the narrow, twisting streets, exchanging homemade cards and sweets wrapped in leaves. As the Russells were still in mourning, they would not join the festivities. Thaddeus sat cross-armed against the balustrade, pouting as he looked down on groups of boys playing games of jacks and cricket.

Ottilie joined him. Not too close—she could feel the resentment pulsating from the top of his tousled hair to the toes of his bare feet—but near enough that he didn't feel too alone while he looked over the crowd.

"I wish we could go down." He strained his neck to better see all the fun he was missing.

"I know."

"Maji wouldn't care if we did."

"But everyone else would."

Thaddeus swung around and speared Nānī, who sat on her mat in the middle of the roof, with a glare. "Would you care?"

Nānī held out her arms, and Thaddeus's chin began to tremble. With a sniff, he launched himself at her, burrowing deep into her embrace. Ottilie turned away and looked out over the city with unseeing eyes.

Behind her, Nānī murmured words meant to ease her brother's confusion and grief. In the kitchen below them, Dilip finished preparing for Christmas breakfast. He might join the merry-makers, or he might just go to sleep in the corner of the room in deference to Maji's death. And farther on, people called out greetings that barely made it through the haze of loss enveloping Ottilie's home.

After Papa died, Christmas had lost its allure. No one much felt like celebrating those first few years. Thaddeus knew nothing about the colorful garlands and cutout stars that had brightened their spacious bungalow northwest of Eden Gardens. He didn't know about the candlelight services they'd attended at St. James's Church, flickering lights reflecting off the gilded angels that watched over the congregation. He knew nothing of his siblings giggling as they watched Papa kiss Maji beneath the little sprig of trumpet vine. "There's no mistletoe in India," he'd say, "so this will have to do."

All Thaddeus knew was the one tradition they kept. On Christmas Eve, they carried their sleeping mats to the roof and slumbered beneath the starry sky. It started when Maji was pregnant with Jemima and struggling to rest in the heat. At only four, Ottilie thought it great fun when Papa led them up the stairs to sleep outside. After that, it became family tradition.

Behind her, Ottilie heard rustling and shuffling, then Nānī stepped near. "He's not only mourning your mother, but his way of life."

"It will be over in five months. Then he can go back to his friends and celebrations."

"A lifetime for a child of six."

"He will hardly remember her, you know. In a year or so, he won't be able to picture her without looking at a photograph. Another few years, and his memories will have faded so that all he'll have are hazy dreams of a laughing woman who fed him rasgulla."

"You've done an admirable job of helping him remember his father, even though he was still a baby when your papa died."

Ottilie ignored her. Plowed ahead with the thought that had been tormenting her all day. As she let out Thaddeus's knicker-bockers and helped Dilip plan Christmas dinner and rubbed Nānī's feet with mustard oil to help stave off the cold that had begun to settle in her chest, Ottilie had toyed with something so alarming and isolating, she couldn't think about anything else.

"Nānī, after you're gone, there will be no one left of the family but me. I'll be the only one who can describe Papa's horrible singing voice and the way Maji smelled of jasmine. The only one who knows that he waved his hands when he got excited and she squeaked every time she saw a roach. And no one will wish to speak of them, because I'll be the only one who *remembers*." A tear slipped free, and she wished very much to be a young child so she could burrow her head against Nānī's breast and be comforted. "We give Thaddeus words. That's all. Words mean less than memories. And he won't have any."

Nānī didn't care about all the years that crowded between Ottilie's want and need. With soft and welcoming arms, she did the work grandmothers all across the globe were meant to do and invited Ottilie to her side. "Sometimes, when we are most alone, the God who sees and knows is closer than ever."

She spoke from experience, Ottilie knew. She'd lost every-thing too. And yet the words didn't bring Ottilie peace. Or assurance. Only a gnawing doubt that was so tangled with yearn-ing, the two were indistinguishable.

Nānī pulled away and cupped Ottilie's cheek. The wrinkled skin of her exposed arm hung like a deflated balloon. She'd lost weight since Maji's death. "Do you believe me, Navasi? That God is never more than a prayer away? That he is always with you?"

Ottilie turned her face so that Nānī's hand fell away. So that her eyes were averted and couldn't be searched. Did she? She used to.

How weak her faith that, when confronted with tragedy, it fell apart.

Nānī leaned over the balustrade. "Your questions are understandable. Expected. God isn't afraid of them."

They laid out their sleeping mats in a row, the air cool enough that they needed to wrap themselves in light woolen blankets. Thaddeus slept all tossed out, his arms and legs open to the night sky. Ottilie turned onto her side, away from her family, and looked through the turned spindles to the building across the alley. The streets were quiet now, families snug in their little houses, children wondering if Christmas Baba would make it all the way to India.

Nānī's even breathing soon settled into the snores that had plagued her for years. Thaddeus rolled over in his sleep and tucked himself against Ottilie, his scraggly toenails scratching the backs of her calves. She smiled. He hated having them cut.

She continued to stare at nothing, unable to shake the sense that despite sleeping inches from her grandmother and brother, she was still very much alone.

Ottilie awoke Christmas morning to the sound of the muezzin calling Muslims to early-morning prayer. She lay still for a moment, listening to the chant. Then the noise of street life took over.

Nānī and Thaddeus still slept beside her. She tried to go back to sleep—the sun was just peeking over the horizon, sending a watery blush over the city—but after many moments of tossing and turning, she gave up. She pushed off her twisted blanket and crept to the edge of the roof. A story below, the winding street already crawled with people ready to start their day. Only the city's minuscule Christian population—smaller in this neighborhood than in the British communities northeast of the Maidan—observed Christmas Day. Everyone else went about their work.

A thin man wearing a *dhoti* carried two buckets of water that hung from a shoulder pole, and beyond him a young boy carried a box on his head and cried, "Sweet meats! Sweet meats!" She stretched her arms above her head, working out the kinks from her back and neck. Nānī had slept in her sari, but Ottilie needed to change out of her nightgown before Dilip awoke and began puttering around the kitchen.

About to turn, she caught sight of a man, newly arrived from Britain—she could tell by his pale skin, untouched by the sun, his perfectly clean white linen trousers and jacket—not a speck of dust marring them—and the bewildered expression on his face. Even from her height, she could tell he was lost and unsettled.

Entally didn't normally attract British travelers. It was mainly populated by Eurasians, Indians, and Chinese immigrants, though some wealthy Europeans had built sprawling bungalows and palaces a few streets over. Maybe he'd been misled.

She turned away, determined to dress and, if he still wandered the street, set him on his way. A frisson of compassion hastened her steps. It was Christmas. No one should wander around lost on Christmas. Papa had told her about being completely overwhelmed when he first moved to India. "You have no idea how different it is from England," he'd always said. "It confuses you at first, and the heat! Even in winter, the heat can feel oppressive."

She donned her layers and layers of British clothing, including the black gown that trapped the sun against her skin, but left her shoes at the bottom of the cabinet. He wouldn't see her feet, and she planned to dress in a sari as soon as he had been pointed in the proper direction.

She crept past the kitchen, still quiet except for the sound of Dilip moving around. Outside, a stray dog dug at the ground, and half a kilometer away, the piggery released its foul odor.

The British man stood a few houses over, covering his nose and looking up at the second-story verandah of a neighbor's house.

Ottilie stepped into the street and craned her neck but saw nothing except for narrow windows, peeling green shutters, and iron framework. She looked again at the man. "Can I help you?"

He scratched his head. "I was told I could find the person I sought on this street, but there are no identifying plaques on the buildings. No numbers. I will admit, though, to being quite tired. I just arrived, set my bags at my hotel, and set off. I should have rested first." He blinked at her, then smiled—a smile that transformed his rather nondescript face into one that was quite appealing.

Ottilie couldn't help but smile back. "You must be meeting someone of great importance to leave so quickly after arrival. And on Christmas."

"Oh! It's Christmas. It had completely slipped my mind. I am looking for someone of great importance. The new Baron Sunderson."

Ottilie shook her head. "Why would anyone think you could find a baron in Entally?" She jerked her chin down the alley. "You're in the wrong part of the city."

The man pulled a crumpled sheet of paper from his pocket and unfolded it. His brows drew together. "Is this Pakanatala?" His pronunciation drew a laugh from her throat, which she tried hard to suppress.

"It is. But I assure you, no British aristocracy live here." She threw a glance over her shoulder at the twisted, narrow road hugged by one- and two-story houses—all featuring crumbling bricks and shabby shutters. Stray dogs rooted through the open sewers, covered only by blocks of rough-hewn stone where people crossed. A baron? He was lost.

"Come," she said, "I'll walk you to the main road and help you find a tanga. Maybe the driver can direct you to the right place."

The door behind her opened, and Dilip called, "Ma'am? Are you all right? Your grandmother is calling for you." From behind him came Nānī's reedy "Navasi? Ottilie, where are you?"

She turned and nodded. "Yes. I'm helping this traveler find the right direction."

"Ottilie?" the man said. "Ottilie Russell?"

She turned back and lifted her brows. "Yes."

His eyes roved her face. "I . . . there must be some mistake."

She crossed her arms and tapped her bare foot against the dusty ground. She should have put on shoes. "I'm certain of my name."

"You're the daughter of Sonia Russell?"

"Yes."

"And your brother is Thaddeus Russell?"

"You're asking a lot of questions for someone I've just met and haven't been introduced to yet."

He bowed. "Everett Scott."

"Well, Mr. Scott, you already know who I am. I'd like to know how. And what do you know about my mother?" Her voice caught, and she coughed into her hand, not eager to offer this man any evidence of her grief.

He continued to stare at her.

"Is there something wrong?"

He shook his head, but his eyes never strayed from her face. Ottilie took a step back, then another. A quick glance assured her Dilip still stood on the verandah. He wasn't large but could probably protect her from this odd man in the straw boater and linen suit, with his questions and unnerving green eyes.

"Happy Christmas!" Thaddeus clattered past Dilip and threw his arms around Ottilie's legs. His upturned face glowed with pleasure, and when he released her, she saw him clutching an orange in one hand and a little tin train in the other. "Christmas Baba came, and look." He thrust the train toward her face.

Ottilie knelt and admired the train, not from Baba but from the coins she'd saved, little by little, from her embroidery money. "It's a lovely train." She spun the wheels, which really moved and had cost more than the simple wooden one she'd originally considered buying. But this one, with its working parts and painted car and shining black steam engine, would bring Thaddeus so much joy.

It didn't make up for his loss, of course, but Ottilie would do nearly anything to ease his sadness.

The British man approached them slowly, his hand held out as though trying to calm a wild animal.

Ottilie stood and pushed Thaddeus behind her. "I don't know who you are, Mr. Scott, or why you're here, but I think you should go."

"I've come to meet with Sonia Russell."

"You can't."

"Please, she's expecting me."

Ottilie swallowed, and her hands clenched around Thaddeus's arms as he peered around her. "Mr. Scott, you can't meet with her because she was killed in an accident last month."

Mr. Scott's mouth fell open. He closed his eyes and wiped a trickle of sweat from his brow before looking at her, this time with compassion instead of disbelief. "I'm so sorry for your loss, Miss Russell. I know how cruel it is to lose a mother."

Thaddeus pulled away from Ottilie and darted around her. "Maji was struck by a horse. Right in the middle of the street."

Mr. Scott laid his hand on Thaddeus's shoulder. "I'm very sorry for it." He went back to staring again, first at Thaddeus then Ottilie. He dropped his grip on Thaddeus and examined them both as though through Papa's microscope. "Do you share both parents?"

Ottilie gasped. "Thaddeus, inside."

Her voice brooked no argument, and he shrugged and ran to Dilip.

Ottilie waved them both into the house, then turned to Mr. Scott. "You are presumptuous."

"I've been sent here for a purpose, and I'm surprised your mother mentioned nothing of my coming."

Ottilie narrowed her eyes. "Being struck down by a horse has a way of obstructing conversations—even important ones."

Mr. Scott sighed. "I must know—was your mother Indian, and is she also Thaddeus's mother?"

Ottilie didn't want to answer. Didn't want to give his impudent question another thought. But if her mother had expected this man, invited him to their home, Ottilie wanted to know why, and she wasn't sure he'd give her the answers she needed if she didn't give him the ones he did.

"Yes, Sonia and Edwin Russell are the parents of us both. My mother was Eurasian—she had a British father and Indian mother. I look like my grandmother. Thaddeus looks like—"

"Your grandfather."

"No, my father. Thaddeus looks nothing like the colonel."

He shook his head. "I meant your father's father. He's the exact replica, except for the brown hair. Your grandfather had blond hair."

Ottilie's breath caught in her chest, and something hard and impossible to ignore fisted her stomach. "You know my father's family?"

"Quite well. They sent me here."

"Why?" she whispered. The English Russells had never contacted them before. Father alluded to some kind of falling out, but otherwise never spoke of his family except to say he had two brothers and a younger sister.

"Thaddeus is . . ." Mr. Scott laughed in a nervous way. "There is no easy way to say this. Your father's eldest brother, Newell, was killed in a carriage accident nine months ago, and he had only daughters. Four of them. They've gone north to live with their mother and her family. The second brother, who died three years ago in the Anglo-Zulu War, wasn't married. That makes Thaddeus the new Baron Sunderson."

Ottilie laughed. "Thaddeus . . . a baron? That's not possible."

"But it is. And your grandmother, Lady Sunderson, has sent me here to bring him home."

7

Ottilie didn't move, didn't blink. The blood traveling her veins turned to ice and made its presence known in the tone of her voice. "He is home."

"Home to England, I mean. He needs to be educated and, eventually, presented to society. He needs to take his place."

"His place is with me and Nānī here in Calcutta."

"Who is Nānī? Your husband?" Mr. Scott's eyes traveled past her and rested on the door Dilip had disappeared into.

"That was Dilip, our servant. Nānī is our grandmother. You're not taking Thaddeus from us. I won't allow it. We've lost too much already. How do I know you are who you say you are?" Her voice rose. "Do you really think I'd send my brother off with a complete stranger to people we've never met? My father never even mentioned his family was titled. He never mentioned his family at all."

Doors up and down the street creaked open, and heads popped out. Mrs. Daniels, a Eurasian woman who had lost her husband to typhoid. Mr. Bashir, a Muslim man who grew the most beautiful flowers in his courtyard. Mrs. Banerjee, who sang opera when the monsoon rains began.

"Are you well, Miss Russell?" Mr. Bashir called. He stepped out of his door, followed by his three very tall sons.

"Miss Russell," Mr. Scott said, his voice soft, "let's speak privately. May I come in and meet your grandmother?"

"No." Ottilie slashed her hand between them. "You may go away." She whirled, heedless of the rocks biting into her feet, and ran from him.

In the house, she shut the door, sliding the bolts on top and bottom. For a moment, she leaned against it, her hand pressed to her chest, trying to settle her heart, which had darted away from him almost faster than her body had been able to.

Then she pushed off and called, "Nānī!"

Her voice echoed off walls and around the sparse furnishings. It drew Dilip and Thaddeus from the kitchen, smelling of cumin and coriander and Christmas breakfast.

She motioned them away and ran toward the bedroom, which was empty. "She's in the courtyard," Dilip said from the doorway, his eyes wide.

Ottilie pushed past him, went through the kitchen, and slammed through the doorway to the courtyard they shared with five other households. Thankfully, Nānī was the only one present.

Not nearly as lush and well kept as the courtyard Ottilie had spied through the doors of the colonel's bungalow, theirs contained a dusty area surrounded by a few *batabi lebu* trees, branches pulled almost to the ground by an abundance of bright yellow fruit. They were lucky to have a well in the center of the courtyard so they didn't have to go far for water.

Ottilie found her grandmother sitting cross-legged against the peeling wall. Her head tipped back, eyes closed and mouth moving, she swirled her fingers through the dust around her.

Ottilie looked at the sky and scowled. Prayer time. She wouldn't be forgiven if she interrupted.

She undid the jet buttons at her wrists and tugged her sleeves up, glaring at Nānī's silent form. She stalked to the fruit tree—pomelos, the British called them—and twisted a fruit from its branch. Shoving her finger into the pebbled skin, she freed the flesh from its thick rind. She tapped her foot against the ground and made quick work of the fruit, though she didn't appreciate its sweet-tart flavor—only the moments it gave her something to do with her hands.

"You are ruining the peace of my morning," Nānī said, not opening her eyes.

Ottilie tossed the remainder of her snack into the weeds climbing up around the wall and licked the juice dribbling down her thumb. "This family's secrets have ruined mine."

Nānī, eyes finally seeing, turned her head. "What do you mean?"

"Someone named Everett Scott from England just told me Papa was from an aristocratic family. Barons. And evidently Thaddeus is the new one. Baron Sunderson, of all the pompous-sounding things. Is this true?"

Nānī's knees cracked as she got to her feet. Ottilie didn't offer her arm to help. She just stood there, the large waxy leaves of the citrus tree brushing her cheek, and folded her arms over her chest.

Nānī crossed the dry space between them and pressed a kiss to Ottilie's forehead. "Happy Christmas. Let's celebrate with your brother, and then we will speak of this." She turned away and ambled into the house as though nothing out of the ordinary had happened.

Ottilie ground her teeth together, barely capturing the shout that clawed her throat. There was no use nagging Nānī. She wouldn't speak until good and ready.

She followed her grandmother's steps, schooling her features into a placid expression for Thaddeus's sake, if not Nānī's.

Breakfast was quiet, save for Thaddeus's boisterous excitement. He ate, one hand scooping fingerfuls of *luchi* and mutton curry—Ottilie had splurged on the meat—the other moving his train around the breakfast platters.

"We won't visit the neighbors today," Nānī said, "out of respect for your mother. No one will expect it."

Dilip began clearing the remains of their meal. "Come help me wash up," he told Thaddeus, and Ottilie was grateful for his perception.

Nānī gripped her wrist. "Come with me. I have something to show you." She raised her brows. "This time help me up."

Ottilie did as she was told, and as she followed her grandmother into the bedroom, her stomach flipped, threatening to spill breakfast all over her feet. Her hands turned clammy, and she wiped them on her bodice.

Christmas morning wasn't meant for secrets. Wasn't meant for revelations and having one's life turned upside down. A small voice urged her to flee. To turn her back on whatever Nānī intended to show her. To pretend Everett Scott hadn't just stumbled into her life.

"Come, Ottilie." Nānī's command spoke louder than that little voice, urging Ottilie's steps forward.

Their bedroom, much like the courtyard, was simple. A little neglected. A pile of sleeping mats in the corner. A cabinet containing their clothing. And the little writing desk that had belonged to Maji—a vestige of their old life. Atop it sat Maji's brush and mirror, and a pot of solid perfume that Ottilie opened and sniffed when she missed her mother. Her fingers itched to twist off the silver cap and inhale jasmine and the comfort that came with the scent.

Nānī sat on the stool in front of the desk and stuck her head beneath the wide middle drawer. A creak, the pull of her finger, and a little hidden drawer popped open where before there was only ornate paneling.

Nānī lifted her head and grinned. "I remember when your papa bought this desk for your mother. It was right after you were born, and at first she just used this drawer to tuck away love notes from him, a curl of your hair, your first lost tooth."

She wrinkled her nose. "Thank goodness I managed to convince her to throw that away. But when the letters started coming, she had something that really needed to remain hidden."

"What letters?" Ottilie approached and saw a stack of envelopes tied with a lilac ribbon. And behind that, another stack tied in scarlet.

Nānī removed the first stack and set them on the desktop. She pushed the drawer closed.

"What about the other letters? Are those Maji's as well?"

Nānī gave her a sharp look. "Those have nothing to do with you and will remain hidden. Some secrets are best never spoken of." She tapped the letters in front of her. "But these . . . well, the secret is out now. Though I didn't know anyone was coming. She'd talked about it, but she must have only recently made the plans. She would have thought she'd have time to prepare us."

"Prepare us?" Ottilie choked on the question. "Maji knew? She knew about all of this and said nothing?"

Nānī held out the letters, but Ottilie refused to take them. She shook her head.

"You must read them, Navasi. They explain it all."

Ottilie squeezed her eyes shut. "I don't think I want to know."

A soft touch against her cheek, as soft as the scent of the jasmine that enveloped the letters, drew her eyes open. "I know. These are hard things. But you need to know."

Then Nānī left her alone.

With a wary glance at the stack of envelopes, Ottilie lifted Maji's perfume jar. It was heavy—Maji had just filled it before her death—the jar itself a Christmas gift from Papa. She twisted off the lid and pressed her fingertip into the smooth waxy surface. With trembling fingers, she ran the scent over her wrists.

Despite the betrayal making her mouth sour, Ottilie held her wrist to her nose and inhaled her mother's embrace. Her kiss. Her hair and clothing and presence.

She shook her head and straightened her spine, then dropped

onto the stool and pulled the letters toward her. With a quick tug, the ribbon came loose, and she eased the first letter from its envelope.

Ottilie's eyes widened at the date—September 22, 1865— only a couple of months after her birth.

My dearest Sonia,

How I wept when I received your letter. We hadn't heard anything from Edwin for two years, and I longed to know he was well. We hurt him terribly, and I've never forgiven myself for my complicit silence. I should have defended him better. That's what mothers do—and you now know that love, don't you?

But I hoped he would see sense and return home. Give up his pursuit of science and enter the church as we'd always planned.

Sonia, don't make plans for your darling Ottilie. She may well have a mind of her own.

I am very glad you wrote. And when Edwin has forgiven us, I pray his letters join yours. For now, I celebrate that Edwin is well and married and has become a father. I've heard such awful things about India—the weather and disease and heat. And the mutiny isn't far from anyone's mind, even these eight years later.

I know you said your people are of no consequence, but if they are ever in Wiltshire, they are welcome here at Hazelbrook Manor.

I leave you now with my eternal gratitude,

Eudora Sunderson

Ottilie stared at the words. Written in gentle, looping script, they told a story of reconciliation and celebration.

And secrets. So many secrets.

Maji had never mentioned her clandestine correspondence.

Evidently only Nānī knew. Had she ever told Papa she wrote to his family?

She riffled through the envelopes, glancing at the postmarks as she went. There were dozens of them. Maji had received three, sometimes four a year. Ottilie chose one from the middle at random and withdrew the fine paper.

I rejoice with you on the birth of your son. Thaddeus is a strong name and one that has a personal connection to our family. Did Edwin tell you it was my brother's name, gone these thirty years? I hope Edwin chose the name out of fondness. He was particularly close to his uncle.

And another, this one not long after Papa died:

When I read the news of your miscarriage my heart broke for you. I had so wanted you to find peace in another of Edwin's children. Oh, Sonia, you have lost too much! In these times, it is difficult to see God's goodness. I continue praying for your health. For Thaddeus and Ottilie, as well. May God keep his hand upon you. I wish you would consider coming to England. I want so much to embrace you, the woman my Edwin loved. To know his children. Please, come home to England. Surely your family misses you. And if they are not able to take you in, we will care for you always.

Ottilie stood so suddenly the stool knocked over and clattered against the floor. There was such familiarity in these letters. This woman Ottilie hadn't even known existed knew everything about her family. Everything about her. Except, it seemed, that Maji had an Indian mother. That their aristocratic British lineage had been diluted.

Ottilie clenched her jaw and flipped through the remaining envelopes. She found the last one and slid her finger beneath the flap, releasing the glue from the paper and tearing the corner in her haste to discover her mother's most recent betrayal.

> *We have already sent a trusted family friend, Everett Scott, to accompany Thaddeus to England. He should arrive not long after this letter. I know it is fast, but Everett's work doesn't allow much time for travel.*
>
> *I hear your grief, Sonia, and I know what it is to lose a son. I have lost three. But your dear boy won't be lost forever. He will only be a couple of continents away, and he will fill the hole left by my sons' deaths—both as far as the barony is concerned and the one in my heart.*
>
> *Oh, Sonia, do reconsider and come with him! Bring Ottilie and make your home here. It's where you belong. Surely, your obligations in India aren't worth sacrificing your health and proximity to your son.*

Ottilie sank to her knees and gripped the edge of the desk. She rested her head atop the cursed letter and took great gulping breaths. Maji knew. She was sending Thaddeus away. When had she planned to tell them? How could she?

"Ottilie?" Thaddeus's soft voice punctuated the sobs that had overtaken her.

"Go get Nānī." She pulled open a desk drawer. Finding a handkerchief, she rubbed at her nose and pushed away from the desk. Scooting across the floor, she pressed against the wall beneath the window and buried her head in her arms.

Thaddeus's loud footsteps sounded as he ran through the house calling, "Nānī! Come quickly! Ottilie is crying."

A moment later, Nānī had Ottilie wrapped in her arms. "You can cry, Navasi. It's a hard thing to learn."

"Why didn't you tell me?"

"I hadn't realized Sonia made the decision, not until this morning when you told me someone from Britain had come.

She'd spoken about it. We talked after your grandmother's letter came asking Sonia if it was possible to send Thaddeus to be educated in England. We knew Lady Sunderson would ask eventually, but I didn't realize your mother had decided." A thoughtful expression crossed her face. "She was leaving the post office when the horse struck. That must have been the letter I pulled from her reticule."

Ottilie glanced at the desk. "It hadn't been opened. You never read it?"

"I couldn't bring myself to. I hid it with the rest and decided to write to Lady Sunderson when my grief had lessened."

"She asked Maji to bring me to England as well. She's been asking her for years to go to them."

Nānī wiped her thumbs across Ottilie's cheeks, catching the last of her tears, then sat back on her heels. "Since your father's death. Of course, your mother couldn't go. Your father's family had no idea he had married a Eurasian."

"And Thaddeus *could* go because he doesn't look Indian. Not like me and Maji."

"Your father only spoke of his family once. He didn't know I heard"—Nānī winked—"but when has not being invited into a conversation ever stopped me from learning what I want to learn?"

"Oh, how can you jest at a time like this?"

Nānī's lips lifted in a soft smile. "Sometimes, it's the only thing that makes life bearable. Anyway, listen . . . when your mother was pregnant with you, your father told her that his father was a baron. That his eldest brother would inherit the title, the second would go into the military, and the third—him—would go into the church. But your father was a scientist, not a minister. He had no interest in being a man of the cloth. He was devoted to his studies. He left on bad terms and came to India. And he never spoke to his parents again."

Oh, Papa. How awful for him. For them. Family was everything. The only place one truly belonged.

"Your mother didn't *want* to send Thaddeus away. But he is the new Baron Sunderson. He has an obligation, a duty, to take his place. And it isn't as if it's an odd thing. Most British send their children away to boarding school around Thaddeus's age. Even Eurasians send their fair-skinned children."

"And they leave the Indian-looking ones here. Yes, I know. It's a sin to tear apart a family like that. I won't have it."

Something like pride glinted in Nānī's eyes. "Will that Everett Scott return?"

"I'm sure he will, but he won't find me receptive to his assignment." Ottilie pushed herself to her feet and held her hand out for Nānī. "I'm sending him back to England. Alone."

8

O ttilie spent a few precious coins and took a tanga to the Great Eastern Hotel. She refused to meet Everett Scott looking dusty and rumpled. To give him any reason to hold her in contempt.

When she had received his note that morning, asking her to join him for tea, she indulged her initial urge and tossed it into the cooking fire. The flames curled the paper, and she couldn't deny her satisfaction in that small act of rebellion. But then she realized that if she didn't go to him, he'd come to her, and it would be harder to set him in his place with Thaddeus present.

She didn't want him wreaking havoc in her home. He'd already wreaked havoc in her spirit.

In front of the elegant hotel on Old Court House Street, she straightened her hat and swept through the door a servant held open. At the desk, a man in a suit asked for her name, then told her Mr. Scott was waiting in the drawing room.

Ottilie passed ladies wearing fashionable gowns and fancy hats, rich Indian men wearing fine silk kurtas edged in taffeta and brocade, and turbaned servants scurrying down the wide halls, carrying correspondence and silver trays and heavy luggage.

She hadn't been inside the hotel since Papa's death. Hadn't

had any reason to visit. No money to spend. But she knew down the opposite direction from the parlor there were restaurants, stores, and merchants set up in little shops. It was said a man could walk in one end of the hotel, buy a complete outfit, a wedding present, seeds for the garden, have an excellent meal, a drink, and if the barmaid was agreeable, walk out the other end engaged to be married.

The hotel was more than a hotel, and Ottilie had never felt more like an outsider. There were only rich Brits and rich Indians. One or the other. No poor little-bit-of-this and little-bit-of-that Eurasians. In her outdated, plain black bombazine gown, she clearly didn't belong. And if the side glances and turned-up noses were any indication, she wasn't the only one who noticed.

She crossed the threshold into a fine drawing room done up in shades of green, brown, and red. Floral paper made the room cozy, along with the carved tables and dainty chairs set up in clusters around the perimeter. An ornate marble fireplace, topped by a large gilded mirror, dominated one end.

When Ottilie entered, someone near the door unfolded himself from a chair and approached. Mr. Scott, looking rested and not at all poor or rumpled or out of fashion.

He smiled that same unnervingly attractive smile, which only made Ottilie's jaw clench.

"Mr. Scott, I only came to tell you there is no reason for us to continue conversing. Thaddeus will not be accompanying you to England."

He tilted his head and studied her a moment before holding out his arm. "Would you like some tea? I loathe it, but I know the empire rises and sets on the stuff."

Ottilie opened her mouth to agree but noticed the interested glances from the people filling the room. All men. They raised their eyebrows and smirked as though knowing exactly why she was there.

Her cheeks burned, and she spun away from Mr. Scott and

his proffered arm. "If you want to speak with me, then we shall walk."

Stalking from the room, she didn't slow her pace until she had reached the dusty street. Far away from the arrogant men and their accusing stares.

Mr. Scott caught up with her as she passed Cuthbertson and Harper Saddlers. "Miss Russell, please, I meant no offense. I just thought we could enjoy a drink and some conversation."

Ottilie stopped and whirled. "Yes, I know what you thought. And I know what every man in that place thought. I am so tired of knowing what other people think. What they think is hardly ever true, yet I'm responsible for making sure they don't think it."

Mr. Scott drew his brows together and tugged his ear—a tell, Maji would have called it. Something that attested to an uncomfortable emotion. Revealed that which a person wished hidden, whether apprehension or confusion or embarrassment.

Probably a mixture of all three.

And it wasn't his fault. He had nothing to do with Calcutta prejudices.

"I'm sorry, Mr. Scott. You wanted to speak with me?"

She couldn't tell him why the men in the hotel were staring and snickering, of course. There were no words that would make the topic polite. But it wouldn't take long before he found out for himself. Eurasian women had a reputation. An unfair and undeserved one, but a reputation nonetheless. British women eyed them with distrust, casting at their feet accusations of trying to lure proper Englishmen from wives and families. And those wives talked to their husbands, whispering slanderous lies that instigated the men to forward and lewd behavior.

In her Indian dress, no one knew. In British fashion, Ottilie's heritage was obvious.

Mr. Scott stepped closer to her, allowing two men in lungis carrying a heavy trunk around them. "I want to set your mind at ease over your brother's welfare. He'll be well treated at

Hazelbrook Manor. Lady Sunderson is a woman I hold in the highest esteem. Nothing will be denied him."

"Except his family?"

"He'll be with family."

"Not with us."

He inclined his head, unable to argue. "I'd like to see Chandpal Ghat again. It was late when the ship docked, and I was so tired I didn't take the time to look around. Will you join me?"

Ottilie knew she should say no. She needed to return home and wash her hands of Everett Scott and his horrible errand. But he sounded so hopeful. His voice soft and imploring. His fingers had gone to his ear again, an endearing gesture.

"Oh, all right." She turned and made her way toward the river.

Mr. Scott drew beside her with a chuckle and kept pace. "Are you always so abrupt in your movements?"

"Only when I'm feeling particularly nettled."

"Am I the one irritating you?"

"It has been happening with increasing frequency since your appearance in my life."

He rubbed his mouth, but Ottilie still saw his quick smile, and she dipped her head to hide her own.

"Calcutta is a vibrant city. I quite like it."

"It's the most British of Indian cities. Maybe that's why?"

"Have you ever been to Britain?"

Ottilie shook her head.

"There's an English veneer to things here. The architecture—I've heard Calcutta referred to as the City of Palaces." He waved toward the town hall, a gleaming white Roman-style building faced with grand columns. "The restaurants and shops and . . . all the Englishmen."

A break in traffic allowed them to cross the street and turn left down Esplanade Row. It was, in truth, a street of palaces. Imposing private homes that faced the Maidan presented a decidedly British façade.

"But this isn't really Calcutta, is it? This isn't *really* India."

Mr. Scott's odd statement drew her attention from a three-story garden house fronted by an ornate iron railing and tall windows. "What do you mean, this isn't really Calcutta?"

"This is Britain's Calcutta. It isn't where India lives. I wish I had time to explore your country."

"You should. Trains leave from Howrah Station every minute to all parts of it. I hear Kerala is particularly beautiful."

A wry smile tipped his lips. "It's also on the other side of the nation."

Ottilie waved her hand. "Oh, that. Such a little thing to worry over."

They walked on in silence for a few minutes, and Ottilie caught herself stealing glances at him. He wasn't as handsome as Victor had been, not in the traditional sense, but his face was arresting, full of strong angles softened by a broad smile and coriander-green eyes that saw more than she wanted exposed. There was kindness in his expression . . . if not in his words.

"You know I won't leave until you allow Thaddeus to come with me."

"Then you'll have a lot of time to travel." She offered him a tight smile. "Why don't you set off tomorrow? I'll help you arrange transport."

They arrived at Chandpal Ghat and stood at the top of the wide, slick steps leading to the Hooghly River, which was crowded with bathers who seemed not to mind the debris from the thousands of ships that sailed into Calcutta each year. The water splashed against the ghat steps, its sound swallowing the argument that brewed between them.

Mr. Scott took everything in, his uncommon eyes gazing out over the men and women dipping themselves, the ferries moving people and goods back and forth to Howrah, the massive ships that deposited and collected and shifted. Standing at the bows of their little boats, *manjees* steered cargo and passengers through it all for a few coins.

"It is nothing like England," he whispered. He turned to her, an intense and disconcerting longing shaping the planes and valleys of his face into something she couldn't look away from. "I wish I *could* disappear on an Indian train. Go to Kerala and beyond. Lose myself in this foreign place. You have no idea how much I wish it." His jaw clenched, and he scrubbed a hand across it as though trying to capture a flood of words he didn't want released. "But I'm needed in England. I have work. Commitments. And I made a promise to Lady Sunderson. She's given me so much. I don't want to disappoint her."

"What is she to you? Who are you that she should trust you with this?"

"I'm the estate manager for Maybourne Park, which neighbors the Sunderson estate. But more than that, I've known Lady Sunderson nearly my entire life, and I am close friends with her daughter, Alberta—your aunt."

Ottilie shrugged. "While that's all very nice, your promise means nothing to me. Neither does her disappointment."

"It was your mother's wish that Thaddeus go."

In the museum, Papa had once shown her an exhibit of Indian weapons. One lethal-looking *kukri* seemed able to slice with only the lightest pressure of its blade. Mr. Scott's words were as sharp. They found their mark and cut straight through, piercing Ottilie's most tender memories. Happy memories.

Memories that were now as tainted as the Hooghly River.

"Mr. Scott," she said in a low voice that made him tip his head toward her in an effort to hear above the sounds of prayer and commerce. "My mother is dead. She's no longer making decisions for my brother. If you take issue with that, you can discover your countryman who killed her and discuss it with him."

Ottilie left him standing on the ghat steps, her heels clicking sharply against the stones as she strode away.

The next day, Ottilie heard Damaris's call as she wandered around Burrabazar.

"Ottilie! Over here."

She spotted her friend standing in front of Firoz Mithai Sweet Shop, waving her arms in a way that drew the attention of everyone who passed.

Ottilie crossed the street, pushing through the crowd of people shopping the market's wholesalers. On their way to buy fruit and wedding jewelry and silk imported from Persia, they stared at the British woman who made no pretense of pale timidity.

"I'm just dying to get my hands on some *ledikeni*. Mother refuses all sweets in the house. Says they will inflame my already passionate nature." Damaris snorted and took Ottilie's arm. "She says God mocked her the day I was born. All she asked for was a child who didn't inherit Father's family trait." She touched one of the red curls swooping beneath her hat.

"Your hair is beautiful." Ottilie steered Damaris through a throng of young boys, faces pressed against the sweetshop window. "And your passionate nature has nothing to do with it or with the sweets you love. It's a gift from God."

Damaris squeezed Ottilie's arm. "And you are the dearest friend in the entire world."

They navigated the small, crowded shop. The scent of sweat, softened by the musky odors of cardamom and saffron, permeated the room. In front of them, a man wearing the head-to-toe white of a servant sent the clerk behind the counter scurrying up and down, picking one or two of each sweet and packing them in a pasteboard box.

"This is my favorite part of India." Damaris grinned.

"Sweets? Or shopping in the bazaar without your mother?"

"Both."

When they reached the front of the line, Damaris ordered a box of ledikeni, a clay pot of rasgulla, and then motioned for Ottilie to choose something.

Ottilie's gaze swept the offerings. There usually wasn't money left over for treats, and she licked her lips in anticipation of the *soan papdi*—a childhood favorite.

Handing over the rolled paper cone, Damaris led Ottilie from the shop. She tapped one of the boys still staring through the window on the shoulder and thrust the pot of rasgulla at them.

"Thank you, memsahib," they said in unison, then sat beneath the window and tore into the treats.

"Thanks, memsahib," Ottilie parroted, scooping a bit of the sweetened flossed gram flour onto her tongue.

"Oh, shush. Now, why did you send a note asking me to meet you here? Are we to shop?"

"Yes, I need more elytra, but I also need to speak with you about a man who—"

"A man! Ottilie, have you met someone?" Damaris stuck her sugar-syrup-soaked finger into her mouth and waggled her eyebrows.

"Not that type of man." Ottilie thought of Mr. Scott's keen eyes and quick grin. "Well, he is that type of man, but not to me."

Damaris popped another ledikeni in her mouth and looked down her nose at Ottilie. She made a sound in her throat that could have been appreciation for the sweet or disbelief at Ottilie's words.

Ottilie shoved her face into the cone and used the moment to compose herself. "Don't be absurd," she said around a mouthful of soan papdi.

"I said nothing." Damaris pulled a handkerchief from her reticule and wiped her sticky fingers on it. She stopped at an open shop where shawls and blankets were piled in neat stacks on shelves cut into the walls. The shopkeeper, a man wearing a white *abaya* and an impressive beard, sat up straight when Damaris ducked to enter and then pulled an embroidered paisley shawl from the top of one pile. She unfolded it and draped it around her shoulders. "This is lovely."

Ottilie watched from the street. She folded the paper around the remains of her treat and tucked it into her bag. She'd save it for Thaddeus. Damaris dropped a few coins into the man's cupped palm, and his eyes gleamed.

When she left the shop, Ottilie shook her head. "You paid too much. I don't know why you refuse to haggle."

"Saving a few coins means much less to me than gaining those coins means to the merchant. Anyway, don't distract me from the conversation at hand. Tell me about this man."

Ottilie quickly corrected her friend's mistaken idea of who Mr. Scott was.

"Your father was the son of a baron and you never knew?"

"Never."

"And you're certain Mr. Scott is who he says he is and is telling the truth?"

"In addition to the letters to my mother, I can't think of any reason he'd travel all this way to lie about that."

"What is the title?"

"Sunderson. They have an estate in Wiltshire called Hazel-brook Manor."

"I've heard of them. If it makes you feel better, they're a well-respected family."

It didn't make Ottilie feel better. It would be much easier to deny Thaddeus his inheritance if they were horrid.

They made their way to the old portion of Burrabazar, becoming lost in the narrow, winding lanes, their heels getting stuck between the bumpy cobblestones. Here the bazaar reminded her of its origins. A place where one could find any type of textile, yarn, or garment. Shops huddled together, shopkeepers shouting from windows and doorways about the superior quality of their dupatta or linen or embellishments.

Hemmed in by a large importer of Chinese silk and a store that catered to European dressmakers with a large selection of calico and lace, Ottilie found the elytra.

The shop was more a niche carved into the wall than anything. A small man, whip-thin and wrinkled, smiled at Ottilie when she stopped in front of him.

"Mr. Sandilya, are you well?"

He jiggled his head and spoke in the accented English of one who had learned another language first. "And your mother? She hasn't been by to see me in so long."

"She has passed, and I've taken over her work."

His eyes and mouth widened, and he lowered his head. "May her soul find redemption."

Maji would say the moment she found death, life found her. There were no endless cycles of rebirth. No striving for release. She'd been a woman of immense faith, none of which Ottilie had seemed to inherit. Though maybe faith wasn't like skin tone or the size of one's foot. Maybe it wasn't subject to the laws of heritage, and Ottilie had only been treating it as such, which was why, when her life tipped upside down, she'd lost it.

Mr. Sandilya cleared his throat, and Ottilie refocused on him. "I need to buy some elytra. Have you any?"

"Yes. Yes." He patted his hands against his spotless lungi, then hopped to his feet and pulled a cloth bag from atop a tray boasting a tangle of anklets. He loosened the string and pulled it wide. Inside, a pile of beetle casings shone and glimmered as bright as the coins Ottilie's work would bring.

He named a price that drew a laugh from Ottilie's throat. "That's robbery. Do you think you can steal from me since my mother isn't here?"

Mr. Sandilya drew his straggly brows and sagging mouth into a look of offense and thrust his fingers through the wiry hairs of his beard. "I wouldn't do that. These are good quality. Better than you will find anywhere else."

For a few minutes while she bargained and argued, Ottilie forgot about Maji's death and Mr. Scott's arrival. She lost herself to the joy of attaining the best deal possible. And she walked away a few coins lighter, having received not only the means to continue her craft, but also a smile on her lips.

Damaris shook her head as they turned down the lane onto the main street splitting the bazaar in two. "It is amazing how well you do that."

Ottilie smirked. "I'm a woman of many concealed talents."

"I have no doubt."

Someone stepped into their path. "Miss Russell."

That voice, cultured and British enough to turn water into the tea he claimed to detest, stole her smile. She turned toward it, ignoring the fine cut of his suit and jaunty angle of his straw boater. Ignoring, too, his grin and the way it turned him from a man overlooked to one who drew attention. Definitely ignoring the way warmth spilled into her belly.

Instead, she focused on introductions. "Mr. Scott, meet my friend Miss Damaris Winship."

He nodded at Damaris, and she offered him a "lovely to meet you."

"What errand brings you to Burrabazar?" Ottilie asked. The English usually shopped the tony and gaslit streets of Chow-ringhee and New Market.

"No errand. Only curiosity." He noted the bag she held in her hand. "And you?"

"Beetles."

"I beg your pardon?"

She eased her hand into the bag and caught an elytron upon her fingertip. Pulling it out, she held it toward him. "The means of my trade."

Pinching it between two fingers, he lifted it eye level. "Beetle wings? What do you do with these?"

"They aren't actually the wings but the casing that protects the wing. The wings are delicate. The elytron is . . . a type of house."

He squeezed the elytron's sides, then released the tension, allowing it to spring back into place. "They are quite resilient. And beautiful." His eyes met hers. Brilliant and rimmed in thick dark lashes, they seemed to say more than his words.

"They must be resilient in order to endure the jab of the needle. And beauty . . . that all depends on the skill of the artist employing them." An unspoken conversation passed between them, and Ottilie found herself in the peculiar position of beginning to like this man who was attempting to upend her life and steal it away.

Damaris's pale, freckled hand took Ottilie's arm. "Ottilie's skill as an embroiderer is in demand. She designs and produces the most beautiful work."

"I would enjoy seeing it one day," he said.

"I doubt you'll have the opportunity with all your travels. When do you leave Calcutta?" The sweetness in Ottilie's voice could have rivaled any finishing-school girl's.

"Where are you going, Mr. Scott? I've traveled all over India with my father and might be of help." Damaris's enviable acting skills were on full display. Had Ottilie not told Damaris about her conversation with Mr. Scott at the ghat herself, she would have thought her friend was truly interested in his plans.

Mr. Scott rubbed his finger along the smooth surface of the elytron. "My only plan is to return to England as soon as possible."

"Then you should book your passage home immediately." Ottilie stepped past him, pausing only long enough to look back and say, "Keep the elytron as memory of your time in Calcutta."

Before she and Damaris disappeared into the crowd, Ottilie glanced over her shoulder and saw Mr. Scott holding the elytron to the sun and smiling.

9

The following day, Ottilie found herself squinting at the linen spread over her lap. After seeing Thaddeus off to school, she had visited with a prospective client, then returned home, changed into a sari, and settled onto the verandah where the light was best.

The gown she worked on was due in two days, meant for a young woman who was leaving India to marry in England and wanted a day dress everyone would talk about. "This gown will be the crowning achievement of my trousseau," she had said, and Ottilie overlooked her self-importance and silly proclamation because of her sweetness and youth. "I've seen your work. You have impeccable taste, and I know you will do something spectacular."

That had been Ottilie's only direction—create something spectacular. She had made a few sketches then and there, asking the young woman which suited her taste best, but she only waved the paper away. "I trust you. Do what you wish."

So Ottilie did. She'd dreamed of swirling patterns in orange thread and green casings splashed across a creamy background. Tendrils that reached and stretched, meant to show off fashionable curves and accentuate a cinched waist. When she woke up the next morning, her spirit bubbled with excitement—for the first time since Maji's death.

This was what she'd been created to do. Not mimic the designs of others but create her own. It took her away from the drudgery of stitching and snipping and working. It took her away from memories that only brought tears.

Ottilie cracked her knuckles, one by one, and sighed at the release. Nānī walked through the door, swatting at the flies that buzzed around her. She hardly made a sound as her bare feet shuffled across the floor. "Are you finished with your lunch?" She sent a scowl at the plate on the ground beside Ottilie's chair, still piled with rice and *machher jhol*, the tomato chutney congealed into an unappetizing mass.

"I forgot," Ottilie admitted. She tied off the thread and bit it free with her teeth. "I'll eat now."

Nānī smoothed her thumbs over Ottilie's brows. "Oh, Boodha, you will look old before your time if you keep working so hard."

"No one cares what I look like, but there are quite a few people in this house who care about their bellies."

"God will provide what we need. He always does."

"That's nonsense. He doesn't always provide what we need. From what I can see, he does the exact opposite and *removes* what we need."

Ottilie stabbed the needle through an elytron, poking a hole into the vivid casing with a satisfying pop. She swallowed and lowered her work to her lap when Nānī's hand cradled her head.

"This world isn't always easy, but God has given you a strong spirit and back. You are capable of doing what needs to be done, and that includes living life without your parents."

A tear slipped from Ottilie's eye and slid off the tip of her nose. It splashed onto a curved elytron, and she wiped her finger across it before the fabric pulled in the moisture. "I don't *want* to live life without them, though. How much more will God take from us?"

Nānī crouched, her knobby knees stretching her sari. She gently slid the bodice from Ottilie's lap and turned it over. "You're looking at things the wrong way. You see only what God has taken." Her hand swept the tidy rows of knots and the sloppy, crisscrossing stitches that would be hidden behind a lining of muslin. She flipped the bodice over, her fingers tripping over the detailed embroidery work. "But not what he has given. Your parents, you, me, Thaddeus, Dilip, we aren't meant for this world. Not forever, anyway. When we die, it's because we are meant for somewhere else. You lost your parents, for a little while, but they went *home*." She took Ottilie's chin in her hand and smiled. "You are so talented, stitching art out of beetle parts. Creating beauty from the ordinary. But even you wouldn't appreciate your work if you only saw it in reverse."

There was a soft reprimand in her words. A calling out of self and into eternity. Ottilie knew Nānī's words were born from suffering and trial. Yet she couldn't help but think that Nānī had left her family—they hadn't been yanked from her. And that made enough difference that Ottilie took the bodice from her grandmother's hands and plucked another elytron from her mother's box.

"I have to finish this."

Nānī pressed a kiss to Ottilie's head. "All right, we won't discuss it anymore today, but I insist you rest a moment. There is enough sunlight yet." She wiped her hands on her hips and lifted the gown. The skirt fell in gentle folds, puddling in Ottilie's lap. "Why, you're nearly done. How quickly you work! And it's beautiful."

Ottilie admired the results of her vision. She hoped the young woman would have the good sense to wear it before leaving Calcutta—it would assure Ottilie more clients for certain. She draped the gown over the back of the chair and got to her feet, holding her hand out to help Nānī up, then went into the kitchen for a cup of tea.

For twenty minutes, she picked at her overdue meal and enjoyed Dilip's company as he prepared spices. They laughed over the silly things Papa used to do when he was caught up in his studies.

"Do you remember, ma'am," Dilip asked, "when he mistook his cup of tea for an inkpot? He spent a quarter of an hour decrying the horrible quality of ink from the new shop and threatening to tell the merchant exactly what he thought of his substandard product until you pointed out he was trying to write his notes with fine Darjeeling."

"Oh, Papa. He always lost himself in his work." Ottilie smiled at the memory as she split open green cardamom pods and released the tiny black seeds into a mortar.

Dilip stirred the coriander sizzling in the oiled pan over the hearth's open flame. "Much like you, ma'am."

She shook her head. "My work is nothing compared to Papa's. It's just enough to keep us in food and clothing, but it means little."

"Why do you say that?"

"Papa's work was in science. He taught and traded knowledge that grew our comprehension of the world around us. My work just makes wealthy women look beautiful." She lifted the heavy pestle and ground it against the seeds, releasing their sweet citrus scent.

"Art offers just as much to the world as science. The importance of one doesn't diminish the other."

Ottilie's heart warmed. "Thank you for calling my work art, but it's hardly that."

"It is. You have a gift. You create pictures not with pastel or pencil, but with things of the natural world. It's easy to make something from nothing, the way someone might paint a portrait, but it requires a special skill to take an item that already fills a role—like the casing of a beetle's wings—and turn it into something else entirely. You help people see possibilities."

A knock sounded on the front door, followed by Nānī's soft tread. She opened the door and slid it closed as she stepped out onto the verandah, her gentle murmurs mixing with a muffled male voice. Ottilie cupped her forehead in her hands. Had her grandmother invited Mr. D'Souza back? She'd thought Nānī had freed her from that expectation.

The door slid open, and Nānī said, "Ottilie, someone has come to visit."

Ottilie jerked her head around, a tense smile on her lips, ready to offer Mr. D'Souza a welcoming but obviously-not-interested greeting. Instead, her teeth slammed together at the sight of Mr. Scott standing beside her grandmother. "Why are you here?"

"Ottilie, offer our guest a drink." Nānī's words were sharp, and she turned toward him. "My name is Gitisha Singh. As you know, I am Ottilie's grandmother." She beamed at him. "You may call me Nānī. Have you had lassi yet?"

"I haven't, Nānī." He followed Nānī's waving hand and sat on the ground as though he made a habit of sitting cross-legged.

Wrapping her pallu more securely around her waist, Ottilie glared at Nānī and jammed the end of it back into place before fetching the jug from the cabinet against the wall. She'd make Mr. Scott a drink, but she wouldn't pretend to be pleased about it. She didn't want this man polluting her home with his expectations and thoughts of ripping apart her family.

She blew a puff of air from between her lips and set a piece of muslin across the top of a ceramic cup, circled the rim with her fingers to hold it in place, and poured out the yogurt. Pressing the bowl of a spoon against the open-weave muslin caused the curd to thin and fall into the cup.

Dilip plucked a couple of small mint leaves from the stack of herbs sitting beside him, and she held out the cup so he could toss them in. She finished it with a dash of salt, a glug of milk, and a stir of the spoon. "Do you like cardamom, Mr. Scott?"

"I'm not sure. I'd like to try it." He watched her as she pinched some from the dish beside Dilip and sprinkled it on top of his drink. She held the cup out to him, drawing back the moment his fingers wrapped around it.

Mr. Scott lifted the cup to his lips, and Ottilie swallowed with him, wondering what he thought of her lassi. Hoping he liked it. Angry she cared.

His lips were coated in yogurt when he lowered the drink, bits of cardamom sticking to them until his tongue swiped at the remains. "It's delicious." He looked at the half-dozen spices in various states of preparation around the kitchen—whole peppercorns, little tin bowls of ground mace and garam masala and turmeric, piles of fenugreek and mustard seeds. "I've never seen so many spices at once."

Ottilie laughed. "You don't spend much time in the kitchen or market, do you?"

"No. My work rarely takes me to those places."

Dilip resumed his duties, emptying the pan of toasted cumin and throwing a handful of mustard seeds into the oil. They popped and released their pungent aroma.

"Ottilie, Mr. Scott has asked for help in purchasing gifts. Maybe he can find what he's looking for at Burrabazar."

Ottilie picked up a cardamom pod and broke it over the mortar. "I have work to do and a gown I must finish."

Nānī plucked the pestle from her hand. "I will do this. I'm an old lady without the energy to help a visitor. You can demonstrate the hospitality Indians are known for." Her words were clothed in gentleness, but beneath them lay a demand. And a warning. "And the gown is nearly complete. It can wait."

Ottilie glanced at Mr. Scott, then leaned toward her grandmother and hissed, "But what will people think, seeing us together? They will gossip and make assumptions."

Nānī gave Ottilie an innocent look. "When have they not gossiped or made assumptions about you?"

Ottilie stood again and glared at her grandmother. If she didn't know better, she'd think Nānī *wanted* Thaddeus to go to England with this man.

"Very well, Mr. Scott." She held her hand toward the door.

They took a gharry to Burrabazar, this time to the spice market. Clutching the seat, Ottilie resisted the bumps that sent her ever closer to Mr. Scott and his boyish charm.

"What really brought you to our door today, Mr. Scott? You don't truly need someone to help you shop for souvenirs, do you?" She didn't look at him as she spoke. She kept her eyes trained on the passing scene outside. The bullock carts and architecture failed to prove as distracting as she'd hoped, though.

His words drew her attention toward him. "I do, actually, need help in choosing gifts, but I also realized you needed to get to know me. It is ridiculous to expect you to send your brother halfway across the world with a complete stranger."

She clenched her hands in her lap, weaving her fingers into a knot that would take effort to disengage. "Mr. Scott, nothing you do or don't do, prove or don't prove, say or don't say, will ever induce me to send my brother to England. In fact, it has nothing to do with you at all."

He uncrossed his arms and dipped his head closer. So close she caught the scent of cardamom on his breath. "Really? Who I am makes no difference in your choice?"

"None."

"Well, what does, then?"

"Nothing. I will not send Thaddeus with you."

He sighed, and the horses stopped. The gharry shuddered and creaked as they climbed from it. It was just after the midday break when most people retreated into their homes and rested in the worst heat of the day, so the market offered them nearly empty streets. Different from the area where textiles were sold, here there were no individual shops or well-kept stalls, only merchant after merchant sitting on woven mats behind wide platters piled high with spices.

As Ottilie walked beside Mr. Scott, she was aware of the glances sent her way. Dark eyes that hid judgment and accusation. The British army's reprisals after the uprising still smelled of death, even in this place of scent and color thirty years later, and they thought she prostituted herself with the enemy. To all outward appearances, she was a woman of no morals. And worse than that, one who rejected her own people. There was no winning the battle. No matter what choices she made, no matter what she wore, which language she spoke, how she behaved, she would never be embraced. Never be fully accepted into society—British or Indian. She was either not enough or too much of one or the other.

They made their way up the packed-dirt street, stopping to sniff chili powder or rub peppercorns between their fingers. As they examined a heap of cinnamon sticks, the spicy scent leaving reminders on their fingers, he interrupted the silence. "Most of the Eurasians I've met have dressed and behaved entirely English."

"That's because most Eurasians believe they are entirely English. They're a separate community far removed from the roots of their Indian heritage. The military no longer allows British men to marry Indian women"—she glanced away, thinking of Victor and wondering if he had only pushed a little harder, they would have let him—"and with the arrival of the Fishing Fleet girls, the necessity of it became obsolete. Eurasians, most of whose last fully British or fully Indian ancestor was two or three generations ago, are a people caught between countries. So they've chosen to identify with the one they believe will bring them the most privilege and ease."

"Does it?"

"Somewhat. They are offered better jobs than native Indians.

They have government posts and work for the railways or as teachers, but they aren't accepted by the English. Not really. You can't convince them of that, though."

"How come you are able to straddle both worlds when they've chosen just one?"

"Because I was partially raised by an Indian grandmother, and my father was an Englishman not beholden to the army. He could marry whomever he wanted, run his household however he believed best. So he never imposed limitations on my mother and grandmother. He admired India without divesting himself of his Britishness." She gave him a wry smile. "I'm not sure that's a good thing, though, because at least most Eurasians *believe* themselves to be fully part of a society. I *know* I'm part of none."

"That can't be true. You have English friends. Powerful ones, if my memory of the Winship name serves me right."

"I have one English friend. One friend, period." She'd been too busy since Papa died to build friendships with the other Eurasian women in her community. Stepping to the next stall, she motioned at the small mountain of fennel seeds. The merchant scooped a pile into her palm. Offering it to Mr. Scott, she let him pinch a few and toss them into his mouth. "What do you think?"

"It tastes like licorice."

"It's fennel. It might taste like an English sweet, but it's an Indian spice." She flipped her braid over her shoulder and pointed at her eyes, hazel like her father's and Thaddeus's. "These are the only thing that gives away my English heritage. And no one sees them when I'm dressed like an Indian. I wear a sari when I can because then I'm only reviled by one half of my heritage instead of both. Sometimes an Indian can tell I'm masquerading, but mostly they see my skin and hair and clothing, they hear that I'm fluent in Hindi and Bengali, and they think I'm one of them. In truth, I belong to no one. And neither does Thaddeus, even though there is no physical attribute giving away his dual bloodline. He belongs to England as much as he belongs to India." She tossed the remaining fennel seeds into her mouth and crunched them between her teeth. The slight bitterness was tempered by a sweet perfume that lingered on her tongue. It was a complex flavor, one that defied understanding. "Which is not at all."

"What if you're wrong? What if he does belong to England, where his father's family has held a title for hundreds of years? What if this feeling of not belonging is meant to lead him to a place he might belong?"

"He'll never belong anywhere without me." Ottilie nodded her thanks to the spice seller and swept down the street.

Mr. Scott's footsteps clattered behind her, and she stopped when he touched her elbow. "He can have a better life in England. Nothing will be beyond his reach."

Ottilie ignored a man selling dried peppers crying, *"Lal mirch! Safed mirch!"* She ignored the musky scent of a hundred ground spices battling with that of cow manure. She looked into Mr. Scott's eyes and could tell he was trying, really trying to comprehend. He had no concept of not belonging. No understanding of living a lifetime somewhere and never finding acceptance. "Have you any family?"

His gaze avoided her, and he shook his head. "My mother died when I was young."

She noticed he mentioned nothing of a father or siblings. Of grandparents or aunts or uncles or cousins. And that made her heart turn toward him. Despite the pain of losing them, she wouldn't give up memories of her parents and siblings for anything. "Then maybe you can't know that they're everything. Especially when you belong nowhere."

"I do know what it feels like not to belong. Lady Sunderson is the closest thing I have to family who will claim me. She is that person to me, as is her daughter, Alberta. They welcomed me when no one else did. I owe them a great deal."

His eyes softened and turned the green of Nānī's favorite dupatta. Ottilie loved that scarf, the way Nānī slipped it over her head when in church. How it had grown threadbare over the years, turning velvety like the petals of an oleander. She couldn't turn away from this memory of her grandmother displayed in vivid color on the face of Everett Scott.

"I don't wish to hurt you," said Mr. Scott. "I only want to preserve a legacy."

Ottilie sighed. They could go around and around, discussing and arguing and repeating. It made no difference. She wouldn't relent, and neither would he. But she had the advantage of being home. He would eventually need to leave. "What will you do if I continue to refuse? You can't stay in Calcutta forever."

"No, I can't. But don't think they'll relent. They will send someone else. They will eventually get what they want."

He didn't sound as though he was making a threat. His words were spoken softly, dappled with regret, yet the result was the same had he said they would kidnap Thaddeus and steal him away from her. Her back stiffened. Her throat closed. And she knew, beyond any doubt, that were she to lose her brother, there would be nothing left tethering her to the joy of her past. The faith of her childhood. The knowledge that she belonged to this earth, had purpose and value.

If Thaddeus was lost, she would be too.

Ottilie and Mr. Scott wandered the spice market, sniffing, tasting, and haggling. Humor tipped his lips, and something like admiration glittered in his eyes as she talked the merchant down by more than half for a silver box with little drawers, each one revealing a different spice when pulled open. He said it was for the cook at his employer's house.

"This is a generous gift for a cook," Ottilie told him as they left the market and he hailed a gharry.

Mr. Scott offered his hand and assisted her up, climbing in after her. "She knew my mother and has always been kind to me." His fingers found his earlobe and Ottilie watched, fascinated, as he tugged and rubbed. "Not many people are."

"Kind to you? Whyever not?" The horses set off, and she nudged him with her shoulder. "Do you have scandalous secrets in your past?"

"Everyone has secrets, Miss Russell."

"A month ago I wouldn't have believed you, but now . . ." She stared down at her hands clasped tightly together in her lap. She kept her nails short so they wouldn't track dirt across delicate fabric or snag on thread. Her fingers were slim—bony, if she were being impartial—unpadded by ease and an abundance of rich foods, and pricked all over by needles. Her hands told a story. They didn't lie. There were no secrets in them.

But people, even people one thought they knew well, were able to hide all manner of things behind familiarity and affection.

Mr. Scott's fingers settled over hers, and she was glad she wore no gloves. That contact, as brief and gentle as it was, made her feel less alone. Less betrayed by those she'd loved most. "I think," he said, his voice as warm and comforting as Nānī's embrace, "sometimes people *want* to be honest, but they aren't sure how. They wish to preserve a relationship or to not be diminished in another's eyes."

Ottilie drew her lower lip between her teeth and looked up at him. How odd that she should find tenderness and understanding in this man who would take from her what she treasured most. "You sound as though you speak from experience."

"It is a story for another day." His gaze caught on something past her head, outside the gharry. "Would you care for a pastry? I've heard wonderful things about that confectioner." With a tap against the wall separating them from the driver, the vehicle stopped.

Ottilie glanced out the window and saw the elegant façade of Federico Peliti. "Maji used to bring me here before Papa died." And she suddenly wished for nothing more than to sit at one of their white cloth-draped tables and enjoy an Italian or French dessert.

Inside, she inhaled the yeasty scent and watched the server behind the counter filling pasteboard boxes with confections.

"What do you recommend?" Mr. Scott asked, leaning toward her.

"Everything."

He ordered a banana cream éclair and a glass of vermut. Ottilie, an orange-ricotta-filled sfogliatella and tea. "It's unusual for an Englishman to dislike tea," she commented.

"It's too bitter for my taste."

"You must try masala chai, then. It is sweetened with jaggery and milk and made interesting with spices."

"I will be sure to visit so you can make me some."

To Ottilie's surprise, she didn't mind the thought. "Make sure you bring the tea. It's too expensive a commodity for us."

"I will bring all the tea in India if you continue treating me as a friend and not an enemy."

"I do like the idea of another friend." She smiled and bit into the flaky pastry. The well-balanced flavors sent her back in time. So many memories were tied to food, and the ones that teased her now were especially sweet. She wiped her mouth with her napkin. "When my mother brought me here, she would dress me in flounces and lace, bows in my hair, and on the way would remind me to behave like a lady. I wanted so badly to make her proud, so I imitated her in every way." Ottilie smiled. "She was so beautiful. Papa said he fell in love with her the moment he saw her. And then she laughed and he fell even deeper." She blinked and took a sip of tea.

"I should like to experience that," Mr. Scott said.

"Me too. Though it isn't likely." She pinched off a piece of her sfogliatella and squeezed it between her fingers. "I will never marry."

"Whyever not?"

Ottilie lifted her shoulder. "I decided long ago it wasn't worth the risk. Somehow everyone either leaves or is yanked away. Is it not better to avoid that kind of pain?"

"I don't think you can, unless you also close yourself off to friendship. But surely there will be someone you will find worthy enough to place your trust in."

"I did once, and now I know I cannot trust myself to recognize who is worthy and who isn't." This conversation was probing too deeply. She was revealing too much. "And you? Is there someone waiting for your return to England?"

Mr. Scott shook his head. "I am not considered a great catch. But I must marry respectably anyway. Someone suitable."

Ottilie waited for an explanation, but none came. She pushed her plate across the table. "Would you care to try it? It's very good." He smiled and split off a piece with his fork. "What makes a woman respectable and suitable?" she asked.

He shrugged. "From a good family, I suppose. Wealth is not necessary, for I am already in possession of an admirable inheritance. Truly, her most important quality will be to have a father or male relative who is a member of Welbourne's." At Ottilie's cocked brow, he explained. "It's a club in Bristol. A well-regarded, long-established one. Full of the wealthy, influential, and acceptable."

Ottilie nearly laughed, but the expression on his face told her to swallow it. "Your greatest wish in a wife is that a male relative belong to a club? And why would you aspire to join one? I thought you were an estate manager."

"And—" he made a quick dash of his tongue across the mouth Ottilie had just noticed boasted a full lower lip—"distant cousin to the man I work for. He will bequeath me everything for he has no children." His eyes shuttered, and he coughed into his hand. He didn't look at her but instead focused on his drink, swirling it in the glass, then taking small sips. Every movement deliberate. "You see, it isn't just a club. It's an inheritance. An indisputable link to all those who came before me. It's necessary for business—once you are in, you have access to some of the wealthiest and most successful businessmen in all of England. But more than that . . ." He tipped the glass to his lips, his eyes turning as deep and fathomless as the Chand Baori stepwell. "It's belonging, Miss Russell."

Ottilie ran the tines of her fork through the creamy filling that had left a trail across the fine porcelain plate. She couldn't look at him. Couldn't see the yearning in his expression that so equaled her own. "I would think a man with such an inheritance would be an attractive catch, indeed. With or without a Welbourne's membership."

"But there are those scandalous secrets, Miss Russell, which I will not divulge, for we have just become friends and I would hate for your estimation of me to be diminished."

Ottilie wished her estimation of him *would* be diminished, for she couldn't reconcile this man who would bring her such great pain but also managed to fill her with compassion and curiosity. They finished their pastries and drinks with nothing left to say, both harboring secrets that remained untold.

Outside, while Ottilie waited for Mr. Scott to wave down a gharry, a British woman walked down the sidewalk, her hand gripping the arm of a young boy in a sailor suit not unlike Thaddeus's, though this one didn't sport any stains and fit the sturdy child properly.

Mr. Scott stepped back toward Ottilie, and the woman drew close, smiling at him. Then her eyes landed on Ottilie, and she jerked her son closer to her skirts. With a sniff, she stepped into the street and crossed the road.

Ottilie stared after the woman and boy for a moment—long enough to release the anger that stemmed from decades of such things. Long enough to school her features. But when she looked at Mr. Scott, his gaze held compassion. And a little fury.

"Are you sure you want Thaddeus to experience a lifetime of that?" he asked. "Because in England, he'll be treated with respect."

"Unless people find out who his mother was."

"How would they discover that?"

Ottilie shrugged. People passed, of course. All the time. Fair-skinned Eurasians who had nothing to lose except a complex history and half their heritage. They looked British and so became British. But Ottilie wondered, when they were alone at night with their thoughts, did they ever dream of sultry summer nights and the gentle fingers of a grandmother who smelled of cardamom? Did they miss the land of their mothers? Did they ever tug at their heavy woolen clothing and eat their bland food and walk around their gray cities, wishing for saris and fragrant oils and color? But more than that, how did they survive when they were only able to admit to being half of who they'd been created to be?

"It wouldn't matter if anyone else discovered who Thaddeus's mother was. He would know. He could never forget, and because of that, he would never *really* belong."

Mr. Scott rubbed the back of his neck. "I'm growing weary of this argument."

"I am as well. I hate to say it, Mr. Scott, but it seems your time here is drawing to a close. I will miss you." Ottilie rapped her hand against the side of the tanga that stopped in front of them. The driver hopped off his seat and helped her up into it. She poked her head out beneath the canopy.

Mr. Scott's mouth twisted into a crooked smile. "So this is good-bye?"

"I'm afraid so. A shame, really, since I've enjoyed our time together. You've turned out to be a rather pleasant man."

He bowed his head, and when he lifted it, his eyes flashed with humor. "I might stay a little longer yet."

She laughed. "Surprisingly, that doesn't disappoint me."

The tanga jerked as the wheels inched forward. Ottilie reached her fingers toward Mr. Scott, and he brushed them with his. Such a brief whisper of touch that she could have sworn it was only the air stirring.

But in that moment, when his fingertips grazed hers, his pointed chin trembling from suppressed laughter, there was a flicker. She pulled her hand to her chest and gave him a single nod, allowing herself one moment to meet his eyes, which had turned as cloudy as the water of the Hooghly. Then she turned in her seat and stared over the driver's head, trying to ignore the odd sensation of having made a decision in touching his hand that upended her life completely but not knowing what she had decided. Or what it had changed.

10

Ottilie could hardly pry her eyes open Sunday morning. She couldn't remember the last time she'd gone to sleep with the rest of the household. The last time she hadn't tossed and turned on her mat, her nightgown tangling about her legs as she mentally counted the jarred coins in the kitchen and subtracted the cost of food and Thaddeus's school tuition.

Nānī nudged her with a foot, her scratchy sole rubbing over the tender skin of Ottilie's shin. "Wake up, Navasi. We worship today."

Ottilie dragged herself out of bed and dressed. Nānī talked her into hailing a tanga, citing her creaking hips, but Ottilie knew it was because her own eyes were red-rimmed, her yawns interrupting breakfast.

Nānī, a dupatta draping her head and shoulders, beamed at their old friends—British, Indian, and Eurasian alike. It was the one place in the city that enfolded God's children into an embrace that left little room for bigotry and arrogance.

Most of the churches in Calcutta were segregated. Papa had loved that Lal Bazar Chapel offered services in both English and Bengali. They'd always attended the English service, as Nānī spoke only a smattering of Bengali and Papa none at all.

It was good to be there. To sit on the cane-back benches and listen to Reverend Hook's message of hope and reconciliation. Afterward, Thaddeus played with friends on the portico, chasing one another and hiding behind the tall pillars. Their shouts and laughter were a balm to Ottilie's tattered spirit.

They ate lunch late, after which Nānī took a nap. Ottilie stitched until her fingers cramped, trying to finish embroidering the shoes of a rich merchant's wife. It was slow, tedious work that required light and a steady hand. She threaded the final knot just as Dilip called her to dinner.

As she sat on her dhurrie and waited while Dilip served Nānī, she let her eyes drift closed. How easy it would be to sleep sitting upright, warmed by the heat of the cooking fire, her lashes tripping together and her head jerking.

"Ma'am?"

Ottilie forced her eyes wide and blinked at Dilip, who held his hand out for her plate. She passed it over and watched as he scooped rice into the center and poured a double portion of ghee over it.

Dilip had made *kumro chenchki*—he knew how much she loved the spiced squash—but she shook her head. "I'm not very hungry today."

"It's your favorite," he said, giving Nānī a pointed glance. Nānī's eyes glimmered, and she insisted Dilip give Ottilie a larger serving. They were in league together. They probably watched her from the kitchen as she worked on the verandah, whispering about how little she ate and conspiring to steal coins from the jar to buy her ledikeni and sfogliatelle.

She ate enough to satisfy them. "Done?"

"But Dilip has made *dalna*, as well, and you like dalna, don't you?"

Ottilie handed him her plate. "I'm done with dinner. Let Thaddeus have mine."

"If you don't eat, you will grow ill." Nānī's voice dipped, fear knitting her words together. "I am frightened you will vanish like the rest. Drift away until you are nothing but a *bhoot*."

Ottilie snorted. Her grandmother, long a Christian, could still revert to childhood superstitions when afraid. "I am not going to become a ghost. I'm not going to vanish. I'm not going to . . ." She glanced at Thaddeus, who was following the conversation as he chewed the last of Ottilie's lentil cake. "Well, you know. Please, you both must stop worrying."

She got up, done with dinner and the conversation. A chilly breeze whistled past the door, and a premonition—likely influenced by her grandmother's words—skittered across her arms, leaving goosebumps in its wake.

She'd changed into a sari after church and had draped Maji's silk and cotton shawl—the one Papa had bought long ago—over her shoulders. She pulled it over her head, hiding her irritation from her grandmother. "Thaddeus, let's go read on the verandah while Dilip cleans up."

Her brother scrambled up and disappeared into the bedroom to retrieve the book, and a moment later, Ottilie sat on the edge of the step. Thaddeus sank down beside her and laid his head on her lap, their well-loved volume of poetry held aloft to her.

"What should I read?"

He looked at her through the thatch of curls tumbling over his eyes. "'A Dream'?"

His favorite. "Of course, little glowworm."

Ottilie flipped through the pages worn from years of love. Worn from her clenching when she'd hidden it beneath the folds of her skirt while the rest of their belongings were being carted away.

Every time she stroked the cover, made velvety by age and touch, she saw Papa tucking an infant Thaddeus beneath his chin, whispering the poem into his clamshell ear. Even then, Papa knew. "He's a little glowworm, but what a great light he makes."

They'd nearly lost Thaddeus. He'd been born too early. He was so small Ottilie feared she'd break him every time she lifted him from his carved cradle. She would stand over him as he napped and hold her hand in front of his mouth, hoping and praying for the puff of air that signaled his steady breathing. Maji had lost twins only a few years earlier. Also born too soon. So very tiny, their little bodies curled together upon the white silk of the miniature casket.

But Thaddeus had survived. And though still small, he brought joy to everyone blessed enough to know him.

"'Once a dream did weave a shade o'er my angel-guarded bed—'"

"Are angels real?"

Ottilie lowered the book and looked down at her brother. His button nose was wrinkled up, and she pressed a kiss to it. "The Bible says they are, though I don't know if they guard our beds."

He gave a sage little nod, and she continued. "'. . . that an emmet lost its way where on grass methought I lay. Troubled, wildered, and forlorn, dark, benighted, travel-worn, over many a tangle spray, all heart-broke, I heard her say, "O my children! do they cry, do they hear their father sigh? Now they look abroad to see, now return and weep for me."'"

"The ant is really Maji, isn't it? Is she crying for us, do you think?"

Ottilie's eyes filled, and she stared at the page of swirling words. How did God expect her to do this? To parent a broken-hearted little boy who'd lost so much when she had no answers to give. No real understanding of anything. The shawl suddenly became a weight too heavy, and she tossed it off. "I hope she doesn't cry for us. And besides, we must remember she isn't lost. She's right where she's supposed to be." The words were bitter and tasted vile in her mouth. She wanted to spit them out. To speak the things really in her heart. But when she peeked over the edge of the book, Thaddeus looked back at her, his face pale and serious. He needed comfort, not her doubts and anger. "Why don't we finish the poem?"

He nodded, and she forced her thoughts into submission. He joined Ottilie now, knowing the poem by heart because of the hundreds of times she had recited it to him so she could feel closer to Papa.

"'Pitying, I dropped a tear: but I saw a glow-worm near, who replied, "What wailing wight calls the watchman of the night? I am set to light the ground, while the beetle goes his round: follow now the beetle's hum; little wanderer, hie thee home!"'" She set the book down and cradled her brother's face in her hands. Upside down, he looked like a wizened old man, all harsh angles and wide eyes. "You are the little glowworm, all light and love. Always pointing us toward home."

His sweet smile eased the warring thoughts that made camp in her mind and tore up her belly in a bid for supremacy.

"To bed," she said. "School begins again tomorrow."

He scrambled to his feet, and his arms wound around her neck. "I love you."

"I love you too."

He pulled back. "You're the beetle."

"The what?"

"The beetle. Going your round. Always working. Leading the way. You're a good person to follow."

He squeezed her tightly, growling the way Maji always had when hugging him good night, and disappeared into the house. Ottilie pulled the book into her lap and pressed her hand over its leather cover. The title, *Songs of Innocence and of Experience*, embossed in gold, spoke to the truth of the poem's meaning. Thaddeus understood it to be a story about a lost mother who required the help of friends to find her way home. But she knew it was the desperate plea of someone who had crossed over into the harsh reality of life. Someone who wanted to find a way back to innocence.

"There's no way back, though," she whispered, absently rubbing her finger across the smooth lettering. "No beetle guiding us, no glowworm lighting up the darkness. It's just me, stumbling around and trying to make sense of it all."

With a sigh, she tugged the shawl off the verandah floor and stood. She had work to do.

A shout drew her attention toward the alley. "Miss Russell! Miss Russell! Please help."

A man dashed toward her, scurrying around piles of waste and scrambling over a tumble of bricks meant for the repair of a crumbling wall.

Through the gloaming, Mr. D'Souza came into view, his jacket flapping and his hand waving. He stopped before her, bent over, hands on knees, and sucked in a few deep breaths. "Miss Russell, I need help. Mother is ill. So ill. I don't know what to do. We've been here such a short time, I haven't met the doctors or our neighbors. No one, really, except you and your grandmother."

The front door creaked open. "I will come." Nānī padded toward her and took Ottilie's arm between pinching fingers. "You see to Thaddeus. I will tell Mr. D'Souza where to find the doctor." A gleam appeared in her eyes. "Unless you wish to accompany him back to his mother's home?"

"I will stay with Thaddeus," Ottilie said, raising her brows.

"Ah well, we tried." Nānī nodded at Mr. D'Souza and set off, the hem of her sari flipping with each step. She held on to Mr. D'Souza's arm and asked demanding questions in a strident voice. "When did she fall ill? What are the symptoms?"

And his answers. "Two days past. Nausea. Watery diarrhea."

Ottilie's heart twisted, and she pressed her hand to her sternum. Not every case of diarrhea led to death. Most did not. Most were not cholera.

But she'd heard whispers a few days ago. A child stricken and an old man dead in hours. And now Mrs. D'Souza, sick enough to send her son begging for help at the neighbor's.

"It is nothing. Nothing to worry about." Ottilie cast a final glance at the alley her grandmother had disappeared down, then draped the shawl over her head, wrapping it around her shoulders to ward off the sudden chill of evening.

Ottilie sat on the verandah, wrapped in her shawl, and closed her eyes. Sleep sang to her, begged her to curl onto her mat, already laid out, and join Thaddeus's slumber. The muezzin had already made the call to prayer, and still Nānī wasn't home. Elbows resting on her knees, she clasped her hands behind her head, desperate to silence the whispered memories of a disease that stole life in hours.

A cicada's song joined with the sound of a nearby celebration in an otherworldly chorus, one that put Ottilie in mind of bhoots and spirits. Hindu folklore said ghosts spoke in a nasal voice. She tipped her head and strained to hear her mother's voice. Not that she wanted her mother to be a ghost, especially a Hindu one, since they were usually miserable, but she *had* died in violence.

And how could anyone know what was truth?

Ottilie stood and walked down the steps, rocks biting into her bare soles and a gecko darting over her feet. Other than a dog foraging through a heap of garbage and a bat flapping overhead, Ottilie saw nothing in the narrow alley. Behind her, Dilip slept in the kitchen near the hearth and Thaddeus on his mat beneath the window. Before her, Nānī was somewhere tending a woman Ottilie had never met. She looked at the sky, squinting to see past the crowded-together houses. "I don't know what to believe anymore."

The dog whined an answer, and her stomach sank. What had she been expecting? A voice from heaven? Answers to questions that had been asked thousands of times, by thousands of people, in thousands of different ways, throughout thousands of years?

Pinching the embroidered edge of her shawl, she drew it close to her cheek. As though anyone could hide from God. She peered past her knuckles and the silk fabric at the sky. As though God saw her.

"Are you there? Are you real? Because I told Nānī I wouldn't vanish, but I feel I have. I'm disappearing. Losing myself and everything I thought was true."

Her spine prickled with a presence, and she dropped her gaze from the incomprehensible vastness of stars and sky and heaven that remained shrouded in questions and doubt.

"He is real, Boodha. These questions you ask." Nānī shuffled down the alley, her shoulders stooped and her hair falling out of its braid. "Even the heavens declare the glory of God, and you've been staring at the sky long enough to have seen it."

"It's not that easy, Nānī." Ottilie reached out to touch her grandmother's shoulder as she drew near. Reassurance that she was flesh and blood.

Nānī clicked her tongue. "I didn't say it was easy, but it is simple."

"I don't know how you suffered all of it and still retained your faith."

"That is simple too." Nānī patted Ottilie's cheek. "I had nothing else left."

The dog foraged nearer, its rank odor reaching them above the smell of waste and cooking. Ottilie sheltered Nānī within the circle of her arms, drawing her away from the animal, and they climbed the two steps onto the verandah. "How is Mrs. D'Souza?"

"She will live, I think."

"What is she ill with?"

Nānī's lids briefly sheltered her tired eyes. She shook her head and shrugged. "It is cholera. When the doctor finally came, he'd already been to the home of five other families with the disease. It will chase life down in Entally. Nothing can be done to prevent the spread of it, I fear."

Ottilie drew the hem of her shawl across her face, pulling it taut over the bridge of her nose. It fluttered beneath the steady cadence of her breathing and offered a flimsy shield against Nānī's pronouncement.

Again. She'd go through it again. How could she keep her family safe? Her deep pant drew the fabric toward her mouth, and she yanked it from her head. How could she survive it? And even worse, how would Nānī and Thaddeus survive if it took her?

"We can't stay. We must leave."

Nānī leaned her forehead against the heavy door. She rested her hands on either side and muttered a string of Hindi too fast for Ottilie to catch. "Where would we go? This is our home."

"I don't know." Ottilie sounded breathless, and no wonder, with her heart pounding as though she had run from one end of Calcutta to the other. "We could go to Benares and seek shelter with your family."

"They will not have us. They'd be glad to see us perish. Except for maybe Niraja . . . she might have forgiven me enough to care whether I am alive or not."

"Forgiven you for what? What is this awful thing you've done that is worth so much heartache? Would they truly wish you taken by a disease rather than offer you protection?"

Nānī studied Ottilie for a moment. Then she offered a resolute nod and pushed open the door. "Sit in the chair and light the lamp."

Ottilie was watching the flame dance within its glass when Nānī returned, carrying the secret stack of letters tied with a scarlet ribbon, and she sank into the chair, pushing against the cane back as tension stiffened her spine. "I thought you said I couldn't read those. That some things are not meant to be known."

Nānī shot Ottilie a withering glance. "And you have visited *that awful man* after saying you never wanted to see him again, so I suppose we both are permitted to change our mind."

Ice rushed through Ottilie's limbs, and she could hardly move her lips from their frozen state. "What man?"

"The colonel. And his wife." Her grandmother hissed the final words.

"How do you know I've seen them?"

Nānī waved her hand. "It doesn't matter. But you have, and you've taken your brother as well, haven't you?"

Ottilie nodded.

"If you are going to spend time with him, you should know what he's done." She thrust the letters into Ottilie's lap. "I am going to bed."

When Nānī left, Ottilie's hands shook as she slipped the ribbon from the envelopes. Each one boasted a jumble of feudatory and British-Indian postage, the stamps garish and bright against the creased white paper.

She opened the first letter and, once she got into the flow of reading Hindi, was drawn into the secret life of two sisters, bonded by a privileged childhood and a clandestine faith in a foreign God. Ottilie's aunt, Niraja Singh, had married shortly before Nānī. It had been arranged from childhood, and the man was less distantly related to the maharaja than their family was. According to descriptions of the wedding, everyone had been pleased with the match.

It's too bad you settled for someone of such low consequence, Gitisha, for I would have liked you to experience the honor of having a wedding such as mine. And I know what you will say, that a Christian must have a Christian wedding and marry a Christian man, but I've met your soldier, and I don't think him any more Christian than my prince. I don't trust him. And not only because he works for the British East India

Company. There's something cold about him. Something that won't be warmed by our sun, no matter how many years he spends in India.

Ottilie read for an hour before coming to a letter, its ink blotched and the words running together as though they had gotten wet. And when she saw the reason why, she knew the water had been tears.

> *Pitā is dead. Accused of inciting a mutiny among the sepoys. He knew the soldiers were coming and warned me to stay away from the house, but I couldn't let them take him away without trying to help. I told them Pitā was a courtier, a member of the royal family, but they cared little about that fact and a man— more of a boy, really—pushed me down so that I struck my head against the floor. When I awoke, Father was gone.*
>
> *He is gone. Accused of crimes he didn't commit.*
>
> *I wish your British husband had been here to intervene. Maybe he would have proved useful. Send me the Bible. I fear there is nowhere else to turn for comfort.*

Ottilie swiped away the tears that wet her cheeks. Poor Nānī. So far from her family and experiencing tragedy alone. The flame flickered, and Ottilie saw the candle had burned down and was only a nub now. She fingered through the remaining envelopes, knowing she needed to sleep but wanting to finish so she could better understand her grandmother.

She placed the stack of correspondence in her lap and withdrew the last one. And then she wished she hadn't. She read the lines, penned in small, stiff letters so unlike her aunt's previous looping script. Letters that spoke of barely restrained fury. Words that ended a friendship born of blood and laughter, family and secrets.

I've just had word that your husband was involved in the process that led to our father's death. It has been confirmed through my husband's connections. Lies and misunderstandings, that's what your colonel propagated. I am heartbroken not only because I have lost Pitā but my sister as well. You made your choice when your head was turned by his smart uniform and flattering words. You made your choice when you turned your back on our family and home and religion (and do not think me a hypocrite because I spent a moment of youthful arrogance believing in a god who spilled blood on a cross; I've since learned my error). I am making a choice now. You are dead to me, Gitisha. I pray your soul doesn't spend eternity trying to atone for your great sin. I pray you do not pay a thousandfold in this life for what you and your husband have done.

"Oh, Nānī." Ottilie pressed the letter to her chest. She said nothing else, but her questions and doubts, such niggling things at first, grew until she could only think one thing.

What if the Bible was wrong? What if there was no forgiveness, just endless cycles of trying to get it right? What if, when Nānī married the colonel, she tied herself to an unscrupulous man who'd been responsible for his own father-in-law's death, and that choice cast ripples of death and heartache, expanding outward until it consumed everyone Nānī loved?

What if Jesus was just another faraway deity, one that demanded and took? Even worse, what if he was make-believe, made up of no more substance than the flame sputtering beside her?

11

fter putting the bundle of letters back in their hiding place—hoping never again to have to see them—Ottilie unrolled her sleeping mat next to Nānī's. Normally she slept beside Thaddeus, loving the sound of his childish murmurs and even breathing, wanting to be close in case he had a nightmare. Since Maji's death, they came frequently.

But tonight Ottilie wanted to see the darkness through beside her grandmother, who had lost so much. And endured even more.

Before the sun appeared, Ottilie dressed in a blue blouse and yellow sari, both trimmed in red and gold embroidery. It was her best clothing. She braided her hair, allowing it to fall over her shoulder. After only a moment's hesitation, she pulled open one of the drawers on her mother's desk and removed the wooden jewelry case. Slipping the clasp, she lifted the lid and ran her fingers over the set of *kadas*, the gold bangles given to Nānī on her wedding day. Piece by piece, Nānī's jewelry had been sold to pay for Papa's debts and their living expenses, but these she refused to sell. And when Ottilie had turned eighteen, Nānī said they were hers.

Ottilie took one of the bracelets and slipped it on her wrist. Encrusted with three rows of tiny Madras pearls and boasting a trio of gems—sapphire, emerald, and diamond—it lay heavy against her skin. She donned the matching one, then draped the pallu over her head.

Without a mirror, Ottilie could only guess how she looked—like an Indian woman with no claim to British blood. No connection to an English colonel who'd cost her grandmother everything.

Something behind her rustled, and Ottilie turned to see Nānī semireclined on her mat, leaning against her elbows. Her hair had come undone and fell in a glorious curtain of barely gray silk down her back. "Do you plan on marrying today?"

"No."

"Then why are you dressed like a bride?"

"I'm dressed like an Indian woman."

Nānī lifted her brows, and a knowing smile curved her lips. "Are you no longer in mourning?"

"I will mourn forever. My clothing will not change that."

"Are you no longer English, then?"

Ottilie shook her head. "I'd rather not be."

Nānī sighed and heaved herself to her feet. She wore only a cotton blouse and petticoat, and her midriff rolled over the bleached fabric. She reached for Ottilie's face, her hands warm and gentle. "Your clothing will not change who you are."

Heat spilled into Ottilie's limbs. "What did you expect me to think after reading those letters? I want nothing more to do with that part of me."

"I didn't give them to you so that you would feel justified in rejecting your father's heritage. I gave them to you so you would understand. So you would know why I don't want you and Thaddeus near *him*."

"I will go further and remove myself from everything that ties me to the colonel."

Nānī shook her head. She took Ottilie's hands, and her eyes fell to the kadas. She shuddered, then kissed first the right, then the left bracelet. "If you do that, you remove yourself from everything that tied you to your father as well. England has done terrible things to our country in the name of prosperity. Even in the name of God. But it is not all bad. The people are not all bad. Think of your father, who was birthed on its soil. He was a good man who loved India. He loved you. He loved your mother and Thaddeus and me. Do not reject everything he was because some men don't know the God they profess."

The God they professed. The God she professed. "Who is he?"

"Your father, Navasi?" Nānī drew her brows together.

"No."

Her eyes lit with understanding. "Ahhh . . . you are asking a question you must discover the answer to yourself. If I tell you who he is, then it will be my understanding of him you make your own. And that is very unwise. You can't lean on the understanding of others, especially in matters of faith. You must learn the truth of it from the Lord."

"That isn't helpful, Nānī." Ottilie withdrew her hands from her grandmother's grasp and clasped them behind her back.

"No, I don't suppose it is." Nānī turned and bustled back to the mats. "Help me roll these and wake your lazy brother. I am hungry."

Nānī held her shoulders at an unmistakable angle, spine straight and head erect. Ottilie would get no advice this morning. She smoothed the length of sari she'd tossed over her shoulder so that it fell neatly behind her back, then went to tickle Thaddeus's feet.

Ten minutes later, with everyone dressed and Thaddeus having submitted to a brush and cloth, they joined Dilip in the kitchen for a quick breakfast of lentil-stuffed *poori*.

They ate standing, the mustard oil Dilip had fried the bread in making Ottilie's eyes water with its pungent scent. As she tore off portions of her meal and chewed, she noticed Thaddeus's gaze traveling between her and his food.

"You look pretty, Didi," he said, his mouth full of beans and bread. "I like you better in yellow than black."

She pinched his chin. "I think you're right. Perhaps I will swear off black clothing forever." God help it be true. She shook her head and placed her attention firmly back on her meal. How easily she slipped between doubt and faith. The one bleeding into the other. Both mixing together until she couldn't separate them.

A firm knock sounded on the door, and Dilip went to answer it. Nānī brushed a crumb from Thaddeus's face and urged him to finish eating so he wouldn't be late for school.

"I don't want to go to school," he said, his voice uncharacteristically petulant. "The boys make fun of my clothes and say I'm poor."

Behind her, Ottilie heard Dilip speaking in quiet tones to the person at the door, but she saw only Thaddeus's frown. The prematurely sad eyes. The school trousers that were inches too short and the collar that had been turned up and stitched more than once in an effort to hide the holes.

It all pointed toward failure. Her failure. She'd managed to keep food in his belly and school fees paid, but that was all.

"Who is at the door, Dilip?" she asked in an effort to distract herself.

He came back into the kitchen and slipped a note into her hand. The fine cardstock bore a grimy fingerprint smudge.

"What is it?" Nānī asked.

"It is from the woman I was to see today. She had promised me enough work to pay for two months of school fees. She says she's heard of the cholera outbreak in our neighborhood and has asked me to stay away for now." Ottilie lifted her eyes and met Nānī's.

"Does that mean I don't have to go to school?" Thaddeus's question bounced around the room, sounding more like joy than the fear tightening Ottilie's stomach.

He didn't know. Didn't know that education was their way

out unless she wanted to marry Mingel D'Souza with his Portuguese-speaking mother and five rooms. "Thaddeus, go get your lunch and books. It's time to go."

He grumbled as he stomped from the kitchen.

Ottilie pressed her hands over her eyes. "What will we do if all the work stops?"

Nānī made a sound in her throat. "We will survive."

"But how do you know?" Ottilie drew her hands away and twisted them together in her lap. "Previous experience says survival is not only unlikely but a fairy tale."

Dilip's hand found Ottilie's, stilling their mad grasping. "You will be fine, ma'am. You and Thaddeus both. I know this."

Ottilie threw her hands in the air, tossing off Dilip's grip. "The both of you. Neither one of you knows anything of the sort. I feel as though I'm living with a couple of soothsayers."

Thaddeus trudged back into the kitchen, the strap securing his books flung over his shoulder. "I suppose I'm ready to go."

Another knock sounded at the door, and a stone dropped into Ottilie's stomach. She couldn't take more bad news, and she waved Dilip away when he stood. "I'll get it."

She took Thaddeus's arm and propelled him toward the door. She'd get her brother off to school, then see about visiting Damaris. Maybe her friend would know of any ladies looking for an embroiderer. Hopefully word hadn't spread too far that another cholera outbreak was sweeping through Entally.

She swung open the door to reveal Mr. Scott, his hand lifted as though about to knock again, but instead he said, "Good morning."

"You're still here." The morning's stress made her words short, but she was glad to see him. A friendly face, a brilliant smile, something to break through her fear.

"That's a rather inauspicious greeting." He leaned his arm against the doorframe, his jacket brushing her shoulder, and she angled toward him.

"I thought you were leaving for England."

He held up a package. "Tea. I can't leave until you try to make me a convert."

Her remaining dread dissipated like clouds after the monsoon beneath the force of this charming diversion. "We will have to hurry, then. I've heard England is lovely this time of year. You wouldn't want to miss the arctic chill of a northern winter."

If Ottilie thought Mr. Scott's smile was profound, his laugh was positively transformative. He was an unassuming man, only his fine green eyes setting him apart as anything other than ordinary, but this . . . It was enough to set her free from fear. Enough to make her forget, for a moment, all the heartache she'd seen and still faced. Almost enough to make her forget she despised the English.

And she wanted more of it. More of him.

Someone jostled her from behind, and Thaddeus pushed his head past her arm. "Hello, we met in the street on Christmas. I'm Thaddeus Russell."

Mr. Scott bowed his head, and his eyes glimmered. "Hello, I'm Mr. Scott, though you can call me Everett, if you like. Your sister can, too, but she might think that kind of familiarity is reserved only for friends."

Thaddeus's face squeezed into a crooked expression. "Aren't you her friend?"

"I'm not entirely sure yet, but I do hope so." Mr. Scott glanced at Ottilie and lifted his brows. "I came for tea and to see if you and your brother want to see the circus tonight."

"The circus!" Thaddeus's whoop turned to a cry of dismay when Ottilie told him it wouldn't be possible because he had to go to school the next day.

She didn't know who looked more disappointed—her brother or Mr. Scott.

"I will still get up for school, even if I get no sleep at all," Thaddeus declared.

"Come now, Navasi," Nānī said, poking her head around the door. "Thaddeus can miss one day of school, can't he?"

Ottilie whirled. "You think that wise?"

She nodded, and their eyes met over Thaddeus's curly head. "I think, given the circumstances, it very wise."

In her words Ottilie heard a cautionary message. Thaddeus would enjoy a day of fun at the circus. Cholera cared little for dreams and plans, and if Ottilie lost the rest of her clients or if anyone in their household became sick, Thaddeus was facing a hard time. They all were.

And this day might offer them a sunny memory to think back on.

Mr. Scott looked so pleased when Ottilie finally conceded to allow him to escort her and Thaddeus to the circus that evening that she was left feeling as though she were doing him a favor instead of the other way around.

As she readied herself, she couldn't think about anything but the way his eyes had glowed, how he had seemed so comfortable sitting in their kitchen drinking masala chai, the way his nose wrinkled and lip curled as the tea pooled in his mouth and he pretended to like it.

"You must not patronize me, Mr. Scott. If you do not like it, we are more than willing to take it off your hands and put it to good use." She had sent a sidelong glance at Dilip, who knew how much she loved tea.

Mr. Scott forced the swallow down, then gave a slow nod. "You can have it."

"You aren't a very good Englishman, are you? Tea runs through their veins, as far as I know. And don't you work for a tea merchant? How very strange." Ottilie took his cup and handed it to Dilip, taking a surreptitious sniff of the wafting steam and barely restraining her desire to take a sip.

"There are many reasons I'm a terrible Englishman, Miss Russell, and that is the least of it."

Ottilie recalled the deep sadness that manifested in his voice and gaze. Suddenly the tea held little appeal. She only wanted to ease his burden in some way. Make it known that he didn't have to be a good Englishman to win her regard. Her affection.

How he had caught both so quickly, she didn't wish to think on. She was certain it had to do with some lack in herself. Was she destined to follow her grandmother's and mother's paths? Even after being singed by Victor's betrayal? She was a fool. More so because Everett Scott had made it clear he would only consider someone connected. Someone suitable.

And she was neither of those things.

Even now, ensconced in a fine gharry, its large red wheels eating up the distance to the Maidan, where Chiarini's Royal Italian Circus had pitched its tents, she shook her head at her own folly. Everett Scott might well be charming and kind, but he was also her enemy. Sent to take Thaddeus away from her. He was as British as Victor and the colonel, and so wasn't to be trusted. Both of them were charming in their own way too.

Her father had been the only British man worth knowing. The only one deserving of her esteem. She looked across the vehicle toward Mr. Scott, who stared pensively out the window as they rolled down Chowringhee Road, and forced herself to take his measure. There was nothing particularly captivating about him. Average in height and appearance, he didn't command attention. He wasn't the type to stand out. So why did she wish for him to notice the way the yellow silk of her sari lit her complexion? Wonder what she would see in his eyes if he took his gaze off the view outside the window and turned it toward her? Her heart was a rebellious, stupid thing, pounding over this ordinary Englishman.

Thaddeus jostled her as he leaned over the window ledge, his rear sticking up and wiggling as he waved at passersby with more energy than Ottilie thought possible for a child who'd spent the day at school.

She tapped his back and urged him to sit still and not fall into the street.

"We've made good time," Mr. Scott said, looking at her for the first time since he helped them into the conveyance. "Would you like the driver to take us to see the Ochterlony Monument and Eden Gardens?"

"Yes, that would be lovely." Ottilie hadn't been to Eden Gardens in years, and Thaddeus was again trying to flip himself out the window. "Plus, Thaddeus needs to get his wiggles out. Thank you, Mr. Scott."

"Please, we know each other well enough now that I believe it's acceptable to call me Everett."

She inclined her head, and he studied her. She turned to look out the window, but from the corner of her eye saw his perusal continue. "Is there something the matter, Mr. Sco—Everett?"

He pressed his lips together—to suppress a smile, she was sure—and shook his head. "Not at all. That dress—the Indian way of dressing—suits you."

"I wore a sari the other day when we went to the market."

"Yes, but that one boasted not a drop of color or stitch of pattern. You look lovely in these vibrant tones."

Heat filled her face. "Thank you. I wasn't sure you would appreciate me casting off my English mourning when going out."

He tipped his head. "It does seem soon to wear such things, but I'm aware enough to understand my sensibilities and customs aren't shared by the rest of the world."

"Have you forgotten half my blood is dripping with English sensibility?"

"Not at all, but you've never been to England, so it seems reasonable to assume you haven't fully embraced British ways."

Ottilie snorted. "My father always said the English in India are more English than the English in England. I've had plenty of exposure to your customs." His customs, not hers. Nani's eyes would roll back if she could hear Ottilie now.

He tilted his head and studied her again, much like a scientist would an interesting specimen beneath a microscope. "You haven't embraced much of that part of yourself, though, and it seems you're eager to cast the rest of it off."

Ottilie turned and stared past Thaddeus's head, out the window and over the grassy Maidan. She could see the circus tent, white and red stripes calling everyone to witness its wonder and be entertained. She didn't answer him. Couldn't explain this need to distance herself from her grandfather and everything he'd done. From every Englishman who'd insulted her and cast aspersions on her character because of the shade of her skin. From Victor, who had been so ashamed of his feelings for her that he had insisted on secrecy. From Everett, even, who conspired with a stranger and her dead mother to separate what was left of her family.

India hadn't always been kind to her, but there was room to be absorbed into its fabric. England was . . . constrictive. Narrow. Insular. England conquered and forced the world to conform. India embraced. It took the best, and sometimes worst, of a hundred cultures and wove it into its own tapestry. England was a colorless land that plodded on in an attempt to usurp the native beauty of conquered places. India reached for the grandeur and charm of other places and made it her own.

Ottilie looked at Everett, who waited patiently for a response. She only said, "You can't reject something that never allowed you entry to begin with."

"Look!" Thaddeus scooted onto his knees and poked his arm out the window, finger pointed at the tall Ochterlony Monument.

Everett leaned toward the window and took in the wonder of it. "I've never seen anything quite so tall. Odd combination of styles, isn't it?"

Ottilie couldn't see it past their heads, but she could picture it from memory—gleaming white and proclaiming its own importance as it stood sentry over Eden Park's lakes, pagodas, and flowering trees. Designed by an English architect, the monument took from Syrian, Egyptian, and Turkish style and celebrated a British East India Company major general in defending Delhi against the Marathas.

"Everything about it is odd," Ottilie said. "But the gardens are beautiful."

"Let's take a stroll, then." Everett slipped a watch from his vest pocket and nodded. "We have plenty of time." He knocked against the box, and the gharry-wallah brought the horses to a stop. Everett descended first and helped Thaddeus, then Ottilie out. He told the driver they would walk from there and sent him on his way.

They moved down the tree-shaded road cutting through the Maidan, staying to the fringe as palanquins held aloft by sinewy men and carriages sheltering fair English women passed by.

"I've heard this is called Respondentia Walk." Everett held out his arm, which she took.

"It is. It's said to be the prettiest place in Calcutta." She watched Thaddeus, who moved a little ahead of them, his curious gaze touching each richly appointed vehicle as it rumbled by, his fingers reaching for overhanging branches heavy with custard apples.

"It is strange to be walking in a park alive and vibrant with color when, back home, everything is cold and gray."

Ottilie nodded. "Father always said he couldn't abide English winters. They made him want to crawl beneath the covers and never leave his bed."

"Yes, the winters are harsh—relieved only by the candles and gifts of Christmas. But the rest of the year is beautiful."

Ottilie gave him a sideways glance, and he laughed.

"It's true. I don't believe Bengal offers the changing leaves and vibrant colors of a Wiltshire autumn. It certainly doesn't have green plains dotted with sheep or pretty villages nestled together."

She smiled. "You paint a lovely picture, but nothing in England can be as beautiful as this."

"Maybe one day you will see for yourself the beauty England has to offer."

"I don't think that likely." She brushed her hand down the front of her sari, Nānī's bracelet slipping down her arm and settling in a heavy circle around her wrist. "At least here I can wear color after death and blend into a crowd."

They rounded a man-made lake ringed with spindly palm trees and stopped as a Burmese pagoda's seven-tiered roof rose before them. Thaddeus ran ahead and alighted its steps, standing outside the prayer hall that housed a golden-robed Buddha. Another teacher sitting securely on his throne, unaware the city was already populated by thousands of gurus and mystics pointing to thousands of gods.

"I understand wanting to belong," Everett said, his voice low. "Truly. More than many people, perhaps."

There was a longing in his words Ottilie identified with. She shifted closer to him. Tightened her hand on his arm.

He smiled at her, then stepped after Thaddeus. She let him go, sensing his need to distance himself from his confession, and watched the two of them talk in serious voices. Everett clasped his hands behind his back, and Thaddeus mimicked him.

Steps alerted Ottilie to the presence of others, and she stepped off the path and into the grass.

In a cloud of imported perfume, a young woman swept by on the arm of her gentleman. Ottilie didn't take offense at the woman's narrowed eyes and turned-up nose. Hardly noticed it, common as it was on the face of the English.

But her words, said in a voice purposely loud enough to carry, and directed at Thaddeus in his too-small sailor suit and Everett, both as English-looking as she, cut deep.

"What a shame they now allow natives into the gardens in the evening. It wasn't so a few years back, when the area was restricted to people of good breeding."

Thaddeus looked back at Ottilie, his brows making sharp slashes across his brow.

"You really should have the boy's ayah stay with your carriage," the woman continued, "instead of allowing her to enjoy this place. It's meant for us. Not them."

Everett's throat constricted with a hard swallow. "And by 'them' you mean the Indians? Those are the people who aren't allowed in this garden in the middle of a city in India?"

The pain that had stabbed through Ottilie at the woman's cruelty mellowed, and she lifted her hand to her lips, meaning to cover her smile. But she couldn't catch the laugh that bubbled over when the woman huffed and stomped off so suddenly that the man with her stumbled down the steps.

Everett shook his head and ushered Thaddeus back to her. "I'm sorry."

"You have nothing to be sorry about." She glanced at her brother, wishing he didn't have to hear such things. "We are used to it."

Thaddeus wrapped his skinny arm around her waist. "People always say things to Ottilie but not me. I think it's because I look like my father and she looks like Maji."

Ottilie pushed his hair back from his forehead and pressed a kiss there.

"I don't know why it makes a difference, though. If people would only get to know Ottilie, they'd realize she is the best person in the entire city. The country. The whole world!"

His exuberant declaration eased the remaining scrap of hurt, and Ottilie smiled at him. "You might be the only person in the world who believes that, but yours is the only opinion that matters."

Everett's hand found her bare arm, the warmth of his fingers searing her skin. When he spoke, his voice was warmer still, and his words filled her belly with heat. "He is most definitely *not* the only person in the whole world who believes that."

Ottilie bit her lip, knowing she shouldn't assign him motives he most likely didn't hold. Knowing he was only being kind and trying to ease her embarrassment. But deep beneath her breast, a flame sparked. She knew she should douse it. Blow it out, and extinguish its light. Because she couldn't—wouldn't—make the same choice Nānī had. A choice she would have already lived to rue herself for had Victor not been a coward.

Father might have been a wonderful, kind English husband, but Ottilie knew most of them were like her grandfather and thought nothing of taking and discarding Indian women.

No, she couldn't care for a British man. Not again. The colonel and Victor had proven that unwise.

Beneath the canvas tent, a crush of people shoved to take their seats. Everett circled his arms around Ottilie and Thaddeus, pushing through the crowd. He found an empty bench only a few rows back from the ring.

Thaddeus soon moved from his place beside Ottilie to her lap in order to better see over the hat of the woman in front of them. "Do you think they'll have trick riders?"

Everett nodded. "The advertisement said they would."

And there they were, a parade of horses manned by men and women in outlandish costumes, standing on bareback. Thaddeus bounced and clapped his hands. He whooped just as loudly as anyone else in the tent. When Ottilie's gaze met Everett's, she mouthed her thanks. She couldn't remember the last time her brother had this much fun.

As the evening progressed, she realized it had been even longer since she had. She began to relax when a cage containing three Bengal tigers and their tamer was rolled center stage. The tension in her jaw and neck released as she watched the acrobats flip and twirl and soar through the air. She pressed her hands to her cheeks as the clowns tumbled together with their oversized costumes and painted faces.

When she laughed, Everett leaned near, and over the din of the crowd cheering the performers, she heard him say, "It's good to see you enjoying yourself."

The circus was another world, the evening a dream. Outside the tent, away from the scent and sound of a thousand people and animals, life waited for her. But inside, Everett's shoulder bumping hers, Thaddeus balancing on his tiptoes so he could see a pair of elephants standing on barrels, it seemed very far away. For a few precious moments, she forgot about loss and disease. She forgot about the worry of paying school fees. She forgot about the grief that followed her family.

Thaddeus looked at her over his shoulder, his eyes bright and reflecting joy. "Can we come back tomorrow night? I'd like to see it all again."

"No, little glowworm. Tonight is a night for magic. It can't last forever." She chuckled and pinched his chin when he pouted, but his gaze soon returned to the show. "Thank you for this," she told Everett. "We've been in such deep mourning, Thaddeus has forgotten what it's like to enjoy himself."

"And you."

She smiled. "And me."

"I'm glad to have a part in it, then." He turned his attention back to the performers, but his throat moved beneath a heavy swallow. "I know it's no comfort, but I've seen how suffering can produce good character. It makes people resilient. Compassionate toward others. The things they accomplish are made more beautiful because of the strength it took to persevere."

"Look, Ottilie!" Thaddeus tugged on her arm. "That man is swallowing a *sword*."

She took a moment to watch the impressive feat, but Everett's words clung to the fringe of her thoughts and wouldn't release her. She lowered her voice so as not to disturb Thaddeus and said, "But why? Why must we suffer, and why do some people suffer so much more than others?" The sounds of clapping and trumpeting elephants were at odds with the heaviness of her question. With her need for an answer.

Everett was quiet for a moment, his heavy brow wrinkled as he thought. She liked that he didn't offer her a trite response. Wasn't the type of man to offer glib words. He reminded her of Damaris. "I think maybe, sometimes, God has called those people to great works. Perhaps their purpose is greater than living a quiet life. The suffering they endure might be necessary to prepare them for it."

A desperate prayer stuck in Ottilie's throat, and she swallowed hard. *That's not what I want.* "What if all that person *wants* is a quiet life? A simple one."

Everett's soft smile was a tender benediction, but his words were piercing arrows. "God is omniscient, is he not? He knows if a person is suited for his purposes."

And if that person isn't sure the god of the Bible is any different than the thousands cluttering temples across this country, then what? The thought was for her alone. There was no use in causing Everett to think the young Baron Sunderson was being raised by anyone other than a committed Christian. Her doubts and questions weren't ones people talked about. They isolated her. Made her unique in a way she didn't care for. Did anyone else wonder these things? Did they ever speak of them?

Were they ridiculed or cast away when they did?

All around, people were standing and shuffling down the aisles toward exits. Thaddeus stared at the empty space where only moments ago animals, clowns, and acrobats entertained the crowd. He turned to her and clasped his hands against his chest, eyes shining and a grin spread across his face.

"Are you ready to go home, little glowworm?" Ottilie asked.

He nodded, and Everett had him hop onto the bench and then his back. They walked out of the crowded tent and started across the trampled grass of the Maidan.

"Are you all right?" Everett tightened his hands around Thaddeus's ankles when he turned to look at her.

She nodded. "Have you . . . suffered much? Do you feel it was worth the character it produced?"

Everett's face was lost to shadows, and Ottilie wished she could see his expression. Make out the shade of his eyes, which revealed so much of what was going on inside his head. His heart. Above him, Thaddeus lifted his hands to the sky, reaching for the stars that spangled it. Grasping for the heavy orange moon.

"I have suffered," Everett said softly. "Maybe not as much as you because there was only one I could claim as my own. Only one to lose. I suffer still at her absence."

They reached the street, and Everett waved for a gharry. He lifted Thaddeus above his head and set him on the seat, then helped Ottilie inside. Following her, he sat next to her, not across as he had earlier. Thaddeus spread out on the opposite seat, resting his head in his hands.

"Do I think it was worth it?" Everett said, just as the gharry set off and Ottilie thought he'd forgotten the rest of her question. "I don't know if that's the right question. It's not as though we have a say in the tragedy we endure. It happens and we grow. Or it happens and we wither. I hope I've grown from it. I hope my mo—I hope what I've experienced hasn't been wasted on me."

He'd been about to say mother but stopped himself, and that told Ottilie all she needed to know about the pain Everett Scott had endured. The knowledge made her scoot nearer to him, her arm brushing his. She touched his hand but said nothing. She didn't need to. A cord of shared sorrow knit them together as surely as threads of gold attached pieces of elytra and glass to fabric.

The rest of the ride was washed in silence, only Thaddeus's sleepy murmurs breaking it. But Ottilie's heartbeat was loud in her ears when Everett turned his hand over and captured her fingers, his thumb drawing circles against the underside of her wrist beneath her grandmother's kada. Chowringhee Road was lined with gaslights, and as the light of one filtered through the open window, she noticed his long, tapered fingers around hers, his nails clean and cut into perfect crescents. Blue veins showing stark against his fair skin. He had the hands of an aristocrat, and his kindness and honor testified to a character stronger and better than any man born to a family of noble blood. If trial had produced such a man as Everett Scott, she could fan the hope that her own suffering meant something.

When they arrived at the alley leading to her house, Everett lifted Thaddeus to his shoulder and carried him over the dusty street. She blinked when she entered the house, surprised to see the room lit by a gas lamp.

Dilip bolted from the chair in the corner and rushed toward her, his face a mask of fear. "You're finally home."

"What's wrong?" Ottilie glanced around, seeing nothing disrupted, no reason for him to be awake instead of sleeping near the fire in the kitchen.

"It's Nānī," he said, his voice going hoarse. "She's ill. I think it's cholera."

12

Ottilie's knees weakened, and she crumpled. Dilip's arms were around her before she hit the floor, and she hung heavy from them, drawing in a deep breath of air that seemed too thin. "No," she finally managed. "You must be wrong. She was fine before we left."

She forced herself to straighten and pulled from Dilip. Looking away from his pale, sorrowful face, she noticed Everett still holding Thaddeus. He shifted his weight, deep lines creasing the area between his brows, and met her eyes. His gaze spoke as clearly as words could have. *It will be all right.* His presence grew more solid. More comforting. It would be all right.

"Dilip, go get Thaddeus's mat and set it out in the living area," Ottilie instructed. "He'll sleep in here tonight."

"Ottilie," Everett said as soon as Dilip disappeared into the bedroom, "go to your grandmother. I'll get Thaddeus settled."

Her nose burned, and she blinked against the burn of tears. "Dilip must be wrong. Nānī is just overworked."

Dilip returned, and after one quick glance at Ottilie and Everett, he looked away and unfurled the mat.

Everett secured Thaddeus against his hip and laid a hand on her shoulder. "I know you're scared. Don't waste another moment in here. Cholera is a fast-moving disease."

His words released icy fingers that gripped her chest. For a moment, her heart ceased to beat, her lungs didn't expand, and everything stilled. Then her feet were moving so fast that she tripped over the hem of her sari in her haste to reach Nānī.

The room was dark, lit only by a lamp on Maji's desk. Ottilie gasped and covered her nose with her hand, and tears spilled over it. A low groan filled her throat, and she worked to keep it from escaping. From vocalizing and making real what she knew to be true.

That scent . . . it took her back in time, surrounded by the fishy odors of her father's and siblings' excretions. She'd never forget how it crept between the floorboards and seeped into her clothing. And every time the memories of that lonely dark day freed themselves from the place she'd hidden them, they were saturated with stench.

The same stench that surrounded her now.

She forced her hand down and lifted the lamp. Followed the soft glow to Nānī's side. Curled around herself, moaning and clutching at her stomach, Nānī seemed to have shrunk in the few hours Ottilie had been enjoying the sights and sounds of the circus. Ottilie set the lamp on the floor and touched her grandmother's shoulder.

"Oh, Navasi, I feel wretched."

"I know. I'm home now."

"I'm so thirsty."

Ottilie lifted the cup near Nānī's head and, supporting her with an arm, helped her drink. Nānī licked her cracked lips and took greedy swallows.

"Only a little at a time." Ottilie pulled the cup away.

Nānī sank back to the mat, and in the lamplight, her sunken cheeks and eyes looked cadaverous. Ottilie shivered and tucked the coarse wool blanket more tightly around Nānī. Ottilie had been so young the first time cholera visited them. She hadn't known to worry at first. But within a day, they were all dead—

Father, Jemima, and Nathan. She and Dilip were alone, abandoned by the rest of the servants, who had left the moment they realized what it was. India had been plagued with cholera epidemics for a hundred years. They had known what was coming.

But Ottilie hadn't. It wasn't until her siblings were lost in hours that Ottilie discovered the horrifying truth.

"Nānī . . . I think you have cholera."

"Yes. The evidence is in the pot."

Ottilie glanced at the chamber pot a few feet away, the source of the foul odor. She knew without looking that it contained the proof the doctor would need to diagnose Nānī.

The doctor.

"Dilip," she called, her voice shrill and desperate.

He appeared less than a second later.

"The doctor? Go fetch the doctor."

"Mr. Scott has already left for one."

Ottilie's heart settled back into her chest. "Bring me the mustard oil." He disappeared, and Ottilie moved to Nānī's feet. "I will rub them for you."

"Ah . . . you are too good to me, my darling Boodha."

"I have every right to worry, Nānī. Don't tease me now."

Ottilie could just make out the outline of her grandmother's features, but she saw the sharp lines of her nose and jaw soften. "I know. This is another thing you must overcome."

Dilip entered and handed Ottilie the jar. He crossed the room and crouched in the corner, resting his head in his hands. Ottilie recognized his position as one of prayer, and she took comfort in it. She crossed her legs and took Nānī's right foot into her lap. After pouring a pool of mustard oil into her cupped palm, she rubbed her hands together, releasing the sharp odor. She lowered her nose and sniffed, clearing out the scent that predicted loss. Then she brought her fingers to Nānī's ankles, rubbing deep circles around them and down to the arch of her foot. Up the sole and around each toe.

Nānī sighed. "If there is anything I will miss, it is this. Make sure to teach your grandchildren to rub your feet, Navasi. There is nothing better."

"Do not say you will miss anything. You will heal."

"I am old."

"You are healthy."

"And so tired."

"We need you. I need you." Ottilie clenched her teeth and took Nānī's other foot in her lap.

"I am ready."

"I'm not, Nānī. Now, stop talking. You grow too weak." Not everyone died of cholera. Mrs. D'Souza had recovered. Ottilie ignored the faces of all those who hadn't. Ignored that her family seemed especially susceptible to the disease. *I don't have any more strength. If you take Nānī away from me, I will break.* She prayed to a God she wasn't sure existed, not sure if she was more afraid he did.

"Navasi, I must go."

"Stop, Nānī!"

"No." Nānī pushed up on her elbows with a gasp. "I must *go.*"

Ottilie scrambled to her feet and called for Dilip. They helped Nānī to the pot, Dilip holding her up and Ottilie lifting the folds of her sari. When she finished, Dilip helped her back to the mat and, with movements as gentle as any mother tending to her babe, lay the blanket back over her and kissed her cheek. He smoothed his hand over Nānī's hair and whispered a prayer in Bengali over her. Then he approached Ottilie and did the same. A kiss to the cheek, a hand against her hair, and a whispered prayer.

Ottilie stood, fixed to that spot where the moonlight, free from its heavy cloak of clouds, spilled through the window, and followed his gaze to the contents of the chamber pot. "It's cholera."

"Yes."

"Will she die?"

"I pray not." He covered the pot with a square of muslin and lifted it. "I will clean this."

Ottilie returned to Nānī and sat at her head. She removed the tie that bound her grandmother's braid and unwove her hair. Carefully lifting Nānī's head to her lap, she rubbed those same deep, even circles from temple to crown.

Nānī lifted her hands, already shrunken from a loss of fluid, and folded them over her stomach. Her eyes drifted closed. Ottilie thought she slept, but then she said, "I never meant to hide it from you, what the colonel did. I only meant to protect you."

"You don't have anything to explain, Nānī. I'm not angry with you."

"I loved him. The way he looked at me . . . and what a fine figure he cut in his uniform. But he loved the company more than he loved me." Nānī made a spitting sound. "Love is a terrible thing to base a marriage on. Don't be taken in by it."

Ottilie grimaced, remembering the warmth of Everett's hands and gaze. "Can you tell me what happened after you found out?"

"I stopped speaking to him."

Ottilie blinked and untwined Nānī's hair from around her fingers. "What do you mean, you stopped speaking to him?"

"Just that. I showed him Niraja's letter and never said another word." Nānī's voice was weakening, the words fading.

"But . . . how? How do you not speak to your husband?"

"You can say a lot without saying a word."

"He stayed with you another four years, though."

Strength seemed to fill Nānī's body, and her voice became strident. "He was always a stubborn man." She motioned for the water, and Ottilie allowed her a tiny sip. "I will rest." Nānī rolled onto her side and slept.

Ottilie didn't move. Every few minutes, she laid her hand on Nānī's back, reassured by the gentle lifting. Her mind moved over Nānī's story. How she'd said not a word to her husband—

who surely deserved much worse, but still. Not a word? If her grandmother had the strength to do that, maybe she could survive this disease. Maybe she would live to demand Ottilie rub her feet with mustard oil and to tell her over and over, a hundred times, that love wasn't good for marriage.

And if Nānī lived, then Ottilie promised she'd marry Mr. D'Souza. She'd gladly trade a marriage of passion for one of security if it meant Nānī would be the one teaching Ottilie's children how to rub her feet with mustard oil.

Everett didn't return for hours. The sky turned black as pitch, with coal and factory smoke blotting out the stars. Turning the moon into a weak, watery thing barely holding on to its supremacy.

Nānī moaned and tossed upon her pallet. Ottilie had never wished for their rosewood beds and stuffed mattresses more. Until this moment, she hadn't known how much they would miss their servants. One to wave a fan over Nānī's sweating body, one to fetch water and cloths, one to sit in the corner and sing ancient songs in Hindi, songs from Nānī's childhood that brought comfort.

"Dilip," Ottilie called.

Still crouched in the corner of the room, he startled and blinked up at her, his eyes glazed with otherworldly thoughts.

"Will you sing?"

"Sing what, ma'am?"

"Why must you always call me that?"

"He must, Navasi." Nānī's reedy voice spilled into the space between Ottilie and Dilip. "It is what keeps the distance between you safe. And he knows you are meant for another."

Ottilie's gaze darted to Dilip, who still crouched near the wall, his head dipped low. They were friends, like siblings, weren't they? "Who am I meant for, Nānī? Not Mr. D'Souza."

"Not who, but where. Meant for another place."

"What is this nonsense?" Ottilie shook her head and pressed the back of her hand against Nānī's cheek. Her skin, papery thin, burned.

"The pot." Nānī bolted upright and wrapped her arms around her middle. Dilip launched to his feet and snatched up the pot on his way to her.

As she retched into it, empty heaving that released only the drops of water Ottilie had rationed out, Dilip rubbed her back. Nānī wiped the edge of her sari over her mouth and sank onto the mat, heavy breaths lifting her chest and releasing a rattle.

"Oh, where is Everett with the doctor?" Ottilie stood and went to the window. She saw nothing but the shadowy outlines of her neighbors' homes, dilapidated buildings sheltering families with their own grief and struggles.

"He will come." Dilip's statement contained a deeper meaning, and Ottilie turned to look at him. Her nails dug into the soft wood casement, naked and unvarnished, splinters piercing beneath them. "He will not leave you to this alone."

"I'm not alone. You're here."

Dilip smiled, shadows of what she'd always thought they'd been on his lips. She realized he'd never allowed her in, not truly. She wanted to run to him. To find comfort in his arms the way she had when Papa and her siblings had been taken. But Nānī's words made her cautious, and she planted her feet.

She couldn't find relief in Dilip's touch any more than she could find it now in Victor's. Unfortunate that she felt, and gave, solace best through a hug. The holding of hands. In drawing near and breathing the scent of a person.

Where was Everett?

She crossed the room and lay beside Nānī. There was no room on the narrow mat, and the floor bit into her hip and shoulder, but she tucked her nose against the curve of Nānī's neck and inhaled. "I love you."

Nānī turned to face her. Her eyes had sunken even farther into her face, and her tongue seemed too thick to fit inside her mouth. Her fingers found Ottilie's cheek. "You are stronger than you think."

"Not strong. I'm a reed brought low by the sickle."

"Oh, my Boodha. That reed is sound and supple. It is woven into the very mats we sleep on and provides lasting comfort. It can be trampled upon, rolled up, and shoved in a corner, yet it still maintains its beauty. It still renders what it was meant to be."

"It is nothing compared to a stuffed mattress." How had Nānī pulled these earlier thoughts from her mind and twisted them into a lesson? A smile tugged Ottilie's lips.

"Bah. A stuffed mattress is a weak thing. Like the Europeans who brought them across the continents. They grow flat and useless after only a season in our city. They weren't made for this place." Her gaze sharpened, and she pulled back. Ottilie could see the lines creasing Nānī's face, the deep crevices on either side of her mouth. Her skin had taken on a dullness that wrapped Ottilie's chest in iron fetters.

"Ottilie?"

Bile filled Ottilie's throat. When had Nānī last called her by her given name? Not Navasi or Boodha? She didn't know what it could mean. Didn't want to know. She sat up and turned her face away. "I will get you some buttermilk. We should buy some bottle gourd tomorrow. Dilip, will you go to the market in the morning?"

"Listen." Nānī's fingers plucked at the hem of Ottilie's sari. "Look at me."

Ottilie obeyed. The expression on Nānī's face made her wish she hadn't. "What is it?" she whispered. "You're scaring me."

"You aren't meant for this place anymore either."

Tears clogged Ottilie's throat. Papa had been like this, too, at the end. Delusional and making little sense.

"Don't look at me like that. I am not confused."

153

"I don't understand what you're saying, Nānī. Of course I belong here. This is my home. Where would I go?"

"England." Dilip's voice wended its way through the stale room.

Nānī sighed as though relieved of a heavy burden. "Yes." She closed her eyes and rested her hands on her chest. Ottilie stared at them, at the loose skin gathering around her knuckles. At the crisscross of veins and narrow ridges of gathered flesh.

Dilip stood, lifting the basin of vomit. "I will clean this out."

When he left, Ottilie studied her grandmother in the light of the lamp's flickering flame. She looked closer to death than life. And it had happened so fast. Every person in Ottilie's life had left suddenly. Without warning. She remembered this feeling well, after Papa's, Jemima's, and Nathan's deaths from cholera. After Maji was trampled by a horse in the middle of the street. Why did God think her capable of handling more of the same?

Why did Nānī?

She had no faith in herself that she would be able to survive it again. Which wouldn't seem so hopeless if her faith in God remained unconquered. She bowed her head and gripped her hair, pulling at it until it fell from her braid in a curtain that shielded her from the eyes of an unspeaking, uncaring, too-far God. *I don't know if I'd rather you exist and watch over us with so little regard or not exist at all.*

Her stomach felt empty, as though doubt had consumed the fragile thread of hope bequeathed by life's grief. It had taken so much. Too much.

"Navasi?"

Ottilie released her hair and looked at her grandmother.

"My legs hurt so badly."

Her groan spurred Ottilie forward, and she took Nānī's foot into her lap again. Her hands kneaded the cramping muscle, easing tender and tight spots. She hoped Nānī felt all the love Ottilie had stored up inside of her in the touch.

A moan tore from Nānī's throat, and Ottilie jerked her hands from the thin skin just barely protecting her grandmother's spindly legs. "I'm sorry. Did I hurt you?"

Nānī sat up with more strength than seemed possible and gripped Ottilie's arm, her nails digging in. "Bring me your grandfather."

"The colonel?"

"Bring him to me. I've done a great wrong."

"I can't leave you."

"I'll go." Dilip set down the pot and disappeared from the room before Ottilie even had time to wonder what Nānī meant to do.

"Navasi?"

"Yes, Nānī?" Ottilie ran her hands around the back of Nānī's calf, teasing out the cramp that had bunched the muscle into a tight ball.

"You and Thaddeus. You will go to England."

This again? She released her grandmother's leg and lifted the lamp, holding it near her face. A thin sheen of sweat glistened against the gray pallor of her skin, but her eyes were clear.

"They only want Thaddeus. He can . . ." The word caught in her throat, loathsome and bitter. It felt like a betrayal of her mother. Of Nānī herself. But she spit it out. "Pass. I cannot." She set down the lamp, and it cast grim shadows. Ottilie lowered the wick, and they shrank.

"I had a dream."

"That I moved to England?"

"No. I dreamed you stayed in India." A wild look entered her grandmother's eyes. "Since I told you and Dilip about the first part of my earlier dream, I've been wondering what the rest of it meant. I couldn't make sense of it. The mausoleum was full, but I wasn't in it. Neither was Thaddeus. But I had another dream tonight. Another that showed me who was in it."

"I was in the crypt." Ottilie sighed. "Nānī, you can't expect me to upset our entire life because of a dream."

"But I saw your parents and siblings again. And I was with them. But you were not. And the mausoleum was full. If you stay in India, you will be lost. You will be lost to India. And lost to us. You will be lost to God. But in England, you will find him. You will be found. You must leave. Promise me you will leave."

The front door creaked open, saving Ottilie from having to answer. After some muffled conversation, Everett entered the room, followed by a somber-looking Englishman wearing a dark suit and carrying a bag.

"I'm sorry it took so long." Everett knelt beside Ottilie and lowered his voice so only she could hear. "Many would not come. I only found Dr. Adley because I stopped at Reverend Hook's— Dilip told me to—and begged him to help. He's in the front room, if you want to see him."

Ottilie nodded but didn't leave her grandmother's side. There was little comfort Reverend Hook could offer.

Dr. Adley hunched over Nānī, prodding her belly, feeling her throat, and peering into her eyes. Then he stood and took Ottilie's arm, directing her to a far corner of the room.

"Don't worry, Doctor. I know." Nānī's voice lacked its normal volume but still held the imperious tone she'd grown up using with servants.

"You don't know anything, Nānī," Ottilie said, turning her attention to the doctor, whose eyes reminded Ottilie of a gaur's. Soft and mournful, they were dark in his pale face.

He ignored Nānī and spoke in a hushed voice. "I'm sorry. Keep her comfortable. Cholera is hard on people her age."

"It's hard on everyone."

"Very true. This area has seen more than its share of outbreaks. If possible, do not drink from the well. Send away for water to be brought to you from a well in a neighboring community."

"That will cause undue expense."

"The cost of ignoring my advice will be higher. Cholera is spread by dirty water. There has been a cluster of cases in this area, and that tells me the wells are contaminated. Do not drink from them. If you have no choice, boil the water—all water—for one full minute. It will kill the pathogens."

Ottilie looked at the cup sitting on the floor beside the lamp and nodded. Was that all it took? Had they only to boil water and her father and siblings would have lived? Could God not have given Nānī a dream about *that*? "I will do it."

"She is very ill. Try to have her drink, but . . . as I said, cholera will be hard on her." He glanced at Nānī, who lay supine on her mat, hands curled into claws over her stomach. "There is a chance she will survive, but the disease progresses quickly, and she's severely dehydrated."

"Dehydrated?" Ottilie turned the unfamiliar word around her tongue. "What does that mean?"

"She's lost much of the water in her body. That is how cholera kills. I wish there were some way to restore it, but with the vomiting and diarrhea, it's nearly impossible. I'm sorry."

Ottilie bowed her head, and he left. A moment later, Everett touched her arm, and she turned toward him. "Must I lose everyone?"

He said nothing, only pressed her head to his chest. The warmth of him seeped through the thin fabric of her blouse, and there, trapped between his heart and touch, she found comfort, if not peace. There were no answers. Only the steady thrump-thrump-thrump of his heartbeat. It was enough for now.

"I'll stay as long as you need me," he said.

"And then?"

"Then I'll stay a bit longer."

"And then you'll return to England."

"Eventually." He sighed, and his fingers found the little hairs curling at the nape of her neck. He twirled them in a gesture too intimate for friends. For whatever it was they were. "I will miss India. It's a complex place, is it not? So many contradictions wrapped up in the most beautiful and terrible packaging. I've never seen such glorious sunsets. Or diseases that strike down entire communities in days."

"Don't you have cholera in England?"

"Not in twenty-five years."

Nānī's words came back to her. *I had a dream. You must go. Promise me.* India would never be rid of cholera. It was as tangled up in its land and water as cast-off threads in the bottom of her sewing box. A chill swept over her, prickling the hairs on her arms. The disease would stalk her always. It wouldn't be satisfied until it consumed everyone she loved. And she only had Nānī and Thaddeus left.

She pulled her head away from Everett and craned her neck, eyes seeking her grandmother. Nānī looked so small—smaller than usual—curled into a circle on her side. A little cry escaped Ottilie's throat, and she pressed her hand against her mouth.

"Let me tell you about my home." Everett led her to her mother's desk and pulled the chair out for her. Then he sat at her feet, one leg stretched before him and the other bent, where he rested his forearm. He looked comfortable and casual. As though he belonged there, in her home, beside her.

Ottilie kept her eyes on Nānī, but Everett's voice was like a breeze. His words cooled her fear, drawing her thoughts toward images of green hills and clouds as fluffy as soan papdi.

"Wiltshire couldn't be more different from Calcutta. Should you ever travel there, you'll find mild weather in the summer and crisp winter days. Even at its hottest, it never reaches the heights of Calcutta in January. My favorite season is autumn, when the leaves change, turning trees to sunsets that rustle with every breeze. There are plains and hills, villages crowded with thousand-year-old stone cottages winding around narrow streets, and good people. It's the prettiest place in all of England."

She watched Everett as he spoke of his home. Saw the longing cross his face. Her stomach sank, and she twisted the fabric draping her lap with nervous fingers. From the moment she'd met Everett, she'd wanted him to leave. To go back to his home among the grazing sheep and chilly nights. But then he'd somehow wended his way into her life. Into her heart.

She couldn't pinpoint exactly when it had happened. Maybe the moment their fingers touched outside Federico Peliti's, or maybe just a few hours ago when he spoke with her about loss and strength, but she no longer wanted him to return to England. She wanted him to stay in India. With her.

What a stupid thing to want. Everett had been sent to India only to fetch Thaddeus and take him to her father's ancestral home. It was clear by the yearning in his voice that he was leaving soon.

Her father had been an unusual man. He'd thrived in the heat and chaos. He lived for the history and diversity, both natural and human. He hadn't walked around, mopping his sweaty brow with a linen handkerchief, complaining of lazy servants and heavy air. But most men weren't like Edwin Russell.

No, Everett would not make India his home. Gone, his unassuming, cozy presence. Gone, his quiet thoughtfulness and integrity. Gone, the gentle stirrings of his touch and voice.

Gone.

As effectively as Father and Maji and all the rest.

Because Wiltshire, England, seemed as far from Calcutta, India, as heaven was from earth.

Ottilie heard the front door slide open. Soft voices came from the front room, and then steps padded across the bare floors. A light knock at the bedroom door brought Everett to his feet.

Steeling herself for his appearance, she stood and smoothed the wrinkles from her sari. Straightened the sleeves that had bunched up and twisted. Since Ottilie last saw him, Nānī had given her the letters to read, and she wasn't sure how she'd respond.

Then he was there, filling the room with his large and impressive bearing. His mustache, gray and full, hid his upper lip, but his lower one trembled, and Ottilie's heart softened. Why that should be, she didn't know. She'd hated this man for so long. He'd abandoned her grandmother and mother—though now she knew he'd been driven away—and she'd since discovered his sins to be even more numerous and horrific than that. But the way he crumpled his fine hat in his hands and the way his eyes darted from empty corner to empty corner, purposely avoiding her grandmother sleeping in a huddle on the floor, spoke of a man on the cusp of something pivotal. Whether that would be a good or terrible thing, neither of them yet knew.

"Colonel," Ottilie said, her voice cutting through the still air.

He slid his eyes toward her and gave a short nod.

"I'll be in the main room with Reverend Hook," Everett said, making his way toward the door.

Ottilie followed his progress, wishing he would stay. Knowing he couldn't. This was a family affair, and even with his connections to Papa's side, he didn't belong.

The colonel grunted, and Ottilie saw that he was watching Nānī sleep. He passed a shaky hand over his eyes, the lantern's light shining on his liver-spotted skin and gnarled knuckles. "She is ill, your servant told me."

"Very. Cholera."

He nodded. "The same took your father, did it not?"

"And my brother and sister."

His head jerked toward her. "You lost them all at the same time?"

"Almost the very moment."

"Where were your grandmother and mother?"

"They were visiting Nānī's family in Benares."

He swallowed hard, and even in the flickering flame, she saw him go pale. "I didn't realize your grandmother was speaking with them."

"She wasn't. Isn't. But she wanted to try."

"Do you know, then?"

"Yes. A bit."

He took two small steps toward Nānī and raised his hand, fingers stretching as though he wanted to touch her. As though he could cross a distance greater than the few feet separating them. "I loved her."

"You had a strange way of displaying it."

Outside a dog barked, and the sound bounced against crumbling buildings. It sounded loud in the stillness of the bedroom, and Nānī stirred.

His whisper barely reached Ottilie's ears, but she heard the desperation in it. "I couldn't let his crimes go unpunished."

"He was your father-in-law. And how did you know he was involved? My aunt said in her letters he was not."

"Oh, but he was. The reports were clear. There were letters encouraging mutiny among the sepoys. Complaints about the grease used to wax packaging and murmurings that the East India Company wanted all the Hindu and Muslim soldiers to convert to Christianity."

Ottilie gave a sharp shake of her head. "How do you know his letters encouraged the mutiny? Are you certain it had nothing to do with the fact that they wanted to be free of company rule?"

"Maybe so. But that is supposition. What isn't, what's absolutely clear, is that Gitisha's father was a primary instigator in the uprising." He glanced at Nānī, then approached Ottilie, drawing nearer than felt comfortable. "I do not wish to argue about this. I've spent over thirty years wishing I'd been somewhere else, someone else, so I didn't have to be the one to break Gitisha's heart. But your great-grandfather's crimes were numerous— greater than even these."

"Great enough to have him killed? For what? Wanting the freedom to be governed by his own people?"

The colonel stared at her for a long moment. A hard stare that winnowed away the questions between them. It laid bare the hard, twisted, violent history that warred within Ottilie's veins, and she didn't like what she saw in his eyes. Not justification for his own behavior. Not the proud maneuverings of a company soldier. No, in them she saw naked grief. And a lifetime of regret. And certainty that he'd made a decision worth making.

None of it made sense. There was no putting Colonel Lupton in a category. No assigning him the role of monster or hero. He was a man conflicted. Even still.

"What are you hiding from me?" she hissed through clenched teeth.

"I will not say while Gitisha still lives. I wouldn't like her to know."

"How can you refuse me answers? After everything you've done to my family?"

He walked away, approaching Nānī and standing with his hands clasped tightly behind his back. Rigid and unyielding. The lamp illuminated him from beneath, cloaking him in a sinister light. But when Ottilie stepped beside him, she saw the heavy tug of grief in his drooping eyes and mouth.

"One word only," he said, "then nothing more until I can be sure Gitisha has escaped the knowledge. I've made sure she's never known of it."

Ottilie nodded, her eyes tracking the slight rise and fall of her grandmother's chest. She finally slept peacefully. The retching and cramping had ceased. Ottilie remembered that moment with Father and her sister and brother. Remembered the relief she felt when she'd thought they'd turned a corner.

But it had only been that there was nothing left to bring up. Nānī wouldn't recover. Ottilie knew this now.

The colonel leaned over so that his mustache tickled her

cheek. And his whispered revelation made her wish she hadn't pushed him. Hadn't demanded.

His voice broke in the saying of it. And even though it was thirty years in the past, the memory was seared into the mind of every person—British and Indian—who called India home.

"Cawnpore."

13

Ottilie stood stiff and tall as a palmyra beside the colonel after his revelation.

Cawnpore.

What had that terrible place to do with her great-grandfather? Nānī's family had lived in Benares for hundreds of years. The cities were a week's journey from each other. How did the tendrils of savagery reach across the foothills, forests, and rivers of Uttar Pradesh and twine around the royal Singh family of Benares?

What was the connection?

She started to demand further information, but Nānī's eyes opened and focused on the colonel. She licked her cracked lips.

"You have come, Richard."

"I have."

"Take my hand."

The colonel squatted beside her and enclosed her emaciated hand in his large one. He was a dichotomy, this man with a soldier's bearing, wearing fine wool trousers, a waistcoat, and coat, sitting beside her grandmother like a village potter. He was the villain, but he came immediately when she called. In the middle of the night.

"Are those tears for me?" Nānī's words, weak but still holding a trace of youthful flirtation, wrenched Ottilie from her thoughts.

There were, indeed, tears slipping down the colonel's weathered cheeks. They burrowed into his mustache, but the evidence remained in his glassy eyes. He laughed and swiped at them. "Those are the first words you've spoken to me in decades."

Nānī heaved a sigh and pulled her hand from his. Her arm dropped heavily onto the mat. "So many regrets. Come closer."

The colonel moved to his knees and bent his head toward her. She took his face between her hands and said, "I forgive you."

He made a small sound in his throat, then dropped his head to her breast. Ottilie looked away, feeling as though she intruded on something meant only for them.

"I don't deserve it." His voice was heavy with sorrow.

"You don't," Nānī said. "But I am about to meet my savior. I must forgive as he forgave me."

Ottilie shifted, and the sound brought Nānī's eyes up. "Leave, Navasi."

"But I think—"

"Leave."

Ottilie nodded and, with only one backward glance at the door, left them.

In the next room, Thaddeus still lay sleeping in the corner. Reverend Hook sat in Papa's chair, his head nodding, and Everett leaned against the wall beside him, his legs stretched out and crossed at the ankles. When he saw her, he straightened. "How is she?"

Reverend Hook's head jerked, and he stood. Ottilie waved him back into his seat. "She is weak. She will not survive it." She dropped her head and stared at her bare toes poking from beneath the hem of her sari. "I might not either."

She hadn't meant to say those final words, but they slipped from her lips like rocks.

"Are you feeling ill?" A note of panic laced Everett's question.

"No."

The way he looked at her said he understood.

"Dilip?" she called. He peered around the wall of the kitchen. "Did you pay the doctor?" They hadn't much. A couple of coins that were meant to keep them in food for a few days.

Dilip shook his head, his gaze darting toward Everett before he ducked away.

"I paid the doctor." Everett pulled away from the wall and removed his jacket. He tossed it aside, rolled up his sleeves, and undid the top button of his shirt. He looked ready to settle in.

"Why? I could have taken care of it."

"We are friends, are we not? It was the only thing I could think to do that would ease your burden."

Ottilie could see the same helplessness that weighted her chest, stealing her breath, also afflicted Everett. He ran his fingers through his hair, tugging it into odd angles, and focused on the floor in front of her. "Very well. Thank you."

Reverend Hook motioned her to the chair. She wanted to refuse, but she recognized the exhaustion settling upon her. Her shoulders sagged, her eyes drooped, and her spirit . . . her spirit had long since been battered.

She sank onto the cushion, leaned her head back, and closed her eyes. "I am so weary."

She heard the others settling against the floor, and the peace of the room was undisturbed except for Thaddeus's gentle snuffling. She dozed and waited and, in her less lucid moments, prayed.

Colonel Lupton entered the room, and she jerked upright at the sound of his heels clicking against the floor. "She's sleeping." He stared at Ottilie for a moment, then leaned down and kissed her cheek. "Let me know what happens."

She lifted her hand to the spot his lips had pressed and watched him leave the house. "Well, that's a turn I didn't expect."

"Who is he?" Everett asked.

"Colonel Richard Lupton. My . . . he was married to Nānī."

"That was your grandfather?"

Ottilie nodded. "I've never called him that, but yes."

"What has he done?"

"More than I care to admit, but I will tell you this: after Father died, Maji took me and Thaddeus, who was only an infant, to see him. We'd just learned Father had been careless with his money—he was always more about his books and studies than managing his finances, and he was always much too generous—and we were about to lose our home. Everything, really. Maji hadn't seen her father since he abandoned her and Nānī when she was sixteen, but she had no choice. He cared little and gave less than that."

"Then why has he come tonight?"

"To be absolved, I suppose."

"I hope so. Because it means you will not be left alone if your grandmother doesn't survive."

She stood and slipped across the room. Standing over her brother, she looked down at him, tenderness swelling her breast. She loved him as much as any mother could. In him, she could see Jemima's bright eyes, Papa's intellect, Maji's determination, and Nathan's energy. Thaddeus was all of them, and all she had left of them. And if Nānī left them—*when* Nānī left them—he would be all she had left of her family. She wouldn't allow herself to be separated from him. Not by distance. Nor by this disease.

But the distance offered her a more controlled option. Cholera had its own mind, and she knew, if they stayed in Calcutta, it would one day find what little joy remained to Ottilie. It would find Thaddeus and consume him.

She wouldn't let that happen. She *couldn't* let that happen.

She turned and rejoined Everett near the chair, her decision made. Nānī could go home knowing Ottilie had obeyed her wish.

"I've decided, should Nānī pass from this world, I will allow you to take Thaddeus to England."

Everett's eyes widened, and relief brightened them, but mingled with it was sorrow and regret. "I will miss you desperately."

"No, you will not."

He scrubbed his hand across his face, bristling with day-old growth. "I believe I know my own mind."

"Yes, I'm sure you do, but you will not have a chance to miss me, for I won't be separated from Thaddeus. I will be accompanying you. I will join him at Hazelbrook Manor, and so we shall be neighbors. I know my father's mother—my . . . grandmother—asked Maji in her letters that we come to her after Father's death."

"But she didn't know your father—"

"Yes, I know. She didn't realize Father had married a Eurasian woman. But marry her he did, and Thaddeus and I both carry his blood and Maji's. Those are my terms."

Everett sank onto the chair and gripped his head in his hands. "I believe you would be happier staying in Calcutta. You do not belong in England."

Tears filled Ottilie's eyes. He'd been kind to her, despite their opposing goals, but it was clear kindness wouldn't extend to English soil. She sniffed. "I see."

He glanced up at her and came to his feet. "No, I don't think you do." He grasped her shoulders. "You will not be accepted there. People will look down on you simply because you are Indian. Do you understand? You will spend the rest of your life an outsider."

"I'm an outsider here as well." She pulled from him and strode toward the window. Gripping the ledge, she leaned over it, taking a deep breath of night air.

He neared—she didn't hear him but felt his presence. "I only want you to be happy. I'm not sure that will happen in England."

"It is Nānī's final wish. Plus, I will not be happy apart from my brother. I would stay in India for the rest of my life if it weren't for him. But I want to be free of this disease that haunts us. I want him safe and healthy, growing up with clean air and water." She turned toward Everett and touched his chest, her fingers splaying over his heart. "You said there is no cholera in England."

He swallowed hard, his eyes dipping to her face before skittering away, focusing on something over her shoulder. "There hasn't been for years."

"You promise he will be safe?"

"As safe as any child raised on a great estate in the country can be."

She nodded. "He will go. And so will I."

She became aware of the warmth of his nearness and leaned toward him. Only a breath closer, but enough to change something. Something she wanted changed despite her vow not to fall in love with an Englishman. Not to fall in love with anyone.

"I . . ." He looked at her, his eyes vibrant and flashing even in the gloom. "I will allow it and let Lady Sunderson decide on the particulars."

He stepped away from her and slipped through the doorway into the kitchen.

She pulled the drape of her sari from her shoulder and covered her head. It was a good thing, Thaddeus going to England. He would be saved. And she wouldn't be forced from him. But her heart ached. Nānī would soon be gone from them. And they would soon be gone from India. From the banyan trees and women draped in vibrant silks, from the scent of cumin crushed beneath a pestle and the monsoon rain that brought celebration. From Dilip and Reverend Hook and Damaris and the graves of her family. From everything and everyone she knew.

"But also from cholera," she whispered and forced her heart into compliance.

The sound of Nānī calling drew Ottilie from the window and into the bedroom.

"Navasi." Nānī's plea sounded weak.

Ottilie lifted her sari and darted to her grandmother's side. "What is it? Are you in pain?"

Nānī's shallow breathing sent alarm spiking through Ottilie. "No. Be with me."

"Of course."

Nānī's gaze caressed Ottilie's face, and a small smile tipped her lips. "I love you, my Boodha."

Ottilie drew Nānī's head into her lap. With firm fingers, she rubbed circles around Nānī's temples. "I love you."

"Do not mourn me in black. Promise me."

"I will wear white when you are buried and color every day after."

"I am so thirsty."

Ottilie reached for the cup, knowing it was too late to offer boiled water, and dribbled some between Nānī's lips. "I will have Dilip bring more."

"No more. I'm done." Nānī's eyes opened wide, and a faraway look entered them. "Do not bury me. Go to Niraja. Tell her my love has never wavered. And neither has Christ's, whatever she may now believe. Bring me home to the Ganges."

"You do not want a Christian burial?"

Nānī grimaced. "What does God care about this vessel? Bring me home. Promise me."

Gently cupping Nānī's face between her palms, Ottilie kissed her. "I promise." She lifted Nānī's head from her knees and stretched her body alongside her grandmother's, draping her arm over Nānī's torso and resting her hand where her grandmother's heart beat a faint echo of what it used to be. "I will bring you home to Benares and wear white. When you are poured out upon the Ganges, your feet will trip on the water, and your hands will reach toward heaven. And when you get there . . ." Ottilie stumbled over the plea, hoping, praying, it was real. "Tell them I love them."

"They know, Navasi." Nānī barely moved her lips, and the words were faint. Ottilie could see her grandmother's spirit fading, growing dim along with the lamp nearly out of oil.

But it didn't matter, because the sun was shyly peeking above the buildings, turning the open window into a frame that proudly displayed a painting of purple, red, and orange. "The sun has risen, Nānī. Turn your head so you can see it."

"Oh, I see it already, and he is beautiful."

Ottilie lifted up on her elbow and looked down at her grandmother, who stared at the ceiling. "Nānī?"

A smile stretched her grandmother's lips, the corners of her mouth cracking from want of fluid.

"Nānī?" Ice chilled Ottilie's veins, and her voice cracked.

But Nānī's spirit had risen with the sun.

14

Indian cities claimed a certain chaos made up of colors, the chatter of many tongues, and a press of humanity nowhere else in the world could rival, but Benares topped them all. The city curved with the lines of the Ganges, and twelve days after Nānī's death, Ottilie found herself pressing down streets that passed ghats crowded with bathers, worshipers, and mourners. The water, murky and littered with garlands of marigolds, bright bobbing suns that twisted like reptiles, took everything devotees offered—flower petals, cremated loved ones, the dipping and washing of bodies very much alive. It took and took, giving nothing back but a place to pin hopes. A shaky promise indeed. Every Hindu wished to die and be cremated in Benares, where the cycle of death and rebirth would end, ushering one into salvation. The city was full of the dying, desperate for freedom. The river full of bloated and charred bodies.

Human ash floated from the crematory ghats and covered the buildings, streets, and water. It choked Ottilie until she thought she'd go mad, wondering who she was inhaling. Quickening her pace, she darted down a side street, narrow and twisting, obeying the directions she'd received from the guesthouse servant.

She was glad she'd insisted on leaving Thaddeus with Everett at their rooms. She hoped to leave this place soon. But first,

Nānī's final wish, though Ottilie couldn't understand why her grandmother wanted to be laid to rest in this depressing place.

She came upon the house—a palace, really—and pushed open the unmanned gate. It admitted her with a shriek that made Ottilie hesitate and wonder if it was a warning to leave. Before she could act on her premonition, a small, stooped man unfolded himself from the grass below a flowering tree, its branches aflame with orange blooms. He approached her, taking in the drape of her yellow sari, the fall of her braid hanging nearly to her waist, and when she lifted her arm in greeting, his eyes were drawn to Nānī's kadas that slipped from her wrist and clinked together.

He stared at them a moment, and his mouth dropped open. "Gitisha?" He hurried closer, taking her hand and inspecting the bracelets with his watery gaze.

Startled by the sound of her grandmother's name on this stranger's lips, Ottilie pulled away, burying her hands in the folds of her sari. "My grandmother. I need to speak with Niraja Singh."

He licked his lips, then smacked them together before scampering down the path toward the steps. At the bottom of the stairs, he motioned her forward, then continued on his way, his wide, dusty feet slapping against the marble.

Ottilie entered a spacious foyer, most of the floor taken up by a sunken courtyard open to the sky. She only had a moment to stare at the rich furnishings—heavy antique tables inlaid with gold, ornately carved wooden screens offering glimpses of the first floor, and colorful ceramic tiles—before the servant, now clapping his hands and muttering prayers, urged her on.

"Wait." The servant disappeared through a heavy wooden door, easing it shut behind him. There was a scuffling, some murmurs, and then he reappeared. "Come now."

Ottilie entered the lavish room, the walls covered in flocked damask wallpaper, shades of burgundy and red contrasting with the golden fabric curtaining the windows and draping doorways. The carpets at her feet absorbed her steps, and if the woman sitting among a huddle of carved chairs hadn't gasped, Ottilie wouldn't have heard or seen her.

"You look just like her." The woman rose in one fluid movement from her seat. She wore a sari in vibrant purple, heavily embroidered with gold thread, and took a few timid steps. Ottilie's great-aunt pressed her palms together, dipped her head, and said, "*Namaste.*"

"Hello, I'm Ottilie. Gitisha was my grandmother."

Niraja froze. Her eyes swept upward, meeting Ottilie's. "Was?"

"Nānī died almost two weeks ago."

Niraja sank back into her seat and waved Ottilie toward a nearby chair. Then she covered her face with her hands. They sat there, silent, for long moments. Ottilie studied Niraja's bowed head, tried to picture her as a young girl getting into trouble with Nānī. Tried and failed. This elegant, wealthy woman only resembled Nānī in the most casual way. Eyes and skin and hair and height. All physical features that spoke little of Nānī's quick wit, bold laugh, and gift of wheedling and coaxing.

"Did she suffer?" Niraja asked.

"She died of cholera. It wasn't an easy death."

Niraja looked up, her gaze sharp. "You say that so coldly."

"Do I? Would you rather I weep and wail? Would that make it obvious Nānī was everything to me? I've lost more to that disease than you know. Cried more tears over the taking it's done than you can imagine." Ottilie stood, feeling crushed by the dark walls and gilded ceiling. By this woman's judgment. This woman who had abandoned Nānī and criticized Ottilie's expression of grief. Her numbness. A memory of letters, crumpled and tear-stained, pricked her conscience, but she ignored it. "I only came because Nānī wished me to give you a message. I'm leaving in two days, after I spread her ashes on the river."

Niraja pressed slender hands to her chest. "Did Gitisha turn back to the faith of her childhood?"

"No. She remained a Christian until her last breath. Her final thought was of Christ. And you."

"Me?"

"She wished me to tell you she never stopped loving you. And neither has Christ." Ottilie dipped her head and eased away from her chair. "I will go now. Thank you for seeing me."

She turned and stiffly walked toward the door. A low moan, weighted with an anguish Ottilie well understood, stopped her.

"Please, do not go. You are all I have left of her. Stay a moment. So many years I have wasted."

Ottilie turned and saw Niraja on her knees, arms outstretched. Tears ran in the grooves that had appeared on her face, washing away the remnants of bitterness. Ottilie's heart turned toward her, softened by her love for Nānī. Desperate for a connection with this woman who knew her grandmother, she retraced her steps, stood only inches away. Ottilie reached out, fingertips brushing Niraja's. Then she slipped to the floor and grasped the older woman's forearms. Her bracelets chimed together, and Niraja looked down, her expression twisting with grief, and she pulled Ottilie against her chest.

"All is lost." Her cry tore through Ottilie's pockmarked faith.

"No," Ottilie said, her word muffled by silk. "No, all is not lost."

Niraja's body shook, her voice gravelly. "I blamed her. Hated her. Because of him. She didn't know. I knew she didn't know, but she joined herself with the man, the country, who destroyed my family. And now our parting can never be undone."

Ottilie pulled away and took Niraja's shoulders. "Nānī always hoped for reconciliation. Still hopes for it, I imagine."

"Old things are passed away, all things become new." Niraja disentangled herself from Ottilie's grasp and stood. "Come with me."

175

Ottilie followed her from the room, sweeping by the gape-mouthed servant at the door. Near the stairs, they passed a household shrine. Imposing and elaborate, the carved cabinet held a statue of Shiva draped with marigold garlands and painted with vermilion. A golden censer still burned with incense. The idol's eyes followed her, condemning her clumsy attempts at proselytizing. Rightly calling her a hypocrite.

Who did she think she was fooling? Could a woman plagued with doubt share a message of hope? Her hope had long since been buried.

They climbed the stairs, Ottilie breathing easier when they reached the first floor. Her aunt led her down a hall and through heavy doors. Marble walls draped in expertly embroidered tapestries were broken up by carved niches framing vases of flowers. A large bed boasting posts carved into pineapples demanded attention.

Niraja opened a cabinet. She thrust her upper body deep into it, then emerged holding a wooden box. With a reverent expression, she brushed the top of it, then brought it to the bed. "Sit beside me."

Ottilie joined her, settling onto the thick mattress covered by an indigo-dyed coverlet.

Niraja opened the box and withdrew a linen-wrapped parcel. Setting it between them, she unwrapped it, revealing a leather Bible embossed with a golden cross. "Did Gitisha tell you how this came to be in our possession?"

"She said you stole it from a visiting dignitary." And indeed, when Niraja opened the cover, Ottilie saw the name Frederick George Taylor written on the dedication page.

Niraja giggled, the sound evoking images of two young girls stitched together with whimsy and mischief. "We did. We had an English-speaking tutor who read from her own Bible every morning before breakfast, but she'd been instructed to keep her religion to herself. We were Hindu, would always be Hindu. My father was Udit Singh, cousin to the maharaja. We were proud of our heritage. But we were also curious about everything, and we talked one of the servants into telling us what was in the vistors' bags. When we heard that man had a Bible, we decided to steal it. Of course, we soon learned God commanded his followers not to steal, but we never felt an ounce of remorse over it. Not until I married and my father was killed and I learned who had been responsible for it. . . ." Her eyes shadowed.

And Ottilie saw an opportunity.

"Niraja Nānī, will you tell me what happened? Nānī never did, and from the colonel I've only heard that my great-grandfather was somehow involved in the massacre at Cawnpore."

Niraja shrank before Ottilie's eyes, tucking herself inward, arms pulled into her belly and head bowing beneath the weight of the story. "I haven't spoken of it in decades."

"I'm sorry. No, you mustn't. Don't speak of it."

"I will tell you this." Niraja's fingers gripped Ottilie's wrist. "Pitaji *trusted* Richard Lupton. He allowed him into his home, his family, even his books and papers. That was how he discovered my father's association with Nana Sahib. They'd had a correspondence."

Ottilie jerked her arm away and rubbed at the red marks Niraja's squeezing had left. "Nana Sahib?" Her mouth went dry. Her great-grandfather had been friendly with Nana Sahib? Even now, thirty years after the massacre, every child with English blood, even those whose veins also pulsed with Indian heritage, knew the story. They had nightmares of the man responsible for the violent deaths of so many women and children. English ones, yes, but many of them Eurasian.

"They'd known each other since they were young men. It didn't mean my father was complicit, but your grandfather decided that was enough to justify his murder."

"But was he? Was he complicit? Did your father have something to do with it?"

Niraja straightened and scowled. "My father was an honorable man who simply wanted freedom from foreign invaders. The only thing he did was decry the violence and rape and plundering the British had forced on our land. He had *nothing* to do with the rest of it."

Ottilie swallowed and nodded. She was glad when Niraja turned her attention back to the Bible and flipped through the crinkling pages. Ottilie's family history was a twisted thing, full of secrets and betrayal. She could feel herself drowning beneath the generations and their hidden stories.

"Listen," Niraja said. "'But my God shall supply all your need according to his riches in glory by Christ Jesus.'" She turned the book and pointed at some script cramped into the thin margin beside the passage.

Do you think he will provide for us handsome husbands, Niraja? Because I want for nothing else.

"Did Nānī write that?" Ottilie swallowed against the lump in her throat.

"She did. My father was a liberal man in many respects—we were educated, allowed the freedom to leave the house in a covered carriage on occasion, were given our own rooms—but he wouldn't have tolerated conversion. So one week I'd read the Bible at night while everyone slumbered, and on Friday I'd slip it beneath Gitisha's bed. We never discussed it for fear of being overheard, but we wrote notes to each other in the margins and blank spaces." She lifted the Bible and held it to her chest. "I haven't looked at it since I renounced Christianity after I learned what Gitisha's husband had done." She buried her nose between the front and back covers, taking a long inhale. "You must take it. Gitisha would want that."

"You don't need it? I have a Bible." Oh, Ottilie wanted it. Wanted it like nothing else. Wanted to read and know Nānī's earliest thoughts on faith. Did she have questions? Doubts? Did she wonder why God allowed heartache? Her fingers itched to take it.

"My husband and father are long gone. There is no one keeping me from buying another, if I choose. Give me one more night with it so that I can remind myself of my sister. I shall arrange for a boat. Meet me here tomorrow morning, and we will see Gitisha off to heaven. Then I will send you with the Bible." Niraja stood and crossed the room. "Come see this before you leave."

Ottilie joined her in front of a wall hanging embroidered with beetle wings. Two girls danced on a background of blue, and a dove flew over their heads, its wings created from white shells. A school of fish, their scales made of tiny shining mirrors, swam below their feet in a pool of blue water. And a cross, made to look like a tree but obvious to someone looking for hidden Christian symbols, sprouted bright red flowers that fell like drops of blood onto a cluster of little sheep below it.

"It's beautiful." Ottilie couldn't look away from one of the girls, her braid whipping above her head, arms held out as though trying to embrace the world. It was Nānī, young and free and forever immortalized in elytra.

"It was our statement of faith. We worked on it for a year before Gitisha left for Calcutta." Niraja pointed to the strip of plain muslin about three inches high that separated the girls from the water, making them look as though they hovered over it. "Gitisha always told me she knew exactly what she wanted to embroider there—her secret to faith—but we were never able to finish it. And then she was gone—sent to Calcutta with her husband. I still wish I'd thought to ask her what she wanted to put there. But I never felt right finishing it after my own faith was lost. There have been so many things left unfinished in the years since."

Ottilie glanced at the Bible on the bed, wondering if the answer was in its pages. Would Nānī tell her through words scribbled decades earlier what she grounded her faith in? What she stood on?

Because Ottilie would read it cover to cover if so.

The sun spilled color over the Ganges at Dashashwamedh Ghat when Ottilie and Niraja climbed from the two-wheeled *ekka* cart. Behind them, carved spires rose, and the sun glinted off the golden dome of Vishwanath Temple. Everything was bathed in a soft orange hue, mist rising from the river and making Ottilie remember Nānī's ghost stories. She tucked the urn more securely against her chest.

Niraja shifted the Bible into the crook of her elbow, then took Ottilie's arm. They walked toward the great bank of steps leading to the water. Even at this early hour, bathers and worshipers were about their business, blending everyday life with the mystical. A young boy led his buffalo past a Brahman priest sitting beneath a bamboo umbrella and offering prayers for clients. A knot of women washed clothing near the bank, naked toddlers playing in the rocks and dirt at their feet. And dozens of people, standing waist-deep in the water, offered *puja*, chanting and bowing and performing ablutions.

Ottilie skirted a saffron-robed *sadhu*. His knotted locks of hair, secured with a length of fabric, bobbed with his head as he stared out over the scene. As they passed by, he turned glazed eyes toward Ottilie. She swallowed, seeing so much of herself in his desperate, lost expression. He was seeking enlightenment and freedom in this most holy Indian city, but she could see the doubt and fear behind his mask of vermilion and ash markings.

Or maybe she was only seeing her own reflection in this man she had nothing in common with except a desire to understand.

Niraja dropped a few coins into the sadhu's outstretched hands, and Ottilie noted the skin hanging from his emaciated form. When they were out of hearing, she asked, "Do you think they attain anything in the renunciation of physical comfort?"

Niraja glanced back at the sadhu, then sighed. "I know nothing. I was so secure in my understanding of faith and life, first as a Hindu, then as a Christian. But then it all became tangled together—politics and religion and family and love. How can it be unwoven? How can we follow one thread to truth when there are so many knots?"

She sounded exhausted in the trying. Exhausted and defeated. Ottilie took her hand and squeezed. She had no argument to offer, no comfort to give, but she could commiserate. She could understand.

Niraja pointed toward a shabby boat bobbing near a wooden platform at the bottom of the steps. "There."

They picked their way through the crowd, and the wiry boatman held his craft steady as they boarded. Niraja gave him terse directions, and he pushed them from the ghat. His muscles quivered as he rowed them away from the crush of people looking for answers and blessings and holiness.

Before them, smoke rose from the shore, and the warm woody scent of burning sandalwood tickled Ottilie's nose.

"That's Manikarnika Ghat, where they do cremations. It's said they've been burning bodies there, night and day, for four hundred years." There was a morbid satisfaction in Niraja's voice. Something that told Ottilie her aunt longed for freedom by flame.

The boatman stopped rowing within sight of the ghat, and Ottilie could see stacks of wood, shrouded bodies on stretchers being carried by *doms*—untouchables who handled corpses—and smoky black fires that consumed life. He pulled in his oars and rested them across his knees.

Ottilie turned her head and stared at the sandbank on the other side of the river. Hidden behind a hazy, heavy veil, it offered her a place to rest her eyes. Her mind. Her heart.

She didn't want to leave Nānī here.

She clutched the urn tighter, wrapping it in her arms. Silently begging for release from this ignorant promise. Her throat clogged with tears. How could she shed so many? Surely God had thought to give his creation a finite amount. Would there be no end to them?

Niraja shifted beside her, and her hand found the middle of Ottilie's back. "It is time."

Ottilie shook her head and bowed over the urn. "Must I? I want to take her with me. I'm leaving so many behind already."

"You know there is nothing in there except ash. And this was her wish. She is home, body and spirit."

Ottilie turned her head, still protecting Nānī in the circle of her embrace. "I don't know if my faith is big enough to sustain this. And when I give her to the Ganges, I might lose what's left of it." She sat up straight and smoothed her fingers over the brass. It wasn't a fine vessel, didn't feel smooth beneath her touch, but because of what it held, it had been made priceless.

Niraja's fingers stroked the Bible on her lap, and when she spoke, there was a smile in her voice. "All is not lost, is it? You still have a tiny mustard seed of faith. Cherish it, protect it, and it is bound to sprout."

Ottilie brushed her eyes and sniffed. "And you? Have you lost that humble seed?"

Niraja stared out over the river, toward Manikarnika Ghat and its death play. "It's been a long time since I've thought about it. I wonder if it has been smothered beneath my bitterness and unforgiveness." She gave Ottilie a sharp look. "That's a greater threat to Christian faith than a million other gods. There is no room for it. And if you allow it in, it burns away the blood of Christ as surely as flesh is burned on a funeral pyre."

The metallic taste of regret filled Ottilie's throat and spilled into her chest. She turned away from Niraja, sure her aunt could see the anger burning hot beneath her tears and questions.

A soft arm wrapped around her back. "Do not think it's too late. I'm an old woman and still have hope."

Niraja commanded the boatman to turn them so they faced the far shore. The sun was a heavy globe that shed an orange swath of light. It glinted off the gentle swells and bobbing waves, an aisle runner waiting for the bride to appear.

And Ottilie held that bride clasped tightly to her chest.

"It's time." Niraja closed her eyes and lifted her face to receive the sun.

No. Ottilie wasn't ready. Not yet. She'd just barely begun to heal from Maji's death, and now she had to say good-bye to someone else. It wasn't fair. She could feel the bitterness, having taken root years ago, spread its branches. Could feel it poison her faith. Her peace. She could hardly see her mustard seed beneath its leafy canopy.

She knew this was the moment she needed to decide. It had to end, this exhausting pendulum of believing and doubt. It was clear she wouldn't be leaving only Nānī in India. She must also leave her indecision.

She couldn't face a new home, a new country, a new life without making this choice.

Would she protect what was left of her tattered faith or turn from it entirely?

I don't want to live in a world where there is no promise of something after. No thought of seeing my family again. Without believing in your sacrifice, your love, Lord, nothing makes sense, and it all seems pointless. I can't exist if it all means nothing.

"Here I am, Lord," Ottilie whispered. "This is all I have to give you."

She pressed a kiss to the top of the urn and then removed the lid. *If I have to tell myself every morning that you are real and you are love, I will. And if my faith never grows, it will be enough.*

She extended her arm and tipped the urn, watching as a sudden breeze, so light and cool it must have been breathed from heaven, caught her grandmother's ashes and spread them over the river. "I love you, Nānī. Go meet your groom."

Niraja made a sound in her throat and shuddered. "May I join you soon, *behan*. My God, my God . . . forgive me my sin."

Ottilie's silent prayer joined her aunt's cry. *Let it be enough. Whatever is to come, whatever I must face, let it be enough.*

After Ottilie scattered Nānī's ashes, she and Niraja were returned to the ghat steps. They said nothing as they climbed out of the boat and made their way through the crowd that had only grown in size. Niraja invited Ottilie and Thaddeus to stay with her, but Ottilie declined for two reasons.

Thaddeus had to go to England, and she wouldn't send him alone.

And Niraja, in the couple of days Ottilie had known her, had grown too dear. She was already filling the empty places left by Nānī's death. Her hennaed hair and complaints about her aching feet drew Ottilie to her in a way that felt comfortable. And dangerous. For that reason, Ottilie wouldn't stay with her another moment. Benares had frequent outbreaks of cholera.

Ottilie hugged her great-aunt and said good-bye, taking the Bible into arms that desperately needed filling. She promised to write when she arrived in England. Then she left, hurrying through the smoke-filled alleys toward the guesthouse—toward Everett and Thaddeus—her head covered with her pallu and her nose with her hand.

She wanted to leave this city that courted and welcomed and prepared for death. But she had one more errand that would mean another night's stay.

She didn't know how accessible beetle wings were in England, but in Benares they were plentiful. And Ottilie would buy enough to keep busy. To create and design. She couldn't take India with her to England, couldn't take its sun and monsoons, but she could take her art. She could take, as Dilip called it, her gift. Tears pricked her eyes when she thought of her old friend.

Dilip was settled at Mr. D'Souza's—who felt an obligation to offer whatever help he could after exposing Nānī to the disease that took her from them—with the promise of work and pay. But that didn't stop Ottilie from feeling as though she had failed him.

She'd promised Dilip a visit before leaving Calcutta for England. They would only be in the city a mere two days, seeing to the buying of appropriate clothing and selling belongings they could not bring with them. Visiting the South Park Street Cemetery and saying good-bye. But she wanted Dilip to know how important he was to her.

"No, ma'am, do not look back," he had said. He caught the tear tracing her chin and pressed it to his lips, his eyes saying things he had never had the courage to speak before.

"I didn't know." She reached for him, wondering if she should stay. He was comfort. And memories. And so very dear.

And also, it seemed, able to read her thoughts. He shook his head. "You must go. Nānī's dream . . ."

She scoffed. "What is a dream?"

"But I see, too, what he has come to mean to you. And you him." His hand found the back of her head. "You are not meant for me. Nor meant for here."

"I am meant for nowhere. I have no home."

"You will, Ottilie. Home was never meant to be a place." He'd smiled then, before crossing into the big house with five rooms and closing the door.

Thinking on her poet-servant, Ottilie shook her head. She would create art but also a commodity. Maybe, when Thaddeus was settled and Ottilie had nothing to fill her days, she could pick up her needle and establish a profession that would keep her from being a financial, as well as social, inconvenience. She wouldn't take more from her father's family than they wanted to give, and she preferred to take less.

Everett and Thaddeus were at breakfast when she arrived at the guesthouse. Run by a Eurasian couple, it offered clean bedding and a jolly hostess. Her husband worked for the railroad and traveled often, so she spent her days caring, cooking, and cleaning for strangers who were soon made to feel very much at home.

When their hostess saw Ottilie standing inside the dining room doorway, she ushered her to a seat across from Thaddeus and near Everett, her chatter easing the room's awkward silence. There were two German men, wealthy and young and intent on adventure; a British couple who cast glances at the rest of the table but said nothing; and an American woman—a zenana missionary—who lit up the room with her blond curls and bright chatter.

After breakfast, they set out on the ten-minute walk to Godowlia Market. Thaddeus hopped beside Ottilie, eager to explore and run. The city, crowded and chaotic, offered much to see for a little boy who had spent days cooped up on a train. He would dart twenty feet ahead, peeking into shops and staring up at ornate temples as he waited for Ottilie and Everett to catch up, then repeat the action.

Ottilie laughed while he watched wide-eyed as a snake charmer, wrapped in multicolored robes and playing a *pungi*, drew a cobra from its basket with the weaving of his head and instrument. Everett stopped, hands on Thaddeus's shoulders, mouth open.

Ottilie leaned toward him, careful so Thaddeus wouldn't hear. "The snake can't hear the music. There's no magic to it. It only thinks it's under threat."

"But it can still attack, can't it? It seems a dangerous profession."

"It can if it hasn't been defanged or had its mouth sewn shut."

She watched the show for another moment, satisfied when the snake opened its mouth to reveal teeth, then tossed a coin onto the mat beside the performer. He deserved to be paid, if only for putting himself at risk and not being cruel to his snake.

Everett's fingers tightened on Thaddeus's shoulders and pulled him away. "Let's find something less perilous to watch." When he'd successfully distracted Thaddeus, Everett turned to Ottilie. "What do you need to get at the market?"

"Elytra. Nānī has been sourcing hers from the same vendor since she was a child. First it was the grandfather, then the father, and now the son. I can get them in Calcutta, but it's much less expensive here. And the quality is better."

He gave her a look that made her stomach churn.

"What?"

"Are you planning on . . . working in England?"

Ottilie gave a slow nod. He said *working* as though it were something terrible, something to do in secret. "Eventually. How else will I support myself?"

"Your family is capable of supporting you."

"But will they want to? I'd rather not be beholden to them, especially when I don't know what kind of reception I'll receive."

Everett pulled off his hat and ran his hand through his dark hair before replacing it. With a sigh, he met her eyes, and she could read in them all kinds of questions. Doubts. Fears. Her heart leapt to her throat. She'd once seen those questions in Victor's eyes. She stepped away from Everett and trained her gaze on Thaddeus, who stood near the street, risking trampling and filth in order to watch a *mahout* drive his elephant.

"I don't know what kind of reception you'll receive either," Everett said, his voice soft. Endearing. Compassionate. "But they won't abandon you. You will want for nothing."

"Except the need not to feel like a burden. An unwanted houseguest forever dependent on people who wish me a continent away."

"You don't know that."

"I suppose we will just have to see what happens, but I'm not going to England without any means of supporting myself. Plus, I love my work. It connects me to Nānī and Maji and all the women before them who used needle and thread to tell stories." She remembered the piece her aunt had shown her, the declaration of faith, and knew every time she created something beautiful, she was declaring something of her own—independence, value, creativity. "I will always embroider."

"Embroidering is fine. It's a perfectly acceptable pastime for a gentlewoman, but going into trade?"

"There is no reason to discuss this until we understand better what my role will be." She nodded toward an alley ahead. "I believe that's the way to the shop."

Everett allowed her to end the conversation, but she could see trepidation in the set of his shoulders and the way he pressed his lips together. She much preferred his smile.

They passed a pile of rags, and Thaddeus poked at it with his shoe.

"Thaddeus, please don't touch things like that. You have no idea what they hold." She was thinking of vermin, but a skinny leg appeared, followed by an arm covered in lesions, then an arm ending in a stump wrapped in a dirty bandage. She grabbed Thaddeus and scooted back as a man unfolded himself and peered at them through eyes set in a face covered in folds and bumps.

Ottilie steered Thaddeus away from the leper and hurried away.

About to turn down a twisting, narrow street hemmed in by stalls and shops, Ottilie realized Everett wasn't with them. She turned and saw him holding the man as a mother might comfort an injured child, his hand cradling the leper's head against his chest. Ottilie blinked, her thoughts freezing, unable to make sense of the sight. She glanced left and right, wondering if anyone else saw what was happening and was gratified to see a crowd of people forming a ring around Everett. They looked at each other in confusion, asking questions no one could answer.

"Didi, what is he doing?" Thaddeus asked.

"I have no idea."

Everett pulled away, removed a watch from his vest pocket, and tucked it into the man's healthy hand. When the leper tried to give it back, Everett shook his head. He turned and slipped through the crowd, the people staring after him in wide-eyed wonder.

Ottilie stared too. When Everett reached them, he ruffled Thaddeus's hair and nodded down the street. "Ready?" he said as though he'd not just done something extraordinary. And insensible.

"Are you going to explain what that was about?"

"I felt a stirring to help."

"I suppose England has no leprosy, just as it's free of cholera? It must be a shock to see so much suffering."

"There are very few cases of leprosy in England, yes, but there is still suffering. Still poverty. I never want to grow so accustomed to it that I feel nothing when I see it."

Ottilie bit her lip and turned away, not wanting him to recognize the truth—that she had become so used to pain, she hardly noticed when she passed it on the street. She held so tightly onto her own sorrow that another person's seemed small and unremarkable in comparison. "You gave him your watch."

He shrugged. "It's a trifle. My employer gave it to me for Christmas a few years ago."

"Do you give all your belongings to the destitute?"

He smiled crookedly, and Ottilie's breath caught at the beauty of it. "Not all of them. But that man, I'm assuming, is garnering no sympathy here. What if my kindness is the only thing he receives today that isn't revulsion and rejection?"

Sharp, jabbing pain shot through her chest. It was conviction.

And shame. But also the stitching closed of a wound. She understood what it was to be reviled and rejected. And Everett proved, in the moment he embraced the leper, that he was a man who would never treat her the way so much of the world did.

There were people who loved for no other reason than that they were called to it. And that brought her healing. And hope.

She took Thaddeus's hand and began walking, unsure how to process all the thoughts and emotions flooding her soul and mind.

"Are you all right?" Everett asked.

"I think so. You've just given me much to think about. I've never met a man like you. A man born to privilege, but who shows so much concern for those who weren't."

A strange expression crossed his face. "I'm not that man, Ottilie. I wasn't born into privilege."

"But you're related to a man of means. You hold an esteemed position. You're educated. You have a secure future."

"Yes, but what I am now isn't what I've always been. We have a lot in common. Neither one of us quite knows where we belong. We're both only a gossiping tongue away from being as alone and destitute as that man behind us." He sighed. "All we can do is marry well. Then maybe our background will be overlooked, and we'll be accepted—if not for who we are, then for what we've become."

"Your club member's daughter." Her lips tipped into a wry smile. "Seems an inconsequential thing to build a marriage on."

"Perhaps. But all that will come from it—the connections and business prospects and the promise that my children will be accepted—is not at all inconsequential."

His words spun a bleak picture and needled her with the painful reminder of Victor's betrayal. She hadn't been good enough for him. And she wasn't good enough for Everett.

But his words also knit them together in a way Ottilie had never experienced with someone before. At least not a person of no relation.

It felt good to be understood. Even if it meant she was losing her heart to a man who could promise her nothing.

15

FEBRUARY 1886

I t took just over three weeks aboard the SS *Sirsa* to get from Calcutta to London. Not enough time to grieve the leaving of everything familiar, including the burial places of her family, or being so far from Dilip and Damaris. Not enough time to make sense of a world without Nānī. After Ottilie's seasickness abated during the second week of travel, she had stood at the rail, looking out over the ocean, straining to see India. She saw nothing but water meeting the horizon. And for one brief moment influenced by a childhood full of magical moments, she thought maybe crossing the world would help release the trauma that settled atop her like so many stones.

But now she was in England, traveling over a frigid, barren land in a hired coach, and she still felt weighted down by what had come before. Even the future was shadowed with fear and regret. Thaddeus, his head in her lap and his legs stretched out across the seat, shifted. He curled onto his side and tucked his hands beneath his face. Ottilie smiled and raked his hair from his forehead, her gloves catching on the curls and mussing them. He looked so handsome in his new suit, his hair neatly cropped. She resettled the blanket over him. Her own nose, ears, and fingers were stiff with cold. They had made a game of puffing air when they first disembarked the ship.

Everett sat across from them and cleared his throat. "I'm sorry we couldn't stay in London for a while. It's a wonderful city with much to see, but I've been away for so long. Now that I'm close to home, I feel an urgency to return. And your grandmother sold her London townhouse after your grandfather died and it became clear Birdie wasn't going to find a husband after half a dozen London seasons. Hazelbrook is only a thirty-minute ride from Chippenham. We should be there soon."

His eyes didn't settle on her the way they had before, that warm coaxing way that made her feel as though she could tell him every secret thought her heart harbored. The farther they got from India, the further he drifted. Maybe he was only distracted. Eager to return to his comfortable life and important work. But suspicion needled her.

It had started onboard, once she had finally been able to pull herself off her cot and walk the perimeter of the ship. She'd leaned on Everett's arm for support, her legs still weak and shaky. He held himself apart, perfectly courteous, but nothing more. Nothing to indicate all they'd shared. The friendship they had developed. The spark that lit between them.

On the train to Chippenham, as they passed empty brown fields and crumbling brown houses and drab little brown villages, his posture grew stiffer. His gaze ever more distant. When he took her hand to assist her into the carriage at the station, he touched her only long enough to see she didn't topple to the ground.

With each moment that passed, the gulf between them widened. Her spirit grew more bruised. And she didn't know why.

Except for a half-formed thought she hated to give credence. She knew Everett could never care for her the way she did him, but had he, once they stood on British ground, decided even her friendship wasn't worth the risk?

"It's all right. I have no desire to see London."

He nodded, then turned toward the window. "You'll like Wiltshire. There's nothing much to look at now, but in spring everything comes alive. And the manor is peaceful, surrounded by forest. You can walk to Elbury or Maybourne Park."

"Will I be welcome at Maybourne Park?" Her soft question drew his head around.

"Why would you be unwelcome? I live there. My employer is generous with me. I have sufficient time to visit."

"It's only that you've been so aloof since we left India. Are you wishing we'd maintained a more indifferent relationship? Will my presence put you in an awkward position?"

Understanding dawned, and the expression in his lovely eyes became familiar and dear once more. "You will always be welcome wherever I am."

Ottilie took her first deep breath since leaving the ship. Frigid air swirled in her lungs, sweeping out the apprehension. She needed Everett's friendship. Coveted his esteem. This unassuming man, with his transforming smile and compassion, had become something more to her than a friend. Something more, even, than a lover. He was more than Victor had ever been.

She couldn't pin a word to it. Couldn't, in any of the four languages she knew, articulate what he was. She only knew she felt strength in his presence. Belonging. A rightness to everything. She shivered and wrapped her arms around herself.

"Are you very cold?"

She laughed. "Of course. Aren't you?"

"Here." He scooped Thaddeus into his arms and settled beside her, laying her sleeping brother and his blanket over their laps. Then, bracing his feet on the opposite seat, he lifted her hands and removed her gloves, one finger at a time. She could only watch, transfixed, as he freed her from the leather. He took her hands between his and held them to his lips, then blew, his breath bringing warmth to her fingers. Her hands. Her arms and legs and chest.

She swallowed and met his eyes. Couldn't look away.

"I'm used to the winter," he said in between puffs. "You'll soon find yourself accustomed to it as well. I've learned my hands stay warmer in wool than leather." He rubbed her hands roughly, then tucked them beneath the blanket, setting her useless gloves on the seat beside him. "I'm sorry I've been inattentive. And even sorrier it has caused you to doubt my affection. I hold you in the highest regard."

He looked as though he wanted to say more, his expressive mouth forming words that stayed firmly in his thoughts, and Ottilie allowed a foolish hope that he *would* say more. But he didn't, and she realized how wise he was. Nothing more could be said without jeopardizing their friendship, his plans to marry well, and her seemingly forgotten vow not to marry at all.

Thaddeus stretched, throwing off the blanket. The chill was opportunistic and vicious. Ottilie leaned over him and yanked it back up off the floor. She clutched it to her chest, letting it drape over her skirts.

"It's too cold to be unwrapped, Thaddeus. You'll become ill." Her words created those fascinating puffs of air above him.

He laughed, eyes widening when little clouds spit from his mouth. "I wonder when it will snow." He threw himself onto the floor of the coach with the energy little boys put into everything, and knelt beside the window, fingers gripping the ledge and nose pushed to the glass. "It's like a frozen fairyland, just as you said, Everett."

Ottilie met Everett's gaze, and their smiles matched. But behind his, she saw a slight pulling away. A tremor indicating hidden thoughts. She couldn't question him, not with Thaddeus so near, so she ignored the worry. She had enough of her own; she didn't need to borrow his.

Thaddeus slid up onto the seat opposite them, and his belly grumbled. "I'm hungry."

Everett crossed his legs, resting one foot over his knee, and leaned back. The picture of easy confidence. A man who knew he was right where he belonged. "Good for you, then, that we've arrived." He looked out the window. "Welcome home."

"This is not a house." Ottilie stared out the window over Thaddeus's head at the structure that seemed to rise out of the ground as though it had been snapped into being by God's fingers.

She'd grown wide-eyed as they passed beneath an ornate gatehouse, three stories high and featuring dozens of leaded windows, gables, and a domed wooden door that would have intimidated an army. But this . . . this stately sandstone building with the peaked roofs and chimneys pointing toward heaven was something entirely outside the realm of *house*.

"My father grew up here?" She sat back and glanced at Everett, whom she'd been leaning over.

"This has been your family's country home for almost three hundred years. Your father, your grandfather, your great-grandfather all grew up here. And now Thaddeus."

Ottilie sank into the seat, squeezing herself into the corner. "We can't live here."

"Why not?" Thaddeus asked. "I want to live here." He pressed his face back against the window.

The horses' clopping hooves stopped, jarring the coach to a halt. Everett scooted near and touched her arm. "It is overwhelming, I know, but it will soon feel like home to you."

Edwin Russell had provided Ottilie and the rest of her family with a lovely life. Before he'd died, they lived in a rambling bungalow with a beautiful garden. They'd had a dozen servants and never wanted for anything. But that life seemed shabby in comparison to this. Why had Father left it behind to forge something different halfway around the world? Why had he left this privileged existence for an unknown? The thought unsettled her. Why would anyone want to leave such a place?

The sun, just starting its descent, cast light over the manor, and its stones seemed to glow from within. It called a welcome but repelled with its grandeur at the same time.

A confusing message. One Ottilie had no wish to unravel.

But here she was, and Thaddeus had already toppled to the ground when a man wearing a handsome livery of deep green opened the door. Everett preceded her, and when she didn't immediately follow, he poked his head back inside the carriage and offered an encouraging smile.

"It will be all right, Ottilie. I won't leave until you're ready." He held out his hand, a tempting invitation. One she ignored in favor of the coach's frozen safety.

"Give me a moment, please."

He dropped his hand, gave her a soft smile and slow nod, then ducked back out. Ottilie slid across the seat and peered out the window. He'd left the door open, and she could hear Thaddeus's exclamations.

Two lines flanked the coach. Staff on one side, and two women on the other. Her grandmother, whose black gown seemed more an extension of her body than mere clothing, and her aunt. They both had Father's deep-set eyes, and grief lined their faces. Traits Ottilie could also claim. But that was all she recognized in them. There was no pull to make herself known. No transcendent connection. They didn't notice her hiding in the carriage. All eyes were on Thaddeus, who was brushing the dirt from his knees and shaking out his legs.

"That was the longest journey I have ever taken," he said so gravely and full of self-importance that everyone laughed. "I need to get my wiggles out."

Lady Sunderson gasped and covered her mouth with her hands.

Thaddeus squinted up at her. "That's what Ottilie always calls them."

"That is what I called them as well when your father was a little boy." Lady Sunderson glanced from Thaddeus to Everett to the carriage. "You said to expect an additional guest, Everett? We got your letter only a week ago, but we've made up a room adjoining Lord Sunderson's. Who is it? A governess? Has Ottilie decided to join Sunderson here?"

"I wasn't completely forthcoming in my letter because it's a sensitive situation. I didn't know how you would want to handle it." Everett glanced over his shoulder at the carriage, and Ottilie was certain he could see her, hidden in the shadows, looking through the wavy glass at a life she couldn't claim. How she wished he'd told them about her. They would have already settled into the knowledge, and Ottilie wouldn't feel as though she had moved to England under false pretenses. "Before I assist your guest out of the coach, first"—he put his hand on Thaddeus's shoulder—"Lord Sunderson, your grandmother, Lady Sunderson."

He had given Ottilie the gift of a few more moments. Enough time to collect herself, settle into the realization that it was time. Time to betray her heritage. And Thaddeus's. Time to say hello to England and her British family. Time to—she pressed her hand to her chest and pushed against the sharp pain that had lodged there—know whether or not this would be a reunion or a rejection.

Thaddeus put his little fists on his hips and turned his face up toward Everett. "I told you I don't like that name."

Everett grinned. "Yes, but it is your name. You will grow used to it."

He'd said that to both of them so many times since they'd boarded the ship that Ottilie was certain she'd hear it in her dreams. Thaddeus had resisted from the moment Everett first addressed him by his title.

Everett leaned forward and whispered something to Lady Sunderson. Her grandmother drew back, eyes wide, then gave a nod and dismissed the staff, who all filed around the side of the house.

A chilly wind swept into the carriage, ruffling the tiered layers of her new wool shawl and creeping past the defenses of her jacket. It urged Ottilie to gather her courage. She couldn't very well sleep in a hired coach. No matter how tempting the prospect.

As though able to read her mind, Everett appeared at the coach door. "Are you ready?" His question wasn't prodding or impatient. She believed, if she told him no, he would give her one of his gentle smiles, turn around, and use whatever means necessary to distract her grandmother and aunt from their reclusive relation.

She took a deep breath. "I believe I am."

"You have faced far harder things, and you aren't alone." He took her hand, and she clung to it. Nothing had prepared her for losing her family. Her fiancé. Her country. Everything that was familiar. And yet she managed to draw breath every day. She could do it again in this alien place. With these people whose blood, if not memories, she shared.

"Thank you." The words slipped from her frozen lips.

She allowed him to help her from the coach, knowing that even though her faith in God was still a shaky thing, her faith in Everett Scott couldn't be any steadier.

16

Miss Ottilie Russell, your grandmother, Lady Sunderson." Everett nudged Ottilie's arm, and she lifted her head.

"Ottilie?" Lady Sunderson stared, her eyes sweeping from the hem of Ottilie's traveling suit to the top of the hat pinned to her head. "How can this be?"

Alberta barked a laugh. "Is this some kind of joke?"

Thaddeus slipped his hand into Ottilie's and moved closer to her, the length of his body pressing against her legs and crushing her skirt. "Didi?" His cheerful smile dropped and was replaced with anxiety.

Ottilie sent a pointed glance toward Everett. She could have this conversation with her grandmother and aunt, but she didn't want to have it in front of her brother. She rested her hand just above Thaddeus's head, hoping Everett would understand her message.

He did.

"Lord Sunderson, why don't you come with me? I will show you the gardens. There's a great grassy hill behind the house that is perfect for rolling down." Passing behind her, Everett squeezed her arm, then collected Thaddeus and took him through the front door.

"Let's go into the drawing room. You must be very cold." Lady Sunderson held her hands in a demure position at her waist, but Ottilie noticed her knuckles turning white from her tight grip. She was a tall woman, sheathed in a black gown that set off the streaks of silver threading through her hair, whose posture and bearing commanded respect, but the nervous way her eyes bounced around betrayed her. And that knowledge calmed Ottilie's prancing heart.

"Thank you," Ottilie said. "I'm not used to this weather. It doesn't get this cold in Calcutta." She'd had five years' practice hiding her emotions. Five years of grief honing her ability to present an image untouched by tragedy. And that skill served her well now, when she most wanted to run to the coach and beg the driver to take her back to Chippenham, London, the Channel, and the Suez Canal that would lead her back to India. They would see nothing but what she wanted them to see. "Shall we, then?"

She sounded as cold as the wind nipping at her bits of exposed skin. So contained, as though this entire situation was nothing but normal. That her palms didn't sweat, sticking to the inside of her gloves, and her stomach wasn't filled with stone.

Lady Sunderson stared at Ottilie, a pinched *V* between her brows, before she turned and went inside. Alberta followed without even a glance. Ottilie sighed and steeled herself for the conversation to come. How little they knew of Papa's life. Not only had he left, he'd told them nothing about it. It revealed more about his feelings toward his home and family than anything he could have said.

As Ottilie walked through a great hall, paneled with waist-high board and batten and tiled with scuffed stone that had felt the tread of a thousand shoes, she reminded herself that these people were real. They had loved her father. Their surprise said nothing about her worth, and even if they rejected her, that wouldn't diminish it.

But, God, please don't let them reject me.

She paused as she passed a two-story nook lined with multi-paned windows and boasting a fireplace cut into the wall, a small table, and a cluster of wispy chairs. Through the wavy glass, she could see the gatehouse standing sentry and, past the wall, the ancient church her family had worshiped at for centuries. This place had roots. These people, her people, knew where they belonged. And they had stayed.

Was she to be sewn into that story? Would she be allowed to claim that history?

Ahead of her, a door creaked open, and Ottilie hurried to catch up. Lady Sunderson led Alberta and Ottilie up a short narrow staircase and into a room done in shades of gold and soft green. The honeyed walls shone just as brilliantly as the stone the house was built from. Light splashed around, bouncing off angles and illuminating every corner.

"Please sit down." Lady Sunderson motioned to a high-back settee topped with a canopy and took the one opposite. Alberta sat beside her mother. "Wakefield, will you please see that Mr. Scott is returned here? Lord Sunderson may be taken to the kitchen for a pudding."

The butler inclined his head. "Of course, my lady."

When he had left, Alberta turned an icy stare toward Ottilie. "Who are you? You can't possibly think we believe you are Edwin's daughter."

Despite the chill in the room, remarkably untouched by the flames leaping in the fireplace, heat swept through Ottilie. Words exploded in her mind, shattering coherent thoughts. She couldn't reach for any of them. Her tongue had frozen in her mouth, and she only stared at her aunt.

"Alberta!" Lady Sunderson turned wide eyes toward her daughter, shifting on the settee. "Enough of that. We will hear her story."

When she turned back to Ottilie, she leaned forward a little, attentive. Ottilie noticed no hasty judgment in her expression. She looked very much like Papa had when he was on the verge of learning something new from one of his old books. All restrained eagerness tempered by unceasing questions. Ottilie blinked back a sudden veil of tears. Papa had looked so much like his mother. Ottilie hadn't expected that.

It was a gentle smile from God. A note of encouragement.

"Edwin Russell was my father, just as he was Thaddeus's. Our mother, Sonia Lupton, was the daughter of an English military man and an Indian woman from Benares."

Silence filled the space between them. It grew so that even the flames hushed their crackling. There was nothing—not neighbors calling greetings to one another, not dogs scuffling and fighting over scraps of trash, not the rhythmic pounding of a mortar crushing cardamom pods—piercing the quiet.

Finally, the door behind them opened, and Everett slid into the room. He sat beside Ottilie and gave her a hand a squeeze.

"Everett," Alberta said, "this woman is claiming Edwin married a *native*."

Ottilie flinched and drew back against the seat. She'd been referred to as a native before, and always with the same disdainful tone dripping from the word. As though being native to anywhere other than England signified a lack of . . . everything. As though her mother and grandmother and all those in her lineage were uncivilized and uneducated. Undeserving of even the slightest respect.

As though the people of India hadn't been building great civilizations while the Celts were collecting berries.

The thought made her sit up straight and lift her chin. She had nothing to be ashamed of.

"My father married a Eurasian woman. He *loved* a Eurasian woman. I am Eurasian. Thaddeus is Eurasian. Thaddeus looks like Father. I look like Maji. But both of us are their children."

"Were they happy?" Lady Sunderson's quiet question drew all their eyes. "Did Edwin and Sonia have a happy marriage? A happy life?" She clasped her hands and leaned forward.

"They did," Ottilie answered. "Before Father died, our home was full of love and laughter. Father adored Maji."

Lady Sunderson pressed her trembling lips together and nodded. "I'm so glad." She stood and crossed the rug that separated them, then cupped one of Ottilie's cheeks. "I have wanted to know you for twenty years. I've imagined you growing from a tiny babe into a curious child, and then into a confident woman. Your mother was so proud of you, Ottilie. Her letters were full of your praise. She told me how Edwin died. How you attended him and Jemima and Nathan. I loved you in that moment. For being with my son when I couldn't." She pressed a kiss to Ottilie's head. "You aren't who I imagined, but you are more than I'd hoped."

All the tightness in Ottilie's chest loosened. She pressed her hand over Lady Sunderson's, still resting on her face, and whispered, "Thank you for saying that."

"This can't be easy for you. Leaving your country, unknowing what our response would be. You are quite brave."

"This is all well and good," Alberta interrupted, "but please, Mother, explain what we're to *do* with her. We can't very well hide her in a cabinet every time someone comes to the house."

Ottilie looked at Everett, a poignant emptiness stabbing at her when Lady Sunderson dropped her hand.

Everett rubbed his temple and grimaced.

"Her presence will cast aspersions on Lord Sunderson," Alberta continued. "What family of good breeding will want to marry their daughter to a lord with Indian blood?"

"Marry?" Ottilie gasped. "He's a child."

"He won't always be a child," Everett said gently.

She met his gaze. "But why should his heritage matter?" Why should hers?

Alberta made a sound of incredulity. "It's the thing that matters most. Of course, looking at him, you'd never believe he was Indian." She cast a glance at Ottilie that seemed to say she

204

didn't believe he was either. "He'll be reviled. Possibly ostracized. Maybe it would have been different before that awful incident at Cawnpore, but now . . . it will damage the reputation of our name. No one must find out."

Ottilie's ribs drew inward at the sound of that wretched city, crushing her lungs and heart. Its name was the backing of an embroidery, all knotted threads and ugly stitches. Except, when turned over, nothing beautiful redeemed it. Everything just twisted together in a story that demonstrated only the atrocity of greed and hatred. A people desperate for freedom, an army looking for vengeance. And what had it accomplished? What was the result of so much violence? Only that she sat here now in the presence of what was left of her family, the legacy of her great-grandfather's and grandfather's involvement casting shadows over her.

"How do you intend to keep Ottilie's relationship with Lord Sunderson secret?" Everett asked.

And Ottilie remembered another man. Another time. *"We must keep this a secret, Ottilie."*

She'd thought it was because she was young—too young to entertain thoughts of marriage—and he hadn't been granted leave to take a wife. But Victor had not even wanted to tell Papa or Maji. Their romance bloomed in shadowy corners and tucked-away gardens, and when Papa had died, it withered beneath his absence, because there was nothing left, nothing at all, making her acceptable.

Resisting the urge to cross her arms over her chest—a protective measure that would give away her insecurity—she watched Alberta, who *had* crossed her arms and was tapping her finger against her lip. Putting every effort into deciding how she would best tear out Ottilie's heart.

Ottilie glanced at Lady Sunderson, but the older woman watched her daughter as though waiting for her to throw a life raft. These were waters none of them had any experience navigating. They were all fighting against choppy waves, unable to swim, and Alberta seemed the only one capable of being captain. Ottilie felt mutinous.

Alberta sat up straighter. A feat, given her neat posture. "What do they call Indian nannies? There's a name for them."

"Ayah." Ottilie pushed the word past the lump in her throat.

"Yes. You will be Thaddeus's ayah. It makes sense, doesn't it, that a child reared in another country would want to have someone familiar attend to him?"

"You would make me my brother's servant?" The lump in Ottilie's throat ossified. Turned as hard and dense as a large ruby she'd seen at the Imperial Museum in some ancient raja's crown. It had glittered and begged to be touched—fire burned within it—but when she reached out to press her fingertips against it, she only felt smooth coldness.

"Would you ruin his chance at happiness? That would be selfish, wouldn't it?" Alberta's words sounded like the ripping of fabric. It was a harsh pronouncement, full of ugly insinuation and preemptive judgment.

"Enough, Alberta." Lady Sunderson finally seemed to come out of her dazed stupor. She put a hand on her daughter's arm, stopping the flow of whatever words Alberta had been about to cast from her lips.

Everett shifted beside Ottilie. "You've always served your brother. Since I've known you, you've put his needs above your own." His voice was soft, inviting. It told her to accept the way things were. That she was being unreasonable, and the situation wasn't so very terrible, after all. "Nothing will change in your relationship, except maybe for what others see. But people will always see what is easiest to understand."

Ottilie collected her fragmented composure, pulling it together into another seamless expression of impassivity. "Isn't Thaddeus too old for an ayah? He needs to learn. In Calcutta, he attended school. What of that?"

Alberta tipped her head. "Maybe a governess would be a better choice. Are you educated?"

"Of course. I went to La Martiniere, Calcutta's best girls' school."

"Then we shall tell everyone you were his ayah in India and will be his governess here. That with all the changes in his life, Everett thought it best you attend to him to help him transition to life in England. And when he's ready for school . . . well, we will have to worry about that when the time comes. Maybe you will hate England and want to move back to India."

"Is that what you're hoping?"

"It would make things easier."

Everett stood and took Ottilie's hand, helping her to her feet. "I will speak with Ottilie now."

He walked her from the room, not stopping until he had her across the drive, through the thick wooden gate set into the wall that surrounded the manor, and deep into the family cemetery.

The Russell family graveyard was nothing like South Park Street Cemetery. Here, the graves were arranged in orderly rows, each one the same distance apart as the next. Tidy paths, crunching beneath Ottilie's shoes with overspent grass, led visitors from one plot to the next. A stone chapel with a pitched steeple hemmed it in on the left. On the right, a gnarled, leafless tree reached its branches over the yard. Beyond, the grounds stretched as far as Ottilie could see, dipping and lifting over gentle hills, dotted with barren trees and ponds. There were no overgrown vines or flowering bushes. No carpets of krishna-chura petals or crumbling mausoleums. This was a neat display of death. Nothing at all like life.

When Everett released her hand, she pulled from him and busied herself by walking along a line of crooked headstones, reading names and dates. Everett had been so intent on leading her from the house, and she so intent on leaving with him, she'd left her gloves on the settee. Closing her eyes, she remembered the soft warmth of the air he'd blown on her fingers in the coach.

She crossed her arms over her chest, tucking her hands beneath her elbows. There was no use wishing for things that could never happen. Shouldn't happen.

Everett followed her—she could hear the sound of his steps, the snapping of twigs and brushing against dead grass—but he gave her a moment.

She used his kindness to pull back from her simmering resentment. The bitterness that always seemed too close to the surface. Aware of the truth behind Niraja's words and her own still-fragile faith—only bolstered by an untried decision.

"I knew this would be hard, but I didn't think I would be forced to deny my relationship with Thaddeus."

"Sunderson."

She turned to stare at him.

He stepped closer to her. "His name is now Lord Sunderson. You can call him Thaddeus privately, for a little while, since he is a child, but you need to begin addressing him properly now that we are in England."

"I'm not calling my brother 'Lord' anything. Everything has changed for him. He's a child. And he hates when you call him that. How do you think he'd feel if I did?"

"Children are resilient, Ottilie. I think maybe this is harder for you than him."

Ottilie sucked in a sharp breath. "What do you know about it? Have you ever had your life turned upside down? Everything has changed, Everett, and I feel as though a God I can't trust is stitching me into a story I don't like."

He didn't draw away from her. Or look shocked at her outburst. He nodded toward a small bench set into an alcove of the chapel wall. "Sit with me." He walked over to it, leaving her to decide whether to follow or not.

She followed. Just as she'd followed Thaddeus to England. She followed because it seemed she was now tethered to this life, and she needed to understand it.

It was a small bench, and her skirts bunched against him. She attempted to tuck them beneath her, without luck, but he didn't seem to mind. He stared at the little graveyard, his long fingers knit together and resting in his lap. She darted a glance at him from the corner of her eye, noting the way his dark lashes swept in soft curves.

"I wasn't born to this life," he said. He looked at her, and she saw hesitation trip its way into his gaze. "I don't take it for granted, but that doesn't mean it was an easy transition."

"You've said that before, but I don't understand. You work for a relative. A tea importer."

"I do. I . . . I'm not ready to tell the story in its entirety. It's one that's not spoken of, even among the people who know. But I want to tell you this." He shifted so his knees pressed against hers and took one of her hands in his. "When my current employer found me, I was lying in a bed beside my mother, who had only a few breaths of life left in her. She had pneumonia, a direct result of the fetid workhouse air and not enough food. For two months, I'd only seen her for a couple of hours each Sunday. They had separated us the moment we walked through the door. I lived for those hours. My mother was . . ." His voice sounded heavy, and he glanced away. "She was a wonderful woman. And my first seven years were full of love. We never had adequate food or warm clothing, but it always felt like enough. One Sunday, they wouldn't allow me to see her. I was told she was ill. The next Sunday, they wouldn't take me to see her either. And the next, when I was told, once again, I couldn't see her, I decided to get myself to the infirmary."

His hand felt cold in hers, and she returned his earlier favor, surrounding it with both of hers and rubbing warmth into it. His other hand inched near, and she took that one too. A small smile played with his lips, and everything in her wanted to see it bloom. She felt she could endure anything, face everything, if she could do it with the memory of his smile urging her on.

His face fell into serious lines again, the promise of sunlight disappearing into a frown, and he pulled away from her, shoving his hands into the pockets of his overcoat. Ottilie bunched the folds of her skirt in her fists and tried to ignore the sting of rejection. It was a silly thing to feel. Everett had promised her nothing. Hadn't even said anything.

Then he looked at her, and words he'd never spoken shouted from green eyes so dark and fathomless, she knew she was at risk of drowning. And there was no one to rescue her, because the only one who could was the one pulling her into the water.

"There was only one way for a boy to be brought to the infirmary. He needed to be injured or ill. And since I couldn't make myself sick, I made myself injured."

His words registered, and she blinked. "You hurt yourself?"

He shook his head. "I made sure someone else did. There was a man tasked with keeping the boys in line. He was unstable, prone to violence when he drank too much. He'd sent a few children to the infirmary."

"Everett, no!" Ottilie couldn't keep the horror from her voice. She imagined Thaddeus putting himself in danger just to see her, and her heart clenched so tightly, she pressed her palm against it to ease the pain.

"I had no other choice. After dinner, he sat at his desk in the little room off the dormitory and pulled out his bottle and cigar. I let him drink a little, then I walked around his desk and kicked him as hard as I could in the shin while screaming, 'I hate you!' It was an effective plan." He gave her a wry smile, then shrugged his coat off one arm, pushed his cufflink through one of the buttonholes on his cuff, and rolled up his sleeve. He turned over his arm and there, along the back of his wrist, were three round, raised scars the diameter of her thumbnail.

"I passed out when he pressed his cigar into my skin and woke up where I set out to go."

Gooseflesh rose along Ottilie's arms and legs, and tears sprang to her eyes. She skimmed one of the scars with her fingertip, eyes meeting his in question.

"They don't hurt anymore," he said. "Every bruise and scar from that beating has healed."

His skin was puckered beneath her touch, and she lifted his arm to her lips, pressing a kiss to each one. "Every scar? There are scars we cannot see that never heal, no matter how much time passes."

She only wanted to ease the memory of his pain, but his eyes widened and his Adam's apple bobbed. And she realized her kisses had revealed too much. She set his arm down and put as much space between them as she could without falling to the ground.

"It got me what I wanted. I don't regret it." When he spoke, he sounded so normal, she wondered if she had imagined the entire incident.

She resisted the temptation to touch her lips. To imagine his skin against them again. Everett had made it clear what he wanted from life. And it wasn't her. His bland response to her touch was his way of offering her an escape from her own impulsive conduct.

She accepted it gladly. "What happened when you awoke?"

"There were only a dozen people in the room, and the night nurse was sleeping in the corner. I crept from bed to bed until I found my mother. Every part of my body hurt, but when I saw her, I felt nothing except joy at knowing it would be all right. I was with my mother. I climbed into bed with her. She whispered my name and held me to her chest and told me she loved me."

"What happened?" Ottilie whispered.

"The next morning a nurse found me and tried to remove me, but my mother spoke harshly to her. I'd never heard her complain or raise her voice until that moment. 'No,' she said, 'you will not take him away from me.' Then she coughed and cried out, and I think the nurse knew that I wouldn't be there long.

"Mr. Fernsby, who is now my employer, found me a few hours later. He cried when he saw my mother. She said, 'Take care of him. Make sure he is never rejected for my sake. I want him to be more than I ever was.' I didn't understand what was happening, and I was escorted out to collect my things. When I returned to the infirmary and wrapped my arms around her, she was dead."

He pulled his coat back over his shoulder and shoved his arm into the sleeve. "Ottilie, I do understand what it's like to have your entire life turned upside down. It's happened to me more than once. I've met grief, and I've lost my home, and I've been thrust into a foreign situation with no idea how to navigate it."

"But how am I to pretend Thaddeus isn't my brother? He's the entire reason I'm here. And I'm to just watch while they embrace him and relegate me to the servants' hall? I'm to be an unwanted visitor in this home the rest of my life?"

Everett scrubbed his hand over the back of his neck. "A governess isn't exactly a servant's position. Though you likely won't be treated like family either. It isn't easy, I know. But give them this for now, until they are able to accept the truth of the situation and determine how to handle it."

"The truth of the situation? That Thaddeus and I are Indian?"

"That they knew nothing of your father's choices. That he had a life and didn't share any of it with them. That he despised them so much, he replaced them with another country, another people." He stood and offered his hand. She took it, and when she got to her feet, he lifted a wisp of hair that had escaped her chignon and tucked it behind her ear. "I don't know how this will be resolved. They may never be willing to risk Thaddeus's security to acknowledge you, but I do know that your value doesn't rest on their acceptance. You aren't unwanted. And never will be."

Everett walked her inside and deposited her back in the elaborate drawing room that suffocated her. She sat on the same canopied settee and assumed the same position—demurely crossing her ankles and resting her hands in her lap.

He said good-bye to Lady Sunderson and Alberta and bowed over Ottilie's hand. "I will see you soon."

When she nodded, he kissed her knuckles, lingering as long as she had over his burns, their eyes meeting and saying things they would never utter. Then he left, and she was alone with her grandmother and aunt.

After several long seconds, Ottilie could stand the silence no longer. "I will act as Thaddeus's governess for the time being."

"What shall we call you? You can't very well be Miss Russell." Alberta looked at her, brows raised.

Ottilie stared at her. "You can't expect me to give up my name." She'd already surrendered too much.

"How will we explain it to the servants, then? I am Miss Russell. You cannot be."

Ottilie pressed her fingers to her eyes, felt them shift beneath her lids, pressure building. *I will not sacrifice any more.* And then a name, one unknown to Alberta and Lady Sunderson, came to mind. It was a connection. A chain of stitches allowing her to claim her family still. "Very well. I will be Miss Singh. It is my grandmother's name."

Alberta gave a satisfied smile and stood. "Well, now that that's settled, I have letters to write."

"Please." Ottilie lifted her chin. "I'm not finished."

Alberta's mouth tightened, but she sat back down.

"Go on, Ottilie," Lady Sunderson said. "I know this is an unorthodox situation, but I want you to feel free to speak with us as . . . well, as family."

"Since that is what we are." Ottilie wouldn't make this easy for them. They might wish to ignore the fact that she and Thaddeus were related and therefore Thaddeus was just as Indian, but she wouldn't allow her brother to forget. "I need to know what is expected of me. How shall I be treated? Am I to be a servant or family member? Or something in between and undefined?"

"You will be treated like a governess. Which is always something in between and undefined, even for an English one," Alberta said. "There is no other way—"

"No." Lady Sunderson touched Alberta's arm, her voice as soft as tussar silk and as rigid as teak. "I will not allow her to be isolated and forgotten. I intend to have a relationship with you, Ottilie. It may be unconventional in practice, but you will be more family than servant."

"The servants, though. What will you tell them?"

"They would never question us, nor would they consider it possible. Who would believe the son of a baron could make such a choice?" Alberta had unattainable composure. She was as unreachable as the bronze Chola statue of Parvati at the museum. But in that moment, she displayed a tell. Miss Alberta Russell, self-contained and perfectly elegant, began to pick at her cuticles.

Ottilie wondered what was making her aunt uncomfortable. It was more than just displeasure at her brother's choice of a wife. It went deeper. Living for two decades on the fringe of society had given Ottilie ample time to observe. And in those hours of watching, she'd become adept at understanding. Her aunt was hiding something.

"Who would believe a member of the gentry would marry an Indian woman . . . ?" Ottilie murmured.

"Precisely," Alberta said. "Especially when the two of you look nothing alike."

Needles stabbed Ottilie's heart. She wanted to convince them that she and Thaddeus were more alike than different. They both loved books and stories. They were both prone to solemnity and overthinking. They were both quick to cry. They both loved having their feet rubbed with mustard oil and listening to Dilip grind spices. Their differences were found only in the color of their hair and skin. Hardly worth noticing at all.

"What was that thing Sunderson called you outside?" Alberta asked.

"Didi? It means 'elder sister' in Bengali."

"Yes. He can continue calling you that. No one here will understand it."

Ottilie's brows tugged together, and her lips pursed.

Lady Sunderson gave Ottilie an appraising look, her eyes sharp with understanding, but her mouth softened in a compassionate smile. "And it will allow you to retain a connection with him. I know we're asking a lot of you, Ottilie."

"Mother." Alberta rolled her eyes. "It is not asking a lot to have her put his needs above her own."

"I have, and always will, put Thaddeus's needs above my own. But I won't lie. I will continue in this charade, but if I'm asked directly, I will tell the truth."

Alberta stood, back rigid, head high, and voice cold. "Well, who will ask?" Then she left.

Her meaning was clear—who would care enough to ask? Who would make the association? Ottilie bowed her head as Alberta passed, more to hide the offense she was sure had bloomed over her face than from any show of submission.

A weight settled beside her, and a soft touch on her arm brought Ottilie's gaze up. Lady Sunderson looked at her with restrained wonder. "I am so happy you're here. I grew close to your mother through our years of letter writing. I always wanted to meet the woman who loved my son enough to build a bridge. Through her, I was able to know of Edwin's life. I knew about his work and successes and failures. Sonia made me feel as though we weren't estranged, and I loved her for it." She glanced at the door Alberta had swept through. "Give her time. She's not as fussy and insensitive as she appears. Life has taught her some hard lessons."

When she cupped Ottilie's cheek and kissed her forehead, the chill in the room thawed. "I will extend grace," Ottilie said.

Lady Sunderson smiled. "Good. Now, let me show you to your room. It is very near your brother's. In fact, a doorway connects the two."

Ottilie didn't tell her they had slept on adjoining mats, nearly always wrapped together, a tangle of legs and arms, since they had lost the house after Papa's death. She had no doubt Thaddeus would ignore his own bed for the familiarity of being near her. And Ottilie wouldn't be able to sleep unless hearing his even breathing and snuffles. "Thank you."

She stood and followed her grandmother back into the main hall. It was a massive room, two stories high, with mellow walls covered in tapestries and dusty paintings of somber people in stiff ruffs and embroidered velvet robes. Everything spoke of established wealth and generations of good breeding.

"This is the great hall," Lady Sunderson said, leading Ottilie to a wide, curving staircase of polished wood. "It's the original part of the house and was built in the fourteenth century." She waved toward the curved bank of windows. "That is the oriel. It is a delicious place to read a book."

They ascended the stairs, passing more paintings, this time gloomy landscapes of misty mountains and stormy seas. At the landing, the first floor split into two wings, and they went left. Narrow carved benches and chairs lined the walls between heavy doors. Puddles of light spilled over the gray slate floor tiles from the recessed windows. The house twisted and turned. It was narrow and snug and filled with sunlight, reminding Ottilie of Calcutta's streets. But she felt no sense of homecoming.

Lady Sunderson opened one of the scarred doors and ushered Ottilie through it.

"I hope it's to your liking." Lady Sunderson walked to the

center of the room and turned in a small circle, her gaze caressing the mahogany four-poster bed, wardrobe, and writing desk. "I realize now how appropriate this is, because it was your father's." She smiled, and it transformed her. Grief had made its mark in the lines running from the corners of her lips to her chin and in the dark shadows beneath her eyes, but for a moment, Ottilie saw she had brought her grandmother joy, and it looked lovely. "Sonia often wrote about how close you were to your father. I think you might enjoy his room. I sometimes walk in here and still feel his presence."

Ottilie ran her hand down the carved bedpost. She recognized the strange sense of past and present stitching together and welcomed it. "I feel it too."

Lady Sunderson took a few steps toward Ottilie, her fingers woven together near her stomach. "I feel as though I've been given a second chance. With my sons . . . well, the prevailing wisdom of the age suggested keeping children at arm's length, not indulging them with too much affection. I didn't realize until they were grown that the distance I held them at while they were children would never be bridged in adulthood. We hardly knew each other, which, I think, is why Edwin was able to leave so fully. I raised Alberta differently. And when Everett came to be in our lives, I indulged him with the tenderness I should have offered my sons." She glanced away, her throat working. "And now I have the opportunity to love Edwin's son and daughter."

"What about your granddaughters? Everett said you had four."

"Yes, and they are dear girls. But their mother has taken them to her family's estate far from here. We will not see them often enough. So, you see, I was quite without grandchildren before you arrived. And I do love them so." She motioned across the room at an alcove. "Your brother is through that door. I'm sure you're probably very tired, so I'll leave you to rest. I'll send someone up in a while to put away your things so you can change for dinner, which is at seven. It's not common for the children of the house to join the family for meals, but we will make allowances for now, as we have years of absence to make up for."

Lady Sunderson was nearly to the door when something struck Ottilie. Answers. Instead of secrets and questions, she could finally get some answers.

"What happened?" she asked.

Her grandmother turned, hand on the knob. She didn't ask Ottilie to clarify. She knew. She sighed and came back into the room. Sat on the edge of the bed and patted the seat beside her.

Ottilie joined her. "I stumbled on Maji's letters, and in one of them, you wrote that you hurt him. That you wanted him to join the church instead of pursuing science. But no matter how I look at it, I cannot fathom something like that causing Papa to abandon you so completely. He loved family."

"It's a hard story to share. More than just a difference of opinion." Lady Sunderson took a moment to hide her face in her hands before dropping them and offering Ottilie a sad smile. "We never understood his love of science. My husband was a traditional man. Educated in the way most men of his standing and generation were—meant to take over the estate and live life the way the gentry have lived it for hundreds of years. But Edwin . . . his curiosity never seemed satiated. He questioned everything. And when he was about sixteen, he questioned the path we'd set for him."

"Papa would have been miserable in that role. And awful at it."

"Yes, I see that now. But at the time, it seemed the thing to do. His oldest brother was being primed to take over the running of the estate. His middle brother had gone into the military. And the third son is meant for the church. My brother Thaddeus, who had always been eccentric, encouraged your father to pursue his scientific studies. Your grandfather refused to financially support him in this, but Edwin was smart and resourceful. He found a patron, one of my brother's associates, who offered to pay for his education at Oxford. In return,

Edwin was to work at one of the man's many archaeological digs for three years after he completed school." Lady Sunderson dropped her head and stared at her knobby fingers twisted into the fabric of her skirt. "Your grandfather was a hard man when crossed. He wasn't used to being defied." Her shoulders drooped, and her words trailed off, as though she'd lost the ability to continue.

But Ottilie needed to know. "What did he do?"

"He used his many connections to threaten the man. He promised ruin—financial and reputation. And the man capitulated. He withdrew his sponsorship. Edwin, rather than follow his father's directives, left school and went to live with my brother. He wouldn't see us or speak with us. I begged my husband to allow Edwin to pursue science, but he refused. We thought he'd eventually come around, but two months later, my brother died, left everything to Edwin, and we lost the only leverage we had left to draw him home—money."

"Papa was never motivated much by money."

"We learned that too late."

"I still can't imagine he would give up his family, forever, for that. It seems so out of character." Ottilie studied Lady Sunderson, noticed her fingers—clenching, twisting, squeezing. "There is more."

Her grandmother nodded. "In the middle of all of this, your grandfather instructed our other two sons to cut off all contact with your father. They didn't want to, but they'd watched Lord Sunderson destroy Edwin's dreams and didn't want to incur his wrath against theirs. They obeyed."

"And Papa was alone."

"Completely." Lady Sunderson lifted her hand, but dropped it halfway to her face, as though too tired to finish the motion. "I will go now."

Ottilie watched her grandmother leave, able to see her father in the narrow shoulders and long neck. She imagined him in this room, poring over forbidden books and dreaming of a future of microscopes and dusty artifacts.

Poor Papa. He had been a bookish idealist, prone to losing himself for hours—days—in some new theory or another. He hadn't been created for conflict. How hurt he must have been, how trapped he must have felt, to have forsaken his family so completely. She closed her eyes and remembered the way his gaze would move around a room while he tried to explain something he'd just discovered. He never realized they all watched him with rapt attention because he'd been mesmerizing, not because of whatever topic had caught his attention.

Bittersweet longing pierced her. How she wished to spend an hour with him again. Fling herself through the years so that she could watch him, hands moving and words trailing, as he gave himself to the subject he most loved. But she'd had him. She'd *known* him.

Ottilie didn't regret the pain of losing him the way Lady Sunderson must.

Weariness settled over her when she recognized that her grandmother's grief must be a heavy weight indeed, one fused with regret and guilt. At least Ottilie was able to mourn free of that burden.

She removed her jacket and laid it over the back of a chair tucked into the corner of the room. Then she settled onto the bed, testing the springs. It would take some getting used to, sleeping in a bed again. She spared a thought for Thaddeus, wondering if he was enjoying his pudding in the kitchen, and the thought wove through her wandering mind that she should seek him out and see that he was all right. But the mattress was so inviting. The blanket she pulled over herself so warm. The fire crackling opposite her so cheerful.

And the journey had been so long. In more ways than miles and weeks.

She welcomed sleep. Where, for an hour, the twisting, narrow corridors of Hazelbrook Manor transformed into the dusty streets of Calcutta and the scent of ground spices perfumed the air. Where nature was allowed to reclaim cemeteries, one had only to show up for dinner, and relationships weren't fraught with complexities better left to poetry and politics.

17

Ottilie pressed her hand to the cold glass and looked out over the sleeping fields. Behind her, Thaddeus sprawled beneath layers of quilts and blankets. He'd crept into her room before the moon reached its zenith, just as he had each of the five nights they'd lived at Hazelbrook Manor.

The sun, made watery and bleak by a veil of wispy gray clouds, promised another cold day. Ottilie rubbed her arms, feeling the prick of hair beneath her wrapper. She never could seem to get warm. Even wearing three wool petticoats and sitting near the fire wasn't enough to dispel the chill that stiffened her fingers.

The sun was hardly bright enough to shed light on the letter she held. She lifted it to the window, eager for the encouragement on its pages to soften the frayed edges of her grief. With evidence of her friend's love, Ottilie thought she might be able to handle England's chill.

Dearest Ottilie,

I hope this letter sees you well settled. I waited two days before penning it. At first, I thought you might need more time to make sense of your new home before having your thoughts pulled back here, but then I realized you might be sorely in need of a comforting voice.

This won't be easy, I know. You have had a taste of it in Calcutta. You will encounter a lot of outright hostility and even more patronizing arrogance. My prayer is that your family will be a buffer between you and society's hatefulness. And maybe that handsome estate manager will be a buffer between you and loneliness. And you needn't bother defending against this, for I saw the expression on your face when we met him in the market.

Write to me soon and tell me about everything. My world is so small here in Calcutta. I am desperate for distraction. I will say good-bye now, for I have nothing of interest to tell you and I hate, more than anything, being a bore.

Your friend,
Damaris

Ottilie pressed a kiss to the letter and set it on the desk before making her way back to the bed.

"It's time to wake up, little glowworm." She ran her hand over Thaddeus's head, down his cheek, and tickled the sensitive area between his neck and collarbone. He giggled and rolled onto his side, then released a great snore. She laughed and pressed her cheek against his. "You can't fool me."

His snores grew louder and more dramatic.

Ottilie jumped up beside her brother and tickled his belly. "Time to wake up, you lazy boy."

His laughter choked out his pretend snores, and he threw his arms around her midsection. His head found the softness of her belly. "Why can't I just share a room with you like we did at home?"

"That's not how it's done here." She stroked his back and pressed a kiss to his wild curls. The first morning after their arrival, Ottilie awoke to a fire crackling in the hearth and the servant Jessamine standing over her with a tea tray, her eyebrows disappearing beneath the frilled cap that covered her hair.

"Are you all right?" Ottilie had asked, gripping the covers to her chest at the sight of this stranger so near as she slept.

"Yes, Miss Singh." But as she arranged the tea service on a table across the room, the maid's eyes kept straying to Thaddeus and Ottilie. With a shake of her head, she left. And later that day, Alberta had made it clear Thaddeus was to sleep in his own bed.

Ottilie hadn't told him that. She only woke before a servant came to light the fires and hustled Thaddeus to his room, where he would sleep for another hour or two.

A shudder ran over Thaddeus's body, and Ottilie carried him across the room to the door that led to his. When she laid him on his bed and tucked the blankets around him, he grabbed her hands and pressed them to his chest. "I miss home, Didi. When can we leave?"

Ottilie's nose burned with immediate tears. "I don't think we can."

His somber little face scrunched. "I'm trying to be patient and good, but I miss Dilip and our house and the river, and, Ottilie, I really miss good food."

A laugh dislodged Ottilie's sympathetic grief. "The food here is terrible, isn't it?"

"It's the worst food."

She thought of the little tin box containing Nānī's spices. She'd tucked it in her trunk, settled among the skirts and jackets, chemises and stockings. She didn't know when she'd have the opportunity to use them, but she was glad for her foresight. "I can't promise anything, but maybe I can convince the cook to allow me to use the kitchen soon."

His eyes brightened, and he squeezed her in a hug. Ottilie heard scraping in the hall outside the door. She pressed her finger to her lips and crept back into her own room, taking a moment to lean against the door and offer a prayer to the still faraway God who promised to provide. She wasn't certain if her silent plea made its way to his ears or fell to the floor like frozen drops of rain, but it was all she had to offer. *Please help make this home. Please don't let us miss India forever.*

The door pushed open, the maid in her black dress and stiff white apron startling. "Oh, I'm sorry, miss. Did I wake you?"

"No. Don't let me disturb your work." Ottilie sat on the edge of her bed and watched the maid go about her business. Outside of lighting the fires, Ottilie never saw her. There were other maids who did most of the cleaning. A couple of footmen, a housekeeper who hurried around looking harried, a butler that struck Ottilie as a little too old to hold the position, two ladies' maids—one for Alberta and one for Lady Sunderson—and the kitchen staff, whom Ottilie had seen when she first arrived but hadn't met. That didn't include the outdoor staff. This maid, though, was the only one who met her eyes. "What is your name?"

The girl looked up from her place kneeling at the fireplace. "Harriet, miss." She wasn't more than fourteen and had a wide freckled face that brought sunshine into the dark room. She finished her work, stood, and brushed her skirt. Lifting a bucket full of ashes and spent coal, she nodded at the fire. "Should be warmin' up soon, miss."

Ottilie approached and held her hands out toward the young flames. "Thank you."

Harriet grinned and left, taking her brightness with her. Ottilie sighed. Breakfast wouldn't be for hours yet. And her sleep since leaving India had been disturbed by dreams of her childhood. By memories of her family, whole and together, sitting in their snug parlor listening to Papa read from one of his treasured books of poetry. Or nestled between Nānī and Maji as they taught her to weave pictures with thread and beetle casings, or attending the little church in Lal Bazar, singing hymns. Songs of innocence that promised everything she'd lost.

Ottilie went to the desk beneath one of the multipaned windows. She pulled open the drawer, which scraped from disuse, and took out the familiar book she'd carried with her from home. The one with the worn black paper cover inscribed with gold. Blake's *Songs of Innocence and of Experience*.

She sat in the chair and stroked it. As a child, she'd begged Papa to read only from *Songs of Innocence*. Even though she'd grown up in a bustling city that was constantly heaving and expanding and forcing itself past its boundaries, her childhood had been idyllic. Their bungalow had featured a central courtyard and back garden, cut off from the nearest neighbor and hemmed in with banana plants and flowering vines.

Blake's poems set in rural England had appealed to her because they were familiar. She turned the pages, taking a moment to enjoy each hand-colored engraving before stopping on "The Lamb."

"'Little lamb who made thee,'" she read, remembering Papa's gentle voice, "'dost thou know who made thee, gave thee life and bid thee feed.'" She finished the poem, wishing the innocent questions Blake posed, coupled with sweet answers, would fill the room and her thoughts with certainty. With peace.

But as her voice drifted away from the final word, she looked up and saw nothing but a strange place where her father's ghost lingered but didn't console. A cold room despite the dancing flames. One full of heavy, sumptuous furniture that refused her sleep.

She could never return to that place of innocence. That place of green beauty and warm regard. She'd been too scarred by life. Too broken by all that had come after childhood. There was the before—before her father died in front of her. Before she watched her sister and brother suffer. Before Maji was killed. Before Nānī told her to leave India and then left them for heaven.

And now Ottilie was in the after.

She flipped forward a dozen pages, finding the poem she'd intensely disliked as a child. Her eyes skimmed until she came to the last stanza, and then her mouth joined the words swirling in her mind. "'Tyger Tyger burning bright, in the forests of the night. What immortal hand or eye, dare frame thy fearful symmetry?'"

No more were there wooly grazing lambs or children asking questions that could be answered within a two-stanza poem. There was only the surviving of each day. The stubborn determination to hold on to whatever shreds of childhood were left.

For the same God who created the lamb had formed the tiger. The same God who had given her Papa and Maji and the echoes of laughter and love also allowed cholera entry to her home.

Ottilie pressed her hands to her head. What a knotted bit of chaos it all was. How to make sense of it?

Everett's gentle words threaded through the patchwork of doubts and questions. *"I know that suffering produces strength of character."*

She tucked the book back into the drawer and went to the washstand. Dropping her wrapper to the ground, she rolled up the sleeves of her nightgown, cracked through the thin layer of ice in the bowl with the ceramic cup, and dipped a flannel cloth into the frigid water.

England was her home now. It was time to stop dwelling on innocence, for there was no going back to it. Instead, she would try to be a person Thaddeus could respect. A person of experience, yes, but also of strength and courage. Scrubbing the cloth over her arms, her skin turning red from the cold and friction, she determined to let go of the past. Focus instead on the future.

And the future was Thaddeus.

The moment Ottilie walked out the door later that day, wind sliced across her face. She drew back and wrinkled her nose. "It's so cold, Thaddeus. Maybe we should stay inside today."

"Please, Didi. I'm bored." Bundled up in long pants, sturdy boots, and a thick coat, he was ready to face a snowstorm. "And besides, Aunt Birdie said it's good for boys to have daily constitutionals."

Ottilie kept her eyes firmly on her brother's upturned face instead of rolling them toward the ceiling, a feat she felt deserved recognition of some sort. "Aunt Birdie" had been filling Thaddeus's head with all manner of cultural expectations during the one hour a day he spent with her and Lady Sunderson.

"*Aunt Birdie* didn't grow up in a tropical paradise where the sun warmed your head in February. It will take time to acclimate to this horrid weather." And everything else about this country.

"If you won't take Lord Sunderson for his constitutional, I will." Alberta appeared, her cloak hanging from thin shoulders and gloves in hand. "I'm headed to Elbury, but I'm in no hurry and can accompany him first."

Thaddeus clapped his hands, and Ottilie ground her teeth. "No, that isn't necessary. I'm feeling a sudden urge to walk, in fact."

She'd cross Antarctica if it meant keeping Alberta from increasing her influence on Thaddeus. In the week they'd been at Hazelbrook Manor, Thaddeus had been made to look like a proper little English gentleman. With his tousled curls trimmed and fine clothing pressed, he took *constitutionals* and had stopped pouting every time someone referred to him as Lord or Sunderson. She could see India slipping from him like an outgrown mantle.

"Why don't we walk together?" Alberta breezed past them, stepping out the door.

Ottilie stared after her. They'd hardly spoken since Ottilie's arrival. Alberta spent many hours each day doing charity in the villages peppering the countryside around the estate—teaching children to read and do sums at the small village school, tending to sick patients at the even smaller hospital, bringing baskets of food to the impoverished. If Ottilie hadn't borne an over-abundance of icy glares and sharp slights, she'd have thought Alberta a saint.

But Alberta had a motive completely at odds with her own. Alberta wanted Thaddeus to be as English on the inside as he looked on the outside. Ottilie wanted him never to forget that India wasn't something that could be bound up in the skin-deep. It was memories and people and home.

The back gardens, hemmed in by the two-hundred-year-old "new" wings, were gray and lifeless. Not a flower peeked its head above the dirt. No small animal scurried or crept. No insects buzzed or collected nectar. She crossed the paved paths that made perfect angles through the cemetery and let her eyes close. If she wound her arms around her stomach, tugged her coat more snugly around herself, ignored the cold biting her nose and ears, maybe she could feel the sun's warmth. She turned up her face and sniffed, hoping to catch the scent of jasmine, of cardamom and cumin, of Nānī's mustard oil, but there was nothing. England held no warmth or scent in winter.

Ottilie caught up to Alberta and Thaddeus, who were pointing out shapes in the clouds that looked like soan papdi floating across the sky. "Look at that one. It resembles a horse." Alberta glanced at him. "We'll have one of the grooms teach you how to sit on one soon. Would you like to ride?"

Thaddeus shrank from her question and shivered. "No. I don't like horses."

"Every gentleman must ride, Sunderson."

Thaddeus's gloved hand reached for Ottilie's, and he pushed against her side. "Do I have to, Didi? A horse killed Maji."

Ottilie crouched and pressed her finger to the tip of his nose, which was red as a berry. "A man killed Maji. The horse didn't mean to do it. It would be good to face your fear, glowworm, but you don't have to do it right away." She stood and squeezed his fingers. "Let's race. I think I'll win."

"You always say that and never do." Thaddeus placed one sturdy boot a foot in front of the other and bent his knees, arms ready to pump him toward victory.

Ottilie matched his stance, drooping only a little when Thaddeus asked Alberta to join them.

Alberta's brows rose to her hairline. "Run? That's hardly a suitable activity for a lady."

Ottilie ground her heel into the frozen ground, leveraging her weight for maximum speed. She wagged her brows in Thaddeus's direction. "Good thing I'm not a lady. Nor am I suitable." She grinned and shouted, "Go!"

As her legs ate up the distance, the wind grabbing her hat and tearing it from her head, she embraced the tightness in her chest. The way the cold air moved down her throat and filled her lungs. Thaddeus began to flag so she, ever so slightly so he wouldn't notice, slowed her pace.

He drew up beside her, his face pinched with effort. She grabbed her side and groaned. "I'm not sure I'll make it, Thaddeus. It's too far."

Her words spurred him forward. She limped a few more paces, then stilled, watching as he reached the shore of a large pond. He turned and waved his hands in the air. "I won! I told you I would."

"You always do," she called. She followed his path, smoothing her hands over her hair, lifting the locks that had fallen free from her chignon and tucking them back into place.

"You dropped your hat." Alberta drew beside her, handing it over. "Not that it would be a terrible thing to lose."

Ottilie took it from her. She ran her thumb over the fading lavender velvet ribbon that trimmed it. It was made of purple felt, a cluster of peacock feathers livening up its homely appearance. "It was my mother's." She pinned it back to her head and strode away. Thaddeus waited for her at the pond's edge, stooping to lift pebbles and clumps of dirt before tossing them over the water's surface.

Behind her, Alberta hurried to catch up. "I'm sorry about your mother. And father. And grandmother."

"And sister and brother."

"Them too."

Ottilie didn't look at her. She heard the compassion softening her aunt's voice, a foreign sound, and didn't want to see it on her stern face. Ottilie survived by ignoring the pain that threatened to engulf her the moment she paid it any heed. She didn't need kindness from Alberta. She needed indifference.

"We've both lost much." Alberta stood near Ottilie, and they stared at Thaddeus—the only one left of their family legacy. "A lot rests on him. Without Thaddeus, the title and estate will fall to a distant cousin none of us has ever met. My mother and I would be left with nothing. We would have to rely on the kindness of relatives willing to take us in. Our drop in status would be a hard thing to bear."

"You would bear it."

"As you did?"

Ottilie jerked her gaze toward Alberta.

"Everett told me of the reduced circumstances you and Thaddeus lived in."

"I didn't realize he'd visited. I would have liked to see him." Ottilie's words sounded strained even to her own ears. She forced her expression into one of placidity when Alberta's sharp glance tried to ferret out the hurt at Everett's neglect simmering beneath the surface.

"He hasn't visited. I was at Maybourne Park a couple of days ago, and we spoke."

"You are close, he told me."

"We grew up together. There were no other children near my class. Not that he is, though at least his benefactor is wealthy enough that it eased the burden of those differences. I was so much younger than my siblings—they'd all gone on to their lives before I was even born—and Everett became like a brother."

"I've wondered since I found out . . . why does he work if he's heir to such an empire?"

"Everett isn't the type to rely on others to take care of things. He likes to be useful. He not only manages the property but also helps in the management of the business."

"It seems odd that Mr. Fernsby would bequeath his estate to a relation so distant he'd not bothered to help them when they went to the poorhouse."

Alberta's cheeks turned red, and she started for the pond and Thaddeus, carefully picking her way over the uneven ground. "Everett told me of my brother's mismanagement. It seems your father cared as little for your future security as my father thought of mine."

Ottilie recognized the diversion, but Alberta's accusation shook Ottilie's voice, her hands . . . and her loyalty. And that deserved defense, for there were already too many things to raise her fist against. "My father was wonderful. I won't listen to you speak ill of him." A crack appeared in her memory of Papa—encouraging, affectionate, brilliant. Flawed.

"How can you not be angry at him? When I think of my father, spending every moment of his life protecting his sons' inheritance while ignoring my future, I could rage in a way that would set all of society against me."

"I had no time for anger. Thaddeus was my responsibility, especially after Maji died. I worried only about survival." She looked at Alberta, taking in the severe set of her mouth, the small lines snaking out from the corners of her eyes, the tightness of her jaw. She was no longer a young woman, blooming with youth and vitality, but family often made up for a lack of beauty. "Perhaps your father expected you to marry."

"I'm sure he did, initially, but he knew that would not happen by the time I reached twenty. He had time to think of me."

There was a story in what Alberta didn't say, and Ottilie sensed there might be more to her aunt than rigid adherence to propriety. "Papa's head was too full of ancient dates and poetry to pay any mind to the future."

"Father always said Edwin was a man without sense." She looked at Ottilie, a wrinkle between her brows, and a door shut. Ottilie could almost see the shuttering of Alberta's eyes. Light dimming. A severing of the fragile strand that connected them. "Your father was foolish. Perhaps even more foolish than we've been led to believe."

The walls Ottilie had erected in her life to protect her heart from innuendo and accusation were as solid as those of Fort William. But in softening toward Alberta, in hoping for a relationship, she'd knocked down a few stones, and it had left her vulnerable. "What are you implying?"

"Only that there isn't the slightest resemblance between you and Lord Sunderson, and everyone has heard that the heat in India makes men stupid and easy prey. If you're any proof, your mother must have been beautiful. Surely my brother wasn't the only one to take note."

Whispers from the past tormented her. Alberta's insults only joined a dozen others. Raised eyebrows when Papa introduced her to colleagues, and discriminatory treatment from teachers at her exclusive school who made sure Ottilie knew British men just didn't marry Indian women after the mutiny, so . . .

So Ottilie probably wasn't Edwin Russell's daughter. Or Thaddeus's sister. Maji might have seduced him, but it was obvious it happened long after Ottilie had been born.

Ottilie replaced the stones that had fallen free from their walls, creating her own elytra-like home. One that couldn't be torn down by carelessness and prejudice. One that left her very much alone. "I'm sure we can send for the marriage certificate, if you'd like to see it." She kept her emotions tucked away. Protected from derision. "My father loved Maji because she was beautiful, yes, but also interesting and kind and good. She was a vibrant bloom against a landscape of wilting English roses. He could not have made a wiser choice."

Alberta studied her. Her eye twitched. Then she looked at Thaddeus again. "I'm just grateful Thaddeus looks nothing like her. And you look nothing like Edwin. It might be enough to keep this house of cards from toppling." Then she strode away.

Ottilie didn't resemble Thaddeus, it was true, but if Alberta had only looked more closely, she would have seen Edwin Russell's fingerprints all over her. And not only in ways beyond the surface.

"I have his eyes," Ottilie said, but the wind stole her words, tearing them apart in a violent show of power and aggression. Who would hear her? Who cared enough to notice?

18

Three days after she'd almost-but-not-quite shared a moment with Alberta, Ottilie slid the door between her room and Thaddeus's closed. She'd awoken worried when he wasn't curled up against her and crept across floors touched by winter. It had been so cold, and he was unused to it. What if he had fallen ill? Or frozen to death in his bed?

She found him wrapped in his blankets, and the gentle rise and fall of his chest beneath her palm settled her nerves before wistfulness swept through her. He'd been sleeping within reach for five years.

She wanted to clutch those fleeting tendrils of childhood and hold them in her fists. Not let go. Because today she'd woken up alone. Who knew what changes tomorrow would bring.

Ottilie was so tired of change.

She tugged at the sash around her waist, cinching her wrapper tighter, and went back to her room. Lighting the lamp on the desk near the window, she took in the scene. Frost iced the glass with delicate lace, and a dusting of snow had fallen on the ground far below. A prickle of excitement urged her closer to the window. She'd never seen snow anywhere but in books. For the first time since coming to England, Ottilie found the surroundings lovely.

She glanced at Thaddeus's door, knowing he would enjoy the sight. Mornings were the loneliest part of days adorned with homesickness. She would love to share this moment with someone.

But Thaddeus needed sleep. And she needed to renew her relationship with one whom she'd pushed away over the last few years.

She opened the drawer, shoved aside Blake's book of poetry, and withdrew Nānī and Niraja's Bible.

Turning the gilt-edged pages, she skimmed stories of creation and sacrifice, life and death, love and jealousy. In the margins were scribbled notes, questions posed by two sisters trying to understand this foreign god, and sketches of the tapestry, in various stages of design, now hanging on her aunt's bedroom wall.

Ottilie stopped in Psalms and read an underlined passage.

My God, my God, why hast thou forsaken me? why art thou so far from helping me, and from the words of my roaring? O my God, I cry in the day time, but thou hearest not; and in the night season, and am not silent.

Niraja, her script feathery and full of lovely loops, had taken up the entire right margin to write, over and over, *Why hast thou forsaken me?*

Ottilie wondered when her aunt had written those words. What had befallen her to cause such thoughts? Her own burned with the same question. *Why, God? Why have you left me to this? Why are you silent?*

A tear dripped from her nose, splashing the page below her fingers. She wiped the water away and saw, written below her aunt's question, in letters small and even, Nānī's response. *Psalm 143:8.*

Hope, fanned by the Bible's flipping pages, surged through Ottilie as she searched for her answer.

Cause me to hear thy lovingkindness in the morning; for in thee do I trust: cause me to know the way wherein I should walk; for I lift up my soul unto thee.

And beside that, another Scripture reference. *Psalm 59:16.*

But I will sing of thy power; yea, I will sing aloud of thy mercy in the morning: for thou hast been my defence and refuge in the day of my trouble.

Ottilie traced Nānī's words, her grandmother's presence so near she could almost smell the fennel seeds Nānī chewed after her meals. Could almost hear her voice, steady and strong, instructing Ottilie how to properly trim elytra. Could almost feel the papery-thin skin of her feet beneath her fingers.

Niraja, there are so many times we're instructed to praise God in the morning. Maybe that's what we must do. Before everyone awakens, pray. And listen. Perhaps he will speak in the quiet.

Conviction passed through Ottilie like a needle through silk. How long had it been since she'd praised God? Sat in the silence and waited on him? She wondered where her faith had gone. Where he had gone. When really she was the one who had left. She set the Bible on the desk and cradled her head in her hands atop it.

I'm here now. Please, Lord, guide me in what I should do. Help me. She thought of the words in the psalm and lifted her head. Outside the window, the sun embraced the hills and valleys. It glinted against the snow, creating fields of diamonds. *Sing aloud of thy mercy in the morning.*

She couldn't claim a beautiful voice, not like Maji and Nānī, but she sang anyway. A made-up song, far from the poetry in

Papa's books, but sincere. She sang words in faith, words she didn't quite believe but wished to. She sang aloud every pain, every fear, every longing. She sang until the clattering bang of metal sounded louder than her song.

Ottilie sat up straight in her chair and opened her eyes.

Harriet stood just inside the door, her bucket on the floor, ashes spilling from it. She clapped her hands over her mouth. "I'm so sorry, miss," came her muffled apology.

Ottilie's face burned, but she looked less uncomfortable than Harriet, who had stooped and was using a small brush to sweep the ashes back into the bucket.

The girl kept glancing at Ottilie, her eyes wide and filled with worry. "I just startled when I opened the door and heard you singin', is all."

"It's all right." Ottilie glanced out the window, noting the sun just barely peeking above the horizon. "You're early this morning."

Harriet smacked her hands against her knees, then stood, a sheepish smile revealing the large space between her two front teeth. "I hurried through the rest of the rooms, 'cause I look forward to seein' you. It makes my morning feel less lonely. I have twelve brothers and sisters at home, you see. We're crammed head to foot in bed, and they're always around. I'm not used to the quiet here."

Ottilie smiled, grateful for the reminder that she wasn't so alone in her loneliness after all. In missing the hum of another's snores. The pressure of a body beside her own. "I understand. And I'm grateful for your early visits as well. The mornings here are so gloomy, aren't they? So cold. It makes one feel as though they are the only person on earth."

"Wait till spring. Everything will grow green, and the lambs will be playing in the fields, and the trees will bloom. The wait of winter only makes it sweeter when it comes. That's what my ma says."

"She sounds very wise. Do you miss her?"

"I see her Sundays, on my half day. I was raised right over the hill, in the village. The whole lot of them liv—"

The door to Thaddeus's chamber slammed open, and a blur of white cotton rushed into the room, ramming into Ottilie's midsection and screeching a jumble of Bengali and English. "I had the worst dream. That you were lost, and I couldn't find you. You weren't there. I couldn't find my way home." Tears tracked down his cheeks, and a shudder shook his little body.

Ottilie dropped to her knees, heedless of the floor biting through the thin fabric of her nightgown, and wrapped him tightly. He pressed his head into the curve of her neck and twisted her braid in his fist the way he had when he was a babe. "No, no. I'm not lost. I'm right here. It was only a dream, glow-worm."

She held him until his sobs turned to hiccups. "You weren't near when I woke, and I thought it was true and I was all alone. Maji is gone, and Nānī is gone, and you were gone too."

"I haven't gone. You only slept soundly and didn't wake in the middle of the night."

He pulled away, and his hand found her cheek, his gaze her heart. "I love you, Didi."

"I love you too."

He looked over her shoulder, his brows knit together and his nose wrinkled. "Who is that?"

The Bengali words had slipped from his tongue too smoothly. Too obviously. Ottilie turned and saw Harriet standing straight and stiff as the iron streetlamps lining Chowringhree Street. Her eyes were wide enough to reflect the flames now dancing in the hearth.

Ottilie whispered to Thaddeus, "English only," then stood and took his hand. "I need to prepare Lord Sunderson for breakfast."

Harriet blinked, and her face turned red. "I'm so sorry, my lord." She scuttled from the room.

"Why must I only speak in English?" Thaddeus asked.

Ottilie ran her palm over the top of his head, smoothing down the thick clusters that stood straight up. "We're in England now, and it confuses people when you speak Bengali or Hindi."

Thaddeus crossed his arms. "I don't like it here. I can't tell anyone you're my sister. I can't help Cook in the kitchen. I can't go outside without someone following me. I can't speak Bengali. I can't sleep in the same room as you. There are so many *can't*s." His face scrunched together. "I miss home."

Ottilie gathered him up again. "I do too, but we need to make this home now."

"How can it be home when nothing feels the way it should?"

Ottilie didn't answer. Couldn't, really. If home was made by feeling, then she didn't think she'd ever know it again.

While Thaddeus worked on his sums and then read through a book of English history, Ottilie pulled out her sewing box and began stitching a set of handkerchiefs. She thought she'd mail them to Damaris, whose friendship Ottilie dearly missed. She saw her friend's wide, welcome smile in the pink zinnia she worked into the corner of the linen. Zinnias for an absent friend.

After lunch, Ottilie led Thaddeus down the stairs to the drawing room for his visit with Lady Sunderson and Alberta. Their days had formed a pattern. Ottilie had breakfast in the dining room with Alberta. Thaddeus ate in the third-floor schoolroom later, while she prepared his day's lessons. Then schoolwork. Thaddeus's constitutional, no matter the weather. Lunch in the schoolroom. An hour-long visit in the drawing room. Then freedom, when Thaddeus played and Ottilie embroidered and they spoke in Bengali and told stories of Calcutta. Tea. Another walk around the grounds. An early dinner in the schoolroom Ottilie felt acted more like a prison. And then bed. The first few days, they had eaten their meals with Lady Sunderson and Alberta in the dining room, but Thaddeus had been banished to the schoolroom after settling in, and Ottilie couldn't stand the thought of him eating all his meals alone.

Everything was regimented. Structured. Monotonous. Ottilie had asked Wakefield one afternoon if he could direct her to the village—she and Thaddeus needed a change of scenery—but he had gravely said, "That's not possible." She was beginning to wonder if Lady Sunderson and Alberta intended to keep her locked away in the manor forever.

The only member of the staff who spoke to her with any kindness was Harriet. The rest either outright ignored her or sent her gazes full of fear and hatred. Even Mrs. Wood, the housekeeper, remained distant. It seemed Ottilie had filled the role of governess whether Lady Sunderson wished for it or not.

Ottilie stopped beside the drawing room door and turned to smooth Thaddeus's hair. She ran her thumbs over his brows and wiped a few errant crumbs from the corner of his mouth. Then she took his hand, and they entered the room.

Lady Sunderson and Alberta were seated where they always were, on one of the canopied settees, but across from them, in the space Ottilie usually took, was Everett. He hadn't turned when she entered, but she recognized the breadth of his back, the straight lines of his shoulders, the precise way his hair ended at the nape of his neck, the curve and pointed tips of his ears. All apathy deserted her, and a thrill shot to her toes.

She hadn't seen him since they spoke in the cemetery the day they arrived at Hazelbrook Manor. She'd grown so accustomed to his presence in Calcutta, to seeing him nearly every day, to their long comfortable stretches of silence and their conversations. He'd become a thread of sorts, connecting India with England, the past and present. He was the thing that bound these two disparate parts of her life.

"Everett!" Thaddeus tugged away from Ottilie and,

unhampered by the proper restraint and cool acknowledgment propriety demanded, darted across the room.

She wished she could too. Tears pricked her eyes. Tears that weren't about grief and loss but of being near someone who remembered the place and the people she loved. She smiled when Thaddeus threw himself at Everett and squeezed his neck.

Ottilie rounded the settee, putting her back to Alberta's disapproving scowl. She couldn't ignore her aunt's voice, though. "That's enough, Sunderson. What a show."

"Let him be, Alberta," Lady Sunderson said. "It's good to see the child smile."

Everett pressed his hand against the back of Thaddeus's head and looked at Ottilie, his wide smile a healing oil poured over the jagged loneliness and heartache that had become her constant companion. It warmed her as surely as the sun and, in this gloomy corner of England, was a more reliable thing to rest upon.

Finally, Everett set Thaddeus away with a pat, then stood and took Ottilie's hand. "I'm sorry my work hasn't allowed me to visit sooner. There was much to catch up on."

His words were formal, his voice affected, but his eyes shown with the gleam she had grown to love in Calcutta and dreamed of in Wiltshire.

"I understand. Alberta has told me how busy it keeps you."

"Would you care to take a walk?" he asked.

She didn't—it had taken nearly an hour to thaw after the walk she'd taken earlier with Thaddeus. "Of course."

Lady Sunderson smiled. "How nice that will be." She went to the bell pull, and when Wakefield appeared at the door, she said, "Please have someone fetch Miss Singh's coat."

Wakefield disappeared with a nod, and Thaddeus's chatter filled the silence as he told Everett about his new room and the bland food and the funny servants who bowed to him or turned into the corner when he entered a room. Jessamine appeared with Ottilie's coat and thrust it at her, eyes narrowed in antagonism.

Ottilie ignored the maid. She wouldn't let the staff's prejudice cast a shadow on her reunion with Everett. She shrugged into her coat and took his arm.

It was just as cold as it had been that morning, but Everett's nearness, his gloved hand resting on hers, which was tucked into his elbow, warmed her. "It's lovely to see you."

He released his smile, free as they were from Alberta's stifling disapproval, and Ottilie's mood lifted. "I've missed you."

"Have you?"

"Of course. We grew to be good friends, didn't we?"

"I believe so."

They passed through the formal garden and crossed the lawn. Once they reached the pond, he led her along it until they reached a cluster of evergreen trees that shaded its south side. Their steps were muffled by fallen needles, and the spicy scent of pine tickled her nose. She inhaled deeply, remembering stories her father told of Christmas trees and snapping fires and riding through the woods. They had all seemed so foreign and exotic to her as a child who'd only known tropical plants and heat and wide, paved streets. Being here, inhaling her father's childhood, softened her toward this place she didn't belong. "Where are we going?"

"The orangery. I thought you might like the warmth of it."

Ottilie had no expectation—she didn't even know what an orangery was—but when they cleared the trees, she gasped. A small multiwindowed building that looked as though it had been plucked from a fairy tale beckoned her forward. It was painted white and sported a domed glass roof, and through the windowed door she could see living things. Green things.

"It was originally used to house just citrus-fruit plants, but now the family uses it as a general greenhouse. The roof lantern was removed when they added the glazed roof, but it's still heated beneath the floor by flues and a stove."

"Heated?"

"It is warm inside."

Ottilie bit her lower lip and pressed closer to Everett in her excitement. Closer than she intended. His arm cradled her back, his hand on her waist, and the look he gave her—the longing in it—was warmer than any stove.

He swallowed and stepped away from her. The way he cleared his throat and tugged at his ear was perhaps even more endearing than his smile. "Right, then. Let's go in, shall we?"

He opened the door, and Ottilie stepped into a place that felt like home. The scent of gardenia, orange, and oleander tugged her heart toward India, and the windows that spanned the walls and roof gathered every bit of watery sun, creating a tapestry of light on the heated floor. For the first time since arriving in England, Ottilie felt she could breathe.

She pulled off her gloves, finger by finger, and dropped them onto an iron bench just inside the door. She unwound her shawl, removed her coat, tugged off her hat, leaving them in a heap beside her gloves. Then she set off to explore the plants, to touch the shiny leaves and sniff the spicy petals. She pushed her face into the feathery fronds of a fern and hugged the spindly trunk of a lemon tree.

"Do you like it in here?" Everett asked, laughing. He plucked a jolly-looking zinnia from its stem and tucked it behind her ear.

"I love it. I'd have spent every moment here if I'd known about it sooner."

"I don't think Lady Sunderson or Alberta ever visit. Otherwise they might have told you about it."

Ottilie looked up at him, catching the flower as it tumbled from her ear. "I'm glad you showed it to me. I'm glad you're here." She laid her hand against his cheek, and he covered it with his own.

For a moment she thought he was going to say something. Something that would fan her hope, would make her forget Victor and his betrayal, but he shook his head and backed away—just one step.

It seemed much farther. Her arm dropped. He was her only friend in England, and she could almost see him layering brick upon brick between them. A wall that shut her out.

He offered her his elbow, but she found no warmth in it now, so she drew away from him and tucked her hands together. They walked the same direction, separated by the width of the path. By so much more she didn't understand.

She was tired of not understanding. She was tired of the loneliness and isolation.

"I miss the friendship we had in Calcutta. This . . . this feels different. And I don't know why."

His steps faltered, and he looked at her, a wounded expression shadowing his eyes. "I've never said aloud this thing that haunts me. Even though I've known since I was ten. It comes between me and everyone. It poisons every relationship I've ever had. And I'm sorry I've hurt you. I didn't mean to. I didn't mean to care for you, because I know we can't ever be."

"Why?" Ottilie whispered. "What is it? Is it because I'm Indian? Poor? Because I have nothing of value to offer? Am I not enough?"

She turned and walked away, unable to keep up the pretense that her heart still beat steadily within her chest. She didn't want him to see her devastation at the finality of his words. She'd been foolish. It was a child's dream, this attachment she'd formed. Yes, she could tell he cared for her. But he'd never once given her any indication he would pursue her. That she was worth pursuing. He'd told her what he wanted—a wife who would lift his status. That would never be her.

But still, in the neglected part of herself where she'd tucked all her dreams, she wondered if they could have the kind of love her parents had shared. Papa and Maji had proven an interracial marriage could work.

A sob escaped her lips. She lifted her skirts and darted toward the door. Her steps beat out the prophecy she'd been running from since Victor had chosen the military over her. *Alone. Alone. You'll always be alone.*

No matter how far she ran, she couldn't escape the narrative God had been fashioning for her—a story of constant loss and never belonging.

She fumbled for the door handle as her breath heaved.

"Ottilie," Everett said, his steps pounding toward her, "wait."

She pushed open the door, and the wind brushed away the tears tracking down her cheeks, leaving only a scattering of frozen imprints. The chill stole her breath, and she tugged the door closed. "I want to go home."

"I'll walk you."

"All the way to India?" Her laugh sounded bitter, full of everything she'd wanted and been denied, given then lost.

"That's a greater threat to Christian faith . . ."

Her aunt's words shot into Ottilie's consciousness. *Oh God, how can I release it? Every time I feel as though I'm climbing out from bitterness, something else steals my peace. My joy. How much loss can I sustain before I'm left with nothing except my anger?*

"I'm sorry, Ottilie," Everett said. "There are no easy answers."

She spun. "Then give me one, at least. Tell me why you resist this . . . whatever this is between us. I know it's there. You know it's there." Her legs and arms began to tremble, and she pressed her hands to the sides of her skirt. Words that had been prancing around her thoughts since they had stopped at the bakery in Calcutta slipped from her consciousness, dripping with disdain. "Is it because my father wasn't a member of that club in Bristol?"

Everett touched her arm, his fingers making promises he couldn't keep. Tenderness softened his mouth, and he closed his eyes. "There is so much standing between us. And yes, that is something to consider."

She pulled away and retrieved her gloves and coat. They were heavy, and she wanted nothing more than for him to give her a reason to discard them and find warmth in his embrace. But instead her words were brick upon brick, dividing them with things left unspoken. "Then there is nothing to be said." She slipped her arms into the sleeves.

"But there is. If only you will allow me to gather the courage I need to say it."

Ottilie stared at him, her fingers twisting the ruff of fur that was meant to keep her warm. How cold she was.

The door burst open, and a tumble of dry leaves ushered Harriet into the orangery. "Miss Singh, you must come. There's been an accident."

19

Harriet's frantic words chased Ottilie across the lawn. *There's been an accident. Lord Sunderson has fallen.*

"Please, oh please, God, my brother. Please." Her prayer churned faster than her steps, and by the time she reached the house, her mouth was dry, her face chapped. She slammed through the front door, ignoring Wakefield's stunned silence. "Where is he?"

"Who?"

My brother. My life. All that is left of my heart. "Lord Sunderson." A sob shook her. "Please, where is he?"

"He is with the family. Miss Russell has instructed you to wait in the drawing room."

Ottilie cursed. The fact that she spoke in Bengali did little to diminish the shock on Wakefield's face. "I will see him now."

The butler only raised a brow, then strode away.

"Tell me where to find him," Ottilie shouted at his back. He disappeared, and she pressed her hands to her chest, trying to hold back the scream that begged release. A maid peeked out from the library, her wide eyes taking up half her pinched face. When she saw Ottilie, she ducked away, but not before disgust twisted her mouth.

"Miss Singh," Harriet's soft voice made its way past the violence that tore at Ottilie, "your brother's been taken to the back parlor."

Ottilie jerked her head around, the shock blanketing Everett's face likely mirrored on her own. "You know?"

Harriet nodded. "Anyone who looked closely enough would. I have enough brothers and sisters to recognize the love between the two of you is more than what has been told to us. And your eyes are the exact shape and color of his."

Ottilie gripped Harriet's arm. That she could feel more connection with the lowliest housemaid than her relatives didn't shock her. But that Harriet noticed what even her own aunt refused to acknowledge landed a blow that made Ottilie's loneliness an even larger, more consuming presence. "Thank you for your loyalty and friendship. And for noticing."

"Come," Everett said, "I'll go with you." He guided her to the back parlor and didn't bother knocking before opening the door.

Thaddeus lay supine on an ornate sofa, his arms resting by his side. Lady Sunderson sat in a chair near his head, worrying a lace-edged handkerchief, and Alberta stood behind the couch, looking down at Thaddeus, her face pale and drawn.

Ottilie raced across the room and dropped to the floor. Taking Thaddeus's hand, she held his wrist to her lips, all the tension leaving her body at the steady beat of his pulse. She touched his face, her hand moving over his forehead, his neck, his chest and abdomen, looking for injury.

His eyes fluttered. "My head hurts, Didi."

His lashes brushed the gentle swell of his cheeks, and when she ran her fingers through his hair, she found crusting dirt and a lump the size of a betel nut. She probed it gently until he flinched. "Sweet glowworm, what happened?"

"He fell," Lady Sunderson answered. Using the corner of her handkerchief, she wiped a smudge of dirt from Thaddeus's cheek. "He was unconscious only a minute, but we've sent for Dr. Dancey. He should be here shortly."

"What are you doing in here?" Alberta circled the couch and sat on the edge of the velvet pillow, wedging her hip between Ottilie and her brother. Ottilie moved nearer Thaddeus's head. "I told Wakefield to keep you out."

"Alberta!" Lady Sunderson said, her soft features sharpened by disapproval. "Why would you tell him that? Of course Ottilie would want to be with Sunderson. And I'm sure the child feels much better now that his sister is near."

Animosity poured off Alberta's stiffened shoulders in waves. It filled the room with an almost tangible hostility. "I was only worried the doctor and servants would talk."

"They're already talking, Alberta," Everett said. "I'm not sure how you expect to keep this a secret for long. You know as well as I that keeping things hidden only causes more problems."

Alberta glared at Everett, but behind the anger, Ottilie could see a frisson of fear. Alberta's façade showed another crack.

Thaddeus lifted his hand, pumping his fingers, and Ottilie took them between her own. She kissed his knuckles in turn, whispering a soft "*sona bhai*" after each press of her lips.

"Stop speaking that horrid language," Alberta snapped. "It sounds absolutely ghastly, and it would be best if no one knew Sunderson could understand it."

Thaddeus sniffed, and a tear slipped from the corner of his eye. Ottilie bit back a rush of words—in English—that would burn Alberta's ears. "I will not allow him to forget the language of his mother and grandmother." She brushed Thaddeus's temple with a kiss. "You did nothing wrong, glowworm."

He turned his head away, and his cries hitched, one atop the other, turning into hiccups as he held them in.

"You'll spoil him," Alberta continued. "He's been indulged and shows a proclivity toward melodrama."

Using her hands to leverage herself against the couch, Ottilie pushed her torso forward, coming within inches of Alberta's prim, priggish face. "When you have children, I will allow you to give me advice. Until then, you will leave the rearing of him to me."

Alberta's chin trembled, and her gaze clouded. "Who do you think you are, speaking to me like that?"

"Who do you think you are? You are nothing to him. To us. You are a stranger who has shown only contempt toward our culture and the love and affection our parents lavished on us. So what if I indulge Thaddeus's feelings? He has lost *everything*."

"He's just been *given* everything. Everett told me how you lived. How poor you were. How Sunderson was ill-treated at school. How you couldn't even afford to pay for a pastry or a doctor."

Ottilie's stomach clenched, and bile soured her mouth. She glanced over her shoulder at Everett, whose arms hung heavy at his sides and whose eyes avoided hers. Everything Alberta said was true. She couldn't deny it. But she hadn't expected Everett to share the extent of those shameful details with this woman. She'd thought their affection for one another meant he'd have kept certain things in confidence. He had been clear about his friendship with Alberta. Ottilie had only thought he cared for her as well.

She returned her attention to Thaddeus. Smoothed the wrinkles from his jacket, and refocused on what was important. "How did he fall?"

Alberta looked away and began to pick at her cuticles with nervous movements.

Ottilie's skin tingled. "What happened?"

Lady Sunderson filled in the silence. "He fell from Tyche."

Ottilie's brow wrinkled. Was that some kind of strange English metaphor? "The Greek goddess of chance?"

Lady Sunderson's lips tipped into a becoming smile. "And Birdie's mare."

"Her horse?" Ottilie stared at her grandmother, mouth open.

"Yes. She's typically a calm animal, but Sunderson panicked

and began kicking when the groom set him upon her. Tyche reared, and he fell, hitting his head on the stall."

Everett spoke the thoughts swirling in Ottilie's mind. "You put the boy on a *horse*?"

Alberta waved her hand in a breezy, dismissive manner. "It would have been fine had he not made such a fuss."

Ottilie jumped to her feet, fists clenched. "Of course he made a fuss. He is terrified of horses. Surely you can understand, given the fact that his mother was *killed* by one. We have already discussed this. I told you Thaddeus wasn't ready yet."

"And I told you all gentlemen ride. This wouldn't have been an issue if he hadn't been coddled his entire life."

"Why was I not part of this conversation?" Lady Sunderson asked. "The two of you seem to be making a lot of decisions—all irreconcilable, it seems—on your own. Perhaps, if you involved me, these things could be worked out without knives being drawn."

Ottilie glanced at Thaddeus, who had rolled onto his side and covered his ears with his hands. His slim shoulders quaked beneath silent sobs. Her belly knotted like thread knocked about by careless hands, and she wished for a dupatta or the fringe of a sari to hide her face. Releasing all her tension and frustration on Alberta felt good in the moment, but it had only frightened her brother. Had only widened the gulf between her and everyone else in the room.

She pressed her fingers to her lips and wordlessly mouthed a prayer of repentance. *Forgive me my bitterness. Help me release it to you.* She sat beside Thaddeus and brushed the curls from his forehead.

Everett approached with tentative steps and cleared his throat. "I'm going to return home, Ottilie. Dr. Dancey is capable. I think you'll like him."

She nodded, eyes still riveted on her brother.

"I'll be back tomorrow to check on Sunderson."

Thaddeus sighed and dropped his hands. "Don't call me that, Everett."

"But it's who you are."

"No, it's not. I'm Thaddeus Russell." His expression pinched. "My head hurts. I want to go to bed." His little face crumpled, and tears tracked his cheeks. "I want Maji, Ottilie. And Nānī. I want to go home. Can we go home?"

He sat up, crying out and pushing his hand against his forehead. He ignored Alberta's chastisement and launched himself into Ottilie's lap. She wrapped him in her arms, gathering him as close as she could. His fingers wound into the hair at the base of her neck, pulling out a strand.

"I want them too." But English didn't fully express her anguish, so she pulled from the more expressive languages of Hindi and Bengali, whispering words she hoped would comfort him in their shared grief. Words no one else in the room would understand. Or judge.

And when all those words were spent, she returned to English. Because she wanted these to be understood. "You are Thaddeus Russell, the love of Edwin and Sonia Russell. The delight of Gitisha Singh. Nothing else you become will change who you are. There is no shame in being only you. No matter what anyone calls you, no matter who they think you are, you will always be Thaddeus Russell."

And Ottilie wouldn't allow the expectations that came with his title to steal that away.

After two days of rest, Thaddeus's headaches and lethargy disappeared, and Ottilie felt it safe for him to spend the night in his own room again. The third morning, after her first restful sleep since his accident, she sat up against the pillows in her bed, a writing desk pulled over her legs. She'd never written back to Damaris. Hadn't had the heart to tell her friend she'd found no acceptance at Hazelbrook Manor. But she'd received two more letters since that first one, keeping her in a steady supply of comfort and love. She owed a response. A truthful one. For Damaris was no fool.

She put her pen back to the paper and allowed herself to write without censorship.

It isn't that my grandmother and aunt seem to despise me. It is more that Lady Sunderson putters around as though too stunned by the death of her eldest son to deal with news of Maji's heritage. And Alberta seems beset by a powerful fear of society—a strange thing, as she's cut herself off from it entirely and holds it in no great esteem. She possesses secrets, just like everyone else in my family.

The servants . . . they do despise me. All but one, a young girl named Harriet who looks uncomplicated but possesses perhaps the keenest mind of anyone in this household. I try to hide it all from Thaddeus—he is so very homesick—but everyone else conspires against me in this and thinks nothing of deliberate rudeness and outright hostility.

I miss you desperately, Damaris. Here I have too much time alone with my thoughts. And I'm afraid those are rather bleak right now.

As she tapped the pen to her teeth, thinking through the ways she could end on a positive note, Thaddeus slammed through his door and climbed into bed with her, twining his arms around her middle. He whispered, "It's snowing."

Ottilie tucked him closer, borrowing his heat. "And you're seven today. Happy birthday, glowworm."

He bolted upright. "I forgot!" He scampered from the bed and climbed atop Ottilie's desk. Pressing his nose and palms against the window, he bounced up and down, rubbing his bare feet together like a grasshopper.

Ottilie pushed off the blankets and reached for her wrapper lying at the end of the bed. "What would you like to do today?"

He stilled. "Can I do anything?"

"Anything. It's not every day a person turns seven."

A hearty sigh escaped his throat. "I want to go home."

"Oh, Thaddeus, I wish we could." He turned, and she patted the bed beside her. When he snuggled back into her arms, she pressed a light kiss to the tender spot that had swelled when he fell from the horse. "Let's not think on these sad things. It's a day to celebrate."

"I've never had a birthday without Maji and Nānī. Or Dilip."

"I know. But I'm here, and we can make the best of it. How about I see if the cook will allow me to make you a special treat? Why don't you go get dressed, and I'll retrieve my spices."

Thaddeus whooped and jumped off the bed. He dashed across her room and disappeared into his own. She could hear him singing a hymn in Bengali with as much gusto as if a choir joined him. A laugh wove its way from her belly to her lips, wrapping around her heart and displacing some of the sorrow that had become embedded there.

With light steps, she went to the desk and took Nānī's Bible into her lap. Already this habit had become as necessary to her as breathing. And the more she filled her mind and spirit with words that brought life, the more steady her faith had grown. If ever the night in her soul consumed her thoughts, she pulled on the Scripture she pored over morning after morning, and while it didn't disappear completely, it hushed enough that she could feel the chill leaving her bones.

"What have you to say this morning, Nānī?" Her grandmother's faith had come after Niraja's but had grown faster. Surer. Stronger. And what Gitisha Singh meant to comfort and guide her sister now, forty years later, worked in her granddaughter's life.

She opened the Bible, letting the pages fall where they may.

A more conscientious student would follow a deliberate course of study, but Ottilie wanted only to pamper her brittle faith. She wanted to indulge in her grandmother's wisdom and take time to ease back into the trust and devotion that had marked her youth.

Today, Nānī's long-ago reflections resonated within Ottilie's fractured spirit. These Scriptures in Ecclesiastes drew her attention because Nānī had circled only a few words in the entire chapter. Usually Ottilie found underlined passages—entire verses—but here, set apart with thick black ink, were the words *dance*, *sew*, *embrace*, and *love*. And in the margins, Nānī's words:

> *Niraja, these are all the things I love best. If I am able to dance and sew and love and be embraced, my life, no matter how it looks, will be a fine one.*

Ottilie had never considered Nānī particularly kissed by fate. She'd been abandoned by her husband, had lost nearly every member of her family, had suffered poverty and a reduced status, had endured much, and yet . . .

From behind the sadness, long-forgotten memories spilled into Ottilie's consciousness. Raising her arms, Nānī laughed, that little bit of flesh that made for homey embraces jiggling as she flicked her wrists. There was singing and dancing and joy. Nānī had taught her daughter and granddaughter to sew—a skill that kept them fed and housed when they'd lost everything—and Ottilie's childhood, in stark contrast to her father's, had burst with love. Nānī had healed with hugs, made every injury better with a kiss. Their hearts had been stitched together with a steady provision of foot rubs and massages and nights lying together beneath starry skies.

Ottilie read the Scripture, speaking aloud those things that had brought Nānī joy. "A time to dance . . . a time to embrace . . . . a time to sew . . . a time to love."

She thought of Maji, who had loved and lived the way Nānī

had. Who had moved with grace, draped in the fluid fabric of an embroidered sari, staying up until their last candle sputtered, her fingertips riddled with pinpricks, the fabric she worked on glinting with thousands of wings. Giving and giving and giving, even when in the giving, it meant she was losing.

The anger that had simmered beneath Ottilie's breast since she learned of Maji's decision to send Thaddeus to England sputtered like a cooking fire doused with water. Maji had made the best decision she could for Thaddeus. Even when it must have felt as though she were ripping out her heart.

And with that realization, the heavy weight of Ottilie's bitterness shattered. Her life had seemed one season after another of plucking and weeping and losing, but undergirding the loss was a lifetime of good things. All the things she loved, her mother had loved, her grandmother had loved.

They'd left her a legacy. And she'd forgotten it.

She closed the Bible, kissed its worn cover, hoping God allowed Nānī and Maji to feel the touch of her lips, and placed it back in the drawer.

And as she saw Blake's book of poems, she recognized a connection of sorts. She had always divided life into two parts—the before and after, the innocence and experience, the good and bad. Before death touched her, and after she discovered the stalking, suffocating presence of fear. Before her faith faltered, and after she learned the ancestry that made her up also made her unacceptable.

But Blake had landed on something. Something she had missed.

Life couldn't be separated into a before and after. Because life's seasons were a mix of both. There was a time to be born and die, a time to mourn and dance, a time to rend and sew. And just because one happened didn't mean the other couldn't. She often pulled mistaken stitches, but she didn't need to discard the garment.

Ottilie covered her mouth with her hands and bent over her legs. *Oh, God, I've gotten everything wrong.* She'd missed so much.

"Miss Singh, are you all right?"

Harriet's gentle voice was a balm on Ottilie's self-recrimination. "I think I will be."

Harriet went about her work, brushing, scrubbing, setting, and emptying while Ottilie thought through everything that needed to be done in order to make Thaddeus's birthday one that would bring him joy. *Dance, sew, embrace, love.* And below that, toward the end of the chapter, *a time to eat and drink.*

"Harriet," Ottilie said, an idea forming, "you like children, correct?"

She laughed. "I'd have to, wouldn't I? Otherwise I'd be miserable at home."

"Do you think, if it was for Lord Sunderson, you'd be allowed to help me today? It's his birthday, and he's asked for a very particular gift, one I can't give him without help."

"I'd have to ask Mrs. Wood first, but I'd like it very much."

"Good. Today we're going to give Sunderson an evening in Calcutta."

India in England. The seams were unraveling and twisting together. And Ottilie could see beauty in the blending. Purpose in the entanglement.

"I don't see why I have to let that . . . that . . . woman in my kitchen." Mrs. Harris, Hazelbrook Manor's longtime cook, stood across the room, arms crossed over her thin, apron-covered bosom. "Ain't right. This is my kitchen."

"Hush. She'll hear you. And it's Lady Sunderson's kitchen, when it comes down to it." Mrs. Wood shook her head and watched Ottilie's movements with suspicion. "It's for the young lord's birthday. His special request."

Ottilie bit back a laugh and unscrewed her tin of cumin seeds, taking a few between her fingers and rubbing until the scent was released. This dark room beneath the ground, teeming with maids in drab dresses staring at her with unconcealed resentment or curiosity, receded, and Ottilie was home. Back with Dilip in their tiny kitchen, measuring spices into the mortar. There was nothing but the summer sunlight filtering through the doors and windows, shutters flung open. Ottilie heard Nānī's humming as she sat on the verandah, slicing okra, and Thaddeus playing nearby with his peg soldiers. Dilip's teeth and eyes gleamed, joy sparking across the handsome planes of his face.

She pressed her finger to her lips and flicked at the bits of crushed seeds with her tongue, recalling, in the taste, every meal she'd shared with her family. She'd give that to Thaddeus today. It would be her gift to him. And maybe he wouldn't struggle the way she had with forgetting the good.

She looked at the ingredients set out before her on the long, scarred oak table that held court in the center of the kitchen. She'd sent a list with Harriet earlier that morning, asking the staff to gather the items she'd need to prepare Thaddeus a feast.

Harriet had returned, red-faced and teary-eyed, saying Mrs. Harris refused to allow Ottilie in her kitchen. Only a conversation between Mrs. Wood and Lady Sunderson reversed the cook's decision, and a couple of hours later, while Harriet kept Thaddeus company, Ottilie faced the daunting task of creating an Indian meal from mostly English ingredients.

There was no bottle gourd or coconut. No *hilsa* fish or *chana dal* or coriander leaves. But Mrs. Harris had reluctantly, and with much complaining, turned over the cod she'd been soaking for the next day's lunch. There were hard yellow peas and cabbages and carrots and fresh milk foaming in pails. It was enough.

Ottilie thought of her conversation with Lady Sunderson before she'd slipped down the stairs to the kitchen. She hadn't known if her grandmother would agree to her idea for Thaddeus's birthday celebration, but she'd seen the spark of interest in Lady Sunderson's gaze.

Ottilie nearly buzzed with excitement as she removed the round metal containers from the wooden box that held Nānī's spices. There were paper packets of dried chilis—green and red—as well as pods of tamarind and, nestled toward the back, small corked bottles of rose water and mustard oil.

"I need four pints of milk put to boil." Ottilie glanced up at the small huddle of kitchen servants near the cook and housekeeper. None responded. One of the maids snorted.

"Mrs. Harris," Ottile said, "would you care to help me prepare Lord Sunderson's birthday meal?"

The housekeeper gave Mrs. Harris a sharp look, then disappeared down the corridor that led to her rooms with a jangle of keys.

Ottilie met Mrs. Harris's gaze, noting the woman's nervous fiddling and tight lips, and smiled. "I know this is an unorthodox situation. I don't mean to take over your kitchen. I only want to give Lord Sunderson the birthday he wishes. And I'd be so grateful for your help. I don't think I can manage on my own, as I only occasionally helped the Russell family cook in Calcutta." She pressed her hand against the sharp pain stabbing her heart. How easily she'd fallen into the role of governess. No one listening would have any idea she and Thaddeus were siblings. That the Russell family cook had been a dear family friend, taken in by her father and educated and loved as though one of his own.

Tears pricked her eyes, and she busied herself organizing the tins of spices in the order she would need them. Only Mrs. Harris's grunting sigh and padding steps alerted Ottilie to the cook's acquiescence.

"I know nothin' about cooking this food."

Ottilie gave her a bright smile. "I will direct you. Here . . . taste this." She dusted amchur powder into Mrs. Harris's palm, who poked the tip of her tongue at it. Her lips puckered, and she wrinkled her nose. "It's made from dried green mangos and adds a complex note of acidity and sweet fruitiness."

"Like lemon but"—the cook took another lick of her palm—"more."

"Many of our Indian spices add more than one note to food. Take, for instance, nigella seeds." Ottilie twisted the lid and sprinkled some of the little black seeds into Mrs. Harris's hand. "We'll use them with the fish." She allowed Mrs. Harris to taste them, then set about measuring the mustard seeds into a large mortar. The weight of the pestle was familiar in her hand, and she ground the seeds beneath it, releasing the aroma of memories and comfort and late-night conversations, and the knowledge that she belonged. Her eyes welled, and she sniffed. "Mustard seeds always irritate my eyes."

Mrs. Harris gave Ottilie a hard stare, then the line of her jaw softened. "You must miss your country, Miss Singh." She lifted a large, dented pot from its hook above their heads and poured milk into it. "I know what that's like. I'm from Northumberland, up near the Scottish border. I haven't been home in over a decade. It never leaves, you know, the longing for somewhere else."

"I expect that is true." Ottilie pulled a head of cabbage toward her and lifted a large knife.

Mrs. Harris directed one of the maids to fetch a pot of water and start soaking the peas. She stirred the simmering milk with a large wooden spoon, pouring the vinegar in when Ottilie directed. "Will you return to India once Lord Sunderson is sent to school?"

Ottilie jerked her head around, and pain sliced through her finger. With a cry, she dropped the knife and yanked her hand from the cabbage, sending a spray of blood across the table.

"What have you done?" Mrs. Harris stopped stirring the milk and bustled over. Taking Ottilie's hand, she tsked. "You're right about having little experience in the kitchen. You cut the tip of your finger right off. You're lucky it wasn't any higher, or we'd have to have the doctor come. Anna, go fetch Mrs. Wood's medical kit. It's on the high shelf in her sitting room cabinet. Kate, bring me a bowl of water and some cloth. Sit down, Miss Singh, before you tumble."

Ottilie, staring at her bloody fingertip, had begun to sway. She followed Mrs. Harris to a stool near the fireplace and sank onto it.

"What were you thinking? You need to pay attention when you're cutting." Mrs. Harris looked up as Kate dropped a square of linen into her lap and handed over an earthenware bowl. She dipped the corner of the cloth into the water and dabbed at Ottilie's finger. "Let's see what you've done."

"What do you mean, will I return to India when Lord Sunderson goes to school?" Ottilie squeezed her eyes closed as the linen turned crimson.

"Only that it would be hard for you to make a life here once your services are no longer needed. Who would marry you? And you'll excuse me for saying so, but no other family would hire you."

"That doesn't matter. What I meant to ask is, when will Lord Sunderson go to school? And where?"

"Why, he'll likely go in a few years, when he's 'bout twelve or thirteen. And he'll go to Eton, which is where all the family attended."

Anna reappeared, carrying a wooden box and drawing the sharp side of Mrs. Harris's tongue. "It took you long enough."

"Sorry, Mrs. Harris. I couldn't find the cabinet."

Mrs. Harris rolled her eyes. "You mean the one that takes up an entire wall, you daft girl? Go stir the milk." She shook her head and opened the box.

"Where's Eton?" Ottilie's fingers trembled within Mrs. Harris's calloused palm, and she forced them still. Drawing on the Scripture she'd read only that morning, which had brought her so much comfort, she silently recited, *A time to get, and a time to lose; a time to keep, and a time to cast away.* But she didn't want to lose or cast away Thaddeus.

"It's a little more than halfway between Chippenham and London. About three hours on the train."

Ottilie's breath swooshed from between her lips. "So he will be home often. Every weekend?"

"Oh no. He will come home for two weeks at Christmas and three weeks in the summer." Mrs. Harris spread a slick of salve over Ottilie's wound, then wrapped it with a strip of cloth.

"But . . . why should they bring him all this way, only to send him off to school?"

Mrs. Harris laughed. "Why should they not?" She set the kit on the floor along with the water bowl and patted her knees. "Now, shall we finish this exotic meal for Lord Sunderson? I must admit, I'm curious to find out how it tastes."

Ottilie stood and followed her back to the stove, where Anna was stirring the milk. Curds had formed, and the chhena was ready to be drained and hung. She went through the motions of preparing the meal, allowing Anna and Kate to cut the vegetables and fish, as well as form the rasgulla balls.

He will be here years yet. Twelve is a very long way off.

20

Ottilie spread her sari over the coverlet draping her bed and smoothed out the wrinkles. Her palm slid over the green silk, the gold embroidery a familiar pattern against her skin.

"It's so beautiful, Miss Singh. Looks like something a princess would wear." Harriet's whisper barely disturbed the hush of the room.

This was a holy moment. Ottilie wasn't just pulling a sari from her trunk, but a legacy. She was presenting her family's story, proclaiming her approval of it, and, in a way, reclaiming it for her brother.

"Has Mr. Scott answered my invitation?" Ottilie kept her words even, made sure none of the emotion that simmered deep inside crept into her voice.

"I haven't heard, miss." Harriet reached a finger toward the embroidered hem of the sari but drew back before touching it.

Ottilie had sent a message earlier in the day asking Everett to join them for Thaddeus's birthday dinner. There hadn't been a response.

She stared at her hands, still stroking the fabric. The linen binding her cut finger was as colorless as the snow blanketing the grounds outside her window. She remembered laying her fingers along his jawline in the orangery. Feeling the hollow of his cheek, the movement as he swallowed. Grazing his earlobe, her touch tangling with his sideburn.

Her wound burned, sending stinging pain toward her knuckle, and she pulled back her hands, clutched them to her chest.

The sun was setting, and a mellow light shone through the window, spilling over her sari. Turning it as bright as Everett's eyes.

"Will you get dressed now? It's nearly time."

Ottilie blinked at Harriet's reminder, and her mind cleared. "Yes. It's time to get ready. Will you help Lord Sunderson dress? His clothing is laid out on his bed."

Harriet disappeared through the doorway, and Ottilie began to remove her gown. She stripped herself of England, leaving only her petticoat, and donned a short blouse. Then she tucked the edge of her sari around her waistband, wrapping, pleating, and draping. The pallu, more ornately embroidered than the rest of the garment, draped her shoulder and arm, the trim falling in a graceful line to the floor.

"Ottilie!" Thaddeus's steps pounded, and his arms wrapped around her middle, head pressed against her back. A sob escaped his lips.

She turned and knelt, drawing him into an embrace of silk and Maji's jasmine perfume. "Glowworm, what's wrong?"

He pulled away, eyes and smile bright on his upturned face despite the tears that stained his cheeks. "I missed you." His hands stroked her shoulders, her back, fingers running along the crisp embroidered edge of her pallu and finding the braid hanging down her back.

A knock sounded at the door, and Ottilie stood. Harriet went to answer it and gave a little gasp when Lady Sunderson entered in a gown of deep aubergine and gray.

"It has been a year since my eldest son's death. Celebrating the new Lord Sunderson's seventh birthday seems a good time to come out of deep mourning." Lady Sunderson ran her hand down the side of her striped overskirt. Trimmed in jet beads, the dress still proclaimed grief and solemnity but was also a statement of moving on. "Harriet, will you take Lord Sunderson downstairs to wait for us?"

With a nod, the maid took Thaddeus's hand and led him from the room.

"You look lovely, Lady Sunderson," Ottilie said once they had left.

"As do you. It's very different from what I'm used to, but I can see the appeal of wearing such a garment in India. The heat must bother you much less than were you to wear all the layers required of an Englishwoman. It's a very elegant look, though you must be very cold here."

Ottilie laughed and drew her shawl from the foot of the bed. It was embroidered with elytra—a swirling, whimsical pattern that represented nothing but the fancies in her own head. She tucked it into the crook of her elbow. "This will keep me warm if the ride to the orangery is too cold. And I have something for you." She retrieved the Kashmiri shawl that had been beneath her own and let it fall open. "Father gave it to Maji before he died."

The soft fabric was a muted red and embroidered with gray silk in a floral pattern. It was a fine shawl, the very best quality, and Ottilie knew from reading her mother's letters that she would have wanted Lady Sunderson to have it.

"Oh, Ottilie, I couldn't. You should keep it." Lady Sunderson touched the edge of the fabric.

Ottilie smiled and draped it over her grandmother's shoulders. "I want you to have it. You were Maji's friend."

Lady Sunderson clasped the edge of the shawl to her chest, and her fingers stroked Ottilie's cheek. "I loved your mother from the moment I knew she wished for reconciliation. I wish I could have met her in person. But I feel she's sent me a piece of herself in you."

Ottilie smiled. "I think she would have liked you very much, Lady Sunderson."

Lady Sunderson turned her head, but not before Ottilie saw the tears shimmering in her eyes. "Would you call me Grandmother? I would so like to hear you say it."

"How would that preserve our secret?"

"I suppose . . . you could only say it when no one else is around. But we would know, wouldn't we?"

In the space of a moment, Ottilie's hope had risen, then shattered. Why she allowed herself to believe Lady Sunderson was extending her an invitation into the family, she didn't know. But she was tired of pretending. Tired of secrets. "I think not. It would be too confusing for Thaddeus."

And me. She would rather be nothing to them than a hushed-up granddaughter, pulled from the cupboard when no one was around. Good enough only for empty moments and lonely corners.

Lady Sunderson pulled her lips inward and gave a slow nod. "I see. That makes sense." She pasted on a bright smile and held her hand toward the door. "Shall we go to dinner?"

As they walked down the stairs, Ottilie draped her shawl around her shoulders, drawing it tightly around her middle to keep the frosty air from biting her midriff. She'd wrapped her sari high, but silk wasn't meant for English winters.

She wasn't sure she was either.

In the time it took for them to go from bedroom to front door, it had begun to snow. A dusting of it swept around their feet as Wakefield opened the door, and ice prickled Ottilie's nose and forehead.

"Where are we going?" Thaddeus asked as a footman assisted him into the waiting carriage.

"It's a surprise." Ottilie forced brightness into her voice. Thaddeus deserved a day of celebration, untinged by everything that had come before and would likely come after. Ottilie knew Lady Sunderson had only offered what she was capable of giving, and she told herself to hold no grudge against her. It would only cause tension and blanket Thaddeus's birthday with awkwardness. She slid onto the seat beside him and leaned down to whisper, "We're going as close to home as possible."

After Lady Sunderson joined them, the horses were encouraged across the yard, wheels crunching over the frozen grass.

"Is Aunt Birdie coming?" Thaddeus asked.

"No, darling." Lady Sunderson gave him a sad smile. "She isn't well today."

Ottilie had been surprised when her grandmother told her Alberta wouldn't be joining them. As much as her aunt seemed to dislike her, she genuinely loved Thaddeus. And she'd been fine the day before. But Lady Sunderson's expression didn't invite further discussion.

It was another peculiarity in her aunt's story.

With merry jangling and creaking, the carriage stopped.

"Look!" Thaddeus cried the moment his feet touched the ground. "What is this place?"

"This is the orangery," Ottilie said. "It's a sort of greenhouse."

"The windows look like the ones in India."

And they did. Arched at the top, with ornate latticework, the orangery seemed to blend English and Indian architecture just the way most buildings in Calcutta did. Light bounced against the wavy glass, drawing them forward. "Wait until you see inside."

"Did you do all this, Ottilie?" Lady Sunderson asked.

"No. I mainly helped Mrs. Harris in the kitchen. The staff was kind enough to carry out my instructions for the decorating." Ottilie didn't mention the threats Mrs. Wood had to leverage when most of the housemaids and footmen refused to acknowledge Ottilie's directives.

"Why should we take orders from *her*?" one young girl sporting a freckled and deceptively cherubic face had said. "My great-uncle was killed by people like her."

268

"He was killed by governesses?" Mrs. Woods raised her fine brows in a warning.

"By Hindus. During the mutiny."

"Miss Singh, are you a Hindu mutineer?" Mrs. Woods asked.

Ottilie shook her head, resisting the urge to lecture on the convoluted, complicated history behind the revolt.

"Well, there. Please carry out Miss Singh's desires for Lord Sunderson's celebration. Unless you prefer to work in a different house."

After that, the maids and footmen did as asked without grumbling, but also without grace. Ottilie only hoped they cared enough about their positions to do a good job. Their regard for her mattered little. Thaddeus's happiness was her only priority.

And he wanted Calcutta for his birthday.

The distinct sound of a sitar drifted toward them, the notes slipping and jolting, skidding and jumping. Ottilie's steps froze, and she glanced around.

"Ottilie," Thaddeus whispered, as though afraid to disrupt the music, "where is it coming from?"

Tears pricked her eyes. "I don't know, but it sounds like home."

The orangery's door opened, and Everett stepped into the cold. Wearing evening attire, dark hair pushed back from his broad forehead, he looked as handsome as Ottilie had ever seen him. The strains of music spilled around him and beckoned her forward.

She held out her hand, and he bent over it. "Miss Russell . . . er, Singh. I shall never get used to the name change."

Ottilie's fingers found her pallu's fringe, and she smiled. "Mr. Scott."

He straightened and released her hand. He'd held it as long as convention thought appropriate, but emptiness took the place of his grasp.

"Happy birthday, Lord Sunderson," Everett said as Thaddeus bounded toward him.

Thaddeus huffed. "Can you at least call me Sunderson the way Aunt Birdie and Grandmother do?"

"I can. At least in private."

"Did you hire the musicians?" Lady Sunderson asked.

"I did. I hope you don't mind, but when I received Miss Russell's invitation, I thought of the lascar seamen I saw in Bristol during my last trip. I sent a message to the captain of one of Mr. Fernsby's ships, asking if he knew of any Indians who had remained in port, as I was looking to hire a couple of musicians." He waved behind him. "He sent two this afternoon."

"We don't mind at all, do we, Ottilie?" Lady Sunderson said. "It sets quite a nice tone. The music is interesting. Very romantic. Shall we go in?"

Ottilie swallowed, forcing away assumptions and conjecture. Why had Everett been in Bristol? To visit that club? To meet a woman who would offer him entry into it? She focused on the task at hand—Thaddeus's birthday.

"May I go in first and make sure everything is how I asked?" She wanted to see Thaddeus's expression as he took his first step toward this small reminder of home.

Everett offered his arm, and they walked toward the building. As she approached, the music grew more distinct, pulling her into something much more personal than a greenhouse. Her heart beat to the tabla, and her palms grew inexplicably clammy. "I hope the servants did my vision justice."

"I believe you'll be pleased. It looks lovely." His hand found her fingers and tucked them into his elbow. "As do you."

The music increased in tempo, along with her heart. And then she remembered another day in the orangery. Everett's words. His certainty that they couldn't be together. "Please, don't toy with me. I've already survived one flirtation I thought was more. I couldn't do it again."

They reached the pavers, light tumbling from the door and

touching their shoes. It danced a merry *kuchipudi*, unaware of the tightness banding Ottilie's chest and shoulders.

"I didn't mean to. I would never dally with you." He put a hand on the small of her back, the warmth seeping through her shawl and sending heat through her limbs, and guided her inside. "I will try to maintain a greater grasp on my admiration for you."

She swung her gaze toward him, a rebuke on her lips.

"I'm not merely flirting with you, Ottilie. Our conversation was interrupted the other day. Please, will you let me explain?"

Against her better judgment, she nodded. She was going to be hurt again. That was as clear as the icicles hanging from the eaves. And she would let him do it. Because nothing she'd ever felt before—not even the heart-stirring ardor she'd experienced with Victor—had prepared her to deny Everett Scott anything he wished.

She didn't want to say she loved him. But she couldn't say she didn't.

"Are you almost ready, Ottilie? I'm getting cold." Thaddeus's fortuitous interruption kept her from embarrassing herself.

"One moment," Everett called. Then to her he said, "We will talk about it later. For now, look." His hands clasped her upper arms, and he turned her to face the room.

For a moment, one exquisite, shattering moment, Ottilie felt as though she'd stepped through a fairy door and traveled to India. Everything was as she'd hoped. The plants—trees heavy with lemons and bright flowers—had been moved from their orderly rows to stand along the perimeter of the orangery, gas lamps hanging from their branches. The air was fragrant with the sweet scents of jasmine and tuberose.

Beneath two towering potted palm trees, the servants had set out a table draped in white cloth, laden with silver covered serving dishes. Tucked behind this were the musicians, dressed in red-belted kurtas and white pajamas. They smiled when they saw Ottilie, bright teeth gleaming behind their thick mustaches. When she approached, their hands stilled on their instruments. *"Namoshkar,"* she said.

The drummer, whose dark eyes glittered like the sleet-pocked sky outside the windows, pressed his palms together and lifted them to his forehead. *"Dhonnabad."*

She spoke in Bengali, his thanks having been spoken in that language, telling them how much Thaddeus missed Calcutta and her gratitude that they had come to play for him.

When he answered, she didn't hear his response. She only allowed the rush of his language to flow over her. Through her. In her. The wave of it tugged her from England's snowbanks, and she spiraled toward warmth and spice and the chatter of parrots in banana plants.

"Ottilie?" Everett yanked her back. "Shall we allow Lady Sunderson and your brother inside?"

Ottilie blinked. "Yes. Of course." She turned so she could see Thaddeus's expression, and Everett went to the door.

The glee on her brother's face when he stepped into the orangery made every bit of work—even the injury to her finger—worth it. His mouth formed a circle, and his eyes widened as he clapped his hands together. "Oh!"

He walked around the room, tugging down branches and breathing in the scent of flowers. Every plant was caressed. Every tree admired. Every bloom adored. Finally, when he'd inspected the entire orangery, he returned to Ottilie and wrapped his arms around her waist. "Thank you." Then he pulled away and sniffed. A slow grin lifted his cheeks, and he craned his neck to see around her.

She laughed and ruffled his hair, forgetting about her wounded finger. When she drew a sharp hiss between her teeth, Everett took a step nearer. "Are you all right?"

"Ottilie cut off her finger when she was cooking."

Thaddeus's embellishment drew a shocked cry from Everett. "What?"

"I did not," she corrected. "I only sliced off a tiny portion of it. Hardly worth mentioning."

Everett lifted her hand and examined the dressing. "Do you need to see a doctor? Do you need stitches?"

"No on both accounts." Her eyes met his, and the concern warming his expression filled her cheeks with heat. "I'm well." She looked away and met Lady Sunderson's bemused gaze.

"How is Alberta today?" Everett asked.

Her grandmother's lips sagged, and she aged in the space of a moment. "It is the first of March. She's taken to her bed."

"I am sorry to hear it."

There was a tightness in Everett's voice Ottilie had never heard before. It attested to something deeper than Alberta's assumed illness. *You must look deeper, beneath what a person shows. There's always a story, Niraja. Things are never what they seem.* Nānī's advice, scribbled between chapters in Proverbs, spoke across the decades. Ottilie had stumbled across the words while she was flipping through her Bible a few days earlier but hadn't stopped to read the passage it was associated with. She'd have to find it again.

Ottilie shook her head. Alberta wasn't her concern. Tonight was about Thaddeus. She took his hands in hers. The golden starbursts surrounding his pupils gleamed with excitement, sparking and spreading so that the green nearly disappeared. "Why don't we see what treats are hiding beneath those dishes?"

They took their seats, her grandmother placing herself beside Ottilie so that Everett was forced to sit opposite her. Then she glanced around. "Where are the footmen? Who is going to serve?"

Ottilie lifted the cover from one of the chafing dishes, and Thaddeus squeaked in delight. The scent of fish spiked with mustard, chilies, and nigella engulfed them. She removed the lid from the rice, lifted a spoon, and scooped a portion onto Lady Sunderson's plate. "Dinner was always very informal at home.

Even when Papa was alive, we rarely had more than one servant present at dinner. And after he was gone, it was only Dilip."

"Dilip wasn't a servant, Ottilie." Thaddeus watched her movements, his expression greedy.

She finished piling Lady Sunderson's plate with food and set it before her. "You're right. Dilip was more like family."

"I miss him." Thaddeus heaved a sigh. "I miss my friends too. There's no one to play with here."

Lady Sunderson lifted her fork and poked her fish with a look of trepidation. "That shall resolve itself, Sunderson, when you start school."

Ottilie, having already served Everett, mounded rice onto Thaddeus's plate, than hers. "Will I continue acting as his governess until then? What shall he do for friends before Eton?"

"Oh, Sunderson won't attend Eton until he is twelve. Before that, he shall attend St. Luke's of Kew. It's one of the finest preparatory schools. Very modern. Alberta heard of it only recently and thought it would provide a good foundation for Sunderson before he goes to Eton. There will be many boys his age to play with there."

Ottilie stared at her. "When will he leave for St. Luke's?"

"Soon, I imagine. Possibly by April so he can become settled before the summer holiday. It is just outside London, near the Royal Botanic Gardens." Lady Sunderson lifted the smallest piece of fish to her lips and tasted it. "This is interesting." She took a larger bite. "I can see why you miss it, Sunderson. Maybe Ottilie can teach Mrs. Harris to make the foods you like. I wouldn't mind a bit of variety. One can only eat so many chicken fricassees and jellies before growing bored."

"I had the privilege of being served an interesting beverage Miss Singh made. I'm sure she's an accomplished cook." Everett smiled at her, but it fell quickly, and a line appeared between his eyebrows. *Are you all right?* he mouthed.

Ottilie shook her head, not looking away. Afraid the only

thing tethering her emotions was the steadiness of his gaze. She didn't want to cry at Thaddeus's birthday dinner. Didn't want to cast a pall over his joy.

Everett, keeping his eyes on her, reached for the spoon and slipped a fillet over her rice. He nodded, and she lifted her fork. He glanced at Lady Sunderson, a quick darting look that brought him back to her faster than the time it would take to make a stitch, but in that moment of loss, her breath hitched and a sob rode the coattails of her heartache.

Something slid beside her shoe. A gentle pressure that reassured her. Protected her from revealing what lay inside. Everett swallowed and pressed his foot closer. It was a comforting embrace. A private consolation.

It might only have postponed what she would surely face later, but it was enough.

She swallowed her agony, took a deep breath, and ate her dinner.

21

"Didi?" Thaddeus padded across her room the day after his birthday celebration, his cheek creased and hair mussed.

She set down the jacket she'd begun embroidering—a plain one she'd decided could use some embellishment—and held her arms wide. "You look like you've rested well." He'd been tired after their late-night celebration and had begged for a nap after finishing his morning schoolwork.

"I did." He nestled into her embrace. "I'm hungry. Do you think Cook will have made normal food?"

Ottilie laughed. "If by normal, you mean familiar to us, then most likely not. I've not had the time to teach her. But I will be sure to speak with her about the possibility of learning." She grinned and went to her wardrobe. "I have an idea." Lifting her spice box from the floor, she ran her finger over the labeled tins and selected one. "Garam masala. Let's go to the schoolroom and eat." She tucked the container into her palm and walked with him to the door. "Did you go for your walk today?" She couldn't face another bitter wind, another frigid afternoon. She'd sent Thaddeus downstairs with instructions to find a maid or footman to accompany him.

He nodded. "Aunt Birdie came with me. She seemed sad." He

skipped down the hall, hopping over puddles of light, gripping her hand as though he were at risk of drowning in one of them.

They ate lunch—cabbage, boiled potatoes, and mutton, all sprinkled with Dilip's spice blend.

Thaddeus stared at the cabbage speared on his fork, then shoved it into his mouth. "Aunt Birdie said I shouldn't eat food that is hot in temperature or spice. She said it will make me passionate and unable to be managed."

Ottilie laughed. "We're from an entire nation of people who manage to survive eating food that actually tastes of something. I think Aunt Birdie is mistaken."

He nodded in agreement, added another pinch of garam masala to his food, and ate with gusto.

They made quick work of their lunch, then walked to the drawing room for their visit with their aunt and grandmother.

"Is that one of your new gowns?" Lady Sunderson asked as soon as they entered.

Ottilie settled onto the settee, and Thaddeus sat at her feet and withdrew his Christmas train from within his jacket. "It is." She'd initially resisted Lady Sunderson's insistence on equipping her with a new wardrobe, but the skirts and jackets she'd purchased in Calcutta before they left port weren't heavy enough to protect her from the harsh wind and cold.

Ottilie found joy in her new gowns' happy colors and patterns. She'd been especially drawn to the one she wore—a walking gown in copper and blue plaid. The colors suited her complexion and reminded her of the vibrancy of Burrabazar. Mounded spices and brilliant saris. Gold and gem-encrusted bangles presented by oily-tongued men who traded beauty for coin.

She fiddled with Nānī's kadas, which she had slipped over her wrist after she'd gotten ready for the day. It was a mixing of British and Indian that at first needled her with its incongruity, but she recognized the practicality of wearing quilted petticoats and wool skirts. And she would allow for a bit of India.

She opened her beetle-wing box, which rested on her lap.

"The colors are becoming, with your complexion and dark hair," Lady Sunderson said. "Although I'm not sure any of our English clothes suit you as well as what you wore last night."

"What did she wear last night?" Alberta asked. She drew a threaded needle through linen bearing evidence of the beginnings of a complex smocking, embroidered with tiny pink flowers.

Lady Sunderson smiled at Ottilie. "A sari, I am told. Beautiful. The color and fabric were some of the loveliest I've ever seen."

Ottilie laughed. "But it was not the thing for early March in Wiltshire. I thought I would freeze on the ride to the orangery."

Alberta's mouth pinched, and she stabbed her needle through the fabric with more force than necessary. "It sounds scandalous. And Mother said Everett was present."

"He has seen me in a sari before." Ottilie scooped her hand into the box and let the elytra spill into her palm.

"Well, as long as no one in society sees you wearing it. Though, for Sunderson's sake, you should refrain from dressing like an Indian. It will draw undue attention."

"Who in society will see me?"

Thaddeus was moving around the room, touching the scattered knickknacks and peeking out each of the windows lining the far wall, and Ottilie's gaze traveled with him.

"I suppose no one."

Ottilie pushed a breath from between her lips and set the box on the delicate table near the settee. She took the plain gray jacket from where she'd set it on the cushion beside her and draped it over her lap, then threaded a needle.

"That's a lovely box, Ottilie," Alberta said.

Ottilie glanced up at her aunt and nodded, not revealing her surprise at having been addressed without displeasure. "Thank you. It was Maji's. I now use it to store elytra."

Thaddeus stopped his inspection of a set of porcelain figurines shaped like dogs and turned from the mantel. "Elytra are beetle wings." He lifted his arms and buzzed a circle around them before pulling three tin soldiers from his pocket and setting them upon the floor at their feet.

"Beetle wings?" Alberta's eyes fell to the jacket.

The piece was utilitarian—dark gray with a short flare in the back to drape over her bustled yellow and green plaid skirt. It sported coordinating plaid ruffles at the bottom of the sleeves, but little else to embellish it. "My mother and grandmother taught me. Nānī learned from her mother." She opened the box and scooped up a handful of the gem-like elytra.

Alberta and Lady Sunderson leaned forward in order to see them in Ottilie's outstretched hand.

"Oh!" Alberta said. "Miss Chadwick was speaking of this in her last letter to me. She said a woman attended a dinner party wearing a gown embroidered with insect wings that she'd had made in India. Everyone talked about it. It seems it was popular fifty years ago, before the mutiny squashed everyone's mania for all things Indian. Lorena said she'd tried and failed to find someone who could make her a gown like her guest's. She eventually visited Madame Laurence, but even that esteemed dressmaker hadn't the ability to provide her with the embroidery."

"It's traditional in certain parts of India. We use beetles from the family *Sternocera*. Expired insects are collected—they don't live very long—and the wing cases are removed. I bought a sackful before leaving India."

Alberta ran her fingers over the completed part of the design. Ottilie had embroidered a meandering pattern of thick gold thread all over the front of the jacket—it had taken days—then begun the painstaking process of attaching paired clusters of elytra, stitching a stamen between them. When she finished, the jacket would look as though it had emerged from a garden. "It's lovely. You are a talent."

"Thank you." Ottilie didn't know what to do with this kind

Alberta, so she dropped her handful of elytra in the box and chose two of similar size to begin stitching. "Nānī used her skill with the needle to support herself and Maji after . . . they were left alone. Then Maji used it after Father died. And I used it after Maji's death. It has served us well. If I ever need to, I can rely on it once more."

"You can rely on us now," Lady Sunderson said.

"Perhaps." Ottilie slid the needle through a wing casing and positioned it on the fabric. "But after you send Thaddeus away . . . there will be no use for me here."

Thaddeus dropped his soldiers and looked up, his eyes wide and startled. "Send me away? Where am I to go?"

How very stupid of me. Ottilie had let the words escape before thinking through how Thaddeus would respond. She'd meant to talk to him about it later, easing him into the idea.

"To school, Sunderson," Alberta said, "as we've discussed."

"Why would you think we'd force you out, Ottilie?" Lady Sunderson asked, hurt coloring her words.

"The school isn't in the village?" Thaddeus cried. He ran to Ottilie, falling to his knees.

Ottilie shoved her jacket away and dropped to the floor near Thaddeus. She gathered him to her and made shushing sounds until his crying ceased.

"Ottilie, don't make me leave you. I don't want to go."

His cries took her back through days and months and years until she was kneeling beside Nathan's bed again, staring with horror as her brother—the first to fall ill—convulsed. Gripping his hand and screaming for Dilip, for Papa, for God, to help. To help her brother. Begging him to stay. *"Don't go, Nathan. Stay with me."* Watching as he was torn from her, violently and without warning. They'd thought it a simple summer fever. Ottilie hadn't had time to prepare. After Nathan left her, she had turned to comfort Jemima, who rested on her bed nearby, only to find Jemima had left as well.

"Please, don't make him leave." Ottilie choked against her tears and pressed Thaddeus's head to her chest. How could she pretend to be all right with it? How could she paste an indifferent smile on her face and tell him she wasn't crushed by the thought of him leaving? "I cannot lose him too."

"Nonsense. You will be able to write, of course," Alberta said, but her voice wavered, and there was no bite in her rebuke.

Ottilie shook her head. "Write? Letters are a terrible substitute for being with someone. How can one maintain a relationship without physical intimacy? There is no comparison." She saw all the carefully constructed pieces of her life tearing apart. Mangled seams and dangling threads. There was no way to repair that which she had tried with all her might to patch together.

"I developed a lovely relationship with your mother through letters." Lady Sunderson's voice was soft. "Your closeness will not suffer."

Ottilie couldn't hold back a short laugh. "Relationship? You didn't even know my mother was Indian. You knew *nothing* about her."

Lady Sunderson reared back, her chin trembling and eyes turning glassy. Ottilie looked away. She wouldn't apologize. Not now, when they sought to tear from her the only thing that kept her from wishing she could follow the rest of her family.

Lady Sunderson set aside her work and turned her attention toward Thaddeus. "Darling, you were so excited when you heard you would be attending school and making friends. We talked of it just last night at dinner."

"But I didn't realize it was far away. I thought it would be like my school at home. That I would only be gone for the morning and afternoon."

"England is your home, Sunderson. You'd best begin to accept that." Alberta took up her fancy work and focused on her needle.

The misery on Thaddeus's face puddled Ottilie's belly with

helplessness. When Ottilie had decided to allow Thaddeus to move to Hazelbrook Manor and take the title, she hadn't realized she was giving up all right to him. She hadn't realized she would have to watch others make decisions based on tradition instead of what was best for Thaddeus. If Lady Sunderson decided he would go away to school, away he would go. And there was precious little she could do to stop it.

"Please," she tried again, desperation making her voice brittle, "must you send him away so soon? He's not ready."

"He hasn't been brought up to inherit a title." Lady Sunderson fiddled with the brooch clasped near her collar. She looked at Ottilie, hurt still evident in the deep grooves running from the corners of her lips toward her chin. But there was also forgiveness in her expression, whether Ottilie wanted to admit wrongdoing or not. Forgiveness and empathy. And Ottilie remembered she wasn't the only one who had lost those she loved. "He needs to be properly guided. He will receive that at St. Luke's. Here . . . Ottilie, you do an admirable job with his academics—no one can fault you on that—but he must study more than math and reading and French. He must learn to be a gentleman."

"He's only a child."

Thaddeus shuddered within her arms, a sob wracking him.

Lady Sunderson swept toward them, her skirts swishing the floor and releasing the scent of roses. She bent and cupped Ottilie's jaw in her palm. There was kindness in her face. Kindness and rigid inflexibility. Her grandmother was knit into the fabric of an empire that had conquered half the known world. There would be no dissuading her.

Ottilie sniffed and rested her chin on Thaddeus's head, tucking his face against her neck. "Please."

She couldn't lose him this way. She would be alone. Trapped in abeyance between worlds. With nothing to do and no one to care for.

"My dear," Lady Sunderson said, "Sunderson is a child. But

more than that, he is a baron. He must begin to think and act as one. An entire estate relies on him."

The road to Maybourne Park wove through a forest of beech and oak. Stripped of their warm-weather finery, the trees reached supplicant arms toward heaven and offered a counterpoint to the lush forests of West Bengal. Ottilie ached for those groves of banyans and mangroves, palms and kapoks. For the warmth of a cheerful sun. For a cozy home of three rooms and knowing she would always find belonging in them. For sleeping mats pushed together on the roof and a tangle of arms and legs.

A sob rose to her throat, but she caught it and forged toward the only person she trusted to be gentle with her anguish. She'd yet to visit Everett's home, but she needed him now. She didn't know how she would be received, but he couldn't send her away. Not with her hope so low.

There was no one else in all of England for her to turn to.

At the edge of the treeline, Ottilie paused. Rising before her, its four chimneys and cupola wrestling with the feathery clouds that spun fairy tales across the slate sky, a stately Italianate house stood its ground. It was as symmetrical and graceful as Hazelbrook Manor was immortal. The wide steps leading to the entrance welcomed her.

No artifice or twisting halls. No buried secrets or hiding places. Maybourne Park exclaimed itself with candid gentility. As she walked toward it, there was a loosening in her chest. A freedom to breathe. Everett was within the walls of that estate.

Everett, with his slow smile and always-right words, would help ease the frantic beating of her heart. Everett, with his soft touch and quiet spirit, would soothe the jabbing hooks of her anguish.

Before she could approach the house, he stepped from it, as though sensing her need. He held up his hand to shield his eyes from the weak sun that couldn't possibly be producing enough light to blind his vision, and he stared at her a moment, as though trying to make sense of her presence in this place. His home. His world.

She stopped, allowing him to come to her. Not wanting to force herself onto him the way she had in the orangery. How mortifying that had been, confessing her feelings, making demands.

He jogged down the steps and stopped three feet from her. "What happened? Is something wrong?"

She nodded.

He grasped her upper arms. "Tell me, Ottilie. Is Thaddeus all right?"

"He's fine."

His face sagged with relief.

"I am not."

His eyes caressed her face as his hands traveled up her arms and gripped her shoulders. "Are you hurt? Is it your finger?"

"They're sending Thaddeus away. To school."

"Oh, Ottilie. You had me worried!" He pulled her toward him, and she allowed herself a moment to rest against his chest, her ear pressed against the rough wool of his jacket.

"They're sending him in a few weeks, Everett. I feel as though I've been deceived. Why would they go to all the trouble of bringing him to England if they only planned to send him away after he got here? I can't allow it. I just can't." She shivered, and her teeth clacked together.

"Come. Let's go inside."

"I despise everything about this country, but the weather is worst of all. Every time I step outside, it takes hours to warm up again. It's as though the cold seeps into my bones and burrows there."

"Do you regret coming, then?" Everett offered his arm as they climbed the steps.

"I . . ." Ottilie pressed her gloved hand to her middle. Did she? As much as she hated the cold, Thaddeus seemed to thrive on it. His daily constitutionals had made him sturdy and red-cheeked—Ottilie resented having to say Alberta had been right—and the plentiful milk and meat had filled out his form. He hadn't had so much as a cold, despite her fears over the icy wind and unpleasant temperature. "That's a difficult question to answer. Thaddeus is alive. But we're to be separated. He is thriving. I am desperately unhappy. He's treated with respect and honor. I'm shoved aside and forgotten." She darted a glance at him. "That sounds wretched."

"It doesn't. You're allowed to be unhappy about your present situation. But you aren't forgotten. Never that."

The door opened, and he guided her past an astonished butler, across a black-and-white tile hall, and into a lovely drawing room done up in shades of turquoise and red. On the walls, Ottilie recognized Mughal court paintings, their vibrant colors and gold frames a striking contrast to the wood paneling.

She stood in the center of the room and turned, taking it in. "It's lovely." A painting of a beautiful woman, bedecked in bangles and a jeweled turban, caught her attention. A parrot rested on the woman's fingers, which had been stained with henna, and outside the window behind her, a jungle of fruit trees and a sunset the color of blushing mangos filled the scene.

Ottilie's breath caught. Longing, intense and poignant, burrowed beneath her ribs.

"She reminds me of you," Everett said, coming to stand beside her. "I sometimes stare at her and wonder who she was. What she was like."

"She was in love."

There was a smile in Everett's voice. "How do you know that?"

How did she? She could reference the henna and jewelry, make up something about the symbolism of the fruit and bird, all declaring an upcoming marriage. Telling the story of a bride.

But it wasn't that. She could have just been a princess. A wealthy woman posing for a portrait.

No, Ottilie saw it in the woman's cloudy gaze. In the gentle way her fingers curved, allowing the bird to perch. In the slope of her shoulders and angle of the necklaces, all pointing toward the woman's breast, rounded over a heart that told stories of romance.

Ottilie saw herself in the woman. But there was a difference, and the pain of it made her unable to answer. They were both in love. But the woman in the painting was secure in it. Comfortable and aware. Accepted.

Ottilie was none of those things.

The woman was home. Ottilie didn't think she'd ever find home again.

"Does your employer collect Indian art?" she asked, evading Everett's question.

"He does. He's spent a lifetime building his plantations into the largest and best producing in all of India. His father was one of the first Brits to cultivate tea there. His grandfather and great-grandfather owned plantations in China. He used to spend great swaths of time in India, but now he has overseers who do that work."

"Did he return to England permanently because of you? He took you in, did he not?"

"He did, but I doubt that was the reason he stopped going to India. We aren't close. I am nothing more than a distant relation, and he will never claim me as anything else." Everett drew his brows together and stared at the portrait. Then he blinked and shook his head. "Would you like some tea?" He stepped toward the pull hanging on the wall. "I'm told the new blend they've developed is excellent."

Ottilie shook her head. She'd been distracted by the paintings, but now her mind turned back to the reason she'd come. Comfort and guidance. She was in desperate need of both. "Everett, what am I to do about Thaddeus?"

He sighed. "He must go to school, Ottilie. You have to understand that."

"I do. But why so soon? Why so far away?"

"We're not a people known for being particularly open-minded"—he gave her a rueful smile—"and Thaddeus will have to conform in order to be accepted."

"Accepted by whom?"

"By society, of course."

Ottilie's gaze swept him, from the top of his perfectly styled hair to the tips of his shoes. She counted him among one of the best men she'd ever known. And yet even he seemed caught up by what society expected. What they wanted. "Why should something so nebulous, so changing, matter? Why should we care if they accept Thaddeus? If they approve of him? Why should you care? I don't understand any of this. You, Alberta, Lady Sunderson—you are all willing to make decisions because of people who care nothing for you."

Everett looked past her. He ignored her words. Ignored her? "He has a responsibility to adapt to his new home. People must know what to expect from him. And he must give it. He doesn't live only for himself. He's obligated to make choices that benefit the people who rely on him—the rest of his family, those living on his estate and in the villages, the farmers who provide him with an income, his descendants." As he spoke, his expression grew increasingly blank. His fingers worked the buttons of his vest, and his vibrant eyes turned as dull as the landscape outside.

"You speak of more than Thaddeus, don't you?"

He lifted a hand to her cheek but didn't touch her, dropping his arm before she could lean into it. "I never meant to hurt you."

"I know. Perhaps I saw more between us than you intended."

"No, you didn't. You saw exactly what was there. I failed you in my inability to conceal how I felt for you. I have obligations, you see. A responsibility to conform." His throat worked, and the hollows of his cheeks shadowed. He curled his lower lip between his teeth.

She remembered her initial thoughts of him—that his face held no arresting quality. Nothing that would make a woman stop and notice. But now it was impossibly dear. She didn't care if he noticed. Didn't care if he misinterpreted her motive. She stared. Committed to memory his broad forehead, heavy brows, sharp nose and chin. The way his eyes gleamed and snapped. The wrinkles across his forehead that she wished to smooth.

"Don't," he said. "Don't look at me like that. No one deserves it less."

"That may be so, but I offer it to you anyway."

"You may regret it when you hear my story."

You must look deeper, beneath what a person shows. There's always a story, Niraja. Things are never what they seem.

Nānī's words bolstered Ottilie. Maybe in the understanding, she would see a resolution. Some way to overcome what Everett thought insurmountable. "Tell me."

He led her to a settee tucked into the corner of the room. Sitting beside her, he leaned forward, resting his elbows on his knees, hands loosely folded. "It is hard to confess that which is meant to remain hidden. My employer, whom you know as my cousin, Mr. Charles Fernsby, lost his wife twenty-seven years ago. They had no children, but from what I understand, he loved her immensely. When she died, Mr. Fernsby gave himself to his work, but he's not a cold man, and he eventually found comfort in the arms of a maid."

Ottilie's mouth turned sour, and she longed to reach for him. It was one thing to have an Indian mother. Quite another to have an unwed one.

"You're probably able to deduce where I'm headed with this." She nodded.

"My father—how strange to refer to him that way—went to India for a year. The maid, Agatha Scott, stayed at Maybourne

Park, left only with a gold and sapphire ring and the promise of a quiet wedding when he returned."

"Why didn't he marry her before he left?"

"She refused him. She knew, once they wed, he would suffer socially for her sake. She wanted him to be sure his affections were strong enough to withstand that. And she assumed that if he returned and still felt the same, they would be. She didn't realize, when he left, that she was already pregnant. I think she would have made a very different decision."

"What happened then?" Ottilie asked, although she could imagine. A pregnant maid wouldn't last long in a grand house.

"She was kicked out of the house without references when it became impossible to hide. She went home, but the situation became unbearable when I was about a year old. She left to find work for the same reason she had the first time—her father was a brute. But this time he'd turned his violence against me. She sent a letter to Mr. Fernsby, but there was no answer, and she assumed he'd forgotten her while traveling, just as she knew he would. She supported herself for a few years by taking in laundry, but then she became ill. It started as minor episodes of breathlessness, but they came more frequently and more violently." He gazed past Ottilie, seeing and remembering. Silent as he thought of his mother and all she had suffered. Then he refocused and continued. "Eventually she couldn't work. She tried, Ottilie. She really did, but every effort brought on a fit that had her gasping for breath."

"Of course she tried." A thought occurred to her. "Did she sell the ring your father gave her? Was it valuable?"

"She refused. She saved it for me, knowing it would pay for school or a start in business. I still have it, though I never look at it.

"When Mr. Fernsby returned to England and discovered her gone, he looked for her. He never stopped, for he truly loved her. No one knows what happened to the letter she sent. Perhaps it was lost in transit or the housekeeper destroyed it. Whatever the reason, he was too late to save her."

"But not too late to save you." And Ottilie was glad. Not for his suffering, of course, but that Everett had been found. That he had found Thaddeus. And her. "When you said he would never claim you, you meant as his son."

"Everyone knows—we look too much alike for him to be anything other than my father—but no one speaks about it. I will always be the poor relation, the cousin dependent on Mr. Fernsby's benevolence. Even after he dies and I am no longer poor."

"But if everyone knows, why not speak of it freely?"

"That isn't how things work. As long as people can *pretend* not to know, they have an excuse to accept me among them, at least superficially. But if forced to acknowledge the truth, if I insisted on making it an issue, there would no longer be a buffer between me and their rigid principles. I would make myself a pariah, and not even my father's money and influence could help me."

Ottilie leaned toward him and rested her hand on his cheek. "This isn't so much a barrier, Everett, as a hurdle. I care little for acceptance into society."

He covered her hand with his own and closed his eyes, pressing his forehead against hers, the slip of his breath tickling her lips and causing them to part in anticipation. But only his voice crept across the air, his words kissing her when she wanted his mouth. "My heart, my love."

Such a short space to cross. It didn't take much—a slight push forward, an inclination of her head—and she grazed his lips. He sucked in a draught of air, a man drowning. Ottilie knew she could give him life. Could save him from loneliness and isolation. And they would be knit together. Whole.

But he pulled back and set her away from him, his hands gripping her arms as though unsure whether to release or clasp. "No . . . you don't understand. I *can't* be with you, Ottilie. Not because I have nothing to offer you or because my history might destroy your future, but because . . ." He released her and scrambled from the settee as though it were on fire.

She saw then what he wouldn't say and watched as he stepped back, the sunlight streaming through the windows shadowing his face. Ice that had nothing to do with the weather swept over her. "Because *my* history would destroy *your* future."

22

Thaddeus hunched over his schoolroom desk, copying out of *Penny Whistles*. Lady Sunderson had given him the poetry collection by Robert Louis Stevenson a week after they arrived. Thaddeus had inherited their father's love of verse. It was a family trait that wove them together.

Ottilie told him to come to her room when he finished his copywork, then made her way down the steps and the hall. She tried for a little while to work on an old reticule that needed sprucing up. A trim of fringe here, a stitch of embroidery there. But her sorrow spilled over, threatening tears, so she set the bag aside and clenched her teeth. She'd spent too much time grieving Victor. She knew how it went. Eventually the ache would diminish and become bearable. She'd think of Everett less and less until, one day, she'd think of him not at all.

Eventually . . . but not now. It hadn't yet been a week.

A tear splashed her cheek, and she dashed it away. She laid her hand on Nānī's Bible and lifted a desperate prayer. *Let me forget him soon.*

But she could still hear his steps pounding after her as she darted from the drawing room, the house, his presence. "I have to marry well, Ottilie. The future of Mr. Fernsby's business depends on it." His words pursued her, and she couldn't outrun them. The future of the *tea business*? That was the future Everett chose to prioritize?

Then he had caught up to her, and she gripped her knees and hunched over the bare ground at the treeline that would have swallowed her whole if she'd been faster. If the cold air hadn't seized her lungs.

"Do you understand?" he asked. "I must become a member of that club. It will legitimize me. Not only will I have access to a large pool of wealthy business owners committed to helping each other be as successful as possible—thereby helping me make Mr. Fernsby's holdings stronger and more productive than ever— but I will also belong. In a way I've never belonged anywhere."

"But you could belong to *me*." She covered her mouth with her hands and squeezed her eyes closed. "And I could belong to you. Why is that not enough?"

He drew near. A whisper away. "I've spent my entire life wanting to bridge this divide between myself and my father. I want him to be proud of me. To know that I was worth his effort. To prove I am worthy of his trust and legacy. Of this inheritance he will leave me. He has been a member of this club for decades, as was his father before him. It is my family legacy. The only one I am permitted to claim."

"And you cannot claim it with an Indian wife?"

"I need two nominations and the majority vote. No one else will nominate me unless I bind myself to the family of an established member. I have tried and failed too many times already, and Mr. Fernsby made this suggestion, knowing my inheritance would make some man, some woman, overlook my past. I am honor bound to follow his guidance in this."

"Honor bound to . . . Everett, do you hear yourself? He's cared for you only enough to give you money, but not his name. You owe him nothing."

"But what about my children? Do I owe them nothing, as well? Because if I marry someone suitable, if I can maintain a membership at Welbourne's, then they would belong in a way I never have. I cannot burden them with my own fate." He shook his head, all the brightness absent from his beautiful eyes. His lips had pulled into a sad frown when she needed to see his smile.

Ottilie blinked away his image and flipped through the pages of the Bible until she found what she was looking for. She hadn't noticed Niraja's original thought, cramped against the underlined passage, when she'd initially read Nānī's answer. And she wanted to know what had brought about that response. *There's always a story.*

Gitisha, your British soldier is wed to the East India Company. You've heard Father talk. They aren't to be trusted. Traded with, yes. Married to? Never. I worry for you.

Ottilie read the tiny printed words Niraja had underlined, and they screamed accusation. Four verses that would later be validated.

These six things doth the Lord hate: yea, seven are an abomination unto him: A proud look, a lying tongue, and hands that shed innocent blood, an heart that deviseth wicked imaginations, feet that be swift in running to mischief, a false witness that speaketh lies, and he that soweth discord among the brethren.

And Nānī's now familiar handwriting, looping out a rebuttal.

You must look deeper beneath what a person shows. There's always a story, Niraja. Things are never what they seem.

"Oh, Nānī. How wrong you were." Sometimes things were exactly as they seemed. And sometimes stories did little to soften the blow.

Ottilie closed the Bible and put it away. Her eyes were drawn outside the window, where the sun, shyly peeking over a hazy cloud, watered the ground with tender rays.

The day after her visit to Maybourne Park, a late-season snowstorm had blanketed the estate in a foot of snow, forcing them all indoors. Then it began to melt, pocketing the lawn with muddy puddles—"muddles" Thaddeus called them—slurping at their boots and conspiring to trip anyone who dared to walk across it.

But today it looked dry.

Thaddeus stepped into her room, hair sticking up in every direction. "I've finished my work."

Ottilie glanced out the window again. "Let's go for a walk."

"It isn't time for our constitutional."

She rolled her eyes. "I think we can break schedule and enjoy the morning while the sun is out. You've been spending entirely too much time indoors, and you're beginning to look pale."

Thaddeus glanced toward the window and nodded, a grin brightening his face. "The sun, the sun, the sun is out . . ." His song remained when he disappeared into his room, and it stirred within her the fragile cord of hope and faith that had nearly snapped at Everett's confession.

She'd run from him, his words trailing her all the way back to Hazelbrook Manor. *I would belong. My children would belong.*

And the words he hadn't said tore at her, vicious dogs baring their teeth. *You don't belong. You will never belong. We would never belong.*

But his children would be accepted. For them, and for the father who wouldn't claim him, and for a tenuous grasp on respectability, Everett would continue walking that in-between place of gray shadows where there was no space for her.

Thaddeus dashed through the door that joined their rooms, coat buttoned crookedly and hat askew. She smiled. "Come here and let me take care of this."

After she straightened her brother and donned her own coat,

gloves, and hat, she lifted her needle and thread, as well as the final handkerchief she was working on for Damaris. A set of six, each boasting a different flower meant to represent their friendship. This one, an oak-leaved geranium, sported two-toned lilac and magenta petals tucked into bushy beetle-wing leaves.

They made their way to the front of the house, where Ottilie took a seat on the stone bench hidden in the shadows of the wall dividing the house from the cemetery and chapel. As she stitched, Thaddeus ran up and down the long drive that traced the front of the manor. He did cartwheels in the grass, throwing himself into a heap when his energy was spent, then leaping back up and dashing away again. A young boy needed space and freedom.

The sun's kindness worked to disperse the remaining wisps of sadness clinging to her, and Ottilie urged her thoughts outward to the things that mattered most. Her brother, laughing and tumbling. A gift for a friend that she hoped would bring a smile.

When had she last been free to laugh? To embrace joy? To experience light and life and pleasure without darkness grabbing for her, clawing her faith to shreds and grasping for her happiness? She couldn't remember.

Thaddeus was happy. He laughed and played and enjoyed his freedom. She could rejoice in that alone.

The crunching of gravel alerted her to someone approaching, and she took her eyes off Thaddeus, who was rolling around in the grass like a wolfhound.

"Miss," Harriet called, waving a letter, "this was just delivered."

The thin envelope sported a trail of stamps—Indian stamps—and Ottilie grinned when she recognized Damaris's handwriting. There hadn't been enough time for Damaris to receive Ottilie's letter, but reading her friend's words always brightened her mood.

Harriet shivered and curled her arms around her torso.

"Go inside before you catch a cold. It's not warm enough to go without a shawl or coat."

When Harriet left, Ottilie set her embroidery aside and slid her finger beneath a corner of the flap, releasing the glue. The letter was short. As brief and pithy as Damaris herself.

Darling Ottilie,

I've done it. I've convinced Mother and Father I would be better off in England. I'm not proud of my methods—I hope you don't find them offensive—but I took to wearing a kurta and pajamas around the house. Mother nearly fainted. I explained how terribly hot British clothes were. How little sense they made in India. I became involved with an Indian suffrage organization. I hope my work with them has some lasting effect, but truth be told, I can change much more in England with my writing than I can here.

I did everything I could to convince my parents I was less of a risk out of India than in it.

And I will be leaving soon, my dear friend. I will most likely stay with my aunt for a while in Bath, which isn't far from Elbury, and then we will go to London until the end of summer. I hope to see you soon!

With love,
Damaris

Ottilie pressed the paper to her nose and inhaled the attar of sandalwood that her friend rubbed on her wrists every morning. Damaris would soon visit, and the sun seemed brighter already.

"Good news, I hope." Alberta crossed the drive and stood before Ottilie.

"Yes. My dearest friend, Damaris Winship, will be returning to England."

"Lovely." Alberta sat beside her and watched Thaddeus, who had thrown himself on his back, arms and legs akimbo, and was tracking clouds passing across the sky. "He'll be leaving soon. You must prepare yourself."

"How can I? Prepare myself to lose the only thing in this world that matters to me? The only person I have left. You ask the impossible."

Alberta flinched. "I know you hate us. Hate Hazelbrook Manor and Elbury and all of England. But we're still your family. Maybe you could look outside your relationship with Sunderson and consider there are others in your life you could claim."

Ottilie's thoughts froze, and she shook her head. "I should look toward others? I should claim others?" Her laugh, cynical and twisted, drew Alberta's head around. "You rejected me the moment I stepped from the carriage. Your unkindness toward me has encouraged the staff to treat me with indifference, at best, and callous prejudice most of the time. You have repeatedly told me that my presence threatens my brother's happiness when my entire life has been devoted to him. I am not the one who needs to do anything." She stood, clutching Damaris's letter and the handkerchief to her chest. "And I don't hate Elbury because I have never been permitted to see it. Hazelbrook Manor, though . . . how could anyone love a prison?"

Unwilling to disturb Thaddeus's happy break, she stalked the other direction, moving beneath the arch that separated the main part of the house from the stables and outbuildings, and rounded the wall.

She picked her way around tumbled gravestones marking the resting places of people who meant nothing to her but should have, tucked herself behind the church, and waited for her spirit to settle in this place she never could.

Ottilie had, in the three days since her conversation with Alberta, worked hard to avoid her grandmother and aunt. She couldn't face them. Couldn't hide her anger. She sought out Scripture in Nānī's Bible that spoke of acceptance and peace, hoping her grandmother's words would soothe her bruised spirit, but the pain hadn't lessened. She'd only managed to seal it with a layer of varnish that kept it from bleeding into every day.

She sat with Thaddeus in the schoolroom, convincing him history trumped playing outside, but Harriet had opened the windows before breakfast, filling the room with the sweet scent of early spring blooms.

Gripping his pencil, he scribbled through a misspelled Anne of Cleves. He threw it down, and it rolled off the edge of his desk. "Please, can we be done?"

Ottilie retrieved the pencil and glanced across the room at the window spilling light over the worn rug. She'd known when she'd awoken that it would be a beautiful day. Warmer by at least ten degrees than all the rest they'd experienced in England. Maybe warm enough to release her from the chill that seeped into her bones and the sniffling that plagued her day and night. "We must not give anyone the impression you are uneducated. You will be attending school soon, and I won't have them say you are any less than the other boys."

"That won't happen." Alberta entered the room, tugging on a pair of gloves. "English schools are less worried about academics and more about how a boy of good breeding behaves."

Ottilie sat straight in her seat, back rigid. Alberta had never deigned to enter the schoolroom. "Perhaps that's true, but his father was invested in education and thought highly of it. I won't allow Thaddeus to remain ignorant like every other boy of *good breeding*."

Alberta stared at her, eyes flinty. Then her gaze slipped toward

Thaddeus, and she softened. "I thought you might like to walk with me to the village."

Thaddeus jumped up from his chair, and it clattered to the floor behind him. "Yes! Yes! Let's go."

"Thaddeus must finish his lessons and—"

"Both of you." Alberta rolled her lips together and looked everywhere but at Ottilie. "You're right. It isn't fair to keep you trapped at Hazelbrook." She smiled. "Good heavens, that sounds like the title of a novel."

"This story has all the makings of one, does it not?"

"I suppose, though I hope it has a happy ending." Alberta took a deep breath. "There is a chill in the air. You'll want to wear a coat. I'll meet you downstairs after you ready yourselves."

Ottilie wished she could refuse, but in truth she was desperate to see the village. Desperate to get away from the heavy paneling and twisting corridors of Hazelbrook Manor.

She tidied the schoolroom, gathered her wrap and gloves, and pinned her hat above the braid she'd twisted around the crown of her head that morning. She had half a dozen other hats that were better quality and more fashionable, but she always chose Maji's.

The walk to the village didn't take long, though the silence between them filled the twenty minutes with heavy awkwardness. They finally came to a small stone footbridge set over the shallow stream that hemmed in Elbury's south side. Crooked houses, leaning against one another as though embracing, jabbed peaked roofs at the sky. Huddled between the gentle swells of hills, the village was a storybook hamlet that was beginning to shed its dull winter coat.

Thaddeus had picked up a stick somewhere along the way and now smacked it against the stones lining the bridge. Ahead of them, the lane spilled onto Brooke Street and was lined with two-story houses sporting gabled roofs and plain, homey fronts broken up by leaded windows and the occasional empty flower box.

"It's lovely." And it was. When Ottilie conjured up images of *village*, she saw thatched roofs and mudded brick walls. Rice paddies stretching toward the horizon. Parrots and monkeys and women walking down unpaved paths, their hips swaying and bangles jangling. Elbury looked solid, as though it had been built a thousand years earlier and would exist a thousand years in the future.

They waited for a wagon to pass before crossing the street. "Where are we going?" Ottilie asked.

"Mr. Ainsworth, who works at the carpet mill, has been ill and unable to leave his bed. He has three young children, so I'm bringing them enough food to last a few more days. Hopefully he'll soon be better. And Mrs. Thomas just had twins. They were born two months early, but both seem healthy enough. I embroidered bonnets and had Mrs. Harris pack some preserves and a loaf of good bread. And I told the vicar I would bring him a book I thought he would enjoy. He's been so lonely since his wife died. His daughter lives two villages over and has five children. She's not able to visit very often. And there's a widow I've been meaning to—"

"Why do you do all this?" Ottilie had known many people who made it their mission in life to ease the burdens of others—Nānī had spent hours each week traveling around Calcutta with a group of elderly Christian women, ministering to the ill and hurting—but as Alberta listed her tasks, Ottilie had noted the desperation in her voice. It was a bowl cupping her never-ending catalog of philanthropy, spilling out duties and refilling just as quickly.

"Why?" Alberta glanced at Ottilie, gave her a peculiar smile, and patted the linen cloth covering the basket. "It's my duty to provide for those suffering in the village. This is our land, after all. Our people."

"I know that, but why do *you* do all this? Why not send someone? You come three or four times a week. Is that common for someone of your station?"

"'God loveth a cheerful giver.'" Alberta took Thaddeus's hand and steered him around the corner.

Ottilie raised her brows but said nothing. Alberta didn't seem cheerful in her giving.

They came to the intersection of Church Lane with Market Place, and Alberta pointed out the square set with a formal garden, a statue of a man on a horse, and a smattering of benches. "This area used to be a thriving weekly market. In my grandfather's day, people gathered to sell meat, produce, and cloth."

Now it featured a tidy row of shops that displayed painted tea sets, feathered hats, and tin trains being ridden by teddy bears.

"The Thomases live above the toy shop," Alberta said, her words getting caught up in the crunch of wheels and clop-clop of horses. She gave Ottilie a side glance and pulled her lip between her teeth before plowing forward.

A bell rang above the door as they entered, and Thaddeus made an immediate beeline for a display of carved and painted wooden soldiers, complete with horses, cannons, and fencing.

"Miss Russell," a man said, coming around the counter. "How kind of you to come. Mrs. Thomas is resting—the babes were up all through the night—but if you'd like to give her a few minutes, I can let her know you're here."

"That's all right. Let her sleep." Alberta set the basket on the counter and removed a loaf of bread and two small jars of jam. "I thought she might enjoy some fresh bread. I didn't think she was up to making it herself just yet." She reached into her reticule and pulled out a bundle. "I embroidered some bonnets for the babies. I hope she likes them."

The shopkeeper grinned, and his large fingers brushed the delicate flowers adorning the linen. "She will love them. How kind of you to think of us and take the time to do this."

Alberta sighed, and when Ottilie glanced at her, she noticed a relaxing of her shoulders. A softening of her profile.

"I'm *happy* to do it."

Ottilie had never thought it possible for a person to glare and smile at the same time, but Alberta managed to send such an expression her way. "Miss Singh, I'd like to introduce Mr. Thomas. Miss Singh has recently come from India with Lord Sunderson."

The man gave Ottilie a frank stare, his face wide and open. Curious. "I've never met anyone from India. I heard you'd come to visit, but I didn't know what to expect."

"I expect something more interesting than I." Ottilie smiled. She liked him. Being looked at with anything other than the distrust and revulsion of the house staff was a refreshing state of affairs.

Alberta resettled her basket over her arm. "Would you pack up a set of those soldiers and have them sent to the house? Lord Sunderson seems to be enjoying them."

After Mr. Thomas, gleeful smile in place, had crossed the store to ask Thaddeus which ones he preferred, Ottilie shook her head. "He has enough toys at the house. An entire set of red-coated soldiers."

Alberta crossed her arms. "Well, now he can have an entire set of French or German ones, as well, and stage a war. The English can't very well fight themselves."

"No, that wouldn't do. Not when there's an entire world to conquer."

Alberta's hand twisted the basket handle, and her lips thinned. "You speak with so little regard for your brother's heritage." Ottilie raised her brows, and Alberta quickly recognized her mistake. "And yours, of course. Though it doesn't seem likely you will embrace it anytime soon."

"My entire experience with Englishmen—especially military men—has been fraught with betrayal and lies. I feel no affinity toward that part of my heritage."

"Well, you say you loved your father, and you seem to trust Everett enough."

Ottilie looked away and began to stroke the velvet dress of the porcelain doll on the table beside her. She *had* loved her father, though he had displayed a shocking lack of judgment and foresight. And Everett . . . Ottilie pinched the lace edging the doll's collar. She couldn't think about Everett right now.

"Anyway," Alberta said, "I like to see Thaddeus made happy. I know there's been so little of it the last year. And this sale will ensure Mr. Thomas can pay a neighbor to make their meals for another week, giving Mrs. Thomas time to rest."

At Thaddeus's exuberant shout, they turned to watch him point out his favorite figures as the shopkeeper collected them. When they finished, Thaddeus bounced toward Ottilie, head bobbing the way it did when he was excited. Just before he reached the counter, he shouted, "Everett!" and tore off through the store, yanking open the door and throwing himself at his friend.

Ottilie hadn't seen Everett since her visit to Maybourne Park. She'd been trying to convince herself she would grow used to the idea of life without him. But seeing his surprised smile flash, meeting his beautiful eyes over a table piled high with books of paper dolls, she realized there wasn't a shred of truth to it.

Thaddeus tugged Everett farther into the store, chattering about his new soldiers and asking why he hadn't been to visit in such a long time.

She would need to speak with Everett. If she didn't, Thaddeus would notice their awkwardness, and his questions would never end. Ottilie didn't think she had ever sacrificed so much for her brother. She gladly worked her fingers to the bone, traveled across the world, and pretended to be a servant for him. But this—pretending she didn't stand there, her heart in Everett's hands—seemed a perilous endeavor.

Everett looked up at them, his eyes first meeting Alberta's in what was obviously a show of nonchalance before sweeping toward her. Had any man ever shown so much in a look? So much yearning and despair, joy and pain glinting from eyes as green as the grass poking from the awakening ground. But this was no rebirth. It was longing cloaked in futility.

"Ottilie."

She couldn't hear her name on his tongue—he spoke barely above a whisper—but she could taste it. She could see it. She could feel it. She wanted nothing more, in that moment, than to nestle against him and listen to him say it, his soft voice rounding the syllables in an embrace more tender than any woman had ever experienced.

"This is all very Shakespearean," Alberta said quietly, so only Ottilie could hear, "but if you're going to say hello, you might do it now, as I still have visits to make. Unless you want me to leave you to him? I'm sure he's willing to escort you home."

Ottilie snapped her head around and frowned.

Alberta rolled her eyes. "I may be a spinster, but I'm not blind."

"Very well." *Courage, Ottilie.* She checked the buttons of her jacket and straightened the flounces at her wrists, then walked over to Everett with as much grace as she could.

"Hello, Mr. Scott." She thought she sounded normal, but Thaddeus looked at her, his nose wrinkled.

"Miss Singh. It's nice to see you."

Oh, this was painful. Ottilie needed to be free of it.

"Why are you speaking to each other like that? Did you argue?" Thaddeus looked between them and shook his head. "Everett, can you come over before I leave for school?"

Ottilie glanced at him sharply. "It hasn't been decided that you shall leave."

"It has," Alberta said.

Ottilie pinched her lips, and her nose began to burn. "I cannot . . . I cannot speak any longer." She looked at Everett but didn't meet his eyes. Her carefully constructed mask was held up by scaffolding made of plaster and desperation. It would crumble if he looked too deeply. "Please, come to visit. We should like that." She took Thaddeus's hand, called a thank-you to Mr. Thomas for seeing to the delivery of the soldiers, and left the store, pride intact.

But little else.

23

Between Hazelbrook Manor's foyer and drawing room, there rose two stories of glass that curved around a grouping of delicate chairs. Lady Sunderson had called it the oriel. It offered lovely views of the drive, the stone wall, and the church spire rising beyond it. Ottilie sometimes found herself pausing within its embrace, watching as the sun rose or set, throwing golden light over the worn stones of the floor. It was, perhaps, the loveliest spot in the house. No one ever found Ottilie there. For a few precious moments, she could close her eyes and feel the warmth on her face, see the red glow behind her eyelids, and believe she was home.

After walking home from Elbury, lunch, and visiting with Lady Sunderson, Ottilie settled Thaddeus into the schoolroom with the few toy soliders he'd carried from the shop. Then she returned downstairs with her embroidery, knowing the oriel offered the best light. She was nearing the end of her work on the jacket and had only a few final stitches to complete it. Damaris's handkerchiefs were also finished, and Ottilie only awaited her friend's visit to gift them to her.

Ottilie was so distracted by the view's loveliness that she walked straight toward the window and didn't notice Alberta until she practically stood before her. "I'm so sorry." Ottilie pressed the jacket to her chest. "I normally find myself alone here."

Alberta stood and dashed her hand across her eyes. "No, please sit. I won't bother you." She turned away, her hands stiff and gripping her skirt.

There was something in the sloping of Alberta's shoulders—a despondency that spoke of deep grief—that filled Ottilie with compassion. "Are you all right?"

Alberta's steps paused, and Ottilie detected a shudder making its way across her aunt's back. "I will be. March is always a hard month for me."

Ottilie sat in one of the seats. "Is that why you didn't want to celebrate Thaddeus's birthday?"

"March first is the hardest day of all." Alberta turned, and Ottilie was struck by the naked sorrow on her face. The longing and desperation.

"Do you want to talk about it?"

"It's a terrible secret."

Ottilie would have let her go if not for the knowledge that secrets had caused so much pain in her own life. "You do not have to confide it. I know there is no reason for you to trust me, except that I am in no position to judge, and you care little for my good opinion anyway. But I have learned that secrets have a way of poisoning everything from the inside out. It's sometimes a blessed relief to share them."

Alberta wavered, literally swaying back and forth between Ottilie and the staircase leading away. Then there was a softening of her expression, a melting away of tension and a release of burden. She approached on soft steps and sat in the chair next to Ottilie instead of opposite her. She offered only her profile.

"Everett knows about it, but it's not the kind of thing you speak of with a man you aren't married to. Mother knows, as well, but she cannot bear for me to talk about it. For seven years I have not said a word. That has been more painful than anything—feeling as though his life mattered so little that he isn't even spoken of."

"Who?" Ottilie asked softly.

Alberta had taken to picking her cuticles, tearing away little strips of skin and revealing raw flesh beneath. "William."

Ottilie shook her head. "Who is that?"

Alberta sighed. "Eight years ago I was in London for the Season. I had been out for three years with no interest. No prospects. I was nearing twenty-one. All of my friends had married or were engaged. I'm no great beauty, I know that, but I'd always assumed, with my dowry and status, I would make a match. Maybe not a grand one, but a suitable one. Father had just begun to show symptoms of the disease that would take his life, and I was desperate not to be a burden. To show him I was taken care of so he could rest. Then I met someone who promised me the moon."

Alberta paused and pressed her fingers to her lips. She would have had lovely hands, the crescents of her nails smooth and white, her skin unlined, had it not been for the reddened areas where she'd picked and bit.

"He didn't give it to you, I take it?" Ottilie knew something about men who made empty promises.

"No. He gave me a baby instead." Alberta dropped her head and clutched the back of her neck. Her words came out muffled. "William Joseph Russell. Born and died March 1, 1881."

Ottilie froze—her thoughts, her movements, her breathing.

Alberta's shoulders began to quake, but when she looked up, her face shone. Tears tracked down her cheeks and fell onto lips that curved upward in a smile. "I haven't said his name since that wonderful and terrible day. He was born too soon and lived but an hour. But his life had value. He merits my thoughts and words, don't you think?"

Ottilie nodded but said nothing. Could say nothing. No wonder Alberta had bowed out of Thaddeus's birthday celebration.

Ottilie had thought her priggishly against the idea of indulgence, but she had, in fact, been sent to bed with grief.

"It was years before I learned of Thaddeus's birth. Mother said nothing, fearing it would break me. And when I finally found out, when I discovered they shared a birthday . . ." Alberta looked out the window, staring past Ottilie at the drive and wall and treetops. "I thought God was redeeming me. Giving me the opportunity to mother. To take back what I had lost."

"But I came with him."

Alberta stiffened. "I wasn't only jealous for his affection." She looked at Ottilie. "You must know that I understand your relationship. I believe there is room for both of us in his heart. It's only that . . . I want for Sunderson everything I wanted for my own son. Even had he lived, I wouldn't have been able to give it to him. We'd already found an adoptive family. A good one who could offer him love and support, but not a position in society. Not wealth. But I dreamed. I dreamed for months. One day . . . one day I could claim my child. One day he would become everything he was meant to be. I don't want that future stolen from Sunderson the way it was from William—be it by death or scandal."

Society again. Desperate for their approval, for position, even as they rejected and disapproved. Here Alberta sat, hidden away in her rambling home, afraid of what would happen if her secret became known. Afraid of what would happen if Thaddeus's secret became known. Afraid. Yet she still talked as though her lost son would have been happier with society's approval than with an unknown family and their love. Ottilie's position engendered most people's pity, but she couldn't help feeling that exact emotion for Alberta, who seemed to have everything Ottilie lacked but was still bound by fear.

"What happened to the father?"

Alberta blinked, and the almost zealous light in her gaze dimmed. "I told him about the baby, and he said it must not be his. He painted me the harlot. Here, in my own house. Father was hosting a hunting party, and my lover"—she spit the word, bitterness rounding the edges of it—"was the son of an old friend. Practically a neighbor. Everett found me in the orangery, and when he discovered what had happened, he insisted the man marry me. But I didn't want to be forced into a loveless life with someone who resented my every breathing moment. What type of life would that have been for a child, anyway? I refused to tell my parents who the father was, and they sent me to a distant cousin in Scotland, where I was supposed to recover from a made-up illness and return home in spectacular health."

"This explains the deep bond you have with Everett. The loyalty between the two of you."

"Everett has been my dearest friend since we were very young. He is the only person who understands the tragedy of my experience. Who understands but doesn't criticize. It was hard for him, to let me suffer alone. To be unable to restore my honor. I think, in a way, I became like his mother in his mind. And he felt he had failed her all over again." Alberta looked at Ottilie. "You asked me, when we went into Elbury, why I do all of it. It's because of this. It's restitution."

They fell silent, the telling of the story a heavy burden that filled the oriel with dashed dreams and frustrated hopes. And then, from outside the window, came the high trill of a birdsong. The soft, sweet call of a warbler looking for a mate. It broke the gloom and ushered in the sun that peered from behind a canopy of clouds and pierced through the windows.

And with it came hope.

For if Alberta had softened toward Ottilie, if she thought enough of her to share this story, perhaps, then, Ottilie would find peace at Hazelbrook Manor. Perhaps she might one day belong here.

Perhaps she might find family and love.

Ottilie spent every moment with Thaddeus over the next couple of weeks. She'd hoped the softening between her and Alberta indicated a chance to convince them of Thaddeus's need to remain at Hazelbrook Manor, but that hope was quickly dashed when Lady Sunderson insisted he go to school. And soon.

Ottilie offered to take a less active role in her brother's education so they could engage a suitable English tutor, but Lady Sunderson remained firm in her decision. Even when Ottilie leveraged her knowledge of Alberta's private pain and begged her to remember the sorrow of losing a child, to consider how it would grieve her, her aunt only shook her head and said, "But he must be educated if he is to be the baron he is meant to be."

Nothing swayed them. Not logical arguments, nor tears.

And now Ottilie sat in the drawing room one final time with her brother, the settee behind them stiff and unyielding. Everett had come as well.

The scene before her was cozy. As soon as they entered the drawing room, Lady Sunderson invited Thaddeus to sit with her while she read from *Pinocchio*, a book she'd recently purchased about a boy who lied and paid a price.

As Ottilie listened to the story, she found herself identifying with the wooden puppet who didn't belong. Who wanted only to be a real boy. To be embraced and loved and know he had something of value to offer. She blinked back tears and sniffed, ignoring the look Everett gave her from his seat beside her.

"Are you well?" he whispered.

"How could I be, when my brother is leaving this afternoon? When they are forcing him away from the last remaining thing familiar to him?" Her response came out in a series of hisses, drawing Alberta's attention. She shook her head, brows slashing above her eyes.

Everett turned his gaze toward Thaddeus, snuggled up between Lady Sunderson and Alberta. "He doesn't look unhappy about it, though. And it is necessary."

Ottilie wanted to lash out—at Everett and Lady Sunderson and Alberta. But instead she looked at her brother and saw that what Everett said was true. Thaddeus didn't seem unhappy. After his initial reaction to the news that he was to leave for school, he had grown steadily more used to the idea until, eventually, he began to talk of it with excitement.

When they had first arrived in England, Thaddeus had been timid and sad. Quiet, with none of the exuberance that characterized little boys. His sleep had been broken up with nightmares, and he often cried out for Nānī and Maji, causing Ottilie to weep, her tears wetting the pillow.

But in the last month, he'd grown lively. His smile bloomed again, the way it had before Maji died. He hadn't crept into Ottilie's bed in weeks. He played and ran and had a jolly time everywhere he went. Ottilie couldn't ignore the changes. She knew time was partially responsible, but so too, she recognized, was the settling in. The structure of days, decent regular meals, and deficiency of illnesses.

And most of all, the expanding of their family. The joy that came from being part of something bigger than oneself. Finally feeling at home. Because here, the boys would see only Lord Sunderson. They wouldn't see poverty. Or parents whose skin and cultures and countries faced one another with bayonets and enmity. Or a person at war within himself.

Ottilie leaned toward Everett. "Does every bit of his Indian blood need to be wrested from him until he only remembers the English? Because that's what they're doing to him."

He stilled at her question, her breath teasing the overlong wisps of hair that straggled near his ear. He sighed and turned to look at her. "They don't mean to do that. It's only that in order to belong in England, Thaddeus must be as English as possible."

"There will be no room for anything else."

"Perhaps. Or perhaps he'll remember anyway." He tipped his chin toward her brother. "I know you've no wish to embrace that part of yourself, despite the great regard you have for your father, but Sunderson is already filling the part. He belongs in England."

He belongs in England. Nothing about her. Everett might well think it better all around if she had never come.

Ottilie pulled herself inward, away from Everett, who sat only inches from her. Away from the settee that offered no comfortable retreat. Away from the knowledge that Thaddeus was Lord Sunderson, an essential part of a dynasty that was admired and distinguished. His ability to speak a handful of Indian languages and eat with his fingers was a charming quirk. And, except for a propensity to turn deeply golden in the sun, there was no identifying mark suggesting he was anything other than what he looked like—a British nobleman.

Ottilie's breath caught in her sternum. She refused its release, knowing it would depart as a sob. She wanted to tear the silly book from Lady Sunderson's hand and tell Thaddeus all about his family, going back hundreds of years. About Nānī and Maji and Niraja and their great-grandfather who wanted nothing more than India's freedom. She wanted to massage his scalp and feet with mustard oil, feed him slices of ripe mango, and tell him stories of maharajas and life before. And she wanted to do all of it in the familiar mix of Bengali and Hindi and English that was spoken in their home.

He could embrace his Britishness—she would allow it for Father's sake—but not if it meant forgetting the rest of him.

Ottilie's eyes burned, and she stared at the cozy scene, an unripe soap nut pressing against her chest, radiating pain up and around and through. After he spent a couple of years at Eton, she wouldn't recognize her brother.

She shifted on her seat, then spoke loudly enough that everyone present would hear. "I cannot allow you to make—"

Everett stood. "I think Miss Singh and I will visit while you spend some moments alone with Lord Sunderson." He took her hand, and she got to her feet, unable to resist without causing a scene.

"I'd like to stay here." She tugged away from him, but his grip tightened.

"I think it best you give them some time."

With no choice in the matter, she followed Everett from the drawing room. He led her to the oriel, where the midafternoon sun was a mellow filter, a softened glow that draped them in gilded light.

"What was that about?" Ottilie crossed her arms.

"I could sense the tension coming off you. You were breathing as heavily as if you'd just run from Elbury."

"Were you afraid I'd do something hasty? Betray my lack of breeding?"

He shook his head. "No. I only thought you needed a moment to collect yourself. I know this is a difficult day. I don't want you to say or do something you'll regret."

"I think they deserve every bit of censure I can offer."

"I'm not thinking of Lady Sunderson and Alberta. They are well aware of your feelings on this matter. I'm thinking of Sunderson. What do you think it would do to him if he knew how angry you are about this?"

"I'm not angry with him."

"He won't know the difference. He will remember it and believe it and wrap it around his life. You mean more to him than any other person in this world. He will not want to disappoint you, so the things you say and do will dictate who he becomes. What he says and does." Everett pressed his lips together, and his eyes shadowed before he turned his back to her. He walked toward the center window, pressing his hand against the glass. "Just think, Ottilie, what words you send him away with."

She inhaled deeply, seeing Everett's wisdom. His experience.

"You aren't only speaking about Thaddeus, are you?" She went to him and, after a moment's hesitation where her hand hovered in the space between them, touched his back.

He turned and caught her fingers, pressing a hard kiss to her knuckles. "If you lay on Thaddeus expectations he cannot possibly live up to, you burden him forever. And when you have come to terms with it all—and you will, for you must—he will still hear your voice."

"You don't even know what I was about to say." She tugged away from him. A cloud scuttled by, and the sun warmed the oriel, baking them behind the wall of glass.

"I have an idea. I know your biggest fear for him—it is a valid one—but I also know there is little you can do to stop it. Sunderson is young, and he will adapt. Trying to stop it is like trying to stop a train by standing on the tracks."

"You mean I will be run over, and he will continue on the tracks laid for him?"

His thumb found the tear that had slipped down her cheek. "I don't want you hurt."

Ottilie laughed. "It is entirely too late for that."

Wakefield appeared and cleared his throat. "Sir, it is time."

Ottilie glanced between Everett and the staid, always-in-control butler. "Time for what?"

Everett ducked his head and took a sudden interest in the carpet beneath his feet. "Lady Sunderson asked me to . . ." He tore his eyes from the floor and winced at her.

"Asked you to what?"

"Accompany Lord Sunderson to school and help him get settled."

Ottilie's head swung toward Wakefield, hoping she'd see something in his expression to refute Everett's words. Wakefield knew everything that happened at Hazelbrook Manor. And she could tell he knew Everett was correct. The butler bowed from the room.

"*I'm* accompanying Thaddeus to school. Alberta and I. It's all settled." Ottilie could hear the tears cloaking her words, and she hated them. Hated the weakness and desperation they revealed.

Everett shook his head, remorse making his face look plain once again. How had she once thought him the most beautiful man she'd ever met? Without his smile, genuine and spontaneous, and the light sparking his green eyes, there was nothing about him that merited her attraction. Nothing. "They decided it would be best if you remained home. They thought you might make it harder for Thaddeus to part ways."

"In other words, they thought I would make a scene. They thought I would act . . . decidedly not British." Her hands began to tremble, and she clasped them together. "Stiff upper lip and all that, correct? I'm lacking it. God forbid I show grief at losing my brother. At being left alone."

He stretched out his arm, hand reaching. "You are not alone."

Ottilie's chest hitched beneath the effort of restraining her tears. Everett had known how important it was that she spend every moment with Thaddeus before they were separated. He *knew*. And his betrayal made her lungs tighten, tighten, tighten. She drew in a heavy breath, but it didn't go deep enough. It swirled in a tight cloud, refusing to fill her. Refusing to refresh.

"Very well. Go." A wheeze followed her words, drawing a startled look from Everett. He stepped toward her. She held up her hand. "I will say good-bye to Thaddeus."

Pressing her fist to her chest, she panted as she walked back toward the drawing room.

They'd betrayed her. Every one of them.

And she had never felt so alone.

Thaddeus was trying to be brave. Ottilie saw it in the way he planted his feet on the drive, hip-width apart, the way his chin trembled, and the way he blinked too much.

She knelt in front of him, caring little about the dust, and placed her hands on his shoulders. "You can be sad."

He nodded. "I thought you were coming."

"I did too. But you will be fine. It will be an adventure with Everett." She wanted to claw the words back as they hung in the air and tell him he wasn't going to be all right. That Everett was the worst kind of person. But even Ottilie could see the excitement sparking behind Thaddeus's tears. He *was* going to be fine. She, on the other hand, felt as though the earth had tipped and everything was off its axis.

Behind them, Lady Sunderson and Alberta stood, collected and altogether composed. Not a tear shimmered in their eyes. Not a tremor shook their well wishes.

No wonder Papa had left this cold, unfeeling place. Ottilie felt stirrings to do the same, as though his discontent flowed beneath the very ground they stood upon. She could throw herself into the carriage and refuse to leave Thaddeus. How would he attend school if she wouldn't part from him? They would be forced to bring him home or risk exposing their carefully constructed story.

The baron and the ayah.

"It is time," Alberta said. "They will miss their train."

Ottilie heard the click of her aunt's watch. So very punctual. How would they respond if she displayed all the anguish and resentment boiling beneath her breast? She could taste the bitterness of it. When Alberta confided her story in her, Ottilie had thought it revealed a softening in her aunt's feelings toward her. Had thought it meant she would consider more carefully the pain she was inflicting. But Alberta remained determined. Unbent before Ottilie's wishes.

Thaddeus placed his cool hand against her cheek. "I *will* be fine, Didi. I know I need to go. But will you be fine?"

She cupped her palm over his fingers, trapping them against her. "I don't know. Without you near, who am I?"

Thaddeus sniffed and swiped his finger beneath his nose. Everett dangled a handkerchief between them, and Ottilie snatched it. She used the edge to remove all traces of Thaddeus's sadness.

Her brother smiled through the tears tracking his cheeks. "I know who you are! You're the beetle."

Ottilie's brows pinched. "The what?"

"The beetle. From our poem. Leading the way and working hard for everyone."

Ottilie gathered her brother to her chest. "Oh, little glowworm. How I love you most of all." All the love she'd had for Papa and Maji and Nānī and her long-gone siblings hadn't just disappeared when they'd slipped from this world. It had remained within her, spilling over onto her young brother. All of it for him. There was no one else, and she had so much love. She'd known the fullness of a heart brimming over and so many to pour it on. Now he was the sole recipient. She couldn't imagine what she would do with herself when the carriage rolled away.

"Ottilie," Everett said, "it's time."

Ottilie's stomach rolled, and her throat began to ache with the press of restrained tears.

Thaddeus tossed his arms around her waist and burrowed against her. "I'll miss you so much."

Ottilie nodded and pressed her nose to his hair, inhaling his sweet little-boy scent.

"You will see her in a few months, Sunderson," Alberta said. As though Ottilie would be satisfied with two weeks at Christmas and three weeks in the summer. As though she hadn't given Thaddeus everything she was, everything she had, and she wouldn't disappear like the mist that hung over Elbury when he left her.

Thaddeus cupped her face between his hands and gave her a very brave nod. "I *will* be all right. I will."

And with that, he allowed the footman to help him into the coach.

Everett's hand found Ottilie's arm, and she didn't have the energy to pull away when he helped her to her feet. "I didn't know, Ottilie, until this morning that they'd decided I would escort Sunderson to school. Truly. I wouldn't have chosen it this way."

"Yet you do it anyway." She looked past him at Thaddeus on the edge of his seat, his fingers gripping the cushion and eyes on her as he peered around the open door. She wouldn't crumble in front of him. She would allow him to leave free of worry for her. As angry as she was at Everett, she saw the wisdom in his advice. She didn't want Thaddeus to take ownership of her needs. He had enough to worry about.

"I owe Lady Sunderson and Alberta so much. I cannot say no."

Ottilie looked at Everett. "There are so many people you owe things to. So many people you refuse to say no to. It is unfortunate I am not one of them."

"I . . . I don't—"

She gave a sharp shake of her head. "No. Yours will not be the last words I hear before Thaddeus leaves." She swept toward the coach and held out her hand. The footman pretended not to see her, so she braced herself against the side of the door and balanced on the step. "Tell me you love me, Thaddeus, so I can sleep with your words in my heart."

"I love you, Ottilie."

She leaned in and pressed her forehead to his. "God go with you, glowworm, and don't forget who you are."

She jumped from her perch and stepped back so Everett could climb in. The coachman, reins in hand, encouraged the horses forward, and then Thaddeus was gone.

And she was left staring at the empty drive.

24

Ottilie went to bed after Thaddeus left. There was nothing to do but hope the pain would leave her alone in sleep.

It didn't.

She dreamed of running and searching and not finding. Through the twisted halls of Hazelbrook Manor, overgrown Calcutta cemeteries, in a boat traveling through the Ganges River full of bloated bodies. Blank eyes and faces covered in bruises. A hand lifted from the water and snaked over the edge of the boat to grab her foot.

With a scream, she bolted upright and kicked away the blanket twisting around her legs. She scraped her hands through her hair, which had tumbled from its pins, and wove it into a loose braid.

Twilight bathed her room in a diffused glow that softened the sharp edges of her nightmare, and she tossed her legs over the bed. Putting her head in her hands, she rubbed with firm fingers, wishing for Nānī's touch. A flask of mustard oil. The comfort of Maji's embrace.

A knock on the door made Ottilie sigh. "Come in."

Jessamine stepped through, a sour look pinching her lips.

"Lady Sunderson wants to know if you will come down to dinner."

"No. I think I will take a plate in my room, please."

Jessamine left without acknowledging her, and Ottilie went to her desk. Her hand hovered over the two books lying atop one another. Nānī's Bible and Blake's poems. She needed comfort. Hoped for wisdom.

"I believe in you. I believe you have a plan and purpose." *I believe. I believe. I believe.* She muttered the prayer like an incantation, hoping the thinking of it made it true. Knowing the believing required much more.

In momentary rebellion, she pushed the Bible aside and lifted the poetry.

Opening the cover, she flipped pages, knowing she needed the camaraderie of Blake's understanding. Her eyes fell to a poem she'd always detested.

> O Rose thou art sick.
> The invisible worm,
> That flies in the night
> In the howling storm:
> Has found out thy bed
> Of crimson joy:
> And his dark secret love
> Does thy life destroy.

It seemed so unfair. The beautiful rose, already pummeled by a storm, killed by an unseen blight. Why had God created the worm, knowing it would destroy what was left of the rose's beauty? Why had he allowed Ottilie to have a brilliantly happy start in life if he was only going to allow it all to be razed? Why had he given her a promise in those honest moments with Alberta, or allowed her to grow fond of Lady Sunderson's gentle touch, if they were only going to betray her deepest wish?

Why had he turned her heart toward Everett when that could never be?

She slammed the book closed and tossed it back into the drawer. It had brought no comfort. Blake's understanding of life's futility and absurd injustice only watered the seed of cynicism that had been planted in fertile soil.

"All right, Nānī. What say you and God?"

She set the Bible on her desk, but when she opened it, she didn't look for her grandmother's wisdom. She sought the Psalms. Her eyes skimmed the pages, stopping to gather words of encouragement like a bee did pollen, holding them to her heart to bring out later.

By the time Harriet came to start a fire, Ottilie had read a dozen poems by men who had known God, had sinned and lived and loved and felt abandoned and destroyed and gathered and built up. Men who believed that where the worm destroyed, new life emerged from the fallen petals and seeds.

Ottilie chose to trust in the God they called on.

She had no other choice.

She closed the Bible and noticed, for the first time, how dark her room had grown. She'd been squinting this last half hour, as the sun had gone to sleep beyond the horizon. Her stomach grumbled, and she realized Jessamine had never brought her dinner.

Of course not.

Ottilie straightened her bodice, then made her way from the room and down the hall, which was lit by gaslight sconces that cast her shadow against the walls. The main floor was dark, and Ottilie was aware of how empty Hazelbrook Manor had become since Thaddeus's departure. He was the light and life of this place. Without him, the rooms echoed with silence.

Depression reached for her with fingers as detestable and unwelcome as the ones attached to the dead bodies in her dream. It snatched bits and pieces of her, hungering for more. She recognized it in the fatigue that made her limbs leaden and the hollowness carved from her breast. What an easy thing it would be to sink into it and give herself over to oblivion. Reaching only for her bed and the nothingness of sleep. Its whisper was lovely.

Ottilie approached the drawing room. At the other end, a doorway led to a short hall that would take her to the dining room. She grasped the door frame, her fingers slipping over the polished wood, and hesitated. She could still slip back into the hall, up the stairs and into her bedroom, her bed, without anyone knowing.

No one would notice. No one would care.

And then the fragment of a psalm, one Nānī or Niraja had underlined with bold strokes, pierced the gloom. *The Lord also will be a refuge for the oppressed, a refuge in times of trouble.*

She must tuck herself away in him. Burrow deep into his word. If she was to avoid going back to that place of desperate questions and doubt, she had to resist the loneliness that stalked her like a tiger did its prey. Giving into it, succumbing to the sorrow, meant not being whole when Thaddeus returned.

And he's only near London. He isn't gone forever.

Soft voices and light drew her across the drawing room and down the short paneled hall. Before reaching the dining room, Ottilie stepped into an alcove shadowing the top of the staircase that led to the kitchen. Here footmen would emerge, carrying trays and platters. But with only two people dining, it was empty and dark.

Ottilie readied herself to meet her aunt and grandmother. She hadn't intended to see them until the next day. Wasn't sure she wanted to, except she'd skipped lunch and was hungry.

"What shall we do with Ottilie now that Sunderson is gone?" Alberta's words stole Ottilie's breath.

"What do you mean? She will stay here, of course." A thread of offense knotted Lady Sunderson's response.

"Of course. I only meant, what will we tell people about her?

We no longer have need of an ayah or governess. She can't just stay on without any role to fill. People will ask questions I don't believe you'd like to answer."

"Oh. That is a challenge, isn't it?" There was the clinking of metal against china.

The conversation fell off, and Ottilie stood in her dark niche. She pressed her forehead against the wall and her hand against her lips. People would ask questions. Why would the ayah stay on after the child had left? There was no reason for her to remain. At least, not one that would make sense to anyone else.

"Alberta, I think I have a solution," Lady Sunderson said. Ottilie crept from her nook and slid against the wall, ear toward the door. "What if Ottilie became your companion?"

Ottilie blinked. How dreadful that would be.

Alberta evidently agreed. "Mother, I hardly think that will work. What will I say, that I enjoyed the conversation of a foreign ayah so much, I decided to keep her on? No one will believe it. Least of all me."

"But you're all alone here, with no one for company but me. You could travel together. Go to London or Bath. Even the Continent."

"I have no desire to go to London or Bath. And I certainly have no desire to go to the Continent. I'm perfectly content living here. You know that. No, we will need to think of something else." Alberta huffed, and there was a clattering of utensils. "Honestly, it would have been so much easier had she stayed in India."

Ottilie gasped and pressed her hands over her face. She'd thought . . .

How foolish she was, to believe one conversation made all the difference. That Alberta's confiding in her meant she cared. Ottilie had only been a willing ear. Someone to listen to a story that had been too long kept quiet. Nothing more.

What a burden she'd become. They would care for her out of

obligation to her father's memory, but she wasn't welcome. She only posed a threat to Thaddeus and an inconvenience to Lady Sunderson and Alberta.

Well, she wouldn't stay where she wasn't wanted. No longer. Thaddeus was gone, and there was no reason for her to remain. She didn't want to. Not in this dark, freezing house where the servants held her in disdain. She wasn't without options. She had a skill that was in demand. Alberta had said her friend was seeking a gown embroidered with elytra. That they were all the rage this season.

Ottilie's fingers found the wings she'd embroidered on her jacket. The smooth casings were expertly attached. The pattern singular and beautiful. She had a gift, one both Maji and Nānī said exceeded their own. She wracked her memory for the name of the dressmaker Alberta had mentioned as one of the most well-regarded in London. Madame Laurence. Pronounced the French way. Well, Ottilie knew embroidery and fashion. She also knew French. And she wouldn't spend any more time at Hazelbrook Manor than necessary.

Ottilie couldn't ignore her stomach any longer. She'd crept away from the dining room after hearing Alberta's terrible words, and Jessamine never had brought a tray to her room. She normally ate with Thaddeus in the schoolroom, but without him here, no one sent up any food. Harriet brought her toast and tea in the morning and filled the carafe sitting on her bedside table with water, but that was all. By morning, even the thought of an English breakfast was appealing.

Ottilie slipped her jar of garam masala into her pocket and retraced her steps from the night before. If luck was with her, she'd reach the dining room before Alberta and be finished breakfasting quickly.

Luck was not with her.

Alberta was sitting at the table, spreading jam on a square of toast. "Good morning."

Ottilie nodded and went to the sideboard. Normally she would take only toast and a slice of bacon or a sausage, but that wouldn't suffice today. Especially when she planned to spend the day packing.

She filled her plate with ham, creamy scrambled eggs, kippers, and toast, then poured herself a cup of hot chocolate and set it all down on the table.

Alberta raised her brow, looking up from Ottilie's breakfast. "Hungry today?"

Ottilie pulled the bowl of marmalade near and spread it on her toast. "I asked Jessamine to bring me dinner last night, but she apparently forgot."

Alberta set her fork down and pressed a napkin to her lips. "I spoke to the staff about their treatment toward you. I . . . I tried to show more kindness and be a better reflection of what I expected of them."

"It's fine. It doesn't matter." Ottilie took the garam masala from her pocket and sprinkled it on her eggs and fish.

Alberta gave the jar a curious look. "What is that?"

"A blend of spices our servant, Dilip, made for us before we left. I meant to give it to Thaddeus when we arrived at St. Luke's, but I forgot when I discovered we wouldn't be traveling with him."

"We didn't make that choice to hurt you."

"Does it matter, when the result was the same?"

"I think it is important to understand the intention behind it."

"You decided I was a risk. Too emotional. Too close to Thaddeus—"

"You really must begin calling him by his proper name."

"I am calling him by his proper name. That title is *not* my brother. You think he is English only, but he isn't. You want to hide the rest of who he is. Pretend it isn't there. Make him forget. It's wrong."

"Those aren't our intentions."

Ottilie lifted her cup to her lips. "Does it matter, if the result is the same?"

They were silent for a quarter of an hour, the only sound their sipping and chewing. Then, as Ottilie placed her napkin beside her plate, Alberta stood. "Would you like to walk with me?"

"Walk with you where?"

Alberta gave her a wry smile. "Do we need a destination?"

These people and their walks to nowhere. Ottilie shook her head. What was one more amble? She would be done with them and their pointless wanderings soon. "Very well."

They went to their rooms to retrieve cloaks, hats, and gloves. Ottilie set Maji's hat on her head, knowing Alberta detested it.

"Thaddeus needs to go to school. It's for the best," Alberta said the moment they stepped outside.

"I'm sure you mean well, but that doesn't mean you're right. I've loved him his entire life, and you've only just met him. Perhaps you aren't equipped to make the best decisions for him."

"Perhaps. But he's here now, and he must acclimate to our way of life."

"And you think tearing him away from all that's left of the life he knows is the best way to accomplish that?"

They walked down the formal garden's central path. Beds containing the brittle remains of flowers and leaves and stalks spread in a radial pattern from a central fountain, turned off for the season. Not a bud nor furl of green brightened the landscape. Gray and brown everywhere. Even the sky was leached of color.

Alberta sighed and pinched a spent bloom from a plant. "I think we've seven years to make up for. He is a charming boy and was obviously loved, but there are rough edges that need filing. How can he become the man he was meant to be surrounded by women?"

Ottilie wasn't sure being surrounded by women his entire life would prove anything other than beneficial. Men had invaded her country. Men had started trade wars. Men had slaughtered innocents—both British and Indian—and men had made a mess of her heart in their pursuit of something better.

"I'm sorry," Alberta said.

Ottilie's steps stopped, and she blinked, unsure what to say. If a response was even expected.

"I'm sorry I've been unkind to you and that set in motion a disregard for you among the staff. I recognize it. I do. It—" Alberta's chin quivered, and she ducked her head. Crushing the brittle flower between her fingers, she dropped it to the ground. "It really had nothing to do with you. I was, of course, shocked when we first met—Edwin told no one he'd married an Indian woman—but I saw everything we'd hoped for disappear the moment you stepped out of the carriage. My pregnancy was a scandal the family barely dodged. I saw the effect it had on my parents, how damaging it was to them. I believe . . . I believe it might have contributed to my father's death. His heart was already weak." Her voice caught, and she turned her head away. "I feared you would be found out. I know society. I left after my son died and never went to another event. Another ball. They call me a 'thornback,' and I suppose it's true. I am unmarried and beyond twenty-six. I made unwise choices that could have ruined my family. I didn't want anyone to take note of me after that for fear that it would all be revealed. I'm desperate for Thaddeus's ancestry to remain hidden. Because if they find out, they won't accept him. He will be left with his title and the estate, but socially? Nothing else. Maybe not even a suitable wife."

She darted a glance at Ottilie. Her gloved hand reached for Ottilie's, and Ottilie, with a little trepidation, allowed the contact. She opened her mouth to speak but was interrupted by the sound of pounding hooves. Across the lawn, they could see a rider.

Alberta shaded her eyes, then raised her hand in a wave. "It's Everett."

Ottilie stepped back. "I think I shall return to the house. Please tell me how Thaddeus did."

Alberta's hand shot out and gripped Ottilie's arm. "No, you should stay. Never let them know how much they've hurt you."

Ottilie's heart stuttered. "How do you know he has hurt me?"

"It is clear to anyone with eyes. He was supremely stupid, but I can't judge him. I once was, as well."

Everett dismounted and walked his horse toward them. When he reached them, his gaze skittered past Ottilie. She didn't insist on being acknowledged. She gave him space and went to his horse, holding out her palm and smiling when it nudged her hand. She ran her knuckles over its muzzle.

Everett greeted Alberta, then said, "Thaddeus was well when I left him. St. Luke's seems like a nice school. Not at all like the one I attended."

Alberta nodded. "That is good to hear. It came highly recommended." She looked between Ottilie and Everett, then gave a tight nod. "Well, I shall go inside. If you'll excuse me." She tightened her hands on the edges of her shawl and walked away so quickly that the fabric caught the wind and flapped.

Ottilie stroked the horse's flank and leaned her head against its firm body. It was a solid divider between them, holding steady and thwarting glances that said too much. She couldn't see Everett, but she could sense him. Sense his energy and remorse and the powerlessness that seemed to blanket his decisions.

"I'm so terribly sorry, Ottilie. About Thaddeus and . . . everything else. You have every right to despise me."

She sighed. "I don't hate you, Everett. I understand your loyalty to Alberta. Truly. I was very angry with you, but I can see you didn't ask to be put in that position."

He was silent for a moment, and she lifted her hand higher

on the horse, sliding it to where she thought Everett stood on the other side. "And the other thing?" he asked.

The other thing. That was all. Not *the love that bloomed between us* nor *all we have become to each other*. Just *the other thing*, which sounded like nothing at all.

"You warned me, before we left India, that we couldn't be together." She'd been foolish and arrogant enough to pursue him anyway. To insist on answers she had no right to. To force him to admit his feelings when they both knew feelings to be unrelated to choices.

He rounded the horse, reins loose in his hands, and came to stand inches from her. "I don't remember that conversation."

"You never spoke the words, but that doesn't mean I didn't hear them. I knew, early on, of your esteem for me. I recognized the spark that lit your gaze every time we were near each other. But I also saw how restrained you were. How you held your thoughts and desire close. You were clear about what you wanted from life—a membership at Welbourne's to help you build Mr. Fernsby's business. A wife who could ease your way."

He looked at her without blinking, saying as much now as he had in India. Silently speaking regret and yearning and despair. She heard him clearly. And she was glad she would soon be far away from this sad story.

Everett's jaw twitched. "I imagine I'll never be able to say these words again, so I'm saying them now. I love you. I wish to God I could marry you and spend the rest of my life erasing the rejection and loneliness life has leveraged against you. I wish I didn't feel my responsibility to my father and his estate so strongly. I wish I didn't want so very much to attain the small bit of him I am allowed. And before I lose my courage, I ask for one thing. I've no right to ask it—I know that—but I want something to remember and dream of before it's all over."

The look in his eyes told her what he wanted, and her head spun. It was an unwise, ill-advised thing to give. But the earnestness on his face as his fingers found his earlobe, the hope flaring in his beautiful eyes, the heartache shadowing all of it, pushed her forward.

Protected from view by Everett's horse, their lips met. He released the reins and his ear, wrapping his arms around her back, gathering her as near as possible, angling his mouth more fully over hers.

She didn't hold back in some coy game of sentimental morality. They didn't have time for that. This moment, this kiss, was all they were allowed. And she would make the most of it.

He pulled back a little, a sigh escaping his throat as though he'd been given everything he needed to live a life tethered to obligation and a possibly loveless marriage. But she hadn't received enough, so she snaked her hands up his back, her fingers tangling in his hair, and pulled him toward her again.

There was desperation and sorrow in their grasping hands and pressing lips. This wasn't a sweet statement of mutual regard. Or a promise of everlasting devotion. This was a rebellious tribute to everything and everyone who meant to keep them apart. It was a hello and a good-bye. A beginning and an end.

Everett's thumb found the tear slipping down her cheek, and she closed her eyes. "I love you," she whispered. "I love you. I love you. I love you."

He pressed his forehead to hers. "My heart." He stole one more sweet, helpless kiss, and she felt the curve of his smile. "How is it you can taste like India when you've been in England for so long?"

She laughed and dashed the tears from her cheeks. "Garam masala. I smuggled it into the dining room and added it to my eggs."

Her lips began to tremble. She gave a short nod and turned toward the house, knowing there was nothing left to say.

25

Leaving turned out to be easier than Ottilie could have hoped for. Less than a week after her kiss with Everett, Alberta said she was going to the village for the day to work with the children at the local school on their spring play. Lady Sunderson was making visits. Ottilie had already decided not to tell her grandmother and aunt her plans. They would only assume she meant to contact Thaddeus—which she did—and make trouble for him at school—which she hoped wouldn't happen. Lady Sunderson had been kind to her. Ottilie was sure her grandmother would try to convince her to stay.

And it might work. Ottilie couldn't deny her desire to be persuaded that she was wanted. That she belonged at Hazelbrook Manor.

But she knew she didn't, and eventually life there would become unbearable.

"Miss, I wish you would at least tell them. They'll worry about you." Harriet grabbed the handle of one of the bags on the floor. "And why can't you tell me where you're headed? What if someone needs to get in touch with you? What if something happens to Lord Sunderson?"

"If you must, contact Miss Damaris Winship of Bath, and later London. I will eventually be in touch with her. But really,

Harriet, you will have no need to contact me. I will keep abreast of Thaddeus." Ottilie took her other bag in hand. She'd decided to forgo the space of a trunk for convenience, and she'd managed to pack all of her Calcutta-made clothing, as well as a couple of newer items—just her favorites that she had embroidered—along with her spice box, books, and embroidery tools. The elytra filled a hatbox nestled in the bottom, beneath skirts and bodices and underclothes. They were her future.

"Is the coach ready?" Ottilie asked.

Harriet nodded, her face tucked into sad lines.

"Don't be upset with me, Harriet. This needs to happen. I'm so unhappy here. And without Thaddeus, there is no longer any reason to burden Lady Sunderson with my presence."

"I don't think she sees it like that."

"No, she likely doesn't, but she will realize when I'm gone how much easier it is without me. She won't have to concoct elaborate stories to explain away my presence. Or worry about someone finding out about my relationship to them." Ottilie started for the door. "Now, come. I must be off."

Harriet followed her down the hall and stairs to the carriage waiting for her in front of the house. Ottilie handed her bag to the coachman and took a last look up at Hazelbrook Manor.

She felt nothing—no longing to remain. No bittersweet memories tugged her back inside. There was only the releasing of shackles and the buoyant joy of knowing she would soon be near her brother.

The coachman didn't offer assistance, so she clambered up the steps herself and held out a hand to Harriet. "You have been my only friend here, and I love you for it. Don't tell them you had anything to do with my leaving. Just let them discover my note."

Then they were off, and Ottilie settled back against the seat, knowing she had, for the first time, made a decision all her own. One not influenced by disease or desperation, but a desire to make her own way. Make her own choices.

No one needed her. Relied on her. It was her alone.
And she could do anything.

Ottilie hadn't realized, as she sat on a train through a country-side beginning to tiptoe into spring, that London would still be ensconced in gray. No hills blanketed in velvety green grass. No wispy clouds darting across a sky as blue as indigo. No plump buds unfurling on branches. No branches at all.

London was gray buildings and gray sky and gray streets and gray people hustling past her, their expressions twisted into gray scowls. She'd hoped, when she arrived the evening before, she had just chosen a particularly depressing area for her lodgings. But now, even when the morning mist had rolled away, nothing cheerful had been revealed. It was just as bleak and depressing as it had been when she approached her boardinghouse.

Ottilie ignored the desire to turn her face back toward the homey charm of Elbury and walked up the short flight of steps to the front door of Madame Laurence's of Regent Street. She carried a worn satchel she'd found in the attic near her own bags, and within it a few paper-wrapped packages—proof of her skill—and her references. She blessed her own foresight in securing them before leaving Calcutta.

Hopefully it would be enough to procure employment. She only had enough money to pay for two more days of lodging. And that would leave nothing for a return trip to Wiltshire.

Ottilie straightened her shoulders and lifted her chin. She wasn't returning to Wiltshire. She could almost feel Thaddeus's nearness—just thirty minutes away by train—and, for the first time in her life, she only had to worry about herself.

She would start by worrying about making a good impression on Madame Laurence.

Ottilie rang the bell, and the door was opened a moment

later by a well-dressed woman wearing a harried expression. "May I help you?"

Ottilie gripped her bag's handle and gave a decisive nod. "I've come to see Madame Laurence about a position she needs filled."

The woman shook her head. "I'm unaware of any position. We've already hired for this Season. Come August, most of them will be dismissed until next year."

Ottilie tried to make sense of those words. Did women in London not buy gowns after August? "And after?"

"After what?"

"The Season is over. Will you have no work at all to fill? What do the seamstresses do then?"

The woman folded her hands primly at her waist. "If they do well this Season, they will be rehired next. In between"—she shrugged—"is not our concern." She gripped the door and gave Ottilie a tight smile. "Have a good day."

Ottilie shifted her bag to the other hand and wiped her sweaty palm against her skirt. "You don't understand. I need work."

"That, too, is not my concern."

Footsteps sounded behind Ottilie, and the change in the woman's expression was nothing short of miraculous. A large smile replaced the pinched lips, and she snaked her arm past Ottilie toward the person behind her. "Mrs. Johns, welcome. It is so lovely to see you. Madame Laurence will be with you in the salon shortly." She ushered the client inside, and Ottilie took the opportunity to enter as well.

The woman led Mrs. Johns toward the room on the left. Ottilie craned her neck and saw plush carpeting, potted plants, walls lined with mirrors in thick gilded frames, and dress forms draped in gowns.

There was a murmuring of voices, and Ottilie crept nearer. If there was some way to get the woman to see her work, she might be willing to allow her an audience with Madame Laurence. Barring that opportunity, maybe she could intercept the modiste and somehow convince her to hire her. For the summer. After which Ottilie had no idea what she was going to do. Or how. But she would worry about that later. For now, she *needed* this particular position. She couldn't afford to spend days crawling through London, trying to find every dressmaker and offering her services.

"Who are you, and what are you doing?"

Ottilie jerked back from the doorway and found herself face-to-face with a formidable-looking woman, her hair pulled back into a severe twist. She was of an undeterminable age, with high cheekbones and tight skin, but sporting a thick gray streak—as gray as the sky and buildings and expressions outside the establishment—that stretched from her left temple. She wore a simple gown of burgundy wool, unadorned but expertly stitched.

"I am Ottilie . . . Russell. I need to speak with Madame Laurence."

"Do you?"

Ottilie nodded. "I heard she has need of an embroiderer, and I am one."

The woman from the front door appeared in the entry and gasped. "I told you to leave." She turned an apologetic smile toward the other woman. "I'm so sorry, Madame Laurence. I've already let her know we have no need of another seamstress." She glared at Ottilie. "And definitely no need of an embroiderer."

"But I am not a typical embroiderer, and I know you are looking for the type of service I offer." Ottilie fumbled at the buttons of her coat. "If you'll only see what I can do."

"I don't believe *you* can offer us anything. We only hire the very best seamstresses in London." The woman moved back toward the door. "You should leave."

Ottilie shrugged out of her coat, draping it over her arm, and turned so Madame Laurence could see the intricate design she'd worked on during her long, lonely days at Hazelbrook Manor.

The jacket was, perhaps, her best work, perking up the plain wool and turning it into a vibrant piece of art worthy of display in any of London's museums.

And *on* any of London's elite.

Madame Laurence showed only one indication of interest as she looked over Ottilie's embroidery—a narrowing of her eyes. Almost imperceptible. "Have you anything else?"

The other woman, standing with her hand on the doorknob, huffed.

Ottilie set down her bag and opened it. "I do." She pulled out the first package and removed the paper, then handed the reticule to Madame Laurence.

As the modiste studied it, Ottilie removed Maji's lone shoe and the shawl—which she had carefully brushed clean. Each one she held out for Madame Laurence's inspection.

"These are well done, but we're in the business of creating gowns. Plus, we have no way of securing the wings. Where would we get them? There is no time to order them from India." Madame Laurence handed back Ottilie's reticule and waved her hand in a dismissive gesture that tossed Ottilie's heart to the floor. "Miss Briggs will see you out."

Ottilie stared at the modiste's back and began to tremble. She couldn't leave without securing employment. She *needed* to work. Needed to stay in London. Needed to take care of herself the way she'd taken care of everyone else. "I have wings. Enough to last until more can be purchased."

Mrs. Johns stepped through the doorway leading to the salon. "I thought I heard you in here, Madame Laurence. I was beginning to wonder if you'd forgotten me." Her gaze swept the room, stopping on Ottilie—or rather Ottilie's shawl—and her eyes widened. "Where did you find that?" She hurried over and took a corner of it in hand. "It's beautiful. Did you embroider this?"

Ottilie nodded, her voice still trapped somewhere between her sternum and her throat.

"I didn't realize you employed someone skilled in beetle-wing embroidery, Madame." Mrs. Johns clucked her tongue and turned toward the modiste. "I was told no one in London could offer these services. And *everyone* wants them. Everyone. Where have you been hiding her?"

A twitch broke Madame Laurence's unflappable demeanor. "I've only just hired her. Brought in especially for the Season. And I shall offer you first option to wear a Madame Laurence beetle-wing creation." She looked at Ottilie and raised her brows. "It will be done in time for the Palmers' ball next week."

Ottilie nodded. She had no idea who the Palmers were or what type of gown Mrs. Johns would request, but she'd work day and night to see it finished.

She'd done it before.

Ottilie started work that very afternoon. She went to the guesthouse, paid for her room, and collected her belongings. When she returned to the dressmaker's, she was directed to the back door, which led her to a flight of stairs.

The narrow, dank-smelling first-floor hallway was lined with doors. Miss Briggs pointed Ottilie to one. The room—if it could be called that—held a bed, rickety side table, washstand, and a meager dresser. No rug warmed the scuffed floor, no curtain framed the grimy window, no artwork brightened the yellowing walls. Nothing of beauty or warmth. She could cross it in six large steps. And she could hardly breathe, the air was so close.

"You'll share the bed with Miss Hale."

Ottilie blinked at Miss Briggs. "I'm to share the room? The bed?"

"This isn't the Langham Hotel, Miss Russell. You are here to work."

"Yes, of course." Ottilie cast one last sideways glance at the too-small-for-two bed. It would be fine. Cramped, but Ottilie had spent years twisted up with her brother in sleep. Hopefully her bedmate didn't snore.

Miss Briggs instructed her to bring her box of elytra, as well as any tools she wished to use, then led her down the hall and pushed open the door at the end. "This is the workroom, where you will spend much of your day."

Ottilie followed her into a room that hummed and buzzed. Along the right side, twenty women sat shoulder to shoulder, working at sewing machines. On the left, near a bank of windows, was a hunched row of embroiderers and those working on lace, buttons, and delicate stitching.

Miss Briggs held up her hand, and the noise stopped so suddenly and completely, Ottilie was left disoriented. "This is Miss Ottilie Russell. She will be embroidering this Season— a particular kind of highly sought-after embroidery. Madame Laurence anticipates her being quite busy when the public hears about our new designs." She looked at one of the seamstresses sitting behind a sewing machine. "Miss Hale, Miss Russell is your new roommate. Please make her welcome."

Then Miss Briggs was gone, leaving Ottilie to stare at a sea of unfamiliar faces displaying very familiar expressions.

Distrust. Dislike. Disapproval.

The women—most of them girls, really—went back to work, and Miss Hale took small steps around the tables, joining Ottilie in the middle of the room at a long table. She waved Ottilie toward a chair at the very end and sat opposite her. "This is where we eat. Madame Laurence doesn't like for us to get crumbs on the gowns, of course, and this way there is no time wasted in going from one room to another."

"That seems efficient. We eat all our meals in here?" Ottilie looked around the room again with the knowledge that she'd likely spend all of her time in it. Similar to the bedroom, there was little to recommend it, but pale light filtered through the windows, which were clean, and the bodies filling the room made it warm.

"We begin work at half past six. Breakfast is fifteen minutes at eight. Lunch is twenty minutes at one. Tea is ten minutes at four, and dinner is at half past seven. Sometimes we are too busy to eat lunch—especially when there is a ball—and we work through the night."

"You work through the night?" The dark circles beneath Miss Hale's eyes and her pallor now made sense. Ottilie had thought her sickly, but it seemed the poor girl was actually exhausted. "How old are you, Miss Hale?"

She smiled. "Oh, I look younger than I am. I turned seventeen this past December."

"And you've worked here long?"

"I apprenticed when I was thirteen and have been here ever since. I'm one of the few who stay on through the year. There are only eight of us. Everyone else is dismissed after the Season ends."

A weight lifted from Ottilie's chest. If Madame Laurence kept some workers on through the year, she would just have to convince the modiste of her worth. She might not need to find different work at the end of summer after all.

"Oh, and Madame Laurence offers us a half day on Sunday. Not many do, you know, so we are very lucky. You are free after two. Most of the girls go straight to sleep, but I visit my father in Kew."

Ottilie sucked in a breath. "You lived in Kew? Near the botanical garden and St. Luke's?"

"Yes. My father works in the gardens. Have you ever seen them?"

Ottilie shook her head, mind spinning. "No, but I would love to."

Miss Hale smiled. "It's a quick trip on the train, and the fare is reasonable."

"Maybe I could join you for the journey next time you go?" Once Ottilie felt secure in her ability to get there alone, she would visit Thaddeus every half day. Once a week. It wouldn't be anything like living with him—seeing his tousled hair and sleepy eyes every morning, kissing him every evening—but it was a sight better than two weeks at Christmas and three in the summer.

"That would be lovely. And, please, call me Penny."

"Thank you. I will. And you must call me Ottilie."

Penny's brows twisted into a question. "May I ask, if it isn't too rude, how you came to have an English name and speak like the women who come in for fittings?"

"My father was an Englishman, a scientist and academic. He met and married my mother in India."

Penny sighed and pressed her hands against her chest. "How romantic. I've always wanted to see India. And China. And everywhere." She grinned and took Ottilie's hand. "But now I have you to call a friend, and you can tell me all about it." Her eyes dimmed, and she looked at her sewing machine. "Later, though. If I don't get back to work, I won't be sleeping tonight."

Penny showed Ottilie where she would work—beside a woman who eyed her suspiciously and scooted her chair away— then returned to her own spot across the room. Madame Laurence had already instructed Ottilie to spend the day working sample designs onto linen squares, as Mrs. Johns's gown wouldn't be ready for embroidery until Thursday—two days hence.

"What are those?" her tablemate asked when Ottilie spilled out a small pile of wings.

"Elytra," Ottilie said, poking through them and organizing mounds based on size. "The casings of beetle wings."

The woman lowered the length of creamy satin she was embroidering jet beads onto, and her eyes met Ottilie's. They were red-rimmed and puffy—evidence of long days doing repetitive close work. "Beetle wings? I've never heard of such a thing."

"They were popular many years ago and have made a resurgence. My family has been embroidering with elytra for hundreds of years. It's a traditional Indian craft." Ottilie selected an elytron and handed it to her.

The woman pinched it between her fingers, then sniffed and tossed it back into the pile. "I'm not sure why England must import Indian embroidery techniques. Or Indian embroiderers. Seems to me we do well enough without either." She pushed her nose back into her work.

Ottilie sighed. She could think of a dozen retorts—none of which would make her any friends. It only promised more of the same. She lifted her scissors and began snipping the elytra into circles, which she meant to use in a pattern that had tripped through her mind as she sat in the train car and stared out the window on a landscape coming alive. Spring buds and pink flowers stretching from branches stitched in gold.

She only had to make it until the end of the week. Then she would see Thaddeus. One day, one week, at a time. Just like she would turn a square of plain fabric into something beautiful and worthy of attention, she'd take her dull, unadorned weeks and make them into something lovely, crowning them with Sundays.

26

Ottilie glanced, for the hundredth time, at her pocket watch, which she'd set before her on the table. She brushed aside the snipped threads that covered the face of it and sighed. It was Sunday, and the hours were crawling by, tormenting her with their refusal to move forward at a reasonable clip.

Thirty minutes. Thirty minutes more, and she could leave Madame Laurence's for the first time in six days and see her brother. She'd written him two days prior but had said nothing of her impending visit. She wanted him surprised. Wanted to see his darling face light up when she told him she lived nearby.

How it chafed, being so close yet unable to ease his unhappiness. She flicked at a rebellious thread and watched the minute hand tick forward.

"Will you stop shaking the table?" Mrs. Alma Follet, the woman who shared her workspace, glared at her.

Ottilie sighed and picked the final thread from her watch, then went back to her embroidering. She'd worked until two o'clock in the morning before getting four hours of sleep and returning to the workroom. Madame Laurence wanted Mrs. Johns's gown finished by Monday morning, and that meant Ottilie had to find hours somewhere else if she was going to visit Thaddeus.

She knotted the thread on the elytron she'd been stitching and cast a glance at Mrs. Follet, who was filling in the outline of a rose with silky red thread on the bodice of a ball gown. She'd been working late into the night, as well, though Ottilie didn't think she'd finish her work in time to take advantage of her half day. Mrs. Follet's eyes were red and drooping. Everything about her was drooping, from the sad little knot of hair at the crown of her head to her shoulders.

"You do beautiful work," Ottilie said, pushing at each of her knuckles in turn.

Mrs. Follet's needle paused its jabbing and pulling, and her lips curled at the popping of Ottilie's knuckles. "Well, a lot of good that does. No one knows or cares it's my hand doing it."

"There's value in creating something beautiful, even if there isn't praise for it."

Ottilie stood and rounded the table. She lifted the gown she'd just finished and held it up, shaking the skirt out to display her design in full glory. The seamstresses had done a wonderful job creating the red silk ball gown with its long ruffled train and gathered skirt. Mrs. Johns, with her dark hair, would look beautiful in it. But it was Ottilie's design that set the gown apart. That would make Mrs. Johns the talk of the evening. She'd stitched a filigree round and round in gold thread, starting at the bodice and making its way down the skirt, weaving in and out of the ruching and black floral appliqués. Springing from the stitching, with elytra in groupings of three and five and nine, she'd created blooming flowers. She'd even stitched a few wings into clusters here and there, marking out little heads and antenna with black thread. The entire effect was a garden come to life.

Mrs. Follet stared up at Ottilie's gown, and her jaw clenched. "If you don't want praise, why are you standing there, preening like a peacock?"

"I'm only pleased with what I've helped to create. As we all should be. If that makes me a peacock, so be it." Ottilie glanced around the room at the women hunched over sewing machines and destroying their eyesight over detail work, all of them wrens in their brown, gray, and black skirts and shawls, blind to the beauty they created with their fingers. Beauty that would adorn others.

And they were peacocks. Every one.

They were just too tired to see it. Too exhausted to claim it.

But Ottilie wouldn't join them. She wouldn't allow drudgery or grief or unmet expectations to steal from her the joy she experienced every time she stitched something worth admiring.

She draped the gown over her arm, careful to keep the hem from brushing the floor, and let her fingers trail over Mrs. Follet's intricate embroidery work. "I'm allowed to find joy in the beauty I create. And if you aren't so inclined to find it in your own work, I will. Mrs. Follet, you are a rare talent. You deserve recognition for it, but if no one ever knows your hands created the gowns they all admire, it doesn't diminish your contribution. You make this tired, dull city a little more splendid." She touched the elytra expertly stitched to Mrs. Johns's bodice. "And I do as well."

Mrs. Follet's shoulders bowed a little more, if possible, and her head hung heavy from her slender neck. Then she blew a curl of hair from her forehead and peered up at Ottilie. "You're an odd one. I suppose that's expected from a foreigner."

Ottilie shrugged. "Perhaps."

She looked over at Penny, who sat behind her sewing machine. The treadle under her foot rose and fell as she fed fabric beneath the needle, but she took a moment to glance up at Ottilie. "I'm nearly finished. Take Madame Laurence that gown, and I'll meet you at the back door."

Ottilie nodded and left the room. Ten minutes. Ten minutes,

and she would join Penny on her walk to the train station. The train that would take them to Kew and St. Luke's and Thaddeus.

Ottilie hurried down the back stairs and knocked on Madame Laurence's private parlor door. She hadn't seen the modiste since she received the sketches for Mrs. Johns's gown, as Ottilie spent most of her day in the workroom and Madame Laurence spent most of hers with clients in the salon.

"Enter."

Ottilie took a deep breath and walked through the door. The room was small and cozy, papered in a cream and burgundy floral pattern and featuring dainty mahogany chairs around a marble-topped table, a curved-arm settee, and screens painted with scenes of rural China. Madame Laurence sat at the table, pencil in hand, eyes focused on her sketch.

As Ottilie drew near, she saw it was another gown featuring elytra.

Madame Laurence set down her pencil and glanced up. "Are you here to show me the finished gown? I'm working on a new design. I believe we will have many orders after Wednesday's ball."

Ottilie draped the bodice over her forearm and pulled the skirt straight out with her other hand, showing off the intricate embroidery.

Madame Laurence's eyes roved the gown, taking on a gleam of approval. "Nicely done. Hang it on the dress form behind the screen in the salon. Mrs. Johns will be in tomorrow morning for her final fitting."

Ottilie nodded and did as asked. Ten minutes later, she met Penny at the back door, and they set off for the train station, a fifteen-minute walk. When they left the alley behind the dressmaker's, crowded with heaps of refuse, puddles of vile-looking liquid, and stray dogs, Ottilie took a deep breath.

And coughed out the smog. "Is there nowhere in London one can breathe freely?"

Penny laughed. "Nowhere. But you will be able to breathe in Kew. This city is filthy and crowded, and fumes swirl around every space not pressed in with buildings. But outside of it, you'll find greenery and air." Penny smiled, bright as the sun. "When we arrive, I'll take you to the botanical gardens. They're so lovely, and I believe you'll find some of the imported plants interesting."

They arrived at the station, Ottilie's heart having grown lighter with each step that moved her farther from Madame Laurence's. It wasn't that she didn't enjoy her work or appreciate it, but she was exhausted. Nothing in Calcutta had prepared her for the never-ending monotony, the sleeplessness, the poor quality food, the lack of ventilation. At least when she worked long hours at home, they were hours she could fill as she wished. She could sit outside on the verandah, her time punctuated by the greetings of her neighbors. Dilip never failed to bring her well-flavored food. And if she wished, she could sleep beneath the stars, waking up to the sound of *adhan* being called and the sun pouring a blanket of rose light over her.

She yawned, visions of Madame Laurence's new design already making her fingers numb and sight blur. She'd heard whispers of a grande fête coming up. It had the rest of the girls in a dither, knowing the work would increase their already heavy load.

Penny took Ottilie's arm. "You'll get used to it. When I first started, I cried every day. The only reason I stayed was that my mother relies on my income to stay healthy."

They approached the ticket counter. "Is your mother unwell?"

Penny nodded. "Consumption. The doctor suggested she go to a sanatorium, but we weren't able to afford the fees, so I went to work. When we've saved enough of my wages, off she goes again."

After they purchased their tickets, they sat on one of the metal benches and waited for their train. Ottilie looked at Penny, who observed the bustle around them, a bright smile on her face.

She was pure and sweet, but also painfully thin, her dark eyes set deep in a face too pale to be natural. She regularly worked into the early morning hours, skipping sleep to keep on top of the ever-increasing workload Madame Laurence foisted on her. She churned out gown after gown, producing faster and better than anyone else. And she never complained. Never huffed or rolled her eyes or wished for anything else. She was grateful for the work. Grateful for the opportunity to send her mother to a sanatorium to find health.

Ottilie, embracing the maternal warmth swelling in her breast, took Penny's fine-boned hand. "You are so good. I imagine your parents feel privileged that you belong to them." There was something about Penny that stole Ottilie's breath. It was more than their immediate friendship, flamed by the sharing of space and food and bed, and more, even, than Penny's fragility, which was overshadowed by her strength of character and the joy that sparked from her wherever she went.

It was deeper. An almost spiritual knowledge that Ottilie had never, and would never again, know someone like Penny—someone who walked as close to heaven as was possible. Someone who seemed to sleep and sew and live only because she was bound to earth by gossamer strands that, given the right resistance, might snap at any moment.

Ottilie and Penny walked from Kew Gardens Station to the gardens. It was a pleasant town, far from London's choking smoke and jaundiced haze. The closer they got to the gardens, the more animated Penny became, tugging at Ottilie's jacket and skipping every few steps.

"It's been three weeks since I've seen Mother and Father. I had so much work at Madame Laurence's that I wasn't able to get away."

"I'll be sure to give you enough time to visit with them alone.

I have an errand I must run anyway." Ottilie hoped to meet Penny's parents, take a quick tour of the gardens, and be on her way, meeting Penny at the station before their train departed.

Penny's shoulders drooped. "Oh, won't you stay with us for tea? They would love your company. You could tell Mother all about India, and it would be sure to cheer her up."

Ottilie's smile wavered. She hated to disappoint Penny, who had become so dear to her since arriving at Madame Laurence's—more so because none of the other women spoke to her. But she had planned to spend most of the day with Thaddeus. Once she was with him, she couldn't imagine leaving until forced to by the train schedule. "Let's see what happens."

Penny brightened, then pointed at an elaborate wrought-iron gate ahead. Beside it, a guard, sharp in his black uniform and cap, kept an eye on those walking by. "Charlie!" Penny gave a cursory glance in either direction before darting across the street, dodging a wagon loaded with lumber to reach the garden entrance.

Charlie's face broke its stoicism for a moment—just long enough that Ottilie could see the fondness he had for Penny. When she reached them, taking no chances with the traffic and waiting for a clear path, she heard Penny's excited chatter.

"I've brought a friend to visit. Is Father inside?"

Charlie nodded. "He is. At the Palm House and will be for a few weeks. Go on in."

Penny grabbed Ottilie's hand and pulled her through the gate and down a tree-lined path. The air was clean, only the slightest bit of chill flecking it, and it smelled of bluebells. Ottilie could hear the quiet murmur of conversation from well-dressed men and women strolling by them, and her heart settled. Relaxed.

The stiffness in her shoulders and neck eased. The nervous energy that coursed through her every waking moment at Madame Laurence's—design and cut and baste and stitch, stitch, stitch—evaporated. Ahead, past the trees, was a wide expanse of grass, sets of gently sloping steps leading to a placid lake, and the largest greenhouse she had ever seen. It reminded her of the orangery at Hazelbrook Manor—though that was much smaller—for they both promised warmth and perfume within the glass walls that sheltered the palms and flowers she'd grown up with.

"Let's walk around the other side." Penny led Ottilie away from the clusters of people taking in the lake view, and they rounded the greenhouse. Penny pointed. "There's the pagoda."

Ottilie followed the direction of her finger and saw, down a clear stretch of grass, an Asian tower poking at the lamb's-wool clouds that ambled across the sky. It was as like the Burmese Pagoda in Eden Gardens as the Palm House was the orangery, sharing only vague similarities in its stacked structure and Asian styling, but Ottilie had a peculiar sense that her worlds were colliding—a reminder of India before her, Wiltshire behind her, all tied up in this enchanted park only a few miles outside of London.

She followed Penny to the front of the Palm House, taking a moment to appreciate the sheer size and engineering of it before walking through the door. A wall of sticky heat struck her, and she could almost hear Nānī's warbling voice weaving around the palms that surrounded them. Could almost reach out and touch Dilip's warm hand. Could almost see the gentle love stirring Maji's lips into a smile.

It was magic, this ability to be carried back in time and across continents just by stepping into a house of glass. Each time Ottilie found herself in an English greenhouse, she felt at home. Except now . . . now a part of her yearned for a cozy orangery tucked beside a pond. Lanterns strung from string, hired musicians playing the music of her childhood, and a cobbled-together Indian feast made with English ingredients.

She yearned for Calcutta, but she reached for something nearer. Something that had become dear when she wasn't looking. Something that she hadn't realized she would miss until she slipped away from the never-ending drudgery of a dressmaker's shop and the constant hum of sewing machines. She missed Hazelbrook Manor.

She missed the clean air and wide expanse of sky, the tidy cemetery nudging against the estate, and the chapel that whispered of Russells past—their births and weddings and deaths.

Her heritage. Whether it wanted to claim her or not. Whether she'd been willing to claim it.

She missed Lady Sunderson and her quiet presence.

She even missed Alberta, who had just begun to thaw when Ottilie decided to run.

And she definitely missed Everett, whose touch and kiss and smile she couldn't escape.

She'd sealed them out, as surely as folding over a hem and sewing a seam kept edges from fraying. She'd been scared of rejection and loss. Again.

In retrospect, she realized she'd never given them the chance to know her. She'd clung tightly to her fears and brother.

Ottilie shook her head, dislodging the disloyal thoughts. "Are you ready to see your father?" She turned a bright smile on Penny. "I'm so looking forward to meeting him."

Penny's elfin face lit up, and two spots of color splashed her cheeks. Ottilie had spent enough time with her to be cheered by the sight. Penny wasn't strong—she often looked pale and wan. She was a tall woman, and her bones poked through her skin at her wrists, clavicle, and jaw, evidence of the deficiency of the food provided at Madame Laurence's. She needed to eat more. Sleep more. Rest more. Sometimes Penny was so still in her sleep that Ottilie held her hand over her mouth, relaxing only when her friend's gentle breath sent a warm puff against her skin.

They explored the rows of potted palms, which grew larger and taller the closer they got to the center of the building, and stroked the velvet petals of rainforest flowers. Ottilie pressed her face into the bloom of a showy orange hibiscus and inhaled its scent. Remembered that life outside of Madame Laurence's, outside of London, was vibrant and alive and colorful.

She'd been astonished at how quickly time went, confined as she was to two small rooms on the first floor of a London shop. In the few days she'd spent embroidering with only a glimpse of the outside through a dingy window yellow with age, spring had finally shown herself.

And she was beautiful. Even in England.

For a moment, Ottilie wondered what Wiltshire looked like. Had the buds burst, canopying the wooded paths in a fleecy veil? Did lambs gambol in the pastures as Everett had promised?

She forced herself to focus on her surroundings and the way light spilled through the green-glazed glass panes. Penny's murmurs of familiarity over each flower, the low buzz of conversation as visitors examined plants, and the gentle swishing of the ladies' skirts a background hum.

"There's my father." Penny started away at a sedate pace, but the closer she got to the tall man bent over a sad-looking palm, the more quickly she went. "Father!"

He turned, and Ottilie's heart ached at the broad smile that spread across his face. His arms went wide, and when Penny flew into them, they wrapped around her in a way that told the world she was his.

Ottilie could almost feel his hug. Her own father had once held her that way. Had once looked at her that way. Had once loved her that way.

Bitterness poked out its head, hissing about life's unfairness, but she squashed it, remembering her aunt's words and not wanting anything ugly to darken her relationship with Penny.

She smiled and walked toward them. Penny's father's eyes widened, but not in the way she was used to—not in an intolerant, distrustful way. They widened and sparkled and lit up, a smile pushing at the balls of his cheeks. He disentangled himself from Penny's arms. "You must be Miss Russell. Penny wrote about you. Such a comfort you are to her."

Ottilie's gaze darted toward her friend. "Am I?"

"You know you are. You make me feel taken care of and looked after." Penny turned to her father. "She's so maternal, Papa. And sometimes I miss you and Mama less because she is near."

He reached for his daughter and gripped her hand. "Thank you, Miss Russell. It has been hard for us to release her, and hard, I know, for her to be apart from us. It's only ever been Penny, you see, so we've been lonely. It does my heart good knowing you're there to care for her." He looped one arm through Penny's and the other through Ottilie's. "I negotiated a half day, so let's go home and visit with your mother. We'll soon have enough—thanks to your hard work, Penny—to send her back to the sanatorium for a few months, so it will be a while before you see her again."

They walked past towering palms toward the door set in glass and iron. And Ottilie felt, for the first time since arriving in England, a coming home. Not in any way she expected, and so far from her heart that beat for Calcutta and its wide streets and ancient river and peculiar patchwork of cultures come together, but in a way that felt familiar. And right.

Fear, sharp and unexpected, pricked at her. She knew how flimsy a thing this belonging was. And how quickly it could change.

"What do you mean, I cannot see him?" Ottilie stared at the butler who had opened the front door to St. Luke's almost as soon as she pressed the bell.

"We don't allow spontaneous visitors during the week. Ever. For anyone. No matter who you *claim* to be." He looked down his straight nose at her, his expression telling her what he thought of her claims.

And if he didn't believe she was Thaddeus's dear family friend, he would probably laugh outright if she claimed to be his sister.

"When do you allow visitors?" She would come back. And if the visiting time fell outside of her free half day, she'd arrange it so that she could come another time.

Her heart constricted. She wouldn't see Thaddeus today. After all the anticipation, she could hardly bear the disappointment.

"The student's guardian must write and ask for a private visitation to be arranged. Such visits are disruptive, though, and we ask they be kept to a minimum."

Ottilie resisted the urge to smooth out the deep line she knew had formed between her brows. Nānī's words floated to her from beyond the Ganges. *Boodha, you'll look like that forever if you aren't careful.*

"Do you mean I cannot request an audience with Lord Sunderson unless his grandmother allows it?"

Her breaths came quick. Shallow. Lady Sunderson, even if Ottilie hadn't left Hazelbrook Manor, would never give Ottilie permission to visit Thaddeus at school for fear he would be found out. There was to be no gossip, no scandal, no link to Thaddeus's past.

Ottilie wondered if it would have been better to stay at Hazelbrook Manor—unwanted, yes, but still present for the two weeks at Christmas and three weeks in the summer that her brother would be home.

Perhaps she could go back during that time. Would she be welcome after her disappearing act? And would it be enough?

No, five weeks a year would never be enough.

A group of boys, smartly dressed in their uniforms, descended the staircase set just inside the door. Ottilie craned her neck, hoping for a glimpse of dark curls and snapping eyes. The butler angled his body in front of them.

"Is there anything else?"

Ottilie dropped her head and allowed herself one moment

to rest her hand against the doorframe. One moment to fully accept that she wouldn't see Thaddeus today. Probably wouldn't see him for a long time yet. "No, nothing."

"Then I bid you good-bye."

The door shut, and she pressed her palms to her eyes. Her brother was somewhere inside that cold, imposing building, and she had no access to him. No right, in their eyes, to see him. She'd come to London hoping to be closer to him. Hoping to see him each Sunday and fill herself with him, enough to make it through the rest of the week, but now the daydreams she'd concocted during the long hours she sat in a hard chair, in a darkening room, with people who distrusted her, lay at her feet. Trampled and small. Laughable.

She scuffed her foot against the step and stiffened her jaw. No. She would see Thaddeus. She hadn't given up everything—her home and people—only to be kept away from him. Even if she had to crawl back to Hazelbrook Manor to beg Lady Sunderson, she wouldn't allow Thaddeus to feel abandoned and alone.

And she wouldn't allow herself to lose the one person she had left.

Everett's flashing smile tripped through her thoughts. Lady Sunderson's soft touch and Alberta's honesty and even Penny's sweet acceptance and Mr. Hale's kind words. But no . . . she didn't really have any of them. At any moment they could turn on her or be lost or decide she wasn't worth their time.

She wouldn't allow that to happen. She would never allow that to happen again.

27

On the way back to Madame Laurence's, Penny sat beside Ottilie in contented silence, red-cheeked and smiling softly. Ottilie stared at her hands and willed her tears away. They arrived at the dress shop just before dinner—a sorry affair consisting of stale bread and a greasy stew that was mostly water and gristle—then got into bed.

Ottilie's eyes fell on Nānī's Bible, and her chest tightened. She turned over, facing Penny's back, and ignored the guilt gnawing at her. Who had time to read with all the work to do? She left her room before the sun rose and returned after it had long since gone to sleep.

But Nānī and Niraja's words, not to mention God's, called to her during the night, filling her sleep with dreams of diaphanous spirits resembling yards of tulle and enticing songs that bound her heart in silk thread.

Beside her, Penny coughed. A deep cough that rattled her chest and left her gasping. She sat upright and clutched her nightgown, the moonlight casting a grubby yellow light over their bed.

Ottilie sat up and put her hand on Penny's back. Beneath the thin fabric, she could feel the bumps and ridges of her friend's spine. So much of Penny reminded Ottilie of Jemima—her sweet spirit and quiet fortitude, but most of all her large eyes, pointed chin, and the bones that poked through skin as soft as satin. Jemima had always looked as though the wind could knock her over, and she'd perished quickly beneath the ravage of cholera.

Fear fisted Ottilie's throat, but she managed to push out the words. "Are you all right?"

Penny nodded. "I haven't been feeling well lately, but I think it's a catarrh left over from winter. I should feel better as the weather warms." She lay back down on her side, facing Ottilie, and folded her hands beneath her head. She looked perfectly well, and Ottilie's alarm subsided.

"Did you enjoy your day?" Penny asked. "I'm so glad you were able to meet my parents. And Mama was happy to host you for tea. They don't often have guests, and you're such an exotic one."

Ottilie settled back against her pillow and smiled. "I don't know how exciting a guest I am, but I was pleased to be there." She picked at the blanket, teasing a loose stitch from the worn quilt. "Your mother . . . she seemed very weak."

Penny's eyes clouded. "It has been nine months since we were able to send her to Bath. She loses so much strength at home."

Mrs. Hale had been carried into the cozy dining room by her husband, who settled her into a chair with as much care as someone transporting a priceless piece of art. He tucked a blanket around her and made sure she had the choicest piece of cake. It had been sweet. And exactly the way Ottilie's father had treated Maji. "I hope she gets better."

"She won't. Consumption is a fatal disease. But we hope to prolong her life with as much care as we can afford." Penny sighed and flopped onto her back. "There's some fancy ball being thrown in three weeks. We'll have so much work in the coming days. I'm glad I got to visit. We may not be able to leave for a while."

Penny closed her eyes, and not a moment later, her soft wheezing filled the room. Ottilie stared through the murky darkness at the ceiling. She'd have to manage her time well if she was to return to St. Luke's the following Sunday. And the next. And the next. Until they admitted her to see Thaddeus. And if they didn't . . .

She couldn't go back to Hazelbrook Manor. Couldn't putter around that grand, empty country house with nothing to do, nowhere to go, no one to love. Couldn't watch Everett find someone suitable to marry.

The walls of their tiny room closed in on her, and Ottilie could sense the darkness clouding her thoughts growing heavier, more difficult to resist. How could she not give up hope when all seemed lost?

She huffed and pushed up from her pillow again. Careful not to wake Penny, she swung her legs over the side of the bed, pulled a match from the drawer of the nearby table, and lit one of the two candles they were allotted a month. Everyone in England thought India a barbaric place, but even at their most destitute, Ottilie had access to kerosene lamps.

The flickering light made a small circle by which she could read, and the pages of Nānī's Bible—*her* Bible—crinkled beneath her fingertips. She knew what she wanted. Encouragement. Hope. Words directly from God's lips that would help her resist the melancholy stealing her peace, her sleep, and the little flame of faith she'd been protecting since scattering Nānī's ashes on the river.

Instead, she found Psalm 88. Her lips moved silently beneath the heaviness of the words.

> I have cried day and night before thee. . . . Thou hast laid me in the lowest pit, in darkness, in the deeps. . . . Thou hast put away mine acquaintance far from me. . . . Lord, why castest thou off my soul?

A tear dripped from her nose, splashing against the page, and she pulled away so they wouldn't wet the thin paper. Nānī's script filled the margin, addressed to Niraja:

> *Oh, my sister, how low I've been brought. I don't see any way out of my trouble. I am alone. Abandoned. Set apart. My husband, a murderer. My sister, estranged. My father, dead. My God . . . oh, my God, he is silent. Where is he? I can no longer see nor hear nor feel him.*
>
> *I don't expect you will write your response below mine. I don't expect you to send our Bible back across India. It will be lost to me like everything else. Your scorn burns as hot as the sun in August. It withers away all we have shared and consumes our love.*
>
> *All is lost.*
>
> *I am lost.*
>
> *Pray for me, sister, if you feel a moment of charity. Even if fifty years have passed, pray for me. Most of all that my faith will not disappear as I sit in this darkness. That it is there, waiting for me to emerge.*

"Oh, Nānī." Ottilie pressed the pages to her chest and felt her grandmother's knobby finger poke straight through to her heart. If Nānī could survive all that had happened, if she could rebuild her faith and hope and joy after losing everything, Ottilie could, as well.

The spark flamed brighter within her.

She lowered the Bible again and read Niraja's response, her breath coming out in a puff and nearly dousing the candle when she saw it addressed not to Nānī, but to her.

> *Ottilie, I fear I never prayed for Gitisha—my bitterness was so great—but I pray for you. Every day, I pray for you. May you find what you are looking for on England's shores. May you*

discover the thing Gitisha once told me was the secret to endur-
ing faith. And when you do, will you share it? I should like to
prepare for the inevitable bitterness and doubt that threatens it.

Ottilie swallowed and set down the Bible. She slipped her legs back beneath the covers and rolled onto her side, tucking her body against Penny's for warmth. Her friend's wheezing had stopped. Her cough as well. Her breathing . . .

Ottilie floated her hand in front of Penny's mouth and counted to five before feeling the warmth of her breath. Her breathing, thank God, had not stopped.

With her arms trapped between Penny's back and her own chest, Ottilie closed her eyes and pictured the unfinished tapestry embroidered by two untried girls. As darkness crowded in on the vision, she saw Nānī's secret—tall green plants crowned with delicate golden flowers, and beneath, the seeds that grew them. Maybe Niraja had known, after all, the secret to enduring faith. Only she'd allowed it to be crowded out by despair.

The mustard seeds were small, insignificant, but protected within the dark, rich soil where they had been planted. That was what a battered faith needed—a seed, only a seed, to cherish. To protect.

Ottilie had always been so worried about what she was losing. Just as Nani had told her the day she pointed to the back of Ottilie's embroidery work, Ottilie had neglected what was given to her. She'd thought she needed something big and strong, when she only truly needed something humble. Something seemingly insignificant.

A seed of faith was her legacy, and it was enough. Enough to protect. Enough to sprout. Enough to grow and propagate and multiply.

And Ottilie, just as she drifted into sleep, knew what needed to be stitched in that space between knowing and doubt.

Ottilie exchanged letters with Thaddeus twice the next week. He told her about his teachers, who made everything so uninteresting, listing only dates and facts and never, ever reading good stories. About the boys who crowded the dormitories at night, whispering long past dark. About his homesickness for India and even Hazelbrook Manor. About how much he missed her and wished they could see each other.

She told him about moving to London, wanting to be near. She promised to visit as soon as she could but didn't tell him she'd already tried. There was no point in raising his hopes. She told him not to divulge her address to Lady Sunderson or Alberta, for she had too much work to do to entertain them. He was young enough to believe her.

Ottilie and Penny filled every hour with stitching. Their fingers cramped and their eyes grew grainy from lack of sleep, but they managed to complete their work and claim their half day. They went to Kew the next Sunday and visited with the Hales. Ottilie told Mr. Hale about life in Calcutta, shared with Mrs. Hale Nānī's secrets for thick shiny hair, and then walked to St. Luke's and again spoke with the taciturn butler.

And just like the first time, the door slammed in her face.

A week later, Ottilie glanced at her watch, set as it was every Sunday on the table before her. Another Sunday. Another hope. Another wait. Another hour. She laid down her work and smoothed out the wrinkles, careful to avoid pulling at the elytra she'd just basted onto the bodice. As long as she came home before dinner and embroidered a few hours before bed, she'd finish the shoes Madame Laurence wanted done by the morning. Then she'd have three days to do the skirt that matched this bodice before moving on to the next project.

All the girls were in a dither at the work required of them. Half of them hadn't been able to take their half day the week before, and all but four of them wouldn't be taking it this time either. Everyone plodded on tired feet, dark circles beneath their eyes and stomachs grumbling between breakfast and dinner, as no one had time to eat lunch.

But Ottilie's fingers flew, whether by God's grace or her own desperation, she didn't know. She sensed resentful eyes on her after she made the final stitches on the bodice and marched it out of the room, down the steps, and to Madame Laurence's parlor. After receiving approval for her work, Ottilie went back to her table and began to tidy up, sweeping the snipped threads into her palm and gathering her tools.

"Are you finished?" Mrs. Follet scowled.

Ottilie nodded.

"And you've no other work?"

"No. Not anything I can't finish tonight."

"You are taking your half day, then?" Mrs. Follet's words were thickened by what sounded like tears, and Ottilie took her attention off the pins she'd been gathering. Mrs. Follet *was* about to cry—her eyes red-rimmed and jaw trembling.

"I am. Are you all right?"

"No, I'm not all right. It doesn't seem very fair that you, the new girl, are able to take your half day when the rest of us are forced to work through it."

"I finished my work. I've not left any of it for others."

"Then you weren't given enough."

Ottilie scratched her cheek, then tucked back stray wisps of hair behind her ear. She glanced at the line of seamstresses sitting behind their sewing machines. "What would you have me do? I don't sew or draw patterns."

Mrs. Follet jerked the gown she'd been working on from the table and shoved it toward Ottilie. "What about this? If you can turn insect parts into something beautiful, then surely you can do the same with thread."

"You want me to finish your work?" Ottilie's brows rose to her hairline.

Mrs. Follet growled and draped the fabric back over her table. "Never mind. Just go. Go and enjoy your time off."

Ottilie shook her head and went to her room to put away her things and retrieve her hat and gloves. Thankfully, the weather had warmed enough that she didn't need her coat.

Before she could leave, Penny appeared in the doorway. "Don't mind her. She's only upset because she hasn't been able to take her half day in weeks."

"That isn't my fault."

"No, but it's hardly hers either. Madame Laurence gives her more work than everyone else. Probably because she is the most experienced. And your embroidery is so singular. Madame Laurence wants to keep you working on the beetle-wing pieces that are all the rage. She's charging a premium for them, you know, because they can't be purchased anywhere else in the city. She won't risk you becoming overworked on plain embroidery when she needs you for pieces the aristocracy are fighting over." Penny took a few shaky steps into the room and sat heavily on the bed.

"Are you all right?" Ottilie pressed the back of her hand to Penny's head, satisfied at the touch of cool skin.

"I am. Just tired. We're all tired, though, so I have no right to complain." Penny smiled, but it was a weak one. "I won't be joining you today. I've no time. Will you stop in on Mama and give her a letter for me?"

"Of course." Ottilie waited for Penny to retrieve an envelope from the table beside the bed and then tucked it into her reticule and walked Penny toward the workroom. They paused just outside the door, and Ottilie saw Mrs. Follet bent over the table. She lifted a hand to her eyes, and her shoulders shook. "Who does she see? On her half days."

Penny didn't ask who Ottilie referred to. "Her son. He lives with her mother here in London. Alma was widowed before he was born, and she began working here as soon as he weaned."

"I didn't realize." Ottilie's heart softened. Mrs. Follet hadn't been kind to her, but if Ottilie's pain at being separated from her brother was so harsh, how much more terrible was Mrs. Follet's at being separated from her child?

Penny blew at the thin hair drooping across her forehead, and her lips fell into a rare frown. "It's very sad. A child of six should see his mother more than weekly, of course, but she hasn't seen him in a month. I hear her crying, sometimes, when I pass her door. She's a difficult woman, but I don't wonder if some of it is rooted in missing him."

Ottilie clutched the gloves in her hands. She really wanted to see her brother, but it was unlikely she would be admitted into St. Luke's.

Mrs. Follet had been so unkind to her, but she suffered tremendously.

Ottilie blew out her cheeks. "Oh, all right." Penny glanced at her, brows knit, and Ottilie shoved her reticule, gloves, and hat into her friend's arms. "Can you put these back in the room?"

She didn't wait for Penny's response. She knew she'd take back her decision if offered a moment to think about it, so she didn't let herself think about it. She gave a little shake of her head and crossed the workroom, stopping before Mrs. Follet.

The other woman looked up and pulled a pin from between her teeth. "Yes?"

"I will do this. You can take your half day."

Mrs. Follet stared at her.

Ottilie rounded the table and held out her hand for the pin. She waggled her fingers when Mrs. Follet didn't immediately comply. "Go."

Mrs. Follet looked at the bodice she was working on. "Can you do this?"

Ottilie studied the design. It was complex, made more so

by the monochromatic color scheme. Cream thread had been embroidered into trailing vines and flowers around the sides of the bodice and down the front in two rows. Mrs. Follet had also sewn glass beads at various spots down the middle sections.

"This isn't done," she was saying, pointing at one of the central vines that stopped a quarter of the way down from the neckline. "And after it is, the lace must be attached to the neckline, and it needs to be finished tonight. I'm not sure you're up for the task."

"I can do it. Go." Ottilie sat, her hip pushing against Mrs. Follet's until she'd forced her off the bench.

Mrs. Follet's fingers found the edge of the bodice, and she tugged a little, as though afraid to hand the project over to Ottilie. "If it isn't done correctly, perfectly, I'll be the one in trouble."

"You'd better leave before I change my mind." Ottilie picked up the scissors and snipped the end of the thread before pulling it through the needle's eye. She expertly knotted it, her gaze on Mrs. Follet's face.

She saw so much more there than a need for control. There was fear and yearning and disbelief.

Ottilie touched Mrs. Follet's hand, which still clutched the fabric. "I know you need this job. I assure you, Madame Laurence will not even know I finished the work. I may prefer beetle-wing embroidery—it makes me feel close to my mother and grandmother—but I'm adept at all forms."

After only a moment of indecision clearly written across her face, Mrs. Follet gave a short nod and left the room.

Ottilie ignored the whispers of the other women, ignored their pointed glances and raised shoulders, and turned her attention toward the intricate work that required a steady hand and all her focus.

Ottilie skipped dinner in favor of keeping her word and finishing the work. She was tying off the final stitch when Mrs. Follet returned just before the nine o'clock curfew. She swept into the workroom, cheeks red and eyes bright, and went to Ottilie.

"Thank you. I don't know why you did what you did, but I'm so grateful. I hadn't seen my son in a month, and your kindness made him so happy. Made me so happy."

Ottilie smiled. "I know what it is to miss someone dear when they are so close you feel they should hear you call to them." Interest sparked in Mrs. Follet's gaze, but Ottilie stood, preventing any prodding questions, and held up the bodice. "What do you think?"

Mrs. Follet's eyes dropped to the embroidery work, and her lips parted around a soft sigh. "I must admit, I was worried, but I see I needn't have been. You can't even tell where I left off. Your stitching is very neat."

Ottilie brushed a wrinkle from the fabric and handed it over. "You may take it down, and Madame Laurence will be none the wiser." She began sweeping the snipped threads and bits of broken beads into her cupped hand.

"Miss Russell?"

Ottilie looked up.

"I'm sorry . . . for the way I've treated you. I've never met someone like you and, well, you hear stories about Indians. But my treatment of you was misguided and ill-founded, and I offer my sincerest regrets. And . . ." She glanced at the wall before meeting Ottilie's eyes. "If you would like, please call me Alma."

Warmth spilled into Ottilie's chest, dazzling as the spices Dilip tossed into his *korai*, spitting and throwing up fragrance the moment they hit the oil. "Thank you for that. You may call me Ottilie."

Over the following days, Alma made sure to address Ottilie by name each morning over their skimpy breakfast of grainy bread, sliced onions, and tea. And with each hour they spent together, another woman showed Ottilie a kindness or chatted with her for a moment over tea or asked her about life in India.

Ottilie awoke early on the third day after everything had changed, and pulled out the long piece of linen she'd stashed in a hatbox beneath the bed. She'd started this personal project after realizing what Nānī had meant to embroider onto her and Niraja's tapestry. She would never have thought her faith would come into itself in this place of constant work, separation, and never-ending hunger, but it had. And she wanted to finish Nānī's tapestry. Wanted to send it to Niraja and give her great-aunt something to bolster her own faith and see her through all the hard things one faced in the growing of it.

Something to remind her that she knew, deep down, how to establish lasting faith already.

Ottilie crossed her legs and teased out the yellow thread. With practiced ease, she threaded her needle and began the repetitive task of filling in the petals' outlines with satin stitching.

After squinting against the dim gray sunrise light for half an hour, Ottilie felt Penny begin to stir beside her. "Good morning."

Penny turned over, and Ottilie gasped at her friend's glassy eyes and the flush that indicated a fever. A quick press of her hand against Penny's forehead confirmed her fear.

She scrambled to gather her supplies, shoving them back into the hatbox. "What's wrong?"

"It's that cough I've had. It's stealing all my energy, and I'm afraid it's settled deep in my chest."

"Well, you must stay in bed and rest. I'll force the cook to give me some of the stock she keeps boiling on the stove."

"Oh, I can't. There is so much to be done."

Ottilie gripped Penny's hand. "You cannot be the one to do it. I will speak with Miss Briggs, and perhaps the rest of us can pick up your work." She rose to dress, careful to make as little noise as possible when she saw Penny had fallen back to sleep while Ottilie freshened up at the washstand.

Kneeling, Ottilie pushed her arms beneath the bed and gripped her spice box. Inside, she found ground dried turmeric, fenugreek, and cardamom pods. She also pinched up a few strands of the saffron she'd been guarding. With silent steps, she made her way from the room and went to the kitchen.

The cook was already there, peering into the oven. Bacon sizzled on the stove, and the scent of chocolate made Ottilie's mouth water. "Are we to have a treat for breakfast?"

The woman jerked upright and waved a greasy spoon around her head. "This is for the madam. You'll get bread and tea, as usual. What are you doing in my kitchen?"

"My bedmate is ill. I'd like to bring her a cup of broth and some warm milk."

"Well, I don't have time for that. Dishes are in the cabinet." She went back to her work, and Ottilie crossed the room and retrieved two heavy mugs from the large, rickety piece of furniture taking up nearly the entire length of the back wall. Setting them on the table, she found a jug of milk and poured a portion into a pot. "Can I heat this up as well?"

The cook sighed. "The milk isn't for the likes of you upstairs. It's for the madam's hot chocolate."

"I don't think she will notice it this once. And I'm sure my friend will get better and be able to return to work more quickly if she could only have something nourishing to eat."

"I suppose." The cook wiped her hands on the apron covering her dress and stood back while Ottilie put the pot to flame and sprinkled the spices into it. After a few minutes, the milk, golden from the turmeric, began to simmer, and Ottilie poured it into a mug. "Have you any garlic?"

The woman sighed and pointed to the braid of garlic near a heap of onions. Ottilie crushed a few cloves and dropped them into the other mug, then dipped a ladle into the boiling stock, careful to keep the scum from floating into it. When she finished her preparations, she thanked the cook and retraced her steps back to the bedroom.

Penny was awake when Ottilie entered, groaning and

clutching her chest. "It hurts so badly. As though I'm being kicked by a goat."

Ottilie set the tray on the table and urged Penny to scoot over so she could reach it. "Hopefully this will make you feel better. I'll bring you up more at lunch, and again at dinner. Drink everything, and eat the garlic at the bottom of the stock."

Penny made a face. "Chew it whole?"

"Yes." Ottilie pointed at her. "You must."

Penny's smile was small, but it cheered Ottilie. "Yes, Doctor."

Ottilie went to the workroom. She'd embroider, eat breakfast, convince some of the other girls to pick up Penny's work—she'd do it herself if she could sew, but she'd never touched one of those machines before—and then talk with Miss Briggs.

Hopefully by the next morning, Penny would be well enough to get out of bed.

28

Ottilie was convinced God set angels on either side of her for the rest of the week, because by Sunday all her work was finished, and she was released to her half day. Confident in her ability to navigate the city and train after her two visits with Penny, Ottilie abandoned decorum and raced from Madame Laurence's as soon as Miss Briggs came to dismiss those who were able to leave.

On the train, she pulled out Thaddeus's most recent letter. Tracing his blocky print, she read the dear words and admired the improvements in his penmanship. That was one area Ottilie had no talent for. She'd never had a fine hand. She would never have been able to teach Thaddeus how to write beautifully.

Two or three times a week, she received a letter from him— London's post was inexpensive and fast—and she was able to follow along with his days, told in rambling sentences and funny anecdotes. He had stopped asking when she would visit, though, and Ottilie felt as though she'd failed him.

When she arrived at the station, she tucked his letters away. Tucked away, too, the disappointment churning in her belly. She'd never meant to be the one who left Thaddeus feeling abandoned. Alone. And she had no idea how to repair the situation. She couldn't very well force herself past the butler.

She walked Kew's pretty streets and found herself at the Gardens' ornate gate, facing the same guard who always greeted her and Penny.

"Did Miss Hale not come today?" Charlie asked, frowning.

"Not today. But I have something for her father."

He waved her through. "He's at the Palm House."

Penny had directed Ottilie to an envelope stuck between the pages of a book and asked her to deliver it. "Don't tell him I'm ill. He already has too much to worry about." She tilted her chin toward the envelope. "That will ease some of his burden. It's the rest of the money needed to send Mama to the Bath sanatorium for a few months."

Ottilie checked the string of her reticule for the fifth time since leaving Madame Laurence's, assuring herself that the ribbon held firm and Penny's money was safe. She would deliver it to Mr. Hale and then set out for St. Luke's. She was sure to be disappointed—the butler seemed a humorless man unlikely to break convention and rules—but Ottilie chose optimism. She didn't think her outlook determined the outcome, but if nothing was going to come of the way she viewed the world, she might as well nurture hope along the way.

Caught up in her ponderings, she nearly plowed into a wall of little boys when she entered the Palm House. All lined up, backs toward her, they listened to a sour-looking man drone on about the history of the building.

She crept along the wall behind them, biting back laughter at the antsy way they swayed from foot to foot, a few pinching the child next in line. One bounced his knees the way Thaddeus always did when excited, head bobbing and arms clasped tightly to his side.

So much like Thaddeus.

Ottilie paused and stared at the child's back. He was small—smaller than the other boys, with dark hair that curled over his ears. She kept her eyes on him as she rounded a massive palm tree, then hurried around the corner and made her way up another aisle, one that deposited her behind the teacher—and facing the small child who had captured her attention.

"Thaddeus," she whispered and drank in the sight of him. He couldn't see her, shielded as she was by a row of Rhapis palms, so she took the moment to impress upon her memory the sight of his sweet face.

He looked well. He'd gained weight, and a rosy hue colored his cheeks. The child next to him leaned down to whisper in his ear, drawing a sharp reprimand from the teacher, and Thaddeus poked his friend in the ribs, a cautious grin tugging at his mouth.

He looked happy. All traces of melancholy had disappeared from his face. He was the boy he'd been before Maji died, all restrained vigor and unaware joy.

What luck! Ottilie wouldn't have to convince the stuffy butler of anything today. She'd sit tight until Thaddeus made his way past her and call to him. She wouldn't give her brother away—wouldn't make it awkward for him—but she would take this chance. She would ask him how he was and kiss his head and hug him tight.

The teacher waved his arms in first one direction, then the other, loudly intoning the layout of the building. Then, with a gesture of his hand, the crowd of boys dispersed, spreading out to explore.

"Remember who you are," the teacher called. "Gentlemen possessed of admirable self-control and somber disposition."

Ottilie laughed and watched her brother's progress. How little this man knew about Thaddeus Russell. He was a sweet boy, but definitely not somber, nor did he show much in the way of self-control. What child did?

But to Ottilie's amazement, Thaddeus wandered along the line of plants at a sedate pace. She could see the excitement coursing through him, but he held on to it and kept up with the boys on either side of him.

They turned down the aisle beside hers and, keeping to the fringe of shade provided by branches and flowering bushes, she stayed a few steps behind.

"So, Sunderson, are these the types of plants you grew up with in India?" one of the boys asked.

"They are familiar." Thaddeus plucked a leaf and sniffed it.

"You're not supposed to tell tales about India, remember, Sunderson?" another boy, this one with a shock of red hair, warned.

Ottilie narrowed her eyes. He couldn't talk about his home?

The boys were quiet a moment while the first one glanced around. "No one is near. Do you miss it?"

"India?" Thaddeus said.

The boy nodded. Ottilie crouched and pressed her face against the plant, straining to see her brother's expression past the thickly entwined branches.

"I miss my mother and grandmother and sister," Thaddeus said, and her heart swelled. "But I don't miss India. Not anymore."

A chill swept over Ottilie's skin, freeing a wave of prickling goose bumps over her arms and legs. How was that possible? He had wept for it on his birthday, begged to return home, and that was only weeks ago.

One of the other boys piped up. "Is England better or India?"

Thaddeus laughed. "India has better food, but England has better boys . . . at least English boys. I haven't met any Indian boys here." He punched the boy's shoulder, and a tangle of arms surrounded him, hands rubbing at his curls and even an errant foot meeting his shin in a good-natured kick. When the tussle ended, Thaddeus ran his hand through his hair and straightened his jacket. "I'm glad to be in England. And St. Luke's is better than my school in India. I wasn't treated well there."

There was a loud outcry, and the boys wondered if they'd ever have the opportunity to go to India and pound the kids who'd treated him so shabbily.

"Well, Sunderson," said the boy whose foot had made contact with Thaddeus's shin, "you have to stay here. You're one of us now."

"I'm glad." Thaddeus turned his face in her direction, and Ottilie could see the confident satisfaction spread over it. The kind that only came when a person knew they belonged. Were accepted.

"Oh, Thaddeus," she whispered.

She watched as the boys made their way down another aisle, drifting farther away. She moved toward a lonely stone bench and sank onto it. *"You're one of us now."*

And he was. The perfect young English gentleman. No one looking at him, listening to him, would think any differently. In a matter of months, Thaddeus had been transformed into Baron Sunderson. India held nothing for him. He'd been absorbed into the culture and family Father had run from.

There had never been such a distance separating Ottilie and her brother before. She could be at his side in moments yet had never felt so far from him. The cord that bound them seemed, in that moment, a tenuous thing. Not thick enough to withstand society, position, and the disparity between them. If she truly cared for him, she'd snip the remaining threads. Release him to his future with nothing holding him back. Nothing and no one posing a risk.

She covered her face with her hands and barely caught the sob eager to slip free of her throat. He was all she had left. And now she had no one.

She alone was left wishing for India. Wishing for what had been.

A hand caught her shoulder, and she looked up into Mr. Hale's kind face. "My dear girl." She stood and let him wrap one massive arm around her shoulders as he looked for his daughter.

Ottilie pushed out a shuddering breath and gathered the tattered remains of her pride. There was nothing to do but tell Mr.

Hale that Penny hadn't been able to come and hand him her wages.

Then she would head back to Madame Laurence's and go about the business of caring for Penny and looking out for Alma. No one else needed her now.

"Lord and Lady Merton are having a ball in two weeks, Lady Sibsly will be hosting a dinner for a Norwegian prince, and we have two bridal trousseaus to prepare for." Miss Briggs stared out at the women assembled in the workroom the next morning, and Ottilie forced herself to listen instead of thinking about Thaddeus. "We are at the height of the Season, and sacrifices will have to be made."

"For us, she means. Not for them," Alma muttered beneath her breath.

Miss Briggs narrowed her eyes and looked in their direction. "Skip dinner, if you must. Work late and get up early. Few of you will be able to take your half days in the coming weeks. You work for the foremost dressmaker in London. Don't disappoint her." With one final sweeping glance over them, she turned and left.

Ottilie scrambled from her chair and rushed after her. "Miss Briggs."

At the head of the stairs, the woman turned. "Yes?"

"I need to let you know that Miss Hale is still ill. The other seamstresses have offered to continue her work. She must have rest."

Miss Briggs sighed and placed her hand on the banister. "See that the work is done, and I won't begrudge her that. If it's not, if she falls behind or the work isn't up to quality, she will be replaced."

Ottilie nodded and watched her descend the staircase. On the way back to the workroom, she checked in on a sleeping Penny, not at all happy to see her friend's lack of color or hear her shallow breathing. And it was no wonder—with no flowing air or ventilation, Penny had little chance of getting well. The room was practically poisonous. Ottilie had tried opening the window a few days earlier, but it had been painted shut long ago and didn't budge. She peered into the cup of broth on the table, pleased to see it empty. But the milk hadn't been touched. She'd replace it at lunch. If she took a lunch.

Back in the workroom, silence had descended, punctuated only by the low hum of the sewing machines and an occasional murmur. Ottilie did take lunch—albeit a quick one. Long enough to run to the kitchen, heat another cup of milk with turmeric, and take it to Penny.

"You must drink this," she said.

Penny hunched over her chest and coughed into her fist. Then she slumped against the rickety brass headboard. "I will." She made a good show of reaching for it, and Ottilie had to leave and get back to work, despite not believing for a second that her friend actually followed through on her promise.

Ottilie had just enough time to spoon a greasy lump of unidentifiable meat into her mouth—how she missed Dilip's cooking!—and gulp half her tea before lunch was collected, forcing the women back to work.

After a few more hours, Ottilie's vision began to blur, and she set the skirt she was working on aside. Standing, she lifted her arms above her head and stretched out the kinks. Their tea was late. Surely they wouldn't be denied tea. They could go a day without food, but drink was another matter entirely.

Before she could retake her seat, Miss Briggs appeared, and everyone turned to her with weary expectation. She motioned to Ottilie. "There is a customer who insists on seeing you."

"Whatever for?"

"She has seen your work and feels you must be present to fully understand her vision." Miss Briggs's lip curled into a sneer.

"Your appearance will be shocking enough. Don't do or say anything that may alienate her."

Ottilie raised her brows and drew herself up straight. "I regularly interacted with customers in Calcutta, Miss Briggs. I am capable of comporting myself with dignity."

"I hope so. Let us go."

Ottilie followed her downstairs and into the salon. She'd yet to enter this room—the seamstresses and embroiderers were kept out of sight on the first floor—and she took the opportunity to look around. It was spacious, with a cluster of ornate chairs and settees surrounding a large round table in front of a wide bank of windows. Screens painted with what could only be French scenery at the back of the room provided privacy. A large gilded mirror took up nearly an entire wall.

"Miss Russell?" Madame Laurence's sharp reprimand drew Ottilie's attention. "Our customer is waiting."

And then another voice, this one just as forceful, but kinder and familiar, spoke in French. *"Ne leur dites pas que nous sommes amies."*

Ottilie's breath caught, and she looked upon Damaris's darling face. *Do not let them know we are friends*, Damaris had said, though Ottilie didn't know why. She schooled her features, blinking away the tears that had risen the moment she saw her friend. She looked at Madame Laurence instead of Damaris, if only because she wasn't an actress and didn't have the foggiest notion how to pretend she didn't know the person she loved best of all outside of her family.

"Miss Winship has quite the vision, Miss Russell, and insisted she meet with you. I admit, her thoughts for the gown are quite esoteric and elude me. Perhaps, with your artistic sensibilities, you might be able to make something concrete out of them?" Madame Laurence—who surely knew French with a name like that—made Ottilie's *artistic sensibilities* sound insulting.

But Ottilie cared little. Here was Damaris, and her presence was a balm to the open wound left from the day before. "I shall try my very best."

Damaris patted the cushion beside her. *"S'il vous plait, asseyez-vous ici."*

Before Ottilie could take the seat as directed, Madame Laurence interrupted. "Oh, my dear, Miss Russell couldn't possibly know French. English from here on out, if you please."

Ottilie bit her lip to keep her laugh from escaping and met Damaris's gaze. She saw her friend's offense on her behalf, but she shook her head. There was no use in taking insult. Once Ottilie was seated, Damaris shifted so that her leg nudged against Ottilie's—a sign of solidarity.

"What is it you were hoping for, Miss Winship?" Ottilie asked.

Madame Laurence pushed a sheet of paper toward Ottilie. "This is what she sketched for us. It's quite . . . spectacular."

Ottilie looked over the drawing and nearly choked on her tongue. *Spectacular* didn't begin to describe the atrocity before her. Within a cloud of what she could only assume was tulle gathered into flounces affixed with roses was an image of a woman swathed in green and violet. Feathers dripped from the waistline and marched down the skirt, and little green circles, which Ottilie assumed were elytra, had been drawn across the bodice.

"It's a peacock," Damaris said with as straight a face as Ottilie had ever seen.

"I gathered. Is this ball you're attending . . . a costumed one?"

"No." Damaris blinked superficially widened eyes. "Do you think . . ." She turned to look at Madame Laurence and Miss Briggs, who had taken the seat near her. "Have you taken me for a fool? Is she the only one willing to be honest? Were you willing to allow me to go out in public and be made a mockery?" Tears sprang to her eyes and slipped down her cheeks. Damaris's acting skills had been honed on her mother, and Ottilie could only stare at her, impressed by the display. "Oh, how terrible that a woman cannot even trust her own dressmaker. *Le chat! Le chat et le pigeon prennent leur thé dans le salon. Le salon!*"

Ottilie easily followed Damaris's exclamation about a cat and pigeon taking tea together. All in French. None of it understood by Madame Laurence. She covered her snort with a cough and pressed her palm to her mouth.

"Now, Miss Winship, there is no reason to get upset. We shall design you a magnificent gown, one worthy of your beauty." Madame Laurence held out her hands, and panic raised her voice an octave.

Damaris lifted from her seat. "*Allez-vous en.* Just go. Leave me with Miss Russell."

Madame Laurence and Miss Briggs didn't wait for Damaris to change her mind. Madame Laurence shot Ottilie a look of what seemed to be regret tinged with relief, then trotted from the room.

The door clicked behind them, and Damaris sank back into the seat. Her face composed itself into the placid lines Ottilie was used to. "I've found you, and you have no idea how happy I am."

"How did you know she couldn't speak French?"

Damaris waved her hand. "I tested her when I first arrived. I said Lady Cartwright told me her establishment smelled of cabbage, and she only understood *Cartwright*, incorrectly assumed I'd merely dropped the viscountess's name, and told me I was welcome. Then she nodded and smiled, pretending she understood, when I knew she couldn't tell if I was speaking French or Malayalam."

Ottilie took her hand. "I'm terribly glad you're here. I've missed you so much. I meant to write you—and I've made you a gift—but I didn't know when you were arriving, and then . . . then I became too busy to think of it."

Damaris studied her. "I can see you *have* been too busy. Too busy even to eat? You have lost weight, Ottilie, and you didn't have much to lose to begin with."

"My life as an embroiderer here is much different than in Calcutta. How did you find me?"

Damaris shrugged. "That was easy enough. My aunt and I spent only a week in Bath before we came to London. I merely followed the string of beetle-wing embroidered gowns that have begun to appear all over Town. I know your work, Ottilie."

Warmth spread within Ottilie's breast, and she pressed a spontaneous kiss to Damaris's cheek. "You have no idea how wonderful it is to see you."

"What happened? Why are you slaving here and not in Wiltshire with your family?"

"It is too long a story. Madame Laurence might return any moment."

Damaris let out an inelegant snort. "She's so terrified of me, she won't be back until I leave."

"You'll have to order a gown now, you know. Otherwise she'll think I ran you off."

Damaris lifted the pencil from the table and handed it over. "Design whatever you wish. I do have a dinner to go to next Thursday, and my aunt will gladly buy me a new gown, if only to prove to Mother that she is capable of caring for me."

Ottilie turned over Damaris's atrocious sketch and began to outline something that would truly complement her friend's stunning figure.

"You really don't look well, Ottilie."

"The Season has us very busy. Every week is a flurry of balls and dinners and the opera. It never ends. There are days we are given only breakfast and tea with nothing in between, or we are forced to skip dinner. We begin work at half past six every morning and sometimes don't get into bed until three the next. One of the younger girls fainted from want of food and exhaustion yesterday. Just crumpled right over her machine."

Ottilie lightly ran the pencil over the skirt, indicating a delicate netting that would be studded with elytra. She'd leave the bodice simple—Damaris had enough charm in that area to pull off an unadorned design. She pinched her lips together, then grabbed the rubber eraser and removed all traces of the netting. Damaris would shine in a gown of complete simplicity. Something that emphasized her beauty and bold features.

She tugged her lip between her teeth and studied her design. There was something missing. Something that didn't quite capture Damaris's spirit. Her brow wrinkled, and she tapped the pencil lead against her teeth. Then she looked up at Damaris with a sigh. "I don't mind the work itself—though I enjoy designing more than the actual stitching, and I'm not offered the opportunity to do that here. It's just the *amount* of work that is overwhelming. The lack of food and sunlight and sleep."

Damaris sat back and clutched her hands in her lap. "It's terrible that nobody gives the women who make us beautiful a passing thought. I wish there was something I could do to ease your burden." She blinked, and then a smile appeared on her lips. "What if I write about it for *The Englishwoman's Review*? It is what I do best, after all. We don't have a broad readership, but perhaps we could mobilize women around the city to protest the poor treatment of seamstresses."

"Oh, don't. If it's found out I had something to do with it, I'll lose my position. And I would hate for anyone else here to get in trouble."

"I don't see how anyone would find out. There are dozens of society dressmakers in London. And think of the change we could effect."

Damaris's face glowed with the thought of her righteous crusade, but Ottilie could only think of Penny, sick in bed. Sick because of overwork and malnourishment and fetid air that couldn't escape through the sealed window. She wondered if an article in one small publication could change the lives of the women she'd come to love. Could she help make a difference for them?

Her life had shrunk to encompass only Madame Laurence's Dress Shop on Regent Street. But if she went back far enough, her life had truly begun shrinking after Papa's death, when nothing felt certain and every decision that took her outside her family or home felt like a risk.

Giving Damaris permission to print this story would be a risk. But if it meant better living conditions, proper food, time to rest . . . perhaps it was one worth taking.

Ottilie felt as though she had been standing for years within a circle of thread, and the more tightly the needle pulled it, the smaller her world became until she was trapped beneath a stitch that adhered her to a life she'd never anticipated. A life of fear and myopia.

"Very well. Write the story. It should be told." For the first time in a very long time, Ottilie felt she'd done the brave thing. She wasn't running from anything—not cholera or death or loneliness or secrets—but toward truth and justice.

Damaris reached into her reticule and withdrew a little notebook and pencil. With a wink in Ottilie's direction, she flipped the pages open. "I always keep this on me. Tell me more about the conditions here."

Ottilie did. She described the cramped, airless bedrooms where it was sometimes hard to draw a full breath. The injuries due to poor lighting and inadequate sleep. She laughed when she told a story about how their stomachs all made noise, protesting the lack of food and sounding as though a poor excuse for an orchestra had taken residence in the sewing room. It wasn't funny, though, and Damaris stopped scribbling in her book, staring at Ottilie as horror crawled over her features.

As Ottilie continued to speak, her arms felt suddenly lighter, and she began to draw again in freedom-inspired creativity. It was like iron fetters falling from her wrists, letting her create from the beauty and goodness welling up within her. Truth set one free. There was no fear in it.

She fell silent and let the idea roll around her mind as she finished the sketch, then held up her design for Damaris's approval.

Her friend's blue eyes lit, and a blush heightened her fair coloring. "Do you really think I might wear something like that?"

The gown would be unlike anything seen in the dining rooms of London's most privileged. But Damaris was unlike any woman likely to be present. For too many years, her friend had been forced into the latest styles, her buxom shape pulled and pinched and squeezed. Ottilie had been embroidering gowns designed by another person for weeks—gowns that created a homogeneous look among England's elite. Damaris deserved something better. She deserved to wear something that would enhance her unique beauty, not dictate it.

"You are the only person I can think of who can wear something like this."

Damaris bit her lower lip and looked between Ottilie and the sketch. Then she nodded. "I love it."

"Good. When will you publish the story about us?"

"We have an issue releasing in two days. I will make sure it's on the front page."

"Your dress will be ready in three days, then, for I'm not certain I'll be welcome at Madame Laurence's if she learns who helped you. Use details if you must, for what is happening here isn't right, and people should know."

Damaris took her eyes off the sketch and propped her chin atop her fist. "What will you do if Madame Laurence discovers your part?"

Ottilie pressed her hands against her knees and blew a puff of air from her lips. "Would you like a lady's maid? Or a companion?" She'd run all the way to Australia to avoid becoming Alberta's companion, but Damaris was a different story altogether.

Damaris tipped her head and chuckled. "As much as I would

love having you around always—I'd be the best-dressed woman in all of England—why not return to Hazelbrook Manor? It's your home, Ottilie. You belong with your family."

"I . . . I left without word. I'm not sure they'll receive me back. And even if they would, I can't live somewhere I'm not wanted. I'm a burden on them, Damaris. I never want to be a burden." A scratching came from outside the door. "We have no more time together, but I ask you to send a doctor to us. My bedmate is seriously ill, and I worry for her."

"Of course. He will be here this very afternoon. Shall I have him ask for you?" Damaris reached into her reticule and pulled out a letter, hesitating only a moment. "One more thing. Mrs. Lupton asked me to deliver this directly to you when I arrived in England."

Ottilie stared at it, bile rising in her throat. Could she not escape the reach of her grandfather even half a world away? But Damaris shoved it toward her, and another scratch came at the door. Ottilie slipped the envelope into her pocket and stood. "You can collect your gift when you return for the gown. I'm so glad you found me, but I must go, or I will never finish it before Madame Laurence hears about the story."

Ottilie hoped it all worked out in the end, for in her pursuit of helping her friends, she might very well have made herself unemployable. And worse . . . tossed out of this place that had become an unlikely home.

Dearest Ottilie,

You may not want to hear from me, for I know we have hurt you terribly. (I tried to say your grandfather hurt you terribly, but my ignorance does not excuse me from having caused you so much pain.) I do want to tell you, though, that Richard returned home the night your grandmother died a changed man.

A broken man.

That is not something I ever thought would be a good thing. But there are many forms of brokenness. There's the type that comes after great grief and trauma. It softens us toward God's Word and his touch. Makes us more compassionate toward others.

And there's the type that sees us shattered into a thousand pieces. Unable to move forward with our lives. Ineffective.

I never met your grandmother, but I prayed for her every day after I discovered her existence. And I know, just by knowing you, that she was a strong kind of broken.

Life has been unfair to you, Ottilie. I'm so sorry for the role I played in that. But you are the type of broken that God shines his light through.

I have seen a change in your grandfather these last couple of weeks. I must tell you that he has recently been brought low by cholera. It has spread far and wide throughout the city. I'm not sure he will survive. But I do not resent him visiting your grandmother because he found forgiveness there.

By the time you receive this, he will have either recovered or not. But I want you to know that his thoughts have turned to you. He calls out your name in his sleep and weeps over his sin toward you.

He is broken, Ottilie. But in the best way possible.

His heart has softened and become fertile ground for the seeds of faith.

Sincerely,
Flora

Ottilie pressed the letter to her chest and leaned against the wall just outside the sewing room. She'd intended to read it later that night, when only her sad little room would be witness to any churning emotions brought to the surface by this unexpected correspondence, but it burned through her pocket and seared her skin. She couldn't ignore it.

He is broken. But in the best way possible.

And joining Flora's words were Everett's, soft and tantalizing, drawing Ottilie nearer freedom than the agony of doubt ever could. *"But I know that suffering produces strength of character."*

Across the continents and over oceans, Ottilie felt the tug of a thread that bound her to the land of her grandmother and mother, but also to her grandfather. The Englishman who had adopted and torn apart and loved and spilled blood upon India's soil.

She couldn't disavow herself from him any more than she could deny the love for Thaddeus bound up in her heart. The colonel wasn't a perfect man. Couldn't really even be called a good man.

But he was a broken man. Broken like her.

The remnants of unforgiveness that had clung to Ottilie slipped, releasing their grasp on her heart and mind. And the same way Everett promised spring would bring the sun, Ottilie felt the warmth of it now, shedding light on that tiny, insignificant seed. It was life sprouting.

29

I believe it's pneumonia."

The doctor's words sprang around Ottilie's mind later that night as she tried to catch a few hours of rest. Beside her, Penny coughed and moaned. Ottilie placed her hand on Penny's back, finding comfort in the rhythmic rise and fall.

Her eyes burned, and she rubbed them, trying to dislodge the gritty feeling. She should sleep. She needed to sleep. But she couldn't sleep. Her mind whirred with worries.

What would she do if she was never able to see Thaddeus? What would she do after the Season, when Madame Laurence no longer needed her services, or if she read Damaris's story and realized Ottilie had something to do with it? What would happen if Penny didn't get well? Should she write to the colonel who, even now, might very well be past reading letters?

Through the darkness, a memory stirred up Nānī's voice. It had been just after they sold their beautiful bungalow and moved into the tiny home in Entally. Ottilie had felt as though she'd lost everything—her father, her neighborhood, most of her belongings, the servants who made life so easy, the privilege and acceptance—as superficial as it was—that came from being the daughter of the superintendent of the Imperial Museum. Everything. She'd pushed herself into the corner of the verandah, her back pressed against the railing, wrapped her arms around her father's copy of Blake's poetry, and wept.

Nānī, back stooped and steps shuffling, found her and eased to the floor, taking the book from Ottilie's hands to set it aside. They wept together.

"How can we survive this, Nānī? How can we live without Father and Jemima and Nathan? What will we do? I'm so frightened."

Nānī had pressed her thumb to the line between Ottilie's eyes, and her fingers, the skin sagging and thin as paper, had cupped her cheek. *"Oh, Boodha. These aren't things for you to worry over."* Then she covered Ottilie's head with her hands and closed her eyes. *"'Peace I leave with you, my peace I give unto you. . . . Let not your heart be troubled, neither let it be afraid.'"*

Ottilie had known Nānī spoke words from the Bible that were meant to comfort and encourage. But they didn't. The worry and fear only grew, as things left unchecked are wont to do.

Ottilie flipped onto her back. She'd had a lifetime of worrying, and not one thing had been changed because of it. Perhaps she would try something different. Perhaps it was time to take Nānī's advice and cast her cares on God.

She tossed the blanket away, got out of bed, and went to the window. Her palm made quick work of the grime. A streetlamp shed dim light over the desolate scene—nothing but a back alley—and she turned from it to stare at Penny's curled form.

Penny had become so dear to her. She was the first person in all of England who had invited Ottilie into her life. The first person, outside of Damaris, to offer the gift of friendship. *And Everett. Don't forget Everett.* But Ottilie had to forget him. Remembering cost too much.

Please, God, I beg you to keep Penny safe. I will pray for nothing else but that. Trusting you with everything else—with Thaddeus and Lady Sunderson and Alberta and my future and Everett—feels like too great a confidence right now. But Penny . . . I will trust you with her.

She crossed the room and pulled her battered hatbox from beneath the bed. From it she removed not only the nearly complete tapestry addition but also Nānī's kadas. Her kadas. They were a perfect match, but she needed the tiny yellow Madras seed pearls for something of greater importance. She knelt beside the bed and, with her embroidery scissors, snipped at the silk thread binding the pearls to the bangle, letting them fall onto the blanket.

When she finished her task, her heart pounded at the destruction she'd wrought. She prayed that if Nānī could see her from heaven, she forgave her, but Ottilie had to finish the tapestry. For Nānī. For Niraja. For herself.

A persistent knock at the door disturbed any thought of finishing tonight.

Upon opening it, she saw Alma and half a dozen of the seamstresses, each holding a candle. Alma held her hand in front of the flame, the light filling the hollows of her cheeks and splashing shadows across her face. "We thought we'd try and finish Penny's work."

Ottilie looked at the women—all young and tired and overworked. All kind and selfless. "Do you sew, Alma?"

"Yes. Not as well as I embroider, but passably well. You can do the buttons and fancy work. We'll each take different pieces and then stitch everything together before breakfast."

"Are you sure?" Ottilie glanced over her shoulder at Penny, who had stirred at the commotion and begun coughing, each spasm flinging out a sharp gasp.

"Yes. We won't allow Penny to be cast away. We're something of a family, aren't we?"

Warmth, as comfortable and lovely as the sun rising over the misty haze that shrouded Calcutta in the morning, pooled in

Ottilie's belly. These women had filled the lonely places in her heart. Had filled them and revealed their limitations.

Family had always been Father, Maji, Nānī, Thaddeus, Jemima, Nathan, and Dilip. There hadn't been room for anyone else. She'd never seen the need for anyone else. There had been people waiting to be gathered to her, but she'd been too afraid to reach out. Too afraid to embrace them. Had built a barricade that kept everyone at arm's length so she wouldn't be hurt.

And they had been there all along.

"I think we have," she told Alma, her lips forming a soft smile that felt somewhat out of place but wholly familiar.

As she followed Alma to the workroom, she discovered something buried within her thoughts that so startled her she gasped and nearly dropped her candle.

"What is it?" Alma asked.

Ottilie shook her head. "Nothing at all." Except she wondered if it hadn't only been Lady Sunderson and Alberta who had shut her out. Maybe she had been at fault as well.

"Would you call me Grandmother?" Lady Sunderson had asked.

It had felt like an insult—only offering a partial invitation. Only in secret. But it could have been an open door. A beginning. A candle lit. A seed, small and insignificant but able to sprout something mighty.

And Ottilie had rejected it.

Over the next three days, they worked their fingers to the bone, not only completing their own work, but Penny's as well. Ottilie skipped meals and tea in favor of bringing her ill friend cups of broth and milk spiked with as many herbs and garlic and spices as she could fit. But still Penny grew weaker. More ill.

By Saturday morning, most everyone else had followed. One by one, they fell victim to a dry cough and fever until nearly all of them were wheezing over their machines and fabric. It hadn't spared Ottilie, and she pushed her face into her elbow as that familiar tickle itched the back of her throat. Her cough set off an eruption of them, and soon the room echoed with the sound of it.

"We all need rest," she said when the noise had subsided. Her words reached every corner because everyone had stopped pushing their treadles to hide their faces in open hands and relieve the pressure in their chests.

Beside her, Alma scoffed. "Not likely."

Ottilie sighed and rubbed her forehead, easing the frown lines she knew had appeared. Everyone was ill. They weren't allowed time to recuperate. The doctor hadn't been called, healing foods hadn't been made, help hadn't been offered.

And no one was getting well.

She stared at the embroidery before her, blinking away the fuzziness that made it swim and waver, and then cracked her knuckles. Each one released a satisfying pop that eased not only the stiffness of her fingers but also the tension in her neck, shoulders, and back. She lifted another beetle wing from the box. The stock she'd purchased in Benares was running low, and she'd sent a letter, along with payment, to the merchant two weeks earlier. Madame Laurence assured her the desire for beetle-wing embroidered gowns had only spread, and there might be work for Ottilie even after the Season.

If Madame Laurence and Miss Briggs didn't read *The English-woman's Review*. And if none of their clients mentioned it to them. A dozen times since Damaris's visit, Ottilie allowed worry to twist her stomach and wished to take back her choice, but she acknowledged God had promised truth to be a higher calling. And she saw it as an opportunity to exercise her reviving faith. To practice it boldly. Each night, in between feeding Penny spoonfuls of spiced broth and milk with turmeric, Ottilie stitched Nānī's mustard seeds. And with each one, she prayed it attached itself as firmly to her spirit as the fabric.

Ottilie stood and shook the wrinkles from Damaris's gown. Made of sage green and ecru striped silk, the skirt draped beautifully, the Watteau back creating fullness without the need for a bustle. Madame Laurence had raised a brow when Ottilie showed her the design. But she only said, "At least it's an improvement on her peacock abomination," and allowed Ottilie to choose the fabric and work directly with the seamstress.

A low whistle drew Ottilie's attention to Alma, who had laid down her work to admire the gown. "That is lovely, Ottilie. I've never seen the like of it."

"I know the client well and thought a design inspired by the aesthetic dress movement would appeal to her."

Alma stood and rounded the table. Her fingers stroked the flounces around the low neckline and shoulders. "It's very simple, though. Are you sure she'll enjoy that style in a gown?"

Ottilie lifted one of the sleeves, where she had embroidered a heavy design of elytra. From wrist to elbow, they would wind around Damaris's forearm, a distinct contrast to the lack of ornamentation elsewhere. "She's a handsome woman with strong features and coloring. She needs little to carry her beauty."

"It will cause talk, that's for sure." Alma shook her head and cast Ottilie a look of admiration. "I hope Madame Laurence appreciates what she has in you. Your skill and creativity will draw her many clients. Pretty soon you will be able to start your own dress shop."

Pleased, Ottilie held the gown against her body and twirled with it. The skirt flared out, the lightweight material as downy and sweet as soan papdi. "If I do, promise me you'll come work with me."

Alma laughed. "You couldn't keep me away."

Someone near the door cleared a throat, and Ottilie stopped midwhirl, her head spinning well after she had stilled. When her vision cleared, she saw Madame Laurence looking at her with a frown and holding a folded newspaper, Miss Briggs beside her.

"If you haven't enough work to fill your time, I'm sure we can find you something to do, Miss Russell. Mrs. Follet."

Alma's eyes widened, and she scurried back to her seat. Ottilie draped the gown over her arm. "I'm sorry, Miss Briggs. I've only just finished Miss Winship's gown."

"Good. She is here for her final fitting, so as long as the alterations necessary are minimal, we can send it with her today."

Ottilie went to hand over the dress, but Madame Laurence held up her hand. "She insists on you attending her, Miss Russell, though I can't see why. Miss Briggs will take you."

Ottilie sent a grin over her shoulder toward Alma, then left the room, her arms swathed in Damaris's gown. As she followed Miss Briggs, Madame Laurence's incensed voice followed her.

"Who wrote these vile lies? I know it was one of you. There is mention of beetle-wing embroidery, and we're the only one in the city who does it."

Ottilie glanced behind her, heart thudding. It was the height of the London Season, and Damaris's publication didn't command a large subscription. It seemed the worst kind of luck that Madame Laurence actually read *The Englishwoman's Review*. Even more pressing, how had she time to read it when the women working for her weren't even given a few moments to eat dinner?

At the salon door, Miss Briggs turned a critical eye toward Ottilie and grimaced. "You could have taken a moment to straighten yourself. You look untidy. And unwell."

Ottilie put a hand to her hair and tucked in the wisps that frizzed around her crown. "I am unwell. We're all unwell."

Miss Briggs lifted her brows, then held her arm toward the door. "Since you've been summoned."

Ottilie dipped her chin and, ignoring Miss Briggs's sharp tone, she stepped into the room.

"Oh, close the door behind you, darling," Damaris called before Ottilie's foot could cross the threshold.

Ottilie's hand caught the knob, and the door clicked behind her as she offered Damaris a bright smile.

And Everett, who sat beside her, a startled gasp.

30

Ottilie leaned against the closed door and gathered Damaris's gown to her chest. "Everett." Her mouth was dry, and she had to force his name from her tongue.

"Hello." He stood and clasped his hands in front of him. His gaze swept her from head to toe, and now she wished she had taken a moment to glance in a mirror and at least straighten her clothing. "You look well."

Damaris laughed. "Liar. She looks ghastly. Ottilie, have you eaten anything at all since I last saw you? Have you slept?"

"I've not had time for much of either, I'm afraid." Ottilie glanced at the door behind her and rubbed her forehead smooth. "But it seems Madame Laurence has had time to read *The Englishwoman's Review*. I will soon be found out."

Damaris tsked and opened her reticule. She pulled out a folded sheet of newsprint and held it out. "As much as I wish Madame Laurence *would* read our humble publication and maybe learn something about decency, it's more likely she saw the article in this."

Ottilie approached, making a wide circle around Everett. She forced her attention to stay on Damaris, laid the gown over the settee, and took the paper. She opened it, smoothing out the crease crossing the center of the story.

At the top, *The Illustrated London News*, and below that, a headline:

Dressing England's Elite a Deadly Choice for Young Women

"How did this happen?" Below the article, an artist had sketched a cartoon of a woman wearing a beautiful dress, a host of ghostly, pale-faced and sunken-eyed girls plucking at the fabric with needle and thread.

Damaris tapped the reporter's name. "I contacted a friend at the paper, and he picked up the story. It deserved more attention than we could offer it."

Ottilie's eyes skimmed the article.

With society's most fashionable flitting through London's greatest ballrooms, resplendent in their gowns embroidered with beetle wings, the poor young women working beneath the demanding and never satisfied hand of court dressmakers live a barely tolerable existence. And some, overworked and undernourished, face more than a reduction in wages for their sacrifice. Death lurks in the corners of those grand salons on Regent Street.

She handed the paper back and coughed into her hand, the rattle of it drawing Everett forward a few steps. She waved him away and took a step nearer Damaris. "There is little doubt Madame Laurence will learn I had something to do with this. But it is a necessary story, Damaris, and I don't regret your writing it. Nor even *The Illustrated London News* reprinting it. Even if I am sent away by teatime, I am glad everyone will know how horrid conditions are for these women."

Ottilie was aware of Everett shifting from one foot to the

other not six feet from her. So near that if they both reached out their hands, she would feel his fingers on hers. So near that she could hear his breathing. Nothing separated them but a bit of carpet and air.

And disparate ambitions.

Her throat began to tickle, and she turned her face away, her cough shattering the peace of the room.

"Are you ill?" Everett asked.

"I am fine." She forced her lips into a bland smile and turned toward him. "How are you, Mr. Scott?"

"Don't." The word came out ragged, as though it had crawled and fought its way between his lips. "Don't call me that. Don't minimize this last month's fear. How could you disappear like that, without a word? Had you no thought for your grandmother and aunt? For me? Do you know how long I have been looking for you?" He crossed the space between them, and his hands gripped her arms, his breath coming fast and uneven, something like a sob catching in his throat. Ottilie stared up at him, the heat beneath his fingers searing her skin with regret. "I have never felt more lost than when I realized you were."

Damaris went to stand before the door, her backside ensuring it remained closed, and took to inspecting her fingernails with zeal.

Ottilie swallowed and looked again at Everett, his brow pleated like a length of silk dropped from its bolt. His chin trembling.

"I never meant to hurt you," she said, "I only needed to leave."

His hands caught her face, and he leaned his forehead against hers. His arms rounded her back, gathering her toward him. Nothing separated them.

Nothing except his illegitimate birth. Welbourne's. Her ancestry.

She pulled away and stepped back. "There was nothing for me at Hazelbrook Manor. Thaddeus was gone. I was a burden on Lady Sunderson and Alberta. My presence caused them constant anxiety. And you . . . you made your plans clear. I didn't fit into any of it."

"I'm so sorry." Everett reached for the chair behind him and sank onto the cushion. He took his head into his hands, elbows on his knees, and scrubbed his fingers through his hair. "How alone you must have felt."

"I did feel alone, but it's not entirely your fault. Nor does the burden rest only on Lady Sunderson and Alberta. I could have allowed them closer. Lady Sunderson, in particular, tried to know me, but I pushed her away. I can see that now. Fear is a powerful motivator. It forces one to erect safeguards, even when remaining vulnerable and open promises more joy." Ottilie took the seat opposite him. "How did you know to find Damaris?"

He smiled, a ghost of the one she loved so much. "Alberta receives *The Englishwoman's Review* and came to me when she recognized you must be the one making the beetle-wing gowns mentioned. A friend had written her months ago, telling her none of the dressmakers offered the service. When I saw Miss Winship's name at the top of the article, I knew if I found her, I'd find you. I was already in London."

"Were you? Why?"

"Looking for you, of course. As soon as Lady Sunderson discovered you'd slipped away, she asked me to find you. But London is a big city, and you had vanished into it. Miss Winship, though, is well known and was easy to find."

Everett had been so close all these weeks, and she'd had no idea. He'd been looking for her, hoping to find her, worried for her. "But you said Alberta brought you the paper. How could that be, if you were here?"

"They left yesterday morning after breakfast and found me at Mr. Fernsby's townhouse."

"They came to London?"

Everett rose from his seat and came to kneel at her feet. He took her hands in his and pressed a soft kiss to each of them. "Of course. Because they care for you, Ottilie, and they want you to come home. They're waiting for you at the Langham, where they have taken rooms."

His arms circled her waist, threading past her hips. He pressed his head to her lap, and his words were muffled against the fabric of her skirt.

"Please, if you don't return for them, return for me."

Ottilie, who had frozen at his display, her hands hovering above his head—desperate to touch him, to thread her fingers into his hair and press him nearer—pushed him away and stood. "Return for you? You were clear I wasn't enough. I could never give you what you need from a wife." She gestured to her face. "When I look in the mirror, I still see a Eurasian who looks more Indian than British. I still see someone who will draw curious glances and vicious gossip. I still see someone who has been rejected, pushed away, forgotten. I still see someone who cannot give you a membership to some Bristol club. I am still someone who will be unable to give you acceptable English children. So what then has changed, Everett? Because it's surely not I."

He'd scrambled to his feet during her speech and now shook his head. "No, no, you haven't changed, and how glad I am of it! I have changed. What I want has changed. I thought I needed to be accepted by society. To have a wife who would ease my way into its ranks. To honor my father and what he is offering me. I've spent my entire life living for others. And now . . . I wish only to live for God. And for you."

Ottilie stared at him, unable to think of anything she could use to protect herself against his admission. She couldn't trust him. Couldn't believe he wouldn't sweep her behind the screen and kiss her, tell her all the ways he would love her, then forsake her when pressured by society. By his father. By his business associates.

And then she wasn't in Madame Laurence's elegant salon

on Regent Street. She wasn't a few steps from Everett Scott, illegitimate son and estate manager and sole heir of a wealthy tea merchant. She wasn't who she'd become since her life had been turned upside down in the space of six months. She was in the Imperial Museum, young and untried and on the cusp of discovering the love her parents had always shared. She was looking into the eyes of a soldier, not comprehending that his love hadn't been forever. His promises had meant nothing. Learning, for the first time, that she wasn't enough.

Someone slammed against the door, and Ottilie jerked from her fuzzy memory. Damaris yelped and scurried away from whoever was insisting on entrance.

Alma came inside, her eyes wildly sweeping the room and landing on Ottilie. "Come quickly. It's Penny."

"Oh, Ottilie." Damaris stared at their little bedroom, her mouth open.

When Alma had raced from the salon, Ottilie darted after her. They had clattered up the stairs, uncaring if they disrupted anyone's work. Damaris and Everett followed.

Ottilie ignored Damaris's shock and ran to the bed. She dropped to her knees and clutched Penny's hands between hers. They were so clammy, and a thin groan threaded from between her lips.

"Penny?" Ottilie pressed the back of her hand to Penny's forehead, gasping at the heat.

Her friend was unresponsive.

"I came to bring her some broth and found her like this." Alma paced behind Ottilie. "What do we do?"

"The first thing you must do is remove her from this room. There is no ventilation. I'm not sure how either of you survived sleeping in it." Everett had settled beside Ottilie and stared at Penny, long-ago memories making themselves plain on his face.

"We've nowhere else to take her. The doctor said she has pneumonia."

Everett's face began to crumple at the diagnosis Ottilie knew meant to him what cholera meant to her. He shook his head, and determination pulled his jaw taut. Then he stood and, with one smooth movement, lifted Penny into his arms. "Very well. Since she can't recover here, we shall take her elsewhere."

Ottilie and Alma exchanged glances. They joined Damaris and followed Everett from the room into the hall, where the other women had clustered, wanting to see what was going on.

At the sound of a dozen pairs of clattering feet descending the stairs, Madame Laurence exited her private parlor and pressed her hand to her chest. "What is the meaning of this?" Her brows knit in confusion when she saw Damaris. "Miss Winship?"

They ignored her and continued toward the door. Madame Laurence snatched at Ottilie's arm. "What is going on?"

"Penny is ill. We're taking her somewhere she can recover."

"She may leave. The rest of you, back to work. We don't have time for this disruption."

Everett turned at the door, his arms cradling Penny as one would a child. Gentle and secure. "Come with us. You are likely to become as ill as your friend if you stay."

"She has work to do. Her place is here." Madame Laurence said *place* in a way that diminished what the shop had become to Ottilie. In that word, there was no indication that she had found friendship within its walls. Nothing to suggest it had become her home since arriving in England.

It hinted at a social position. A spot to work. Nothing more.

But it had been so much more. Ottilie, even knowing it unsafe and exhausting, wavered between wanting to go with Penny and wanting to stay where she could care for her friends. And protect her heart.

Everett addressed Madame Laurence but looked at Ottilie, his eyes soft and grassy, just as she best liked to remember them.

"Her place is wherever she wishes to be. Whether here or at Hazelbrook Manor with her family or wandering Calcutta's markets or . . . or with me."

Ottilie's breath caught, lost somewhere between England and India, unforgiving work and the thrill of haggling over a tumbling pile of elytra, new friends and old, a tidy church grave-yard boasting proper headstones and names and a mausoleum sheltering a family as jumbled as the cemetery they rested in.

Where did she belong? How could she tell?

The pressure in her chest grew until she had no choice but to release it in the same deep, barking cough that afflicted every one of her new sisters.

Alma caught Ottilie's hand. "Go with them. Be with Penny. There need be no decisions today. And you do need clean air to get well."

Ottilie shook her head. "It seems very unfair that I should have that benefit while the rest of you suffer."

Alma pressed Ottilie's hand to her cheek and smiled. Then she leaned closer and whispered, "Go with your friends. Care for Penny and yourself. You can do more good for us out there than in here. You are meant for great things."

31

Damaris insisted on taking Penny to her aunt's town-house. "There is much more room there than at a hotel, and it will give Ottilie time to prepare herself for seeing Lady Sunderson."

No one had argued, and Ottilie soon found herself in a well-appointed and beautifully decorated bedroom, Penny nearly disappearing beneath the many blankets a servant had layered atop her.

Ottilie's hand hovered above Penny's mouth, waiting for her friend's warm breath. An assurance of life.

Penny groaned and shifted her head against the pillow. Her eyes cracked open, and she blinked. "Ottilie?"

"We are at my friend's home." Penny had briefly woken in the carriage, her head propped in Ottilie's lap and her legs stretched across the seat. She'd listened while Ottilie explained that she needed to be someplace where the air was fresh and moving, then drifted back into whatever blackness beckoned.

"I can't . . ." Penny sighed.

"Just rest. The doctor will be here soon, and then you will get well. Everett has gone for your parents."

"No. They will worry." Penny's fingers appeared beneath her chin and pinched at the sheet.

"Of course they will worry. That is a parent's prerogative. But they need to know how unwell you are. Don't think about anything. Just rest."

Penny nodded, and her eyes drifted closed. "I am . . . so glad you're with me."

She fell asleep, and Ottilie leaned back in her chair and ignored her grumbling stomach. It had to be past lunch, which wouldn't have caused her stomach to cramp so painfully if she hadn't skipped breakfast. But she had, and now she wished for something to eat, something to settle her and give her hands a task.

She spied the pull near the fireplace across the room but didn't get up. If the staff in this house were anything like the ones at Hazelbrook Manor, nothing would be served by it.

A moment later, Damaris led the doctor into the room. The same one who had seen Penny earlier in the week. He was young, with a sincere expression, flopping light brown hair, and a natural warmth.

"I'm sorry to hear Miss Hale is still unwell." He drew near the bed, setting his large black bag on it, and took Penny's hand. With a thumb to her wrist, he watched her breathe for a moment before setting her arm down and tucking the blanket more snugly around her. "It is good you've taken her from that ghastly shop. It's no place for someone to recover their health. No place for anyone to live, actually." He turned toward Damaris. "I saw your story. I hope change comes from it."

Damaris murmured a thank-you, and she stood near Ottilie while the doctor examined Penny.

"Well," he said, standing, "I cannot promise she will survive—those with pneumonia don't always—but I like to think that with rest, proper nutrition, and attentive tending, she'll recover. Health favors the young, and she has that going for her." He smiled at Ottilie and Damaris. "As well as friends who care."

He gave them instructions on how to nurse Penny before taking his leave.

Damaris took one glance at Ottilie, then commanded her from the room. "You look only marginally further from death than Penny. I want you to rest. I've had the next bedroom made up for you, so you will be nearby if necessary. But for now I insist you sleep."

She took Ottilie's elbow and led her from the room and into the one adjacent to Penny's. Ottilie hardly resisted. The bed was capped by a filmy canopy and welcomed her into sleep as soon as she laid her head on the pillow.

Ottilie didn't know what time it was when she woke. The room was bathed in light—someone had opened the curtains—and her stomach rolled and complained. She pushed the blankets away and sat up. Her eyes landed on her satchels stacked in the corner. On the table beside her, someone had set a plate of bread with jam and a small silver tea service.

She pinched off a piece of crust and shoved it into her mouth, pouring tea as she chewed. While it cooled, she wandered around the room, touching the knickknacks and admiring the small still-life paintings. Atop the mantel, a bronze clock declared it eight o'clock. Her stomach dropped. She'd slept through an entire day and night. Even now, Penny could be struggling for breath, death camped at her feet. She could be . . .

Ottilie dashed toward the washstand, unbuttoning her bodice as she went, and made quick work of her scrubbing. It took many more moments to dress than she wished, so she merely twisted her hair into a simple braid and, on her way from the room, picked up her teacup, finding comfort in the wafting scents of Darjeeling.

Her nerves jangled again the moment she plowed through Penny's door. Sitting in the chair beside the bed, Everett stared at something between his fingers. He hid it in his palm the moment she appeared, and stood. "I sent her father to bed a couple of hours ago and told him I'd sit with her until someone else arrived."

"He is here, then. Her mother?"

Everett shook his head. "Mrs. Hale left yesterday morning for Bath." He dragged his gaze from Ottilie and let it rest on Penny. "She is the same. Not any better, but no worse either. Damaris was able to help her eat some gruel late last night. Miss Hale said it was better than anything she'd eaten at Madame Laurence's."

"It likely had enough cream in it to make a syllabub."

Everett smiled. "Butter too."

She stared at him, loving the flash of his teeth. The way his face lit up like a gas lamp turned on in the middle of the night.

He swallowed and motioned toward the chair he'd vacated. "Have you eaten? I can ring for breakfast to be brought up."

Ottilie sat. "That would be lovely."

He went to tug on the pull beside the fireplace, then turned back to her. "I brought your things." He blushed. "I see you've changed, so you must have noticed."

"I did. Thank you."

Silence fell, awkward and unnatural. Not like those moments before that had sprung up between them from comfortable companionship. This quiet demanded to be filled, but she had no idea what to say.

Everett began fiddling again with whatever was in his hand.

"What are you playing with?" she asked.

His fingers stilled. "Oh." He looked at the floor and pushed his toe into the plush carpet. Then he took a few steps toward her and held it out. She set her tea on the table between the chair and the bed and opened her palm.

Into it, he dropped an elytron. She smiled at its simple beauty. "Where did you get this?"

"It's the one you gave me at the market. Do you remember? You told me it was to remember Calcutta by."

Her skin prickled, all along her arms and legs, and her breath hitched. "You kept it?"

"I did." He glanced at Penny, then sat on the edge of the bed, his knees knocking against Ottilie's. He reached for her hands and cupped them gently, thumbs tracing circles on her wrists. "You told me that the elytron is like a house, meant to protect the fragile wings. And I realized something while you were away. I realized that you had a house, meant to keep your heart safe. You opened it up, let me in, and I only hurt you. You were vulnerable, even though it required great courage and risk. And I failed you. I don't deserve another chance with you, Ottilie, but I hope for one. I will honor whatever it is you want from me. I will support whatever it is you decide. But . . . please, please, decide on me."

Ottilie tugged her hands from his and dropped her head. She lifted her shawl over her head, hiding her face from him. Hiding her tears. They fell onto her lap, though, so she knew he saw them.

He said nothing. Only gave her the space to think.

"How would it work, Everett? Don't you need a proper wife, one who will help you into your club and society and bring honor to your father's work? You once told me your greatest desire is that your children wouldn't suffer your fate. I wouldn't be able to give you that."

"I would face a thousand scandals with you beside me. And our children would be blessed enough to know the love of a woman as loyal and caring as you. Mr. Fernsby—my father—convinced me of my foolish pursuit of things that do not matter."

She looked at him, past the swaying edges of her shawl. "What did he say?"

"He reminded me that he fell in love with a servant girl and that he never wanted me to be anything but happy. My desire to marry above my station was always driven by a wish to honor his grace in taking me in. To grasp for the only thing I knew of that could connect me to him and my family. But as much as he dreamed of the day when I would join him not only in business, but in society as well, he never wished for me to sacrifice love. Not when everything I never realized I wanted and needed can be found with you."

She laughed, tears dripping into her mouth, the salty taste of them washing away the bitterness that had lodged in her throat when he told her he couldn't be with her. "Are you sure, Everett? I could never live with myself if I knew I'd ruined any chance of you being acceptable."

He stood, drawing her to her feet and wrapping her in his arms. "Oh, my heart. Nothing you do or I do will ever make me acceptable. Nothing society thinks can make me unacceptable. My worth, your worth, is found in God alone. And he says we are accepted." He pulled back and looked at her. "Will you forgive me? Will you accept me? I can't offer you social approval or a world where things will be easy for us or our children. But I can offer myself. My love. A home of joy."

Ottilie removed her hands from Everett's back and reached for his face, her fingers caressing and speaking her answer. And his dear, dear smile answered back. "I will," she said. "Everything you offer is all I've ever wanted."

She tugged the edge of her shawl over his head, and there, beneath her mantle, she kissed him. A sweet kiss, with none of the desperate passion from their first, but containing more in its promise. It was the soft brush of lips and gentle touch of his hands on her back. The feel of his skin beneath her fingers and the taste of breakfast on his tongue.

Ottilie's stomach grumbled, and his mouth curved into a smile.

"I'm very hungry," she said before pressing more firmly against him and tasting his mouth again. "I should like to eat."

Something clattered and hissed, and Ottilie jerked the shawl from their heads.

Behind Everett, sitting up against the headboard, Penny held her finger to her lips, a sheepish expression lifting her brows. "I woke and was so thirsty, but I didn't want to interrupt. My hand trembled when I reached for your tea." Her face burned red, and Ottilie knew it had nothing to do with fever. "I'm so sorry to have interrupted. Please carry on."

Then she sank back into the mattress and pulled the covers over her head.

Everett left after a servant arrived and he asked her to bring Ottilie and Penny breakfast. "Lots of cream and butter in the oatmeal, please," he told the maid with a wink at Ottilie. "More than is seemly."

Penny's fever had broken, and her eyes, for the first time in days, were clear. But she was still very weak, and Ottilie gladly served her. After they ate, Damaris led Mr. Hale into the room. He wept at seeing Penny so well, and Ottilie left.

"You have visitors in the drawing room," Damaris told her as they walked down the hall. "Your aunt and grandmother are anxious to see you. I hope you can work out whatever it was that occurred between you. I want you to have a family again."

"I will try my best, Damaris, but since I arrived in London, I've learned family is made up of more than those related by blood. And before I left India, Dilip told me that home was never supposed to be a place. It is the people. That includes dear friends. And you are the sister I've been desperately missing since losing Jemima."

"That is lovely, for I've always wanted a sister." Damaris squeezed Ottilie's hand and opened the drawing room door. "I will see that tea is sent."

Ottilie's heart thudded, and her rib cage constricted around it. But she took a step forward in faith.

She had only a moment to take in those present—Lady

Sunderson, looking weepy and grateful, and Alberta, whose head was bent so low that Ottilie couldn't make out her expression—before a familiar voice tore through her composure.

"Didi! I'm here!" Thaddeus hurtled toward her and threw his arms around her midsection. "I missed you so much. A boy at school told everyone that he saw an Indian at the door, and no one believed him, but I knew it was you."

Ottilie lifted her brother. He was too large for it, too old, but she didn't care. She wanted him as near as possible, tangled in her arms and legs. As close to a sleeping mat on the roof beneath Calcutta's winter sky as possible. She pressed her nose to his neck and inhaled his little-boy scent. "Oh, Thaddeus. How I have longed for this."

Ottilie had no idea how long they stood like that, their eyes squeezed tightly against everyone else in the room, but it was long enough that Ottilie felt she could put her brother down without tearing her heart from her chest. She set him on the floor beside her but didn't release his hand. She couldn't let him go entirely just yet.

Lady Sunderson approached, her eyes bright and washed with tears. "How glad I am Everett found you. We were so worried."

"Were you?"

"What a thing to ask," Alberta said. "Of course we were."

Lady Sunderson shook her head. "She has a right to wonder, Birdie. We didn't claim her when she lived with us, so why should she think we would worry over her? We allowed fear to cloud our call to truth. And I allowed grief to keep me distant. It was so very wrong of us."

"I only needed to know I was wanted," Ottilie whispered. "More even than you acknowledging me, I needed to know you accepted me."

Lady Sunderson took Ottilie's face between her hands. "Oh, my dear, you deserve to be accepted and acknowledged. More than that, you deserve to be embraced as a member of our family. And you will be."

Alberta approached, stiff and anxious. "Mother is right. I am so sorry, Ottilie. So sorry for everything."

"I am as well," Ottilie said. "We both made the mistake of holding too tightly to our fear and pain."

Alberta wiped at her eyes. "Yes. And we must rectify it. I wish to be your friend."

Ottilie drew Thaddeus nearer, finding comfort in the press of his sturdy body, still small but filling out. "But how can you? It might make life hard for Thaddeus if people know I'm his sister."

Thaddeus tugged her hand, but Lady Sunderson's words caught her attention. "We may not be able to protect Sunderson from the social implications of his Indian ancestry, but that will hurt much less than if he were to lose his sister. Maybe we will just have to allow life to be messy—it so often is—and we can face it. Together, Ottilie. We *will* face it."

Thaddeus tugged again on her hand. "Didi?"

Ottilie glanced down at him. "Yes?"

"Was it a secret that I'm Indian at school too? Because I told all the boys you were my sister. And I sang them Nānī's songs when they missed their parents." He shrugged. "At least until the teachers told me I wasn't allowed to sing songs in anything but English, and I wasn't allowed to tell stories about India. And I put this"—he pulled a little spice jar from his pocket—"on everything I ate. I filled it from your big one and packed it, but I didn't take all of it because I didn't want you to have none. And I wouldn't share it, because there wasn't very much."

Ottilie remembered her fears at Kew Gardens that Thaddeus had forgotten who he was, that he had become so absorbed into England there remained nothing left of India in him. But it seemed she'd only seen one side of his story, and Thaddeus had become a fluid, perfect mix of both.

She knelt beside him and hugged him once more, knowing

she would have to release him to St. Luke's later that day. Knowing it would be all right. He would be all right. Knowing that, in the end, he'd found a home with a group of very English boys, but that he sprinkled India—Papa, Maji, Nānī, Dilip, their little house in Entally—everywhere he stepped.

"No, glowworm, it isn't a secret."

She stood and noticed Damaris had stepped into the drawing room. Ottilie's gaze swept over those she loved best, and she pulled Thaddeus toward Everett, taking his hand and linking them into a cord of three once more.

In Damaris's aunt's drawing room, time became an immeasurable thing, the clock on the mantel ticking the minutes and hours in a way that seemed entirely too fast. Then, in moments when Ottilie stood back from the conversation and tried to imprint upon her mind the knitting together of family and friends, it seemed to stand impossibly still.

Before she was ready, though, Alberta shot her a look of regret, then stood. "Lord Sunderson must be returned to school." She held out her hand for Thaddeus's, but he burrowed even nearer Ottilie, and her expression softened. "What if we all went with you, your sister included?"

All five of them crowded into the carriage that had taken Ottilie away from Madame Laurence's and took it across London to St. Luke's. Ottilie stared up at the imposing brick walls, but this time she was holding her brother's hand. Walking him in, not being shut out.

The door was opened by the same stoic butler before they'd even descended from the carriage.

"Are you sure you want to do this? It will be seen as a public statement." Ottilie peered out the door of the carriage while everyone waited for her.

Alberta glanced at the school, a quick lick of her lips and

nibble of her cuticle betraying her nerves. But then she stiffened and held her head straight. "Yes, we are sure. There have been enough secrets in this family." And then she and Lady Sunderson each held out an arm, ushering Ottilie forward.

Thaddeus had grabbed Ottilie's hand before her feet touched the stone pavers, and he led her in a brisk walk up the path, narrow chest thrust foward. He sent little smiles toward her and waved at the windows of the first and second floors, where boys pressed their noses and foreheads against the glass.

The butler admitted them, and a tall, thin man waited in the foyer, everything about him pinched. His expression, his too-tight jacket, the clasp of his hands at his waist. "Lady Sunderson. Lord Sunderson."

Alberta leaned near and whispered, "That is Mr. Igden, the school's headmaster."

Ottilie's grandmother stepped forward. "Mr. Igden, may I introduce to you my granddaughter, Baron Sunderson's sister, Miss Russell." She motioned with her fingers, drawing Ottilie forward.

Mr. Igden's eyes narrowed as his gaze swept her. Then he made an abrupt turn. "Please follow me. Holman, see that we are brought tea."

The butler gave a short nod and left. They followed Mr. Igden into a cramped private parlor crowded with mismatched chairs. He settled upon a cracked leather armchair. Thaddeus sat at Ottilie's feet. Everett stood behind her, his hand clasping the curved back of her seat and his knuckles brushing her neck. Alberta and Lady Sunderson took a settee pushed up against the wall, hemmed in by a table that boasted a globe and a shelf overflowing with dusty books.

Ottilie didn't trust a person who owned dusty books.

Mr. Igden's next words proved her assumption correct. "This situation needs clarification. Surely you don't mean that Miss Russell is, indeed, Lord Sunderson's sister."

Across the room, Alberta winced, and Ottilie knew she remembered saying almost those same words when first hearing Ottilie's claim.

On the floor, Thaddeus tensed and crossed his arms. "She *is* my sister."

Mr. Igden sent Thaddeus a sharp look. "Mind your manners, Lord Sunderson. You are not relieved of them because your blood flows with savagery." Before Ottilie could even gasp, he pinched his pointed chin. "This is illuminating, I will admit. Lord Sunderson has had trouble acclimating to the school's schedule and rules. He seems unable to control his passions. We have caught him on multiple occasions adulterating his food, telling the other students pagan tales, and goading the teachers with incessant questions."

"He's a child who has lost everything dear to him, and this is an entirely new situation. Of course he is struggling with that," Ottilie countered. How could such a man—so devoid of compasson and even a basic understanding of grief—properly lead a school full of boys? Thaddeus's arms slipped beneath her skirt and around her calf, and Ottilie rested her hand on his shoulder.

Mr. Igden stared at her for a moment before blinking a dismissal. He turned to Lady Sunderson and Alberta. "I recommend, in light of his heritage, we double our efforts to see him transformed into a man of the highest pedigree. He requires an upbringing meant to foster those good, British parts of him so that the *others* will be smothered."

Lady Sunderson smoothed her hands over her skirt. "And how do you propose we do this?"

Ottilie shifted forward. Her grandmother couldn't mean it. Not after the words she'd spoken only moments ago.

Mr. Igden smiled, a simpering smile that did no service to his already ponderous face. "We must be sure he is removed from any connection to his unfortunate parentage. He will not be allowed to speak of India. Nor will he be permitted to alter his food. There will be no letters from . . . Miss Russell." He looked over at Ottilie, but his eyes didn't meet hers. "In fact, I suggest he stay here through the summer in order to create a proper distance between them. I think it unlikely she will be capable of rejecting the heathen part of her. It is much more evident in her than him."

"I will never reject any part of my heritage again." Ottilie's voice rose with her as she shot to her feet. "I made that mistake once, wanting to divest myself of everything English because of men like you, and I shall not do it again. Neither will Thaddeus. You may well take away his food and his sister and his ability to speak of his family and past and country, but you will not be able to invade his mind or spirit."

Alberta stood suddenly, drawing Lady Sunderson up with her. "I quite disagree, Ottilie."

Nausea swept through Ottilie when she realized nothing had changed. She wasn't accepted or loved at all. Her aunt and grandmother weren't willing to defend her. Not when Thaddeus's reputation was at risk. Not when what she wanted went against the order of things.

So when Alberta smiled, her eyes washed with tears, Ottilie could make little sense of it. "Mr. Igden will not be able to take away his food or his sister or his ability to speak of the things that he loves. Indeed, we will be taking Lord Sunderson away from this place." She turned to Mr. Igden, whose mouth hung open in indignation. "There are other schools. And I think Lord Sunderson needs to spend more time with his sister before being sent to one. She said as much, but I thought I knew better. I was wrong. Miss Russell told me only an hour ago that fear is a powerful motivator. But it is not one for which I will sacrifice any longer." She looked at Ottilie, and there was still a measure of doubt lurking behind her bright eyes and stubborn smile. "What do you think?"

In India, the sun rose with alacrity, not just shining but pushing and prodding and filling every dark corner with light. Little escaped it. Since coming to England, though, Ottilie had experienced the gentle nudging of Britain's spring awakening. It peeked shyly from a veil of mist and clouds, a slow coaxing to life. There was more than one way to illuminate. More than one way to grow things. Innocence and experience, knotted together by a hand much steadier than her own.

She reached for Thaddeus and helped him to his feet. "I think I wish to take Thaddeus from this place and go home to Hazelbrook Manor."

EPILOGUE

Wiltshire had been experiencing record-breaking heat that summer. Ottilie fanned her hand at her face and trudged behind her husband up the drive to the newly finished building. Made from the same creamy sandstone as Hazelbrook Manor, the House of Gahana—named for the jewel beetle—rose two stories. Compact and sturdy, it would stand long after Ottilie had disappeared into the earth.

She wiped the sweat from her lip, not knowing if the heat bothered her so much because she'd grown weak in the three years since she'd left Calcutta, or because the baby nestled in her arms made her body a furnace. Either way, she wanted to see their new venture as everyone else would. Not trapped inside a carriage and peering through a small square window.

"It's so lovely," she said, coming up beside Everett and squeezing his hand. The ring he had slid onto her finger when they wed—the gold and sapphire one meant for his mother—gave her skin a reassuring nip. "When will they all be here?"

"Next week. Penny is already settled in one of the cottages and will see that everything is prepared."

"And Sunderson?" She knew already, had made Everett promise her a dozen times, but she needed to hear it.

"He comes home in two days and will be here for three entire weeks."

Ottilie sighed and looked at her daughter. She pushed her fingers through the thatch of black hair sticking straight up from the baby's head and marveled at her beauty.

"Are you ready to see your grandfather?" Everett asked.

Ottilie ran her finger over little Sonia's pursed lips, seeing her mother and father, Nānī and her siblngs, and yes, even her grandfather in the sweet face. She'd received the letter from Flora only a week earlier. The colonel had retired. It was time for them to return home. "I believe so." She gazed at the House of Gahana and knew the good things that could come of pain. "Let's see it," she said.

Everett took their daughter and allowed Ottilie to enter before him. The open foyer was made grand by tall windows and a brilliant gas lamp hanging from a medallion in the middle of the ceiling. Beyond, a wide staircase led to the first floor where, Ottilie knew, two large workrooms waited—one for sewing and one for embroidery and detail work. Both lined with windows that could be opened for airflow.

"Do you want to see the salon?" Everett asked.

She nodded eagerly and didn't wait for him. It was to her left. Ottilie hadn't seen it since Alberta had forced her out after the workmen finished. "I want to surprise you," her aunt had said. "You are not the only artistic one in the family." So Ottilie had stayed away these three long weeks.

She darted across the stone tiles and pushed open the door.

Inside, Alberta, Lady Sunderson, Damaris, and Penny stood, grins spread across their faces. They welcomed Ottilie with clapping hands, and she turned in a circle, taking in the teak privacy screens, bright Agra carpets, and carved furniture—octagonal tables with inlay tops and cane-back chairs, and trunks overlaid with brass. They were dowry trunks, she knew, brought from India to fill with sketches and pencils and needles and thread.

Filled, too, with hopes and dreams. For the seamstresses and embroiderers—many of them poor and alone—who would soon live in the dozen cottages behind the main house. For Ottilie, who hoped she and Everett had built something that would be a place of art and beauty. For the wealthy women who would order one-of-a-kind House of Gahana gowns, knowing those whose fingers had stitched them were making fair wages and working in safe conditions.

"It's lovely, Alberta."

Damaris bit her lip and laced her fingers together below her chin. "Turn around, Ottilie. Lady Sunderson arranged for a surprise."

Ottilie whirled, and there, above a side table set with an Indian tea service and plates of pastries, hung Nānī and Niraja's tapestry. Complete. Whole.

Ottilie gasped and crossed the room, her fingers reaching for it. Finally . . . finally she was able to touch it. The little mustard seeds she'd ruined her bangles for, the delicate golden blooms that bounced above green stems sprouting from a blue-stitched pool. The darting mirror fish and tree that was more than a tree dropping bloodred flowers upon sheep that were more than sheep. So much more. The dove made out of shells that promised life above. And the beetle-wing girls who danced, their hands held high, their feet pounding the ground.

"Oh, Nānī." Ottilie touched one of the girls, and though it was nothing but elytra and thread, she felt closer to Nānī than she had since she'd spilled her into the Ganges. She turned to offer Grandmother a watery smile. "How did you do this?"

"Everett told me about the portion you worked on while at the dress shop, so we smuggled it from the house, and I sent it to Niraja, who stitched your part to the rest of it. She thought you should have it. And we thought you would want it here."

Ottilie turned back to look at it, and Everett came up beside her, his arm wrapping around her waist. "Are you happy?"

"Deliriously." Ottilie leaned her head against his shoulder and stared up at the tapestry that was Nānī's statement of faith. And also hers.

On the backside, she knew, it would seem only a tangle of thread and knots. Imperfect. But it told a story of women as they went about life weeping and laughing, grieving and dancing, living and dying. Walking through seasons that changed, but always, always stitching something beautiful.

One just needed to remember to look at the right side.

AUTHOR'S NOTE

Ottilie's faith journey is my own. Her wrestle with belief and doubt, questioning and frustration, despair and hope, is something I identify with on the deepest level. My faith is hard-won. It's something I struggled for and nearly walked away from. To this day, it is still wrapped up in all manner of complexity.

Being a Christian—following the rules and adhering to the values—was easy for me. It was the believing that was hard.

But God is faithful. And he chases the lost one. The confused one. The isolated one. The doubting one. He chased me.

Like Ottilie, he showed me that all I needed was a mustard seed-sized faith. He would do the rest. So I took that little seed and protected it, waking up every morning and praying, "I *choose* to believe today. Forgive my unbelief." It was enough. Because the alternative was living in a world without grace. Without Christ. Without sacrifice. Without a reason for humanity to pursue goodness. I didn't want to live a life where blood hadn't been spilled out on a cross.

When I began writing Ottilie, I had no intention of giving her this struggle. But in the very first scene, I found myself writing, "A cord of three. Four, if you counted God . . . which she didn't."

"Why don't you count God, Ottilie?" I asked.

And then I saw my faith story spill out on the pages. This is a love letter to my Jesus. My statement of faith. I believe.

And I'm sharing it with you because even a tiny flame chases away darkness.

Every historical novel is an interesting mix of truth and imagination. As an author, it's my job to provide enough detail to immerse the reader in place and setting without overwhelming them with minutiae. For someone who loves research and history, that isn't an easy thing. Much of the background of *A Tapestry of Light* is based on fact. The story itself is entirely imagination.

I first learned of the Anglo-Indian people when I lived in Bangalore years ago. I met a woman who told me she was Anglo-Indian and that her people had descended from the offspring of British men and Indian women. She said they had never been treated very well and were often marginalized, leading them to marrying within their community and creating a distinct culture. Anglo-Indian is the name given to these people starting in 1911. Prior to that, they were called Eurasians. This term came to be derogatory, but I've chosen to use it for historical accuracy and because it held no negative connotations in the nineteenth century. I'm told by Anglo-Indians that they do not, for the most part, find the word offensive today. Their history is a twisted one full of discriminatory laws and inequality. Today, Anglo-Indian leaders are afraid their culture is dying, falling prey to emigration and marriage to those outside their community.

When it came to researching life in Victorian England for seamstresses, there was plenty of information. These poor women were overworked, lived in overcrowded and unhealthy environments, and made little money. In 1863, a young seamstress died from poor ventilation and exhaustion. A magazine picked up the story and sensationalized it with cartoons. There was a cry for reform. However, nothing was done, and the lot for seamstresses continued to be dire for many years.

I first stumbled across beetle-wing embroidery at an exhibit on Indian fabrics at our local museum. I'd never seen anything like it, and that scrap of nineteenth-century trim, embroidered with gorgeous green wings (or casings, as Ottilie enjoyed correcting Everett) still vibrant over a hundred years later, captured my fancy. Beetle-wing embroidery is, indeed, a traditional Indian craft. It grew in popularity as a method of embellishment among the British in India and then traveled to England and graced gowns, reticules, and shoes. I took the liberty of creating a craze in *A Tapestry of Light* for beetle-wing embroidered gowns in 1886.

The Indian Rebellion of 1857 plays an important role in Ottilie's family history. It's a devastating story, one that cannot be explained in a sentence or two. The reasons behind it are complex, many people—both Indian and British—lost their lives (including innocent women and children), and it resulted in a massive change in the way the British viewed India and Indians, which perpetuated almost a hundred years of bigotry and exploitation.

It's no secret that I love descriptive writing, thanks to all the gothic novels I read in high school. My favorite part of writing any book is immersing myself in those places, real or imaginary. Elbury is based loosely on Castle Combe in Wiltshire. Hazelbrook Manor was inspired by Stanway House in Gloucestershire. When I stumbled across the beautiful Frampton Court orangery during research, I knew I had to give it to Ottilie—a place where she could feel the heat and smell the flowers of home. I've never been to England and so had to fill out my descriptions with the help of YouTube videos and photographs. I have, however, been to Kolkata, and it is one of my favorite Indian cities. I tried to be as accurate as possible in describing it. Nearly every place mentioned actually existed, and some still stand. Cuthbertson and

Harper Saddlers, the Great Eastern Hotel, St. James's Church, Federico Peliti bakery, the Imperial Museum (now called the Indian Museum), the Maidan, Lal Bazar Chapel, Fort William, Entally, and more. I actually visited Entally when I went to the Mother House of the Missionaries of Charity, though at the time I didn't know Ottilie or anything about her story. My favorite resource for information on historical Kolkata is *Calcutta in the Nineteenth Century* by Bidisha Chakraborty and Sarmistha De.

I could probably write another book based on the research I did for *A Tapestry of Light*. The history of Indian-British relations, embroidery, Victorian fashion (check out *A Victorian Lady's Guide to Fashion and Beauty* by Mimi Matthews), Benares (known today as Varanasi), and the Fishing Fleet girls fascinates me. As I'm limited on space, though (my books already push the upper limits of my allowed word count), I'll leave off here and wish you happy travels. As romantic as going back in time sounds, I'm so grateful we only have to log on to a computer or open the pages of a book to experience life and culture in different places and ages.

ACKNOWLEDGMENTS

I don't know any book published in the history of book publishing that was written by a single person. Every single one is a community effort.

Thanks to the Bethany House team, who continues to bless me with grace, expertise, effort, and creativity. A special thanks to my editor, Jessica Sharpe, who manages to turn my books into something worthy of their covers; Jennifer Parker, who designs those covers; Amy Lokkesmoe, without whom I'm pretty sure I'd be selling books out of my trunk; as well as Rachael Wing, Noelle Chew, Serena Hanson, and Brooke Vikla for all of your hard work.

Thanks to Rachelle Gardner, the first person in the industry to see value in my stories. I'll always be grateful to you.

I would be raving mad right now if it weren't for my OWL Adjacent Mastermind Voxer group (whose name grows longer with every book)—Leslie, Hope, Kristi, and Lindsey. You kept me sane and connected through the pandemic and those seasons where I would gladly give up communication and human interaction in favor of writing just *one more scene*.

To a few particular writing friends (there are so many more of you, but I'd run out of room)—Stephanie Gammon, Ashley Clark, Jen Turano, and Rachel McMillan—who answered my questions, discussed publishing, brainstormed, and encouraged me during the making of *A Tapestry of Light*.

Thanks to my friend Tim Hartley, who was the inspiration for that scene with Everett, the watch, and the man suffering from leprosy. Tim's generosity and compassion reminded me not to become so desensitized to pain that I forget love.

I wouldn't be able to write any book set in India without the help of my sensitivity reader, Madhu. She is a wealth of information, always willing to answer questions, and makes sure my books are accurate (with allowances made for artistic license), culturally aware, and reflect my love for India.

And thanks to Debb Hackett, formerly of Wiltshire, for helping me with the British parts of this book. (She also saved me from a pretty scandalous blunder when it came to naming Hazelbrook Manor.)

Thanks always and forever to my husband, Shane, who never begrudges me all the hours I need to write the stories that consume my thoughts. I'm so grateful I had the foresight to marry someone who would eventually go into IT. He would be very expensive to replace.

And to my children, Ellie, Grainne, Hazel, and August. I hope we have created a safe place for you. A place where you belong and are known. I pray you always know you have a home with us. Writers like to talk about their book babies, and I cherish every one I've birthed, but you are my legacy, and I couldn't be prouder. Psalm 127:3.

Kimberly Duffy is a Long Island native currently living in southwest Ohio. When she's not homeschooling her four kids, she writes historical fiction that takes her readers back in time and across oceans. She loves trips that require a passport, recipe books, and practicing kissing scenes with her husband of twenty-one years. He doesn't mind. You can find her at www.kimberlyduffy.com.

Sign Up for Kimberly's Newsletter!

Keep up to date with Kimberly's latest news on book releases and events by signing up for her email list at kimberlyduffy.com.

More from Kimberly Duffy

Determined to uphold her father's legacy, newly graduated Nora Shipley joins an entomology research expedition to India to prove herself in the field. In this spellbinding new land, Nora is faced with impossible choices—between saving a young Indian girl and saving her career, and between what she's always thought she wanted and the man she's come to love.

A Mosaic of Wings

You May Also Like . . .

When his reputation is threatened, Aaron Whitworth makes the desperate decision to hire a circus horse trainer as a jockey for his racehorses. Most men don't take Sophia Fitzroy seriously because she's a woman, but as she fights for the right to do the work she was hired for, she finds the fight for Aaron's guarded heart might be a more worthwhile challenge.

Winning the Gentleman by Kristi Ann Hunter
HEARTS ON THE HEATH
kristiannhunter.com

Luke Delacroix's hidden past as a spy has him carrying out an ambitious agenda—thwarting the reelection of his only real enemy. But trouble begins when he falls for Marianne Magruder, the congressman's daughter. Can their newfound love survive a political firestorm, or will three generations of family rivalry drive them apart forever?

The Prince of Spies by Elizabeth Camden
HOPE AND GLORY #3
elizabethcamden.com

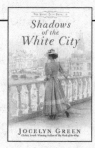

When Sylvie Townsend's Polish ward, Rose, goes missing at the World's Fair, her life unravels. Brushed off by the authorities, Sylvie turns to her boarder and Rose's violin instructor, Kristof Bartok, for help searching the immigrant communities. When the unexpected happens, will Sylvie be able to accept the change that comes her way?

Shadows of the White City by Jocelyn Green
THE WINDY CITY SAGA #2
jocelyngreen.com

 BETHANYHOUSE

More from Bethany House

After receiving word that her sweetheart has been lost during a raid on a Yankee vessel, Cordelia Owens clings to hope. But Phineas Dunn finds nothing redemptive in the horrors of war, and when he returns, sure that he is not the hero Cordelia sees, they both must decide where the dreams of a new America will take them, and if they will go there together.

Dreams of Savannah by Roseanna M. White
roseannamwhite.com

Haunted by painful memories, Olivia Rosetti is singularly focused on running her maternity home for troubled women. Darius Reed is determined to protect his daughter from the prejudice that killed his wife by marrying a society darling. But when he's suddenly drawn to Olivia, they will learn if love can prove stronger than the secrets and hurts of the past.

A Haven for Her Heart by Susan Anne Mason
REDEMPTION'S LIGHT #1
susanannemason.net

In this epistolary novel from the WWII home front, Johanna Berglund is forced to return to her small Midwestern town to become a translator at a German prisoner of war camp. There, amid old secrets and prejudice, she finds that the POWs have hidden depths. When the lines between compassion and treason are blurred, she must decide where her heart truly lies.

Things We Didn't Say by Amy Lynn Green
amygreenbooks.com

◆ BETHANYHOUSE